BRIGHT SHARK

BRIGHT SHARK

ROBERT BALLARD AND TONY CHIU

Delacorte Press

Published by
Delacorte Press
Bantam Doubleday Dell Publishing Group, Inc.
666 Fifth Avenue
New York, New York 10103

Library of Congress Cataloging-in-Publication Data

Ballard, Robert.
    Bright shark : a novel / by Robert Ballard and Tony Chiu.
       p.   cm.
    ISBN 0-385-29887-0 (hc) : $20.00
      I. Chiu, Tony. II. Title.
PS3552.A467B7 1992
813′.54—dc20   91-30932 CIP

Book design by Diane Stevenson/SNAP · HAUS GRAPHICS

Manufactured in the United States of America

Published simultaneously in Canada

April 1992

10 9 8 7 6 5 4 3 2 1

BVG

To Barbara and Douglas
and
Ali and Delia

BRIGHT SHARK

"Are we going to die, Papa?"

The girl's whispered question took him by surprise.

"No," he replied, a beat too quickly. He stole a glance at the nearest fellow passengers. They appeared to be dozing. "Of course not, Princess. Never."

His daughter had just returned from the bow of the vessel clutching her talisman, a souvenir ballpoint pen from the 1964 World's Fair in New York. It had been mailed from the fairgrounds by an aunt who had emigrated to America. The pen, its plastic barrel covered with gaily colored images of a globe, a monorail, and various fantastic pavilions befitting a fairy tale, was far too precious to use for writing. His daughter liked to click its tip in and out, though; he had already replaced the spring twice in three years.

The father waited until his runaway heart calmed, then said softly, "What gives you such an idea?"

The girl shifted from one foot to another and began biting her lower lip. This was a tic that had developed since the start of their journey. Small wonder, he thought, saddened by his inability to relieve her of the many stresses she was experiencing. Even before the present predicament his daughter had been dealing with a cruel personal upheaval, the first prolonged separation from her mother and younger siblings. But it had to be this way; the rest of the family would come later, after he had established a new life. In addition, the girl was just four months shy of her birthday—May 14, coincidentally a day of great joy in the new land that was their destination. Twelve was a frustrating age for a child, for the events captured by a rapidly maturing eye were still subject to interpretation by a mind not fully schooled in adult nuance.

"Our funny young friend who talks on the radio," she finally said, "the one who tries to tell the world we are in trouble. I see all the sailors say good-bye to him, and then he goes away."

" 'Goes away'? What do you mean?"

"He takes a heavy yellow bag and he goes through the red door at the front. You know, the door with the pretty white circle."

The father forced a smile and beckoned the girl to climb into the hammock to lie beside him. He ignored the heat and the humid stench in the cabin and drew his daughter close. Was it so he could comfort her, or she him?

"That is a good sign," he said, nuzzling her cheek. "About our funny young friend and the red door, I mean. Soon he will be swimming outside, where he can fix what is wrong."

"The water here is deep?"

"I believe it is over your head, Princess," he said lightly. "But I have seen what is inside the yellow bag. It is special clothing that allows him to breathe under the water. When he puts on that clothing, he will be able to fix what is wrong. The funny young man looks like someone who does his job well. What do you think?"

She nodded mutely and leaned her head against his chest.

He looked down at the "tiara"—a metal headband studded with fake emeralds and sapphires—that held her auburn mane. His wife would die of shame were she here to see the girl's matted hair. Not that anyone aboard the vessel cared; with fresh water tightly rationed, personal hygiene had become a bigger luxury than even fresh fruit.

The father closed his eyes and tried to take stock.

He understood from snatches of overheard conversations that the crew had begun experiencing difficulties before the passengers boarded; something to do with "maintaining the trim." Accordingly, the captain had ordered the fifty-three newcomers, as well as all off-duty sailors, to remain at the stern, near the massive twin diesel engines. Still, it was hard not to notice that objects had a way of gradually sliding or rolling toward the bow of the vessel.

Then, sixteen hours earlier, one of the engines had seized, even though it was said to be brand new.

The funny young sailor whom his daughter had grown to like was assigned to calm the passengers—don't worry, he joked, that's why we asked them to give us a second engine—while his mates rushed to make repairs. The surge of activity had bolstered everyone's confidence. Surely, with all those skilled men working, the engine would soon be running again.

In the meantime the bow of the vessel seemed to dip ever lower, the roar of the second diesel to grow ever more intense.

Until it, too, started to miss.

The funny young sailor had hurried up front to the radio room. In the deafening silence after the second engine stopped altogether, the distress message he urgently repeated carried throughout the vessel.

The captain had come back to the passenger quarters a short while ago to explain that the lights were now dim because the vessel was operating on emergency power. Unless the situation improved soon, he would dispatch one of his bravest men, an expert in underwater diving, to repair the problem. Everyone had seemed content to take the captain at his word; there had been no questions about the exact nature of the problem. Would the captain have answered them? If so, would any of us have understood his replies? The father was well aware that his own nautical experience consisted of taking his family to the nearby park on weekend afternoons and rowing them around the shallow artificial lake. Surely the other passengers, all city folks like him, were in much the same boat.

The inadvertent gallows humor brought a rueful smile to his lips, the first in too long.

He opened his eyes and glanced about. In the funereal half-light the cabin looked like a way station to hell. The tight rows of hammocks, strung top and bottom along both walls of the long, narrow space and pendant with somnolent bodies, resembled cells in an insect hive. From overhead pipes dangled fifty-three rucksacks, one per passenger, containing hastily gathered documents, photographs, and keepsakes. The floor was luminous with a thin coat of water, the foul spill from overburdened sanitation facilities.

Suddenly the ominous hush constricting the vessel gave way to a roiling liquid *whooosh.*

Was that the funny young man, on his way to save us all?

He felt his daughter stir.

"Papa, the story about the Golden Land," she murmured into his chest. "Tell it again?"

He felt a stinging sensation in his nose. Since infancy his daughter's favorite bedtime story had been the one about a country where people were free to have fun, to buy all the fresh fruits and vegetables they wanted, and to worship as they chose. She no doubt also imagined this country to be filled with wondrous buildings much like the icons on the barrel of her favorite pen. Yesterday, the captain had announced that the Golden Land was only two days distant. But now, with both the vessel's engines silent, it seemed a lifetime away. The father blinked rapidly, willing back the tears.

"I want to see the sun again," she said in a tremulous voice. "Papa, I'm scared. I want to see Mama and my brother and my sisters, and I want to see the sun again."

He hugged her tightly, caressed her face, and said, "You are my love, Princess."

The girl gave him a quick kiss and snuggled closer. Then she began clicking her pen: in and out, in and out, in and out—

The father cleared his throat. No matter how often he repeated the tale of the Golden Land, where the family would reunite and live happily ever after, it never grew stale: "Once upon a time—"

A dull *whump* quivered the bow of the vessel.

There was just time enough for a startled yell, and then the metal skin of the vessel surrendered and the waters of the Mediterranean lunged in.

It was a typically busy late spring evening at Cantler's Riverside Inn in Annapolis, Maryland. By seven-thirty the line of patrons waiting for a table extended out into the parking lot. Among them was a group of U.S. Naval Academy midshipmen treating themselves to a break from final exams, not to mention from the pizza that had dominated their diets on recent nights.

A black 1988 Honda CRX pulled into the lot.

The midshipmen's desultory chatter trailed off when they noticed the woman emerging from the car.

"How old do you think she is?" whispered one of the gawking cadets.

"Twenty-eight, thirty maybe . . . but who's counting?"

The woman had dressed for the muggy weather in an outfit—baggy white T-shirt, faded gray cargo shorts, running shoes—that accentuated her rangy frame. Locking the car and hitching a knapsack over one shoulder, she adjusted her sunglasses and started striding toward the restaurant.

"Think she's meeting somebody?"

"A twin sister, if we're lucky."

One of the cadets hesitated, then stepped forward to ask if she might like to join their table for dinner.

"I've already got a date," the woman replied, stifling a smile. Definitely cute, but barely older than her baby brother. Nor would he be so aggressive were she in her work clothes. "Thank you anyway."

Inside the restaurant the harried manager softened when she gave him the name of the man she was to meet. "Oh, yes, the captain. Right this way, please."

The manager led her through the main room, bustling with diners cracking steamed crabs over newspaper tablecloths, and out onto a terrace that overlooked one of the inlets of the Severn River.

A man in his early fifties sat at a table, beer in hand, paging through a thick book by the last light of day. Although now a college professor, he still had the short haircut and erect bearing of a former Navy skipper.

Propping her sunglasses atop her head, the woman began to make her way toward him.

The man spotted her coming and stood. "Lieutenant Edna J. Haddix, my favorite eighteen-hundred."*

"My favorite skipper," she said, accepting a kiss on the cheek.

---

*1800: *In Naval Officer Billet Code, an oceanographic specialist ticketed to the U.S. Naval Oceanographic Office, or NavOceano.*

"Sorry I'm late, Jack. I didn't expect so much construction on Route Fifty."

"I'd rather row a dinghy up the Mekong in a monsoon than drive here from Washington," he grumped, motioning her to a seat. "But no harm. Emily won't be back from visiting her folks until Thursday. She can't stand to be around me during final exams."

"I thought you left your temper at sea. Anyway, aren't professors supposed to tyrannize their students, not their wives?"

"Very funny, E.J., only you got it backward. See this book? The definitive text on hydrodynamics. If you ever have trouble falling asleep, just read a paragraph or two. Well, today I received an essay that totally misconstrued the test question. Trouble is, it was from my best student . . . who, I might add, happens to be female."

Haddix grinned; when she first met Jack, on a mission in the Western Pacific several years ago, his views on women serving in the Navy had been considerably less charitable.

"Do you have to rub it in?" he said with mock annoyance. "I was wrong about not letting your kind wear uniforms, okay? Now, where was I? Oh, yes, so I took another look at my question. Damn thing was just ambiguous enough to allow a different interpretation."

"And now you're backchecking her logic, to see if her answer might also be correct. Same old Skip." Too decent for the Navy, she thought, her latest grudge against the service's casual chauvinism still fresh. Two days earlier Haddix had been tasked to a new mission; if she'd only gotten the careful briefing that any male 1800 would have received, she might not have had to drive all the way to Annapolis to see a friend who could fill in the blanks.

"Let's get you something cold to drink," Jack said, signaling the waitress. "What've you been doing with yourself these last two years? Still running robots?"

"Affirmative. You should see some of the goodies they're putting aboard my . . ." At the edge of her vision Haddix glimpsed somebody waving at her from a table across the way. It was the flirtatious midshipman she had passed in the parking lot. The cadet's smile suddenly froze when he noticed the man with whom she was sitting.

"Friend of yours?" asked Jack acerbically.

"He volunteered to become one."

"One of the Academy's basketball stars," Jack said. "I had him last semester. Decent student, a better athlete. Something tells me he's going to be dropping by my office soon. Want me to say you're my niece, or should I give him your name?"

She laughed. "No, just my rank. That should put things in perspective for him."

The waitress arrived.

Haddix ordered a beer, then said, "Skip, what happens to a ship when it sinks? What kind of trail does it leave?"

The question surprised him. "Navy's sending you fishing."

She nodded.

"And you need a crash course in search-and-recovery. Okay, what can you tell me about the circumstances . . . anybody hear her die? Any debris float to the surface?"

"I, uh, I think we better keep this theoretical."

He studied her for several moments. "Damn, you've been to Suitland."*

She met his gaze but remained silent.

Jack snorted. "Same old No Intelligence Service. Fair enough, but give me a moment. Unless I sort things out, I could talk until the sun comes up and still not tell you what you need."

Haddix watched him lean back in his chair. Though forbidden from sharing her brief, she was confident Jack would quickly deduce that the target lay in deep water, since the robots she handled —unmanned research probes rigged with various cameras and mechanical arms—were designed to work at depths beyond the range of even the strongest-hulled nuclear submarine. He might also rea-

---

*Suitland: *Headquarters of the Naval Intelligence Service, or NIS, in the Washington, D.C. suburb of Suitland, Maryland.*

sonably wonder how high a priority the search had if a staff officer like herself was in charge, rather than a line officer experienced in such operations.

A fresh breeze swept across the inlet, ruffling the waters and lifting the edges of the newspaper tablecloths.

The waitress returned with Haddix's beer and started to recite the daily specials.

"I'll have whatever he's having," she interrupted.

"We'll start with a dozen crabs," Jack said. He regarded Haddix. "I assume you don't need a refresher course about pressure."

"Every thirty-three feet down's another atmosphere."

"Correct. At a depth of three thousand feet, you're talking one ton per square inch. No hull ever built can withstand that kind of pressure."

"But they found *Titanic* below thirteen thousand feet, and it hadn't imploded,"* she said.

"You're getting ahead of me, E.J. I've seen wrecks at four thousand feet that looked like the captain had parked her and gone out for a cup of coffee. I've seen others in much shallower waters that looked like a nuclear bomb had gone off. We had one submarine where the entire stern section telescoped forward into the engine compartment. It's one thing to die, another to be squished into goo . . . at least it happened so fast that her crew never knew what hit them.

"The key is the amount of flooding that occurs before the ship reaches her collapse depth. If the hull retains its integrity and remains basically watertight, you'll probably get a pretty violent implosion along the lines of that submarine I just mentioned. But if water's coming in at a fairly good rate, like on *Titanic,* she might well reach bottom mostly intact. Of course, that still doesn't tell you

*Implosion: *A violent inward collapse of the hull caused when water pressure surpasses the strength of the hull and the atmospheric pressure inside the ship.*

if she hit hard or soft, or if she landed in a field of silt or a rocky canyon."

Haddix sipped her beer. "What kind of trail does it leave?"

"The more a ship breaks up, and the deeper she sinks, the easier she is to find," Jack replied. "The heaviest stuff tends to drop almost vertically, just like the ship itself . . . something like a deck winch isn't going to be affected much by even a three-knot current. Lighter objects, though, drift down-current. A ship finding bottom at two thousand feet will have a pretty tight debris field. That same ship sinks to ten thousand feet, and suddenly you're talking a pretty significant field. I believe *Titanic*'s trail stretched almost a mile and a half. In either case, just track from the lightest debris to the heaviest, and it'll lead you right to the wreck."

"Is that how you located the *Challenger* off Cape Canaveral?" she asked.

Jack nodded. "The explosion blew the shuttle apart, but the crew capsule retained structural integrity. Those poor astronauts . . . free-falling for five minutes, knowing there was no way to bail out."

Haddix's eyes widened. "You mean that rumor's true? They actually lived through that fireball?"

"Affirmative. It was the capsule hitting the water that killed them. The impact tore up everything pretty badly . . . hell, we're talking about a debris field where most of the debris was no bigger than that fork. I just wish all of it had been that size." He took a sip of beer. "It was ghastly, E.J. I'd been on more than my share of search-and-recovers, but after that one, when Navy offered me a teaching post at the Academy, well, maybe I just figured these eyes had seen enough."

Haddix shook her head in commiseration. "Funny how in the last few minutes we've mentioned two examples of state-of-the-art technology that failed."

"*Titanic* and *Challenger*," Jack said softly. "We try so hard to conquer nature, don't we? But nature is unforgiving . . . especially the sea."

The two of them fell silent.

Out beyond the inlet a sailboat, a wraithlike silhouette in the gathering dusk, headed gracefully up the Severn for home.

The waitress appeared with a platter of steamed crabs.

Jack ordered another round of beers, served Haddix a crab, and plopped one on the newspaper in front of him.

"Any other questions?" he asked.

She hesitated, then said, "Remains. What might I expect to find?"

"That also depends. If the boat went down more than a year or two ago, not very much."

"Really? I thought low water temperature would preserve—"

"Food chain, E.J., food chain. Nature is not only remarkably unforgiving, but also remarkably efficient. At every depth there are fish, mollusks, crustaceans." Jack twisted off a claw and brandished it. "How do you think our friend here got so plump and juicy?"

She involuntarily shivered.

"Shall I continue, or do you want to enjoy your meal?"

"No, please go on."

"Flesh is the first to go, followed by the bones," he said. "Clothing takes a few years longer, but after a decade or so, just about everything organic aboard the boat will have been consumed. Except leather footwear."

"Hunh?"

"Perhaps the chemicals they use to tan leather are indigestible, but you always find shoes and boots at the site of a wreck. Lots of them, singly and in pairs. Very eerie."

"God, if I'd known all this as a kid, I'd have been a terror at telling campfire stories."

Jack laughed, then said, "When you called this morning, did I hear you say you're leaving the Navy?"

"That's an affirmative," Haddix replied. "In August, to go back for my doctorate. In fact, this'll probably be my next-to-last mission."

"Has Navy tried to talk you into staying?"

"This time, Skip, I was smart enough to just say no."

He smiled. "Listen, Emily and I are having a cookout this week-end. We'd love for you to come, E.J."

"Damn, I'm shipping out Thursday morning."

"Too bad," Jack said mischievously. "There'll be bachelors there."

"This some kind of class project, finding me a guy?"

"Well, it'd be good to see you settle down with someone."

"It's been a while, I'll tell you." Haddix laughed sardonically. "Several months ago I read about a species of shrimp that lives in Death Valley and parts of Nevada and Utah. You know how they cope with the lack of water? By going into a kind of suspended animation—for decades, if necessary—until enough rain falls to bring them back to life. I think I may have turned into a desert shrimp a few years back, at least as far as my social life is concerned."

He reached for his glass but remained silent.

"I don't know, Jack." Usually loath to discuss her personal life, she knew she'd be hard pressed to find a more sympathetic audience. "I used to think it was just the men I met. Even after you weed out the ones who wear nerd packs and the ones who move their lips when they read *TV Guide,* there should be plenty to go around, right? But the real can-do guys never seemed comfortable with the fact that I'm that way too. As for the others . . . well, aren't men supposed to make some of the decisions about where to eat, what movie to see? But now I think it's me."

"What do you mean?"

She shrugged. "I have this real thing about competence. I demand it of myself, and of everyone around me too."

"Nothing wrong with that, E.J."

"Depends on your motive, doesn't it? Mine was so people wouldn't judge me only by appearances." Haddix stared at her plate for several moments. "Did I ever tell you about my father?"

Jack shook his head.

"A decent man, Skip. Educated, good job, only he has one big blind spot . . . he thinks women shouldn't trouble themselves over things like a career. Just find the right man, make him happy, and go through life on cruise control. When the dentist suggested I might need braces, my father was right there with the checkbook. When I said I wanted to go to college, the checkbook stayed shut. Well, damn it, I refuse to be an ornament." She glanced out at the darkened waters. "It's such a cliché, isn't it, trying to earn your father's approval? The trouble is, maybe I've tried so hard to prove I'm competent that I've become incompetent at relationships."

"Bullshit," Jack said. "You were right the first time. I predict the man for you is going to be wearing civvies . . . but look who you've been meeting the last four years."

Haddix grinned and tilted her head toward the flirtatious midshipman's table: "Either kids with zits, or old farts who are married, like you."

"Touché." He raised his glass in sardonic salute. "Now that we've solved your love life, where you off to? Or can't you say?"

"The Med."

"Uh-oh."

"What?"

"Better watch your step, E.J. Navy doesn't go throwing around cushy assignments like that unless they really want you to reup."

DAY ONE:

27 MAY 1988

THE EASTERN MEDITERRANEAN

From the horizon the ship looked like a tramp steamer resting at anchor between voyages. It sat motionless on a glassy sea, flags limp, decks bare save for a few stray cargo containers strewn about the afterdeck, the broad expanse that stretched from its three-story superstructure back to the stern.

An alert observer, though, might have wondered why a freighter would choose to idle in open water a full thirty-eight nautical miles from the nearest landfall, the rock-strewn beaches of western Crete. A few moments at the navigational chart would have pointed up a second incongruity; the vessel lay becalmed directly over the deepest part of the Mediterranean, a submarine rift known as the Hellencian Trench that plunged in spots to almost 15,000 feet.

From closer in, disturbing hints that something might have gone awry aboard the ship: a tall yellow two-legged boom, known as an A-frame, leaned drunkenly out over the stern, seemingly as useless and forgotten as a bent croquet wicket. A massive diesel engine yammered away dementedly on the afterdeck even though the drums and winches of a nearby traction unit stood idle. The crew had also failed to lower from the foremast the three black canvas balls that proclaimed the vessel to have a load under tow.

Only from directly alongside was the illusion of a ghost ship dispelled. Every thirty seconds or so the waters forward and aft boiled angrily as special underwater thrusters kicked in to maintain precise positioning. Although the traction unit stood idle, a thin cable stretched tautly from it up to the top of the A-frame and then down into the depths. And two of the cargo containers on the afterdeck were worth a second look. Normally, these modular steel boxes

* Zulu: *Greenwich Mean Time.*

weren't placed side by side with unusual precision; nor were they painted an eye-jangling electric blue; nor did they whine with 20,000-BTU air conditioners laboring against the rapidly ascending sun; nor did they reverberate with the muffled twang of Charley Pride's *Kiss an Angel Good Morning.*

In fact, *Fanning II,* as the name on the stern read, was not a tramp steamer but a "mud boat"—a 262-foot research vessel custom-built by ONYXX, the U.S. petrochemical giant, to probe the world's seabeds for oil-bearing formations.

The ship's present expedition, however, was on behalf of pure science rather than commerce. It had been chartered from ONYXX by the Ethan R. Gillette Institute of Oceanography, or GIO, of Mystic, Connecticut, to serve as the platform for a fifteen-day study of a micro-section of the Hellencian Trench.

The enormous depths involved—five to ten times that achievable by the strongest-hulled submarine—had stymied previous generations of geophysicists from accurately surveying the underwater terrain. Now, however, there were unmanned deep-sea research vehicles that could transmit real-time video images from the ocean floor, as well as perform manual chores like collecting core samples. The GIO team had been able to borrow from the U.S. Office of Naval Research two state-of-the-art, remote-operated vehicles, nicknamed *Bert* and *Ernie,* along with three officers—an 1800 and two lieutenants, junior grade—to oversee the robots.

On this last Friday in May of 1988, Lieutenant Edna J. Haddix stood by the chart table in the nerve center of the expedition, a windowless "control van" on the afterdeck that had been formed by mating the two electric-blue cargo containers into a single unit.

The control van measured a mere eighteen by twenty feet. Yet in it was crammed enough sophisticated electronic gear to equip a TV studio, as well as the expedition's mission specialists, who operated *Bert* and *Ernie* around the clock in three watches of seven members each. The men and women carried out their duties in the spectral red glow cast by night-operation lights. Theirs was an environment both hermetic and timeless; the only clue that the sun had climbed high over the horizon came from the air-conditioners, whose heightened drone was giving Charley Pride stiff competition.

Haddix, the current watch officer, was hunched over a chart. Like the rest of the casually dressed crew she wore a T-shirt and shorts. Checking the numbers on her clipboard, she turned to study the row of large screens mounted high on the forward wall. Four of these twenty-seven-inch color television monitors displayed real-time images from the underwater vehicles, superimposed with date, time, and depth at which taken; the fifth displayed computer-generated navigational graphics.

Good, she thought; they were almost ready to take the next sample.

Beneath the monitors ran a long console subdivided into three work stations. The station on the far right, next to the forward hatch, was the navigator's; when the deep-sea vehicles were at work, the person manning it, and not the bridge, had command of the ship. The other two stations were for the "flyers" who piloted *Bert* and *Ernie*.

The van wall to Haddix's left was lined with banks of video recorders, shelf upon shelf of blank cassettes, and a laser-disc recorder. Just behind these, tucked into the corner, was a fourth work station that was occupied by *Bert*'s engineer.

Finally, on the wall behind her were two sonar plotters and the chart table. Under the table sat a squat combination safe; over it, a shelf for the all-important stereo gear. The aft wall also had a hatch that led out to the stern.

At the moment Haddix's two deep-sea vehicles were gingerly skating between jagged outcroppings on the eastern face of the Hellencian some 12,400 feet directly below *Fanning II.*

Bert, the larger of the robots, was a rectangular fifteen-foot-long vehicle. It lacked a propulsion system but was rigged with a pair of horizontal thrusters that afforded a degree of lateral mobility. Designed to serve as a research platform, the towed sled's open frame-

work bristled with video and still cameras equipped with SIT*
lenses; high-intensity floodlamps; and sonar scanners and fathome-
ters, all encased in pressure- and impact-resistant titanium housings.

Tethered to the sled was its sidekick *Ernie,* a free-roaming re-
motely operated vehicle, or ROV. Little *Ernie,* though only seven
feet in length, boasted half a dozen variable-pitch thrusters for propulsion and steering. It also carried its own battery of SIT video
cameras, lights, and sensors. Most important, it was fitted with a
pair of multitask mechanical arms.

Both vehicles received commands, and sent back video images
and other data, by way of a fragile fiber-optic cable protected by
two sheaths of steel wrapping. This three-quarter-inch-thick lifeline
emerged from the roof of the control van and ran aft to the traction
unit that sat halfway to the stern. From there it stretched tautly up
to the top of the thirty-foot-tall A-frame tilting out over the fantail,
then angled straight down and plunged into the depths.

Haddix could see by the image on the main monitor—taken by
the towed sled *Bert*'s wide-angle, forward-looking camera—that little *Ernie* was easing into position against a rugged canyon wall. As
soon as the ROV skirted a threatening finger of rock, it would be
ready to bore another core sample with the drill-and-canister assembly mounted on its right arm.

"How's it coming, Ezra?" she asked.

"Almost there, Navy." GIO tech Ezra Schell, *Ernie*'s "flyer," sat
at the center work station at the front of the van, between the
navigator and *Bert*'s flyer. Before him was a Watchman-sized video
monitor mounted just above two sets of steering controls. Consulting the monitor, which displayed images from *Ernie*'s own forward-
looking camera, Schell gently fingered the controls to swing the
ROV wide of the outcrop, then said, "How's she looking, Rollie?"

---

*SIT: Silicon Intensified Technology, developed in the 1960s to capture a coherent
image with 1/200th the light required by the fastest film. Its first application: the
"Starlight" scope, which enabled American GIs to pick off infiltrating Viet Cong on
moonless nights without having to use their telltale infrared beams.*

His question was directed to Roland Vigneron, a French marine geologist manning the *Bert* engineering station in the rear corner of the van. The station consisted of a computer terminal, three small TV monitors, two oscilloscope screens, and a panel of buttons that directed the routing of the various video feeds. The Frenchman glanced at one of the small monitors. The feed from the towed sled's forward-looking camera showed little *Ernie* passing well clear of the outcrop.

"It is looking fine," Vigneron said. "Your tether, it is streaming clear of the scarp."

Haddix said, "Rollie, why don't you throw *Ernie*'s forward feed up on Monitor Two."

"Roger, Navy," Vigneron replied, punching the buttons that would switch the signal.

The five men and two women in the van transferred their attention to the new image; the dicey long-distance surgery was about to begin.

Schell inched *Ernie* to within two feet of the brownish-black wall. He extended the ROV's right arm until the canister touched rock, then toggled the switch that started the drill.

As the bit dug into the chalky surface, Monitor Two blossomed with a bright yellow glow that all but obscured the operation; the light from the ROV's powerful lamps was being scattered by sedimentary particles.

Just then over the sound system, a final quavering guitar chord, followed by a *click,* followed by silence.

"Thank God," navigator Leonard Heppel muttered. He glanced up from the computer that tracked *Fanning II*'s position and automatically made the minute adjustments needed to keep the research vessel steady against wind and current. "Country sucks."

"Yo, watch it," said Billy Ray McConkey, the sonar operator on this watch, as well as *Fanning II*'s resident yahoo. Despite having lived five years in genteel Mystic, Connecticut, the wiry McConkey proudly clung to a down-home mind-set acquired as a youth in a hardscrabble section of Galveston, Texas, and reinforced by two hitches in the Navy prior to joining GIO as a mission specialist. "I don't see no Brie and Chablis on board, Big Len, so how come we got to listen to your fancy yuppie music? New Age, my ass. Same damned four notes over and over, like the dude lost his sheet music or his synthesizer glitched out."

Heppel met McConkey's glare, but the two men let it go. Both had been on enough expeditions to recognize control-van fever. This being *Fanning II*'s ninth consecutive day on site, the physical wear and tear that every ocean voyage exacted was compounded by the kind of high-tech stress experienced by sleep-deprived NASA mission controllers and air traffic controllers. For when *Bert* and *Ernie* operated in terrain as rugged as the Hellencian Trench, even momentary lapses of concentration invited catastrophe. In less time then it took to freshen a mug of coffee or even retrieve a pencil that had fallen to the floor, a jagged face of rock could loom out of the jet-black darkness just beyond the range of the vehicles' lights. Unless reflexes were sharp, the sled and ROV, each valued at several million dollars, might smash into the wall or, worse, sever the steel-sheathed fiber-optic cable.

"Somebody slap on a fresh tape," McConkey growled. "Whose turn is it?"

Liz Trimble, one of two college-aged GIO interns on the expedition, reached for a clipboard hanging on the wall next to the sound system. To accommodate widely varying musical preferences this watch had established a rotation based on drawn straws. She consulted the list, looked at Heppel—who was already holding up a cassette—and said, "One guess, Cowboy."

McConkey followed her gaze and groaned.

Trimble caught the tossed cassette, inserted it into the box, and pressed Play.

Heppel had chosen not New Age but the latest Midnight Oil.

As the rockers from Down Under thundered into action, McConkey made a face. "Damn fool thing, sticking electric wires in a perfectly good guitar."

Five minutes later Schell backed little *Ernie* away from the sheer vertical wall and retracted its right arm toward the sample cage in the ROV's belly. When he uncoupled the canister and secured it in the cage, the others in the van allowed themselves to relax.

"One down, one to go," Haddix announced. She turned to Trimble and said, "Liz, Leonard needs range and bearing to the next target."

Trimble was double-checking the position of the latest sample before logging it. She cast her eyes up the track line, which ran to the northwest, and said, "Len, come to three-zero-nine. It's about twelve hundred meters away. Sam, we'll be dropping below thirteen thousand two hundred feet for the next sample, but bathymetry's showing a lot of bear traps."

"Roger that," Sam Lippman acknowledged from the left front work station. As *Bert*'s flyer he controlled the towed sled's altitude by winching its cable in or out. It was his job to keep the vehicle safely above the ocean floor and out of bear traps, those enticing drop-offs that invariably and abruptly terminated in a towering wall of solid rock. To do so he relied on a trio of console-mounted TV monitors that displayed, from left to right, a sonar plot of the terrain; the traction unit on the afterdeck, to make sure the cable remained unobstructed; and the feed from *Bert*'s wide-angle, forward-looking camera.

At a speed of one and a half knots it would take *Fanning II* forty-five minutes to reach its new position.

Haddix said, "Ezra, time to garage *Ernie*."

"Right, Navy." Schell started his little ROV up toward the sled; during transits like this it was standard operating procedure to tuck *Ernie* inside the cage attached to *Bert*'s belly.

Around the van, crew members picked up half-finished sandwiches and warm sodas. Some chatted about which video movie to rack up when their watch ended; trouble was, each tape on board, even the turkeys, had already been played at least twice.

Haddix grabbed her bottle of Evian and walked over to the *Bert* engineering station. "Rollie, why don't you take five? I'll sit in."

Roland Vigneron nodded in appreciation. An owlishly polite

Frenchman in his forties who was a faculty member of the Oceano-graphic Department of the Université d'Aix-Marseille, he had joined the expedition to gain hands-on experience with the deep-sea research vehicles. Haddix judged him the most capable of the electronics specialists on board. Vigneron stood and headed straight for Billy Ray McConkey, his best friend on the ship.

As usual McConkey had something to gripe about. This time it was the launch that would be arriving in several hours to pick up the party of Greek scientists who had spent the past four days as observers aboard *Fanning II.*

"Yo, Rollie," McConkey said, "what say we talk our way aboard that sucker?"

"But Cowboy, if we go ashore, how do we get back?"

"We charter us a speedboat, *mon ami.* What good's money if there's nothing to spend it on?"

"But who stands our watches?" asked Vigneron.

"Not watches, Rollie, watch. Way I figure it, we only miss one. Got to be some bimbos hanging out near the port, and shoot, us cowboys don't need long to score—" McConkey suddenly remem-bered who else was in the van and lapsed into silence.

On the second day at sea he had tried with comic intensity to coax Edna Haddix into bed, at one point assuming a thick Mexican accent and offering to rejuvenate her with his precious "Oil of Olé!"

Now, settling in at the *Bert* engineering station, she couldn't resist the opening. "Yo, Sonar. Hear about the cowboy who wanted to kiss his girl in a naughty place?"

McConkey stared at his sonar plotters with unusual intensity, acutely aware that all eyes were on him.

"He drove her to Texarkana."

McConkey reddened as laughter filled the van.

Just then a dazzling wedge of light slammed into the darkened van.

"Aw, shut the fucking hatch, for Christ's sake," McConkey barked, and for once everyone else was on his side.

Haddix squinted into the glare, identified the figure who was quickly closing the forward hatch behind him, and scowled.

It was Ariel Kahane, the other GIO intern aboard. "Sorry, Cowboy," the young Israeli graduate student said, removing his sunglasses. He was a tanned, handsome six-footer whose hesitant manner stemmed more from unfamiliarity with the idiomatic English spoken on board than from shyness.

Bet he goes straight for the chart table, Haddix thought darkly.

Kahane blinked until his eyes had adjusted to the dim red light, then headed for the back of the van and Liz Trimble.

Just flirting, or scrounging data again? Though Haddix had no specific reason to distrust Kahane, she had nonetheless mentally nicknamed him "The Carp" after the way he bottom-fed for information.

A few moments later she forced herself to put aside her suspicions. While she was the officer of this watch, the ultimate responsibility for the expedition, and its data, rested with the chief scientist.

Haddix switched one of the *Bert* engineering station monitors over to the laser recorder feed.

The GIO team was visually documenting its underwater work in two ways. The video cameras aboard *Bert* and *Ernie,* which included both stationary units that provided wide-angled views and swiveling units with pan-and-tilt and zoom capabilities, sent their signals up the fiber-optic cable and directly into the rows of VCRs along the van's left wall. The team was using Beta-format machines, which despite their limited taping time yielded significantly crisper images than the more common VHS-format decks. Although the resulting tapes reproduced acceptable full-color overviews, their capacity for capturing fine details was still wanting; the analogue recording process inevitably degraded signal quality.

The solution was an electronic still camera that recorded images not on film or tape, but in digital form, as electronic signals. The techs had installed such a unit aboard *Bert,* slaving it to move in tandem with the sled's pan-and-tilt video camera. Triggered by a red button at the right of the *Bert* engineering station, the camera snapped high-resolution black-and-white frames. These were stored aboard the sled until called up and spooled into a Panasonic TQ3031-F laser recorder, which burned the data onto a write-once disc. Because the signals were digital, they never deteriorated or became grainy. Further, they could be computer-enhanced—electronically sharpened, magnified, and cropped—without harm.

Haddix pecked a few commands into the computer keyboard to retrieve the most recent electronic still. Twenty seconds later an image began to form.

It was a portrait of *Ernie,* taken several minutes earlier by the sled-mounted camera from a distance of thirty feet. The little ROV was poised in front of the canyon wall, its half-bent mechanical arm emerging from a sediment cloud.

Haddix fiddled with several knobs and zoomed in on the canister assembly at the end of the mechanical arm. She continued to up magnification until the canister assembly filled the screen. The picture remained in such clear focus that she could make out silt and even individual pebbles sloughing off the outside of the canister assembly.

Quite a toy, she mused. Too bad her covert task from Naval Intelligence Service—the assignment that had prompted her to drive out to Annapolis to consult with an ex-skipper—was such a long shot. It would've been fun to use the resources aboard *Fanning II* to hunt something more interesting than rock samples.

Haddix sighed and switched the monitor back to the live feed from *Bert*'s forward-looking camera.

The sled had fallen slightly astern as the research vessel towed it toward its next station.

In the flat, shadow-casting glare of *Bert*'s lights, the unfolding terrain resembled the scene of a geological accident. Some primordial force had gouged great chunks out of the nearly vertical canyon wall to the right. Slightly below sat a ledge—a fragile balcony perched over the black void, thought Haddix—on which boulders, one the size of a skyscraper, teetered precariously. If this stretch of the Hellencian Trench were to be thrust above water, could even the most skilled mountaineer scale it?

The sled's bow slowly started angling to port.

Haddix switched her computer over to the stream of navigational data. Len Heppel had not changed *Fanning II*'s course; there must be a crosscurrent caused by irregularities in the wall.

Now, up ahead to starboard, Haddix spotted a sizable gap in the rock face. In order to take a quick look-see with the forward-looking camera, she needed to pivot *Bert*'s bow against the current. Haddix was about to activate the sled's horizontal thrusters when she remembered the telephoto lens on its pan-and-tilt camera.

She quickly swapped feeds and keyboarded several commands.

The camera began panning clockwise and tilting downward.

As the sled slowly neared the leading edge of the gap, its lights penetrated the indentation and reflected off the walls of a surprisingly spacious vertical column not unlike an exposed elevator shaft. How far down did it reach? Haddix angled the camera lower.

Hold on. . . .

She cranked the zoom.

Some forty feet below the sled the shaft widened out into a sloping terrace covered with silt and . . . could it be?

"Navigator, all stop and hold this position!"

Startled, Heppel keyed in a command, then swung around to glare at Haddix. "What the hell? How's about a little warning next time, Navy?"

"There's something to starboard," she replied over the growing whine of engines crashing into full reverse.

The ship shuddered as its twin screws labored to halt its forward momentum.

A strangled yell now from *Bert* flyer Lippman, who had sloshed hot coffee onto his lap in his haste to grab his control stick. The sled had been gliding below and behind the ship, held at a constant altitude by the steady flow of water past both it and its two-and-a-half-mile-long cable. *Fanning II*'s unannounced slowdown, though, caused the flow to suddenly diminish. The sled responded by penduluming forward—and, more ominously, downward. Lippman began hauling in cable as rapidly as he dared, his eyes glued to the monitor showing the traction unit; if he winched up too fast, the line could jump the drum and jam or snap.

The others in the van, quickly as alert as a pointer scenting a quail, stared at the images filling two of the large monitors on the forward wall: a swooping overhead from the *Bert*'s forward-looking camera and a steadier sideways shot from its pan-and-tilt camera.

Haddix ignored the bewildered comments flying around her. Damn, the angle was bad; she couldn't deflect the pan-and-tilt camera enough to get the target in full frame. Did she have time to dart the sled into the approaching crevice, then dart back out before it slammed into the far wall?

No sweat, she thought, her fingers attacking the keyboard.

As *Bert*'s corkscrew to the right became apparent on the large monitors, the van filled with protests.

"Get her the fuck out of there, Navy!" Heppel yelled. "Up, Sam, pull up on the cable!"

That's better, Haddix thought. Now, if I can just line up the camera . . .

"Wall dead ahead, Navy, wall dead ahead!" shouted McConkey. "Range, less than seven meters . . . hard to port, now!"

Haddix was oblivious to the sonarman's alarm and to the terrifying images of impending catastrophe flashing on the main monitor. Her eyes glued to the small screen in her console, she waited until the target was smack in the middle of the screen, then pressed the red button at the right of the console to fire off an electronic still. "Three-seven-two," she said, reflexively calling off a frame number for Liz Trimble to log.

"Jesus, we're going to hit!"

Haddix's eyes finally darted up to the main monitor.

Bert's forward-looking camera showed the sled closing slowly but inexorably on the far wall.

Galvanized by an adrenaline surge, she kicked the thrusters to port.

It was too late.

No one in the van could feel the actual collision, but they all flinched, as if gut-punched, when the impact caused the pictures from below to suddenly dance with a multitude of ghosts. Another sickening gauge of how hard the sled hit: An avalanche of sediment and rocks began streaming down past the cameras.

"Up, up! Pull up!"

"I'm trying," flyer Lippman said through clenched teeth. "God damn you, Navy. . . ."

Bert had recoiled some three feet from the initial collision; now it began to swing back toward the wall.

"Watch your tension!"

Lippman glanced at the gauge that registered the forces on the cable. "Fourteen thousand pounds," he called out. "Sixteen thousand, fourteen thousand . . . shit, I hate this!"

Hit and bounce, this time higher up the rock face but still with enough force to scramble the images—and to set off a beeper and a flashing red light on the console in front of *Ernie* flyer Ezra Schell.

"Oh my God, the garage door's open," Schell said. "If *Ernie* slides out . . ."

Under the red night-operation lights flyer Lippman's sweaty face seemed drenched in blood as he desperately continued to winch up *Bert.*

Hit and bounce, yet higher up the wall, the pictures from *Bert* momentarily freezing.

"That cable snags, we're dead!"

Hit and bounce again; this time, though, as the image from the forward-looking camera stabilized, the high-intensity lamps illuminated not the looming wall but open water.

The relief flooding the van lasted a heartbeat before it turned to wrath.

"That was a real asshole move, Navy," Heppel snapped.

"This ain't no Top Gun school," McConkey chimed in.

"Sorry, guys," Haddix said lamely, feeling as mortified as the time her parents had caught her sneaking back into the house two hours past her curfew. "I thought I could get in and out real quick."

"Atlantic Fleet says you're famous for that," McConkey shot back.

She let it go; the others had good reason to be furious. Covert intelligence assignment notwithstanding, as watch officer she had no right to jeopardize the expedition by haring off after something glimpsed out of the corner of her eye.

"Still holding station, Navy," Heppel said.

Haddix called to Schell, "Ezra, *Ernie* okay?"

"He stayed in the garage. I better run a systems check, though."

"Roger. Sam, what about *Bert*?"

"Forward-looking and pan-and-tilt cameras transmitting normally. Check out the electronic still camera, please?"

"Right," Haddix said, turning to the keyboard. "Len, please hold position until we finish damage control."

Twenty seconds later the image she had captured from the bottom of the crevice began to paint itself on her screen. Only the top two thirds materialized—the rest was lost to snow and streaks—and the image was badly oversaturated and out of focus. Still, it clearly showed the smooth floor of the terrace to be broken by something that possessed compound curves.

Haddix sagged with disappointment; the object could not have come from the long-lost vessel on which she had been briefed.

From behind her Liz Trimble said, "Hey, E.J., put that up on the main monitor."

Haddix punched a button.

"Hell, looks like one of them inflatable love-dolls," McConkey said.

"You'd know," Haddix replied, automatically massaging the digital enhancement knobs on her console.

The van fell silent as the image slowly sharpened into a close-up of an ebony vase decorated with breathtakingly intricate spirals. The vase lay on its side, two thirds buried in silt, but appeared to be intact.

After a while Len Heppel said, "Anybody got a clue?"

"I remember something like this from an art appreciation class," Liz Trimble volunteered. "It may be Minoan, which makes sense, considering where we are. Off Crete, I mean."

"When was Minoa?" McConkey asked.

"One or two thousand B.C.," Trimble replied.

"Well, hell, this cowboy needs a new pair of boots. Let's go get it."

"It may be a copy you can pick up at Woolworth's, or whatever the Greeks call their five-and-dimes," Heppel said.

"And it could be the real McCoy, in which case some museum is going to make us fucking rich," McConkey said.

Haddix was grateful the others had switched their attention from her reckless actions to her intriguing discovery. Still, she felt a palpable disappointment; she hadn't been sent to the Med to dig up a vase. She stood. "Dr. Stathoplos, the taller scientist? Isn't his wife an amateur archaeologist? And if it is an antique, we better figure out if we're sitting in somebody's EEZ* before we pluck it."

"Aw, Navy, you're no fun."

"Sure I am, Cowboy. You're just on the wrong wavelength. One of us better go get Rick and Mrs. Stathoplos."

The others continued to gawk at the monitor, the romance of their find a tonic to the tedium of their mission and the high tension of their recent crisis.

Finally Haddix sighed, reached under the engineering station for her knapsack, and said, "Rollie, if you'll relieve me, I'll go get them."

She pushed open the forward hatch and winced; the sunlight streaming down from the cerulean skies was turning the surrounding seas into a giant mirror. Slipping on her sunglasses, Haddix started forward toward the superstructure.

*EEZ: *Exclusive Economic Zone, which extends beyond a nation's territorial waters.*

■ ■ ■

Dr. Rick Wolfe, the mission's chief scientist, sat in the mess hall on the main deck of *Fanning II*. Flanking him were the two Greek scientists, Stathoplos and Los, who had been invited aboard as observers because some of the core samples were being taken inside their nation's EEZ. As the two men, and Mrs. Stathoplos, continued to chat animatedly in their native language, Wolfe traced idle patterns in the film of reddish grit that covered the tabletop. The fine particles, which coated every surface of the ship, had been Saharan topsoil until they were kicked up and borne north by the ill wind known as the "sirocco."

Why had the ship just come to a halt? More to the point, since he had volunteered to pinch-hit on the upcoming midwatch for one of *Ernie*'s flyers who had taken ill, why wasn't he in his cabin, napping? But the Greeks had decided to depart a day early, and Wolfe thought it polite to spend some time with them. Until five minutes ago they had been sounding him out about coming back to participate on a bilateral geomorphological expedition, but what in the world were they discussing now? Probably which spiffy restaurant to hit for dinner, he thought darkly as he surveyed the half-eaten breakfasts on the table. Was his envy merely a sign of fatigue? Or did it in fact grow from the acute sense of anticlimax that had dogged him the past few days?

Now forty-one, Wolfe had spent the better part of five years trying to get his expedition off the drawing board. He, his twenty-six-member GIO team, and the three Navy specialists had come to this end of the Med to gather data on continental drift, the theory postulating that Earth's land masses sat atop giant tectonic plates that were in imperceptible but perpetual migration. The 450-mile-long Hellencian Trench was one place where the African and Eurasian plates were thought to grind against each other. By methodically collecting core samples from both sides of the abyss, Wolfe hoped to help validate the theory.

In the oceanographic community, though, there was a definite pecking order to the projects receiving funding and equipment. He had learned the hard way that studying the Hellencian's strata composition did not rank high. In addition, science grants had grown progressively harder to come by during the Reagan years, and the competition for the handful of suitable deep-sea research vehicles, all of which belonged to the U.S. Navy, was fiercer yet.

Still, Wolfe had lobbied and fought. As he used to say to his wife and friends, it was like running against a multiterm congressman. But his persistence finally paid off. The previous winter the Navy had unexpectedly agreed to lend him *Bert* and *Ernie* for three weeks, for they had judged his expedition perfect for field-testing a new fiber-optic cable long enough to reach the Trench's great depths.

Access to the robots proved the key that unlocked other finite resources. Wolfe's superiors, mindful of GIO's rivalry with the more prestigious oceanographic programs at Woods Hole and Scripps, had within a week helped him stitch together the necessary grants and persuade ONYXX to charter him a mud boat. The next six months had passed in a blur of seventy-hour workweeks as Wolfe fine-tuned the mission objectives and itinerary, recruited his team, negotiated to keep costs within budget, and even joined another oceanographic expedition to learn how to operate the unmanned deep-sea vehicles.

Now, ten days after boarding *Fanning II* in Athens and nine days into the painstaking task of drilling core samples, excitement had given way to apathy, enthusiasm to ennui. Wolfe smiled ruefully; he was starting to behave like one of his neighbors back home in Connecticut, a newly retired fireman who complained of finding himself lying awake nights, waiting for the bell to ring.

Wolfe looked up as Edna Haddix strode into the mess hall, her ever-present knapsack slung over one shoulder.

Like everyone else aboard ship he was intrigued by the 1800 the Navy had assigned to oversee its vehicles. The paradoxes surrounding her had been best articulated by Billy Ray McConkey back in Athens on the morning the crew assembled. Spotting Lt. Edna J. Haddix, USN, in crisp dress whites, as she led her two junior officers up the gangplank, Cowboy had blurted, "What's a girl like her doing in an outfit like that?"

McConkey's confusion was forgivable. One out of ten members of the armed services may have been female, but very few of them resembled Haddix; her looks were the kind that could easily have aroused desire among the men in the crew and jealousy among the women. Yet she also radiated a self-sufficiency that tended to disarm both envy and fantasy. In fact, McConkey's question remained unanswered for the simple reason that no one had yet summoned up the nerve to ask it of her.

Haddix approached the table and said, "Mrs. Stathoplos, gentlemen, we've stumbled across something I think you'll want to see. A vase . . . possibly Minoan."

The four people at the table quickly rose and followed Haddix toward the van.

"Yes . . . Kamáres," Demetra Stathoplos exclaimed as she studied the magnified electronic still displayed on all five of the large monitors. Space in the van was now at a premium. As word of the find had gotten out, some members of the idle watches had begun drifting back for a look, as had several of *Fanning II*'s crew, who normally stayed well clear of the afterdeck.

"Early Minoan," Mrs. Stathoplos continued. "Perhaps two thousand B.C., either from Kamáres or Knossós . . . look, not one crack or chip on the surfaces we see. This is incredible! Why it is not completely buried in silt?"

"There must be a microcurrent flowing down and out of that shaft," Rick Wolfe ventured. "E.J., did you feel anything when you approached with the sled?"

Haddix nodded.

McConkey cleared his throat and said to Mrs. Stathoplos, "Ma'am, how much might that pot be worth?"

"This is hard to say. You do not find too many Kamáres in one piece, but perhaps the other side has much damage."

"Shouldn't we, like, retrieve it for closer study?"

Wolfe cut in: "Demmie, we're almost thirty-eight miles from the nearest land."

"Yes . . . ?"

"That vase didn't just fall over the side of some pleasure boat."

"I see what you suggest," she said. "Of course. I think it comes only from a Phoenician trading boat which sinks."

McConkey whistled. "You mean there's more of this old stuff lying around?"

"Is quite possible," Mrs. Stathoplos replied.

Wolfe could feel the others in the van perking up—they were no doubt as bored with retrieving core samples of mud and rock as he was—and sensed that his next decision would go a long way toward defining whether, years hence, his crew looked back on this mission as drudgery or high adventure. The serendipity of stumbling across this one vase had already energized them; what if they could find more treasures? On the other hand, there was a simple bottom line that he could not ignore: This expedition's on-site time ran nearly $2,000 an hour.

He turned to the chart table to scan Liz Trimble's neatly penciled entries. Since *Fanning II* first took up station over the Hellencian, the weather had been even better than projected and the time lost to equipment snafus negligible. Overall, the mission was nearly fourteen hours ahead of schedule. Further, the current watch was right on its goal of one core sample every two hours. It was now shortly past nine-thirty A.M. Mrs. Stathoplos would be aboard only three more hours. What the hell, Wolfe thought, they could all use the R and R.

"E.J."

"Rick?"

"You've got two and a half hours left on your watch. If Demmie's willing to share her expertise, why don't we spend it trawling for treasure?"

"Roger that," Haddix replied, a smile spreading across her face. She quickly gathered her crew and, drawing upon the briefing she had received over the crab dinner in Annapolis, began to plot strategy.

The shaft in which the vase lay was notched into a towering 1,500-foot wall of rock to the east of their present position; some of the debris undoubtedly lay atop the canyon rim high above *Bert* and *Ernie*. Had the mission been purely archaeological, they would have "mowed the lawn," or meticulously tracked back and forth across the entire area, climbing and descending as needed. Pressed as they were for time, though, shortcuts were in order.

The prevailing northwesterly current would have carried the relatively lightweight vase an appreciable distance, Haddix reasoned. *Fanning II* would therefore slowly tack up-current, zigzagging in half-mile legs, or "lines," across the plateaus gently receding to the northwest. In trying to spot a debris trail that led to a Phoenician trader, *Bert* would fly thirty feet above the bottom, providing fifty-foot-wide overviews, and *Ernie* would scoot in for close-ups while also exploring nooks and crannies. This pattern was to a careful search as driving the Pacific Coast Highway was to getting a feel for California, but it represented the most efficient use of their scant time.

As Liz Trimble punched a Beach Boys tape into the cassette deck, navigator Heppel headed *Fanning II* north-by-northwest.

The first line yielded another vase that had shattered on impact.

On the second line they came across some encrusted utensils that Demetra Stathoplos identified, with palpable disappointment, as late Roman from the second century A.D., and more pottery sherds.

Shortly after eleven A.M. navigator Leonard Heppel brought *Fanning II* around for the third line.

Haddix glanced about the van. There were still about twenty people inside, but many were members of the other watches, whom she usually saw only at mess. She spotted Lieutenant (Junior Grade) Jeff Kabelo over in one corner. Haddix had assigned her two subordinates to separate science crews so that each of the three watches would have its own naval officer; Kabelo manned sonar on the twelve-to-four.

Vivaldi started to swirl over the sound system.

"Look at that!"

Up on Monitor Two, which carried the feed from *Bert*'s pan-and-tilt camera, an object that appeared to be a manhole cover was leaning against the base of the rock wall, half buried in silt.

Haddix suddenly came to alert. Trying to suppress the excitement from her voice, she said, "Zoom in."

Vigneron, at the *Bert* engineering station, tapped in a command.

Haddix studied the image. "Rollie, can you come in tighter?"

"No, Navy, I cannot."

"It looks like a hatch cover," navigator Heppel volunteered.

"Navy, you want me to go in for a closer look?" asked Ezra Schell, who was flying little *Ernie*. "Navy?"

"Hunh?" Be cool, Haddix told herself, be cool. "No, that's okay. The stuff we're looking for's about thirty-five hundred years older. Oh, uh, Rollie . . . just for the record, why don't you grab an electronic still. And put it on the reference tape."

"Yes, Navy. Liz, three-seven-six," Vigneron said. He hit the red button at the right of the console to capture the image, then retrieved the frame and burned it onto the time- and date-stamped video that was recording the sled's wide-angle forward camera.

Fifty feet ahead the cameras picked up another jumble of sherds that they passed over without pausing.

"Watch your altitude, Sam," McConkey called from the sonar table. "Coming up on a ridge, one-five-zero meters dead ahead."

"Roger that," flyer Lippman replied. He began winching in cable to climb *Bert* over a ridge that angled across their path.

On the far slope of the ridge, near the end of the third leg, they made a find that caused Demetra Stathoplos's eyes to gleam with excitement—and McConkey's with avarice. A dented and corroded metal chest the size of a bread box had come to rest in a field of jagged rocks. The impact had popped its cover, allowing some of its contents to escape and cascade down into a shallow gully.

Little *Ernie* hovered over the site, sending up pictures of a gully awash in coins.

"I'll be damned," McConkey said. "It's like one of them arcade games. You know, the kind where you try to scrape the coins into the payout chute?"

Demetra Stathoplos studied the close-up from the ROV's zoom lens, settled back in her seat, and said dismissively, "Roman."

"They worth anything, ma'am?"

"Perhaps tourists, they will pay several thousand drachmas each for them."

When McConkey remembered how little several thousand drachmas had bought back in Athens, his face fell.

The fourth line yielded yet more sherds, as well as an amphora that had landed in silt largely intact, though the impact had cracked the vessel.

Demetra Stathoplos stood and stretched. "Minoan, but Late, not Early. I think maybe it carries precious oils for trading, or maybe for the cooking. A nice piece, except for the crack." She moved to the chart table, where GIO interns Trimble and Kahane were plotting the finds. "See these different periods? The trade ships, they sail this route for thousands of years. Is interesting historically, but I think maybe we do not find the Phoenician."

Fanning II was slowing to begin its final line when *Bert*'s forward-looking camera picked up a large, oddly shaped shadow looming ahead and to the left.

"Ezra," Haddix said, "target at eleven o'clock. Can you give me a fly-by? Rollie, throw up *Bert*'s pan-and-tilt."

Vigneron switched one of the sled's feeds onto a large monitor as Schell continued flying the little ROV toward the target.

It was a four-foot section of metal plating that had obviously been ripped from a ship's hull by an immense force; though the sheet was three-quarter-inch thick steel, it was as warped and mangled as an empty beer can at a fraternity party.

"Looks like World War II," McConkey said softly, "and it

must've been one hell of a bang. Hope some of those poor sonuvabitches got out."

"Electronic still, please," Haddix said. "A couple here. . . . Ezra, circle it. Let's get a couple from the back."

Schell carefully swung *Ernie* around the debris.

The sheet was still attached at several points to a tightly curved span that had been part of the superstructure.

"What the hell did that come off of?" asked Sam Lippman from the *Bert* work station. "Any idea, Navy?"

" 'Fraid not, Sam," she replied, trying to hide her elation. "Ezra, clear your tether. Len, we better get onto our last line."

Haddix turned to the chart table and stared at Trimble's neatly marked chart. First a hatch cover and now a section of pressure-hull plating; could she have found the long-lost vessel?

The fifth line started out over a rugged patch of terrain, then sloped down to a fairly level terrace. They passed scatterings of sherds, then came across a six-foot-tall urn that was broken but not shattered. Demetra Stathoplos identified it as Late Minoan—"a nice specimen that can be restored; many small museums would like to have it"—and surmised it had carried fresh water for the long journeys from one Mediterranean port to another.

"Van, Bridge," the intercom squawked.

Navigator Heppel leaned over and flipped a switch: "Bridge, Van here."

"Right. We've been hailed by the launch coming to offload passengers. Her ETA is twenty minutes."

"Roger that, Bridge."

The three Greeks in the van stirred; preoccupied by the unexpected hunt for antiquities, they had neglected to pack. Rick Wolfe intercepted them as they headed for the forward door to say he would meet them by the port gangway after finishing the final few hundred yards of the last line.

Up on the monitors silt was giving way to rocks as the bottom began to rise again.

"Sonar, how tall's this ridge coming up?"

"I make it about three-five meters, Sam."

Flyer Lippman pulled back on his stick to climb *Bert*.

"Hey, what's that at two o'clock?"

There, almost lost in an outcropping of dark gray rocks, lurked an amorphous black shadow.

Vigneron swung *Bert*'s pan-and-tilt camera to starboard and zoomed in.

The sled's lamps were too weak to fully illuminate the target.

"Ezra," Vignernon said, "you can swing *Ernie* over there, please?"

"You got it," Schell replied, hitting the ROV's controls.

As *Ernie* drew nearer, the blob began to take on shape.

"Okay, guys, kill all the underwater lights," Haddix said, her voice loud in the hushed van.

The request went unheeded; everyone was too busy trying to comprehend the surrealistic vision of a neoprene skin-diver's suit in such an unlikely place.

The ROV had closed to inside fifteen feet.

The suit, obviously empty, was badly shredded, particularly about the legs. The air tank was missing, but fastened to its waist was a weight belt that had dragged it to this great depth and now held it facedown in a craggy cavity.

"I said all underwater lights off," Haddix repeated, an edge to her voice.

"Steady as she goes, Ezra," Wolfe interjected. He turned to Haddix. "This is pretty interesting stuff. Don't worry, we'll be under way in just a few minutes."

She stifled a retort and began threading her way through the press of bodies toward the *Bert* engineering station.

Suddenly, on one of the large monitors, the wet suit lurched up from its resting place.

The collective gasp subsided as soon as the people in the van realized it had only been pressure waves from *Ernie,* agitating the water.

McConkey hummed the opening notes of *The Twilight Zone* theme; the laughter he elicited sounded hollow.

The ROV began maneuvering around to the far side, its passage causing the suit's torso and head to bob up and down rhythmically.

Haddix finally reached the *Bert* engineering station and keyed in the commands to shut off the vehicles' lamps.

But before she could hit Enter, an indelible close-up filled the monitor and froze the room. On the forehead of the suit, standing out boldly against the ebony neoprene, was a light blue insignia—a circle enclosing the Star of David.

"Israeli frogman," McConkey murmured. "Poor sonuvabitch died pretty far from home."

Every screen went black.

"Sam, bring *Bert* up one thousand feet," Haddix said.

Lippman automatically began winching in the sled's cable.

Rick Wolfe was the first to break the stunned silence.

"What the hell do you think you're doing, E.J.?" he barked, pushing his way toward her.

She unzipped her ever-present knapsack, drew out an envelope, and handed it over.

Inside was a single sheet of stationery. Wolfe glanced at the letterhead and frowned. Then, as he read the note, the color drained from his face. Composing himself, he turned to the others in the van and announced, "Until further notice, this expedition is under the command of Lieutenant Haddix."

"On whose authority?" navigator Heppel asked.

"My director at GIO. They're the Navy's vehicles, and it seems they want them back."

"Can they do that?"

"Affirmative," Haddix replied, conscious that all eyes were swiveling to her. "Consider what you've just seen to be classified. Our Greek visitors are not, I repeat, are not to know about that wet suit. And until further notice this van will be off limits unless I have personally cleared you to enter. If Dr. Wolfe and Mr. Kabelo would please remain behind, I'd like the rest of you to leave and reassemble by the traction unit."

The others, thoroughly confused, began to file from the van.

She turned to Kabelo. "Jeff, I'm tasking you to keep everyone on the afterdeck until the Greeks are gone. And when you see Parkhill," she added, referring to her other j.g., "have him to report to the van."

Haddix switched her attention to Wolfe, whose shock was turning to anger. "Rick, I'd like you to baby-sit the Greeks right onto that launch. Then inform Captain Nichols about the change in command, and tell him I want a blackout on all ship-to-shore radio traffic."

"Anything else?" he replied tightly.

"Yes. I need a fix on this position. Please drop a transponder over the side immediately."

Wolfe glanced around and saw Kabelo herding the last of the people from the van. As soon as the door closed, he wheeled and said, "Are you getting off on this little power trip, E.J.? What the hell's going on?"

She met his eyes squarely. "As of this moment you are not cleared to know. I'm sorry, Rick."

"Not cleared to know? Jesus, lady, you are jeopardizing a scientific expedition—my expedition!—and I have a right to know why." He waited until it became apparent that she had nothing further to say, then stormed from the van.

Haddix locked both of the van's hatches and dug from her knapsack two cables and a portable CD player.

This black unit looked normal but its new innards, courtesy of NIS's fabled Q department, would have left the technicians at Sony *ahso*-ing in wonderment. Haddix inserted the thinner cable into the box, then crossed to the *Bert* engineering station and dropped to one knee. The van contained enough outlets and jacks to stock a small electronics shop. She'd secretly added yet another, beneath this console, that ran up to an antenna hidden in the tangle of wires on the roof. After plugging into this jack she used the second cable to patch the black box into the work station's computer.

Haddix flipped the box's Play switch.

A small red bulb lit up; the encrypter-transmitter was ready.

Now she took from her knapsack a trio of three-and-a-half-inch computer disks. One held the daily transmission frequency, another her daily initialization, or "handshake," code, and the third the daily alphabet; all data was encoded so that anyone idly rummaging through the disks would get only gobbledygook.

Haddix called up a DOS prompt and typed in her maternal grandmother's maiden name. In response the machine loaded a hidden program that translated the gobbledygook into English.

Working quickly, she started a file onto which she copied the transmission frequency, initialization code, and alphabet for 27 May. Then she typed out her message. After reviewing it she entered the Send command.

The red bulb on the box began to flash; encryption under way. Forty seconds later the bulb returned to a steady glow; transmission sent.

Haddix logged the computer back to its normal drive, unplugged the box, and stored it, the cables, and the disks. Then she began calling up on the large monitors certain of the images recorded over the last three hours: the electronic stills of the hatch cover and the crumpled pressure-hull plating, as well as *Ernie*'s videotape of the wet suit.

Hot damn, she thought. They were close to it. Real close.

The rump end of the midnight-to-eight shift in the communications room of the U.S. Naval Intelligence Service headquarters in suburban Maryland was never quiet for the simple reason that the majority of America's warships sailed in time zones where the sun was well over the horizon. Signal traffic from the fleets bounced off one or another of the Fleet Satellite Communications System birds orbiting in fixed position above the world's oceans and were captured by the giant National Security Agency antennae at Fort Meade, halfway between Washington, D.C., and Baltimore, Maryland. There, Cray supercomputers sorted through the addressees and then electronically relayed each dispatch, via secure fiber-optic cables, to the intended recipient. Total elapsed time from transmission to arrival at destination, including any necessary decoding: less than two minutes.

An NIS communications clerk yawned, took another sip of coffee, and moved over to a chattering line printer to clear a rapidly growing backlog of flimsies. One of them caught his eye. "Hey, Dave," he called out. "Remember Haddix? That foxy eighteen-hundred that was through here about a month ago? She's out in the Med playing Mata Hari . . . sending in Delta cipher and everything. Boy, I'd sure like to bust her code."

Hearing no response, the clerk looked across the room to find his buddy assiduously studying a clipboard. He suppressed a groan, turned, and found his worst fear confirmed.

The watch officer had slipped into the room, and now the dyspeptic Commander Feeney was bearing down on him like a greyhound destroyer scenting a kill, her starched skirt snapping with every stride.

"Mr. Arnold, what is the procedure for Delta dispatches?"

"Ma'am! We are to forward them without delay to the senior intelligence officer!"

"Mr. Arnold, I don't see the senior intelligence officer present in this room. Do you?"

"No, ma'am!"

"Then I suggest you forward that dispatch before I do some busting of my own."

"Yes, ma'am!"

The clerk curled Haddix's decrypted message into a tube, slipped the tube into the pneumatic system, and punched in a routing code.

The senior intelligence officer on duty skimmed the flimsy and shook his head. It was from the Med, from a civilian oceanographic expedition, for Christ's sake, and the code name on it dated back at least ten years, to before NIS changed its nomenclature.

He turned to his computer and typed BRIGHT SHARK.

Data quickly filled the screen. When he saw the person to be contacted, he snorted derisively—since when did the Department of Energy begin participating in intelligence operations?—and reached for an outside line.

WASHINGTON, D.C.

1017 Zulu/6:17 A.M. local time

In a second-story bedroom of a house off Connecticut Avenue, in the northwest sector of the capital, Clifford Zeman awakened at the first ring of the bedside telephone. A man in his mid-fifties, Zeman had upon retiring from the Navy joined the Department of Energy; he was currently an undersecretary charged with monitoring international transfers of nuclear materiel and technology. Clearing his throat, he picked up the receiver. "Yes."

"Mister Zeman, this is Schaal at DOE Security. There's a secure call for you from Suitland. Are you able to take it?"

"Affirmative. Give me a moment to switch lines." Zeman's telephone was a government-issue STU III. He depressed the Secure button and said, "Okay, I'm on scrambler."

"Right, sir. Hold on while I transfer. . . ."

There was a click, and then another voice came on. "Am I speaking to Mr. Clifford Zeman?"

"Yes, you are."

"Commander Bill O'Connor, NIS. Are we secure?"

"Affirmative, Commander."

"Sir, we just got word of a Bright Shark event, and it says here you're the man to notify."

Bright Shark . . . the Israeli enigma. Zeman allowed himself a small smile—it had taken two appeals to the chief of naval operations, or CNO, to obtain the unmanned deep-sea vehicles for that civilian expedition to the Hellencian—and then his mind kicked into gear.

"Commander, this one's a joint DOE-CIA operation designated Top Secret," Zeman said; in the wake of the Jonathan Pollard affair all U.S. intelligence agencies were still running painstaking searches for additional Israeli penetrations. "For the moment DOE's assuming the point position. What's our status?"

"Sir, the probe has established visual contact with debris from the target. Depth of debris, twelve thousand five hundred feet. The target itself has not been sighted, but it is believed to lie within a two-mile radius. They are presently holding station pending further orders. Also, there's a microwave transmitter on board from a previous geophysical survey. They are standing by to Satcom images, pending a secure relay. Report ends."

"Thank you, Commander. We'll take it from here," Zeman said, breaking the connection and direct-dialing DOE Security.

"Trouble, Cliff?" his wife Jeanne said softly from the other side of the bed.

"Hmmmh? No, I don't think so, dear. Just some loose ends from a long time ago." And if we can unravel them a bit more, he thought, we might be able to conclusively prove that a certain U.S. ally has been promiscuously selling fissionable material to Jerusalem for quite some time. Zeman's smile faded as he rubbed his face. Damn, he'd have to shave and shower in the office. Then he returned his attention to the phone. "Schaal, Cliff Zeman again. I've just been alerted that an operation code-named Bright Shark is breaking. Go into the system and see if we have any agents familiar with it. I'll hold."

Zeman switched on the speaker phone, picked up pencil and pad, and began to draw up a plan of action. It would take most of a day to scramble one of his men out to the Med. How experienced was the senior naval officer on site, and how thoroughly had he been briefed?

"Sir? I've pulled up the roster of agents."

Zeman saw Jeanne stand and pull on a bathrobe. "Go ahead, Schaal," he said, waving her to stay put.

She ignored him and padded from the room.

"Bruckner, Cornelius, retired 1974, deceased 1979. Herrman, Gerald, retired 1985 . . ."

As Schaal continued down the list, Zeman was surprised at how names from the past were still fresh in his mind, and at how easily he could still attach faces to the names. "Hold it . . . Seattle office, isn't he?"

"Yes, sir."

"Good. Find him, get him aboard a military jet. Call in whatever chits you need to." Zeman picked up his pad. "Now, there's a civilian ship off Crete with some sensitive data to microwave. Navy owes us a few favors . . . ask them to divert a relay plane into the area and send me the bill. Next, request NavOceano to transfer their assets over to Bright Shark for the duration. When they cut those orders, perhaps they could instruct the probe to pursue the

target until we get a direct link up. Three, I want a list of all hands
aboard that research vessel on my desk by oh-eight-hundred. Four,
see what clearance each of them holds. Five, call Ann Davis and ask
her to get to the office ASAP. That's it for now, Schaal."

"Yes, sir."

Zeman quickly dressed, grabbed his briefcase, and went down-
stairs.

Jeanne was standing by the door to the garage, a lidded com-
muter's mug of coffee at the ready.

"You shouldn't have."

"I only had time to microwave some instant," she said.

Zeman leaned over to give her a peck. "Hey, what's wrong?"

"Tomorrow? Nora's new boyfriend and his parents are coming
out to the country for the weekend, remember?"

"Of course I do. Brunch at eleven-thirty. Piece of cake."

"Tell me another one," she said with a wry shake of her head.
She handed Zeman the mug, opened the door for him, and patted
his rump affectionately as he stepped through it.

THE EASTERN MED

1029 Zulu/1:29 p.m. local time

Several of *Fanning II*'s crewmen were transferring the duffel
bags of the departing academicians down to the Greek naval launch
moored beneath the port gangway.

Back at the fantail Rick Wolfe knelt beside the A-frame as he
prepared to launch a bright yellow transponder.

This twenty-inch-high unit consisted of two hemispheres of high-
impact plastic that shielded a vacuum-sealed glass bubble. Packed
inside the bubble were electronics designed to communicate on

preset frequencies with the pollywog, or acoustic send/receive device, that hung over the side of the ship, as well as batteries to power the gear for up to one year. Attaching sufficient weights to the positive-buoyancy transponder made it sink to the ocean floor. There, depending on the command sent down, it could emit pings that announced its location, switch to a silent mode, or, when instructed to "release," burn through the wire that moored it to its weight and thus resurface. In case it came up at night, there was a blinking white beacon light atop the plastic housing to facilitate retrieval.

Wolfe jotted down the send/receive frequencies of the transponder nearest the railing. Removing its magnetic arming plug, he wrestled the seventy-pound unit overboard. As the yellow ball floated gaily on the bright blue sea, he payed out 300 feet of wire, enough to suspend the transponder safely above the bottom. Then he fixed a heavy length of chain to the end of the wire and toppled the chain into the water.

Within seconds the transponder disappeared into the depths.

Wolfe turned and proceeded forward to bid the Greeks goodbye.

"A most interesting conclusion to the trip," Stathoplos said, extending a hand. "Now we regret that we are leaving early. But Dr. Los, and my wife and I, thank you for having us on board."

"Our pleasure, Yanni." Wolfe turned to Demetra Stathoplos and added, "You have my word we won't disturb any of the artifacts."

"That is most kind of you, though you do realize that they are in international waters, as far as artifacts are concerned."

"The plates we're after are tectonic, not Kamáres," Wolfe said. Then, still smarting from Haddix's peremptory actions in the van, he added, "Unless, of course, Lieutenant Haddix decides to cut new orders."

"I think that one, she is what Aristophanes has in mind when he writes *Lysistrata*." Seeing the blank look on the American's face, Mrs. Stathoplos said, "A play about women who will not, how do I say this, who will not give themselves to their men until their men stop making war."

Wolfe chuckled ruefully. "Demmie, I'll fax a detailed chart by Monday, and I'll send along a videocassette as soon as I can."

"There is no need to hurry, my friend. The treasures, they go no place until my country develops submersibles like yours." She laughed. "That is after I am dead. Maybe you will come back to do an expedition with my husband, and we retrieve them together?"

"That would be my pleasure."

A crewman approached to announce that the launch was loaded. Wolfe and the Greeks started for the Jacob's ladder.

Thirty feet forward, up on *Fanning II*'s quarterdeck, a lone figure pretended to sip a can of soda as he leaned against the railing and studied the activity down on the afterdeck.

Not a person had entered the control van since Wolfe emerged to launch a transponder, which meant Haddix was in there alone. Damn, why wasn't she coming out to bid the Greeks farewell? Even with all those instruments to monitor, there was always the chance she might spot the momentary spike that would appear in the polly-wog data and the echo sounder plots.

The man on the quarterdeck nervously jiggled his can of orange Fanta, which was surprisingly heavy. He felt alone and confused; if only his friends had seen fit to provide him with a code book, so that he might ask for instructions by shortwave. The man finally screwed up his courage—the situation demanded that he act, de-spite the risk—and slowly sauntered to the starboard side of the ship, opposite the departing launch.

Down on the afterdeck he saw Wolfe give a final wave, cross back to the van, and knock on the door.

Now, the man thought; now, while Haddix was distracted.

A fast glance in both directions to make sure no one else was within sight on the quarterdeck, and then he drew back his arm, flung the soda can over the side, and watched it tumble in a glisten-ing arc into the sea some thirty-five feet below.

It sank from sight with astonishing swiftness.

As it plummeted past sixteen fathoms, a pressure switch tripped, splitting it longitudinally; both halves continued their downward journey.

Fifteen hundred feet down, one section exploded with a dull *whump.*

Precisely six seconds later, so did the second.

In approximately fourteen minutes, if his friends were listening as promised, they would detect this crude summons for help—and soon thereafter begin hurrying in reinforcements.

THE ISRAELI-OCCUPIED WEST BANK
1101 Zulu/2:01 p.m. local time

The Israeli families who built Herzl, a "new village" in the occupied territories just north of the town of Beit Fajjar in the Judean Desert, always felt good when Leon Rose arrived for a weekend at his country retreat.

Understandably so, for Rose was a national celebrity: a superb military tactician who helped guide his country through four wars in which its very survival had been at risk, and later an impassioned politician who advocated keeping the vast tracts—the Northern Territory, the Golan Heights, Gaza and the Sinai, the West Bank— won back from the neighboring Arab states since 1948. Currently, as punishment for his role in the Lebanon misadventure of the early 1980s, Rose was serving as a minister without portfolio; but that could change momentarily, for the fragile coalition government in Tel Aviv was proving woefully inept at dealing with the *intifada,* or Palestinian uprising, now dragging into its sixth month.

There was also a second, more practical reason why the settlers looked forward to Rose's visits. Simply put, he was one of the most heavily guarded men in Israel. When Rose arrived, so did agents of Shin Bet, the national internal security service, and a platoon of Defense Forces soldiers. And as long as he remained in residence, the citizens of Herzl didn't have to guard their perimeters against the disgruntled Palestinians whom they had displaced; professionals did it for them.

Rose, on the other hand, rarely looked forward to his trips to the "new village." Once, when both he and his nation were young, he had reveled in a certain Spartan chic. Now, at sixty-two, he was put off by the sight of raw cinder-block houses huddled close together, as if for succor, and by yards that were barren save for tenuous saplings that would deliver no shade in his lifetime. Even more depressing were the settlers themselves, mostly second-generation sabras who took perverse pleasure in self-denial; at Herzl, for example, there was only one television set, in the community center, and not a single air-conditioner. To Rose their abstemiousness suggested an attempt to atone for childhoods they judged too comfortable. Yet in choosing to carry out the expansionist vision of a small clique of political and religious leaders even farther to the right than Rose, they were compounding Israel's domestic problems and draining its scarce resources.

Still, he kept coming to Herzl because he needed to be seen championing the settlers' right to build wherever they chose. The political fissures splitting his nation were widening. Soon, the leaders who favored accommodation with Israel's blood enemies would be totally discredited; soon, the increasingly conservative electorate would look for a man who could restore the pioneering zeal.

When that day came, Leon Rose aimed to be ready.

Meanwhile, there was discomfort to suffer. For instance, Rose had intended to spend the coming weekend at his flat in Tel Aviv. But some sort of fair was scheduled in Herzl, and he had been asked to serve as its grand marshal. When his press aide learned that a television news crew would be present, Rose had grudgingly accepted, though not before privately cursing the Americans, both politicians and the media, for jointly inventing the concept of the "photo opportunity."

In a few hours, when the sun lowered and the late afternoon breezes freshened, he would be able to do his reading outside. At the moment, though, he sat in his den, wearing but a pair of swimming trunks, perspiring heavily despite the efforts of two large fans to speed the stifling desert air past him.

The papers Rose had brought to Herzl were a series of recently declassified French Army monographs from the mid-1960s that evaluated the tactics used against the Algerian secessionists. He put down a technical report on how General Jacques Massu had managed to effectively cordon and search the winding streets of the casbah in Oran. Would those tactics work against the *intifada*? Perhaps, Rose reflected. Yet though the French had won many battles, they ultimately lost the war; that must not happen here.

He glanced mournfully at the picked-clean carcass of half a roasted chicken. The other half sat invitingly in the refrigerator, but a recent political poster had spurred him to do what a decade of nagging from wife, children, doctors, and friends had not: start on a diet. The poster, borne on a protest march in Jerusalem by a Palestinian girl of no more than eight years, featured his name scrawled across a photograph of a villain from one of the *Star Wars* movies, the grotesquely obese Jabba the Hut. Even the Israeli soldiers had laughed. Rose regarded his sweat-glistened belly and sighed. Two weeks of dramatically reduced intake, and he was still cinching his belt in the last hole.

A car pulled up in front of the house. Rose knew it was too early for his wife, who wouldn't be arriving until after four. Curious, he climbed out of his chair and wandered out into the living room.

The soldier on duty was opening the door to admit Rose's press aide, Ehud Nir.

"Leon, you're not going to believe this," Nir said, triumphantly waving a manila envelope. "Peres has gone mad!"

"What have you brought, Ehud?"

"A draft of a Labor proposal . . . they are thinking of increasing the cotton textiles quota from Taiwan!"

"A rude shock to us all," Rose said, unable to rid his voice of sarcasm. His old mentor, Dayan, had been right: to practice statecraft one must first wade through the sludge of petty politics. Judging by the enthusiasm of his press aide, Nir must have calculated that the fledgling Israeli cotton industry would bitterly resent the merest suggestion of a raised quota. Which meant that Rose would have to say something about it in his remarks at the fair opening, which, of course, would appear on the nightly news. What had that senile media manipulator Reagan wrought? Or, more precisely, his drink-addled public relations expert, Deaver?

The phone rang.

He snatched up the receiver. "Rose."

"Have you heard the news?" It was Ephraim Levenger, an old comrade-in-arms now highly placed in Mossad, the national intelligence agency.

"Shamir was caught in bed with Peres, and you have color photographs."

"Have you heard the news?"

Rose frowned; it was not like Ephraim to be so—so stiff. "No, my friend, I have not heard the news."

"Ben tells me our underwater listening station in Haifa detected two explosions precisely six seconds apart. A signal from one of our stringers." Ephraim paused, as if what he was about to say were too painful to utter aloud—or as if he couldn't guarantee the security of this line. "Perhaps the pilgrims are no longer missing."

Suddenly, Rose felt as though he were free-falling into a glacial crevasse; now was definitely not the time for old secrets to resurface. "It has been, what, twenty years?" he said carefully. "Tell me, who is the second party?"

"An American scientific vessel."

"I see. And Washington has sent us formal notification?"

"I am sure they will," Ephraim replied sardonically, "as soon as they can obtain a hard confirmation."

So the Americans were not sharing the news, which could only mean that they planned to investigate the find themselves. Amid this devastating news, also some hope: the Americans had not yet reached their quarry. Rose pondered the situation for several moments, then said, "It is a sensitive area."

"Yes."

"Is it possible to, uh, to gain some time?"

"I will see what I can do," Ephraim replied. "Unofficially, of course."

"Of course. Tell me, are you free for tea?"

"Our usual place?"

"Yes," Rose replied.

"Shall I invite Ben?"

"Yes."

"Fine. Why don't you get us a table. We will be along within the hour."

Rose set down the receiver and stared idly out the window. The young twin girls from next door were playing with the IDF soldiers guarding his house. Across the street Meir's wife sat under an umbrella, rocking a baby carriage. Suddenly, Rose wanted nothing more than a nap. A long nap.

"Leon? Are you well?"

Rose turned to his press aide. "Yes, Ehud, quite well. That was Abie Sofaer over at Justice. The Americans may be offering to negotiate on some matter that neither you nor I are supposed to know about." He winked broadly and started for the bedroom to dress. "Why don't you leave those papers on the cotton quotas here, and I will study them when I get back."

THE EASTERN MED

"**Y**ou're being paranoid about this," Rick Wolfe said to Edna Haddix from across the control van. He had rolled his eyes in disbelief when she'd stowed the videotapes and the laser disc of the sightings in the safe beneath the chart table; he'd gone ballistic when she began flying the sled with a crew of just three. "Look at that terrain down there . . . hell, you're just an accident looking for a place to happen."

"Orders," she replied from *Bert*'s engineering station, her eyes never leaving the large monitors at the front of the van.

In fact, Haddix was only slightly less angry than Wolfe, though for a different reason. Always her own harshest critic, she was kicking herself for having failed to anticipate this critical manpower shortage.

During her cursory briefing at Suitland she had never thought to request that additional personnel aboard *Fanning II* be vetted. Why the oversight—because the previous missions in her four-and-a-half-year naval career had been so uneventful? Because the flattering prospect of finally gaining a command had made her incautious? Because her task of keeping an eye peeled for a long-lost Israeli submarine had seemed so undemanding? Or because in the days before this, her penultimate assignment as an 1800, she had been too preoccupied with planning the rest of her life?

For Haddix had joined the Navy not to see the world, but to finance a college degree. An exceptional student in high school, she had been deeply wounded when her not-so-closet chauvinist father balked at underwriting further education. Your brothers need degrees, he had said; a girl with your looks doesn't. Intent on forging her own way, Haddix won admission to Stanford, where she enrolled in premed courses. She also enlisted in the Naval Reserve Officer Training Corps, which had guaranteed four years of tuition and room and board in return for three years of active service following graduation.

During her sophomore year Haddix briefly dated a graduate student whose personality proved less stimulating than his academic field: stratigraphy, the study of the interrelationships of the various layers of the planet's crust. On a lark she took several geology courses. They exposed her to eminent geophysicists and to theories like continental drift, which held that Earth's seven continents had been a single land mass before slowly migrating apart atop giant slabs of semimolten crust called tectonic plates. The proof of Pangaea, as the protocontinent was known, depended on meticulous data-gathering, deductive reasoning, and, from time to time, a quantum leap of imagination. The field intrigued Haddix far more than pediatrics; she switched majors, graduated with honors, and decided to continue for a doctorate in marine geophysics.

At which point the Navy, never reluctant to swell its roster of Ph.D.'s, made Haddix another offer she couldn't refuse. It would either continue to foot the bill—though every year of graduate work meant an additional two years in uniform—or she could begin working off her three-year debt immediately. Needless to say, Haddix had found this blackmail galling. But her sorry finances left no other option; she had agreed, knowing full well that by the time she finished at the Scripps Institute of Oceanography in La Jolla, California, and fulfilled her military obligation, she would be nearing forty.

Only after arriving at Scripps did Haddix realize that by securing an RA, or research assistantship, and moonlighting on weekends, she could actually self-finance her studies. At the end of her first year Haddix made the most momentous decision of her life. By taking an academic leave and serving her tour of duty, which now stood at sixty months, she would reclaim seven years of her future. The choice pained her faculty advisor, cost her a boyfriend, and displeased the Navy, which did not like to be outmaneuvered.

Still, NavOceano, to which she was assigned, had treated her fairly; Haddix drew not only her share of intriguing military mis-

sions, but also civilian scientific expeditions that would be of considerable benefit when she returned to her studies. Joining Rick
Wolfe's survey of the Hellencian Trench had seemed like another of
the latter.

True, it marked the first time she had been routed through
Suitland to receive both an intelligence briefing and a crash course
in operating the latest miniaturized communications gear.

But it was one thing to become senior naval officer aboard and
quite another to suddenly find herself in charge of a top-security
operation.

Equally bewildering was why, in midmission, NavOceano had instructed Haddix and her two j.g.'s to remain out of uniform for the
duration even as it seconded all three of them to the Department of
Energy. She imagined that agency to be staffed with Geiger-
counter-toting nerds whose idea of fun was discovering radiation
leaks at nuclear power plants. What interest could they possibly
have in an Israeli wreck that had lain at the bottom of the Med for
more than two decades?

And, of more practical concern, was DOE capable of quickly
conducting security checks on Wolfe's team and *Fanning II*'s crew?
The vetting process usually took NIS at least a week, longer when
extranationals were involved. Yet speed was of the essence, for
Haddix was seriously shorthanded. For instance, her imminent
transmission to the beach depended on a microwave transmitter
that the ONYXX geologists had disconnected and stowed away.
Luckily, Roland Vigneron had agreed to help. The adept Frenchman had performed the setup, which included patching a balky
board on the unit, in a cramped utility van, before passing the transmitter into the restricted-access control van. Haddix had apologized
for the inconvenience; but until she knew the security clearance of
each person aboard, she could fully trust only Rick Wolfe and her
two j.g.'s, Kabelo and Parkhill.

At the moment Parkhill was watching over both the afterdeck
and the Israeli intern Ariel Kahane, whose allegiances were un-
clear, while Wolfe navigated *Fanning II* and Kabelo flew the sled.

The relative weights and positions of the three original finds—hatch cover, pressure-hull plating, wet suit—suggested that the objects had streamed off a vessel sinking to the south-southeast. Since receiving orders to continue the search they had been working a single line in that direction. The cameras aboard *Bert* had picked up several more large chunks of gnarled metal; were they in fact the remnants of a common catastrophe?

Haddix got up and crossed to the sonar station. *Fanning II* was returning to the spot where the hatch cover lay half buried at the base of the 1,500-foot-high cliff. She had enhanced the electronic stills of the hatch cover and searched them in vain for some clue to the boat's identity. Should she stop to offload little *Ernie* for another inspection? But if she flew the ROV, who would man the engineering station? Haddix shook her head in frustration and turned to Kabelo. "Jeff, cliff coming up, height four-five-zero meters. Better start your climb."

"Roger that, E.J."

Wolfe glanced over his shoulder. "E.J., you've been standing watch for more than six hours. How long do you plan on going?"

"The target's got to be within a mile. I can keep going until we find it."

MOUNT RAINIER NATIONAL PARK, WASHINGTON

1228 Zulu/5:28 A.M. local time

Mist hung over the stream like pale gray shrouds. In minutes the first rays of the new day's sun would edge around the brooding bulk of Mount Rainier, thirty miles to the east, and begin teasing the still, clammy air to life; and soon thereafter the spectral curtains would eddy and dissolve. For the moment, though, the wilderness remained enveloped in the hush of false dawn.

"Here we are," Wendell Trent said.

"It was closer yesterday," his twelve-year-old daughter, Erica, grumbled, resting the handle of her graphite rod on the ground.

"Time goes faster when there's lots of things to look at. Come on." Trent rebalanced the duffel bag and his own rod before reaching back with his free hand to assist her down the slope to the water.

There, alongside the stream, the silence gave way to the gurgle of the current.

Trent leaned the rods against a tree, then sought out a level site that would remain in the shade as the morning wore on. He unzipped the bag and pulled out a mesh bag filled with cans of soda and beer. Looping the leader around a stump, he lowered the bag into the stream.

Erica picked up a stone. "Dad? Will this wake up the fish?"

"Probably. But we can't catch 'em if they're asleep, can we?"

Erica flashed him a grin, then cocked her arm and flung the stone with all her might. It immediately disappeared into the mist; seconds later, though, they both heard a satisfying splash.

"Those videos you like to rent," Trent said, "don't they start like this? *Nightmare on Friday the 13th* . . . a lonely stream, lots of mist, a mysterious splash. 'Oh, no, Freddie, please don't make me swim in that fishing hole, it's full of piranhas. . . .' "

"Really, Dad," Erica replied with all the archness a girl her age could muster. "That's the kind of junk Matty and his lame-o friends watch. We're into more sophisticated films."

"Oh?"

"Yeah. Last week me and Ruthie and Georgette, we snuck—"

"Ruthie, Georgette, and I."

"Right." Erica accepted the wading boots he held out and sat down on a log to pull them on. "Anyway, we snuck in to see this really neat movie."

Trent recalled seeing a recent coming attraction for a new movie that seemed popular with preteens. *"Big?"*

She crinkled her nose in disdain. "Unh-unh, it was called *Bull Durham,* and it's about this woman who has a thing for baseball players, see, and she has to choose between this cute young guy who's really talented but kind of a guido, or this other guy who's too old now, only he's kind of smart. Kevin Costner, who plays the old guy, he's *soooo* sexy."

He looked over suspiciously. *"Bull Durham*'s rated 'R.' How did three girls your age get into an 'R' movie?"

"Earth to Dad, Earth to Dad," Erica said. "Where do you think San Diego is, Kansas? Me and Ruthie and Georgette, we can get into any movie we want. Georgette's five eight, and when she puts on makeup, we never get stopped."

She stood and clumped around in the waders. "These are really gross. Do we have to wear them?"

"Yup. The water in that stream comes straight off a glacier. Cold as hell." Trent wriggled his feet to seat his own waders.

"Dad, how'd you know it's an 'R'? Did you see it?"

He grunted.

"By yourself? Or with a bunch of pals?"

Careful, Trent told himself, she's laying more mines than we dumped in Haiphong harbor. "No, I went with a date."

"What's her name?"

"Nan."

"How come Nan didn't come with us? Doesn't she fish?"

"Nan and I go out from time to time. We're friends, but we're not a couple. Besides, I saved this weekend just for you."

Erica pretended to concentrate furiously on the lambs'-wool patch on her fishing vest. At that moment Trent suddenly understood what this conversation was about, indeed, what this whole trip was about.

His daughter normally had as much use for nature as she did for boys. Trent had offered to fly down to San Diego from Seattle, where he had found a job following his divorce and his retirement from the Navy, for his Memorial Day visitation. Erica, though, had insisted on coming north for a fishing weekend. *Why do people like to fish, Daddy?* How old had she been when she had first asked that question, three or four? *It's peaceful, honey. Gives you time to sort things out.* So she had remembered his answer, and now, he guessed, there were things she wanted him to help her sort out— which probably meant the new man in her mother's life. A nice guy, Kath had said, divorced, one son younger than Matty. And most important, a lawyer rather than an ambitious naval officer.

That's what had irreparably strained the marriage, the long periods at sea demanded of a fast-track submariner. Early on, before the kids were born, Kath hadn't seemed to mind; in fact, because Trent had drawn several consecutive postings in San Diego, she was able to establish herself there as a landscape architect. After he became the XO, or executive officer, of a Los Angeles–class fast attack boat based in San Diego, she began to begrudge the marathon cruises that made her assume the role of Supermom. Two years later he was offered a similar posting on a Trident-class ballistic missile boat, or "boomer," out of the new Naval Submarine Base in Bangor, Washington. Faced with his continuing extended absences—not to mention the loss of her hard-earned practice— Kath refused to keep playing the good little Navy wife; she stayed in San Diego with Erica and Matty.

The crushing irony was that when both the divorce and Trent's first command, of a "boomer," were already in the works, he had gone in for the annual medical required of all officers over the age of forty. The doctors discovered a heart flutter, a condition that was neither life nor career threatening. It was, however, enough to disqualify him from further service at sea. Unwilling to command a desk for the next fifteen years, Trent filed his retirement papers. They went through the same week as the divorce.

The experts said that children never relinquished the fantasy that their parents would reunite someday. But in this case that's exactly what it was: a fantasy. What could he say to his daughter, that there was no going back, that he was genuinely happy Kath again had a man in her life, not to mention her bed?

And then the sun saved Trent by giving him a chance to change the topic: "Look . . ."

Erica turned to see the right flank of Mount Rainier begin to glow, as if brushed by a blowtorch.

"Come on, hon, the day's not getting any younger." Trent collected the rods and broke open his fly box.

Erica peered in and said, "That one's so pretty."

She was pointing to a red/green/yellow Spruce streamer, the most gaily-colored fly in the box. Trent didn't think it would work particularly well in these waters, but he quickly knotted it onto her tippet.

"Here's your rod," he said. "Got your sunglasses? Good. Now, what we're going to do is wade out to about there, to the left of that fallen log. Ready?"

Trent stepped out into the stream.

Behind him he heard one of Erica's waders splash into the water, followed by a sharp inhale.

"Dad! This water is freezing! These boots don't do any good at all!"

"Sure they do. Just test it with your finger."

Erica let out a little yelp.

"Don't worry, you'll warm up," he said, moving farther into the stream.

"Not so fast, Dad, you're disappearing into the mist."

The spot Trent had chosen was some twenty yards out.

"Okay, hon, why don't you try a cast or two? Just like we practiced yesterday in the parking lot . . . arm back to eleven o'clock, then forward to one o'clock."

Erica gathered line with her left hand, tentatively raised her rod, and started the backcast. She stopped her arm in the correct position but hesitated too long; the line unrolled completely and fell into the water. When she finally started the forward cast, the energy went into freeing the line. As a result the fly shot virtually straight up into the air before falling a short distance away.

"That was fine, hon. Try it again. Remember, look back over your right shoulder so you'll know when to start forward again."

Over the running water now, the muffled *whack-whacks* of a distant helicopter. Trent detected a change in pitch. Must be flying a search pattern; probably some hikers failed to make it off the mountain before nightfall.

Erica made another cast. This time the fly flew through the mist and landed softly at the outer limits of their visibility, some thirty feet away.

"Daddy! I did it!"

Trent freeze-framed the image—her jubilant face outlined by curls of gray vapor—to savor later, after she had returned to San Diego; it was just one of the tricks that divorced fathers learned. Did his kids do the same? he wondered, then instantly suppressed the thought. "Terrific, hon. Time to catch our lunch."

His daughter's face fell. "We have to *eat* them?"

Trent laughed. "No, that's just an expression. Don't worry, I brought sandwiches. Okay, now, make a cast toward that log."

For the next ten minutes, as the sun continued to dispel the mist, father and daughter presented flies that, alas, no trout found alluring enough to taste.

"Come on, hon, let's try another spot a bit farther upstream," Trent said, slipping his sunglasses down into place as he waited for Erica to wade over to him.

Suddenly, from due east, a rapidly approaching basso throb that made the very air around them reverberate. Trent pivoted clumsily in the knee-high water to see a giant black form swooping down on them, so close now that it was blotting out the sun and inhaling the last of the rising mist. He instantly recognized the silhouette: a six-passenger UH-1 Bell, most likely from nearby McChord Air Force Base.

Trent wrapped one protective arm around his daughter—he could feel her shivering through all those layers of clothing—and remained crouched in the stream, squinting up into the rising sun and willing his adrenaline to stop pumping.

Settling a mere hundred feet above the stream, the hovering
Huey whipped the water into froth. Then a *click,* followed by an
amplified metallic voice: "Wendell Trent?"

Trent raised his free arm in acknowledgment.

Another *click,* and the metallic voice boomed, "Captain, this is
Lieutenant Don Hinkle, U.S. Air Force. We got a clearing approximately sixty yards due south of your position. Request you meet us
there."

Trent waved again; the pilot banked and floated past the tree
line.

"Dad? I'm scared."

Trent squeezed his daughter's shoulder and led her toward the
bank. "It's okay," he said. "They're friends."

The Huey had set down in a glade beyond where Trent's car was
parked. Its rotors were still turning. A man in a flight suit—a lieutenant, judging by his helmet markings—hurried to intercept Trent
and Erica as they made their way through the tall grass toward the
craft.

"Don Hinkle," the man said, snapping off a crisp salute. As he
led them toward the chopper, he said, "Sir, I apologize for bush-
whacking you and your daughter. Some brass back East needs to
chat with you soonest. Our orders were to urgently find one angler,
male adult, and one angler, female child, somewhere west of Mount
Rainier. I'm afraid we spooked half the fishermen in the area."

"And all the fish," Trent said, reaching down to boost Erica into
the craft. Then he hoisted himself aboard.

As his daughter regarded the multigauge control panel with
wide-eyed wonder, Trent accepted a headset from Hinkle.

"Wendell Trent here."

"Hello, Wendell," said Cliff Zeman.

"Hello, Cliff."

"When you go off the map, son, you go off the map."

"Yes, sir."

"Kath may be a mite peeved at me," Zeman said. "We had to

wake her up a couple of hours ago to get a fix on you. I assured her neither Erica nor you was in harm's way."

Ouch, thought Trent, his next call down to San Diego was going to be a bitch; Kath had every reason to think that those dreaded middle-of-the-night calls had ended with their marriage.

Backhanded apology—or perhaps friendly warning—tendered, Zeman got right down to business: "Remember Bright Shark?"

"How could I forget?" replied Trent. "I was on that operation when I was a j.g. at NIS, and I was on it again as captain on my way out of this man's Navy. We never did find her."

"It looks like the fat lady's practicing her scales. About two hours ago a civilian research ship came across some interesting debris."

"Where?"

"The Hellencian Trench, west of Crete."

Trent whistled in astonishment. "That's better than six hundred miles west of our search zone."

"Probably why you never found it," Zeman said dryly. "Son, I've been reviewing the files. If that analysis you did of Bright Shark's cargo was correct, this may be what we need to finally shut down the Oslo pipeline for good."

"It's still open for business?"

"Affirmative. Remember when Toshiba got caught selling re-duced-cavitation technology to the Soviets?"

"Sure do," Trent said ruefully. "Had dinner with an old Navy buddy the other month. He says with those new silent-running screws, Ivan's boomers are almost as hard to detect as ours."

"Well, we recently learned there was a silent partner in the deal. A company called Konigsberg, owned by some of our Norwegian friends. That's why I need you on-site soonest. Navy's lending us an A-3 out of Whidbey Island to bring you east for a briefing. You'll rendezvous with it over at McChord."

"Sir, my daughter . . ."

"We'll fly her down to San Diego later this morning. I'm sorry, Wendell, she's going to have to take a rain check on that trout dinner."

"Yes, sir." Trent took off the headset and passed them forward to Hinkle. "Lieutenant, our car and the gear . . ."

"If you'll give us the keys, one of my men will take care of it."

Flipping Hinkle the keys, Trent leaned over to help Erica buckle up.

As the helicopter lurched off the ground, she slipped a hand into his.

He gave it a squeeze, then turned to watch the stream they had been fishing a short time ago rapidly shrink into a thin, glittering ribbon. He was struck by an acute sense of déjà vu. In two decades in the Navy, how many choppers had he ridden into action? It was a part of his past he had not expected to recapture.

At loose ends after retiring, Trent was grateful for the offer from Zeman, an acquaintance from the Navy, to join him at DOE, but had almost spurned it; how could an officer accustomed to having his every command instantly obeyed become a pencil-pushing investigator for a cumbersome bureaucracy? And in fact, it hadn't been easy. During his first year at his new job, before he began to accept the transition from warrior to civilian, Trent's colleagues had regarded him as a surly misfit. One had even openly compared him to Kid Shelleen, the alcoholic gunslinger played by Lee Marvin in *Cat Ballou*. It was therefore ironic, Trent reflected, that having gradually made his peace, having acclimatized to the low-stress world of DOE, he was now being thrown back onto Bright Shark, the unsolved puzzle that had spanned his naval career.

He thought back to 1966 when, freshly graduated from Annapolis, he had drawn a Naval Intelligence tour out at Suitland. At the time Israel was in the midst of purchasing, modernizing, and reflagging British T-class diesel submarines built during World War II. Officially, this fleet was to defend its merchant ships as they plied the Med—even though the combined Arab navies of the era couldn't have sunk a dinghy. The real reason was to transport items Israel wished to keep hidden from the world's eyes.

The subs would rendezvous with friendly freighters out in the Atlantic, far from the marked shipping lanes. After taking on cargo, be it diverted technology or exotic arms, they would submerge and head for home. Once through the narrow Strait of Gibraltar it was a leisurely 2,600-mile cruise to Haifa. NIS analysts grew to suspect that Israel was also using its underwater pipeline to supply its new nuclear plant at Dimona, in the Negev, with under-the-counter fissionable material and heavy water from Western Europe and, it turned out later, even the United States. That was when one wag dubbed the Israeli fleet "the A-Trains," after both the New York subway system's most famous express train and the glow-in-the-dark nature of its freight.

In December of 1967 the newest Israeli submarine, a 285-foot, 1,280-ton boat, left the shipyard in Portsmouth, England, where it had been refitted and set out on its maiden voyage. Instead of heading for the Med, *Dakar,* which was Hebrew for "shark," first turned north. This immediately set off speculation that it was picking up forbidden cargo from Norway, infamous in intelligence circles for its ability to routinely "misplace" large quantities of deuterium oxide, or heavy water, a key ingredient for converting uranium into weapons-grade plutonium.

Several weeks later Israel announced that *Dakar* and its crew of sixty-nine were lost in heavy seas some 150 miles west of Cyprus. It asked four other nations—Great Britain, Greece, Turkey, and the United States—to help mount a search operation.

NIS would ordinarily have dispatched its most senior specialists, especially in view of *Dakar*'s intriguing manifest. But the call came during a period of unparalleled chaos within the intelligence community: one day earlier the North Koreans had captured the U.S. surveillance ship *Pueblo,* and six days later the North Vietnamese launched their Tet offensive against the south.

Which was why Lieutenant (j.g.) Trent had been assigned to the team. And why, when the ten-day search yielded nary a scrap of debris from the stricken submarine, the case had been moved to a back burner.

A year later the Israelis produced a marker buoy bearing *Dakar*'s name that they said had washed ashore north of Haifa, near the

Lebanese border. The analysis Trent ordered up of prevailing currents concluded that the buoy could not have possibly drifted to that particular beach if released one hundred miles west of Cyprus; in short, either the buoy was bogus or the boat had gone down at another site. By then, though, none of his superiors wanted to devote resources to further investigation.

Then, in 1986, shortly after his fateful medical exam but just before his retirement, Trent had participated at the request of the Israeli Navy in still another search, this time south of the original site, nearer the Egyptian coast. Again, nothing.

Yet obviously not the entire United States intelligence community had closed the books on Bright Shark. The research vessel mentioned by Zeman, the one that spotted the debris, may have been a civilian ship, but its presence over the Hellencian Trench, as well as its willingness to quickly pass on its discovery to Suitland, weren't pure coincidence. Why this continuing interest? And, in view of the site, how could Israeli military communications—which were world class—have been so derelict as to place *Dakar* in a totally different sector of the Med?

The questions would be answered soon enough. For the moment all he needed to know was that Zeman was dispatching him to the Med to eyeball whatever lay inside *Dakar*. Many DOE troubleshooters were ex-submariners, but the logical choice was the only man who possessed operational experience on Bright Shark.

Trent began to refocus his attention on Erica and her visible disappointment over their truncated fishing trip.

HELSINKI

To be a sherpa was to sweat the details. Nepalese sherpas, who accompanied teams of climbers up the outsized peaks of the Himalayas, knew a single loose knot might cause a backpack to shift, which in turn could disrupt balance and trigger a fatal fall. Diplomatic sherpas, who laid the foundations for superpower summits, knew a single unanticipated event might cause a precipitate response, which in turn could disrupt negotiations and lead to a nasty falling-out.

In May of 1960, for example, President Dwight D. Eisenhower was to journey to Paris to meet Premier Nikita S. Khrushchev. If their talks proved fruitful, Eisenhower would continue north to become the first U.S. chief executive to set foot in the Soviet Union since Roosevelt at Yalta, in 1945. But the sherpas had not taken into account recent advances in Soviet weaponry. A fortnight before the summit an American U-2 spy plane cruising 80,000 feet above the industrial city of Sverdlovsk was shot down by an advanced surface-to-air missile. Washington, confident the CIA-contracted pilot had swallowed his regulation-issue cyanide capsule and triggered the self-destruct charges built into his plane, flatly denied overflying Soviet airspace. Whereupon Khrushchev trotted out not only the largely intact wreckage of the spy plane, but also the hapless pilot, Francis Gary Powers, and canceled the Paris sessions.

The U-2 precedent notwithstanding, the American sherpas who had set up the latest summit might have been forgiven a moment of quiet satisfaction as they stood alongside most of the Administration's senior advisors in the wings of Finlandia Hall, the soaring auditorium on the shores of Toolonlahti Bay. For they were on the verge of pulling off that diplomatic rarity, a low-risk international meeting.

The President of the United States was at the podium working his way through a speech on human rights. It had been written to sound tough yet statesmanlike, but in fact it was a boilerplate sermon to the choir. The address gave him an excuse to spend nearly four days in the Finnish capital before flying on to Moscow; it would have been impolitic to admit the true reason, which was that he needed time to adjust to the change in time zones.

A round of polite applause now as the Old Man reminded the audience that it was here, in Finlandia Hall, that the civilized nations of the world had in 1975 collectively vowed to accord all citizens a fuller measure of individual liberty. The Soviet Union was making progress in this regard, he continued; wasn't it time for that great nation to redeem its pledge and lift all restrictions on matters like free speech, religion, and emigration?

The Americans backstage were heartened by the vintage zest with which the Old Man delivered his speech.

Second terms were often cruel to those who occupied the White House. For eighteen months now this most popular of politicians had been battered by a succession of unlikely reversals: the emergence of a charismatic new Soviet president equally adroit at politics-by-public-relations; the Iran-*contra* quagmire; the Black Monday stock-market nosedive; the charges of misconduct leveled against several of his most trusted advisors. Now, with the primaries all but over and his successor all but narrowed to one of two men, neither of whom he much cared for, the impending summit was rekindling his interest in governance to the point where he was actually cracking his briefing books. For as the Old Man had recently confided to one senior aide, the visit to the land he had once labeled "the Evil Empire" would allow him to reach out and touch the Russian people—and, well, perhaps it was immodest to say this aloud, but hadn't he usually made the most of his ability to communicate?

Whether or not the sherpas shared the Old Man's dream of turning Moscow into the capstone of his presidency, they knew that he would arrive well rested and well briefed.

They also knew they would be catching the young Soviet leader off stride, his reform policies sandbagged by dilemmas considerably thornier than those plaguing Washington. *Perestroika* had not solved the perennial agricultural shortfalls. Nor the long queues for staples like flour and cooking oil, much less consumer goods ranging from shoes to automobiles. Nor the continuing hemorrhage of men, materiel, and rubles in the Afghanistan misadventure. Nor the ethnic tensions that were erupting, in the form of devastating riots, throughout the captive republics of Estonia and Azerbaijan. In fact, the young president had spent most of the spring prepping not for the summit, but for the upcoming extraordinary session of the Soviet Congress, at which he would have to fend off the conservative dinosaurs of the Communist party.

Two superpower leaders, each with sufficient domestic problems to make a mediagenic summit look like an oasis in the deepest desert; no wonder the sherpas were relaxed. It indeed figured to be a low-risk international meeting—barring, of course, some unanticipated event. Hence, the unofficial watchword of the Moscow talks, borrowed verbatim from the Old Man's embattled attorney general: "No problems."

JERUSALEM

1236 Zulu/3:36 P.M. local time

Among Israel's three and a half million Jews and two and a quarter million Arabs, Leon Rose, according to the polls, possessed a higher recognition factor than the country's most popular television personalities and entertainers, not to mention its elected coleaders, Yitzhak Shamir of the conservative Likud party and Labor's Shimon Peres. Tonic though this was to Rose's ego, it also represented, when secret meetings were convened, a dilemma as substantial as his porcine girth.

The solution—like so many things—lay inside the walls of the epicenter of the Holy Land, Jerusalem's Old City.

Over a span of 5,000 years the dolomitic limestone immediately below its surface has been thoroughly honeycombed with hidden passages and chambers. In fact, it was not unusual for archaeologists to attend the excavation of new building sites just outside the walls; more than one high-rise stands on a layer cake of ruins whose ingredients were contributed by civilizations long dead, from Assyrian to Hellenic to Roman to Byzantine.

In 1967 the Old City became one of the prized spoils of the Six-Day War. Shortly thereafter Israel formed a special unit whose only mission was to quietly chart the world that lay beneath the Arab quarters. Some teams, posing as street-repair crews, wielded sophisticated seismographic equipment to ferret out anomalies that might be tunnels. Others, posing as building inspectors or representatives of the local utilities, investigated likely entrances and exits. No one team was allowed to trace more than a fraction of a subterranean network, and all field data was tightly compartmented. Thus, only the project overseers were privy to the emerging big picture; and the lone copy of that map carried a classification as restrictive as the one slapped on the new nuclear plant at Dimona.

When the special unit's work was done, its director decided to leave the majority of underground warrens undisturbed; in fact, some were currently being used by leaders of the *intifada*. But by closing a business establishment here and evicting a family there, he turned a few of the tunnels into ultrasafe zones for Israel's intelligence agencies. In keeping with Jerusalem's secretive heritage he made sure Shin Bet didn't know the locations of Mossad's complexes, and vice versa. Finally, before destroying the map, he set aside one passageway for officials whose affiliations transcended Shin Bet and Mossad.

Leon Rose was one such official. Which was why, following his unsettling telephone conversation with Ephraim Levenger, he had driven the thirty miles to Jerusalem, entered the Old City through Zion Gate, and proceeded to a restaurant off Habad Street known as a hangout for government officials. Most of the regulars, however, were unaware of the unmarked "private banquet room" at the rear of the ground floor, and in any event would have been denied access to it.

The room opened onto a tunnel that ran downhill and ended roughly three fifths of a mile to the northeast.

Halfway down its dank length was a safe room.

Forty-five feet directly overhead, at street level, a man with a strong arm could throw a stone and strike either the Western Wall of the Second Temple, the sacred site of Judaism also known as the Wailing Wall, or the gilded Dome of the Rock, whence the Prophet Muhammad is said to have ascended to heaven astride his great white horse, Burak. Down here that same throw would have to be made sidearm; though the room was generously proportioned, its low ceiling suggested that the conspirators of antiquity were considerably shorter than today's.

Modern workmen had run in a power line and installed sound-proofing insulation now dingy from two decades of inadequately vented cigarette smoke. But the room had not been fitted with telephone lines or plumbing; this last was the more serious inconvenience, for it meant no running water and no bathroom. In fact, the only amenity was the security agent who came by once a week to sweep for bugs, restock the supply of bottled mineral water, and empty the one modern appliance within, a shredding machine.

Rose had been the first to arrive. Shortly thereafter he was joined by two old Defense Forces colleagues: Levenger of Mossad and Ben Goren, now risen high in the Defense Ministry. The three men sat in folding metal chairs around a swaybacked card table, silently pondering a bathymetric chart of the waters west of Crete. Goren's experts had triangulated on the pair of timed underwater explosions and marked the position of the American research vessel.

Finally, Goren spoke. "We will have one of our submarines in the vicinity of the ship by tomorrow morning. It will serve as a communications platform for Ephraim's agent."

"Can we not raise him directly?" asked Rose.

"Unfortunately, no," Levenger replied. "His transmitting equipment is short range. We can broadcast messages to him, but only in the clear. No one thought to give him a code book."

Rose returned his attention to the chart. "A pity. Tell me, my friend, how is it that you have someone on that boat?"

"This is the third scientific expedition to the Hellencian Trench that has deep-diving vehicles," Levenger replied. "We covered the other two as well."

"The discussion is academic," Goren observed. "Even if we have the capability to directly instruct Ephraim's agent, whatever he can do to delay the Americans is no more than a nuisance."

"True, Ben, if the Americans are already scavenging *Dakar*," Rose said. He turned back to Levenger. "You think perhaps they are not?"

The Mossad official shrugged. "A find such as *Dakar* does not remain a secret for long. Yet, our sources in Washington have not been able to ascertain even who exactly conducts this operation. Furthermore, they report no unusual movement of U.S. Navy ships in the eastern Med . . . which suggests that the research vessel does not request support at this time. Why? One possibility is, they are still trying to confirm their find."

"Let us pray this is so," Rose said. "I propose that until we hear to the contrary, we assume that the Americans continue to search."

Goren sighed. "Even if they have not found our submarine, they will. Even if we stop this ship, they will send another. I say we ask the Foreign Ministry to file a formal protest. May I remind you that *Dakar* is a warship, and therefore remains our property under international law? It is illegal to attempt salvage."

"Fine, Ben," Levenger said sarcastically. "We file a protest, then what? Do we request the Hague to assign a jurist to that site? Or station our navy over it forever? Anyway, I do not think the Americans want to salvage anything. I think they only want a look inside. Do you agree, Leon?"

Rose, chin in hand, continued to stare at the chart on the table with unseeing eyes. Suddenly he turned to Goren and said, "This Hellencian Trench, it is like a wadi?"*

"A very deep wadi . . . in some areas, more than five thousand meters."

"At what depth are the Americans working?"

Goren shrugged. "We plan to ask Ephraim's man for that data. Why?"

"I am thinking back to the Sinai campaign, to the morning this accursed adventure began," Rose said. "The Egyptian half-track which pulls the launcher has broken down near the bottom of a wadi. The crew cannot fix the half-track . . . typical, really, the Egyptians, they have no way with machinery. Anyway, can you guess what they are doing when we came upon them? The crew is placing charges under the rim of the wadi. If they win the battle, they come back and dig out the launcher. If not, we will never find it."

Rose carefully placed both elbows on the table, clasped his hands, and leaned forward. "So tell me, Ben, if we can set off a landslide in this Hellencian Trench, nothing more than an underwater wadi, really, can we not bury *Dakar* until the end of time?"

Goren thought about it, then replied, "That is possible."

"Well, there," Rose said, unlocking his hands and turning them palms-up for emphasis. "We shall send a submarine, and we shall instruct it to fire as many torpedoes as necessary to set off an avalanche."

"Leon, Leon, this is not a Hollywood movie," Goren protested, fingering the chart before them. "This location that my men plot, the bottom here is around thirty-eight hundred meters. . . ."

"So?"

*Wadi: *Arabic for "gully."*

"Our antisubmarine torpedoes are effective to only one hundred eighty meters."

"Then I shall call Mother and demand a torpedo with a nuclear warhead. That should do it."

Both Goren and Levenger blanched, though for different reasons.

Goren was the first to regain his voice. "Good God, Leon, have you no idea of what happens when such a device is detonated underwater? First, the noise . . . I guarantee you it is enough to break eardrums at every listening post in the Mediterranean. And then, a column of irradiated water shoots high into the air, where the fallout can be carried every which way. Look at the map: Greece, Turkey, Egypt, Libya, all lie within three hundred miles. You will make Chernobyl look like a practice drill, and you will make Israel a pariah among nations."

"Besides," Levenger said, "this is not the kind of request you make casually. When is the last time you talked to Mother?"

"January," Rose replied smugly, enjoying the surprise on the faces of his two friends. "In Vienna."

"The contact was not authorized."

"I do not need authorization to trade war stories with an old battlefield acquaintance."

Levenger mulled over this unexpected revelation, then decided to let it drop. "Not even Mother can deliver you such a torpedo."

"You are right, as usual, Ephraim," Rose said. "But Mother's superiors can. And I believe they shall, once they understand that we are in this together . . . that they have as much to lose as we."

Without warning Ben Goren triumphantly slammed a fist down on the table. "Mother's superiors will never give us a nuclear warhead, no matter what the reason. But we recently acquired an intelligence report that suggests they are field-testing a high-explosive sub-killing torpedo rated effective to eighteen hundred meters. If the topography is favorable, that is enough to bury *Dakar*. I think this one, they may give us."

Rose sneaked a glance at Levenger, who was now gnawing on a

fingernail. A good sign; Ephraim only did that when his mind was focusing on matters operational rather than strategic.

"Perhaps Mother can serve another function as well," Levenger said at last. "You know how sensitive the Greeks are about their territorial waters. This American ship, perhaps Mother can help convince the schmucks in Athens that it does something illegal."

Rose and Goren broke into broad smiles at the sweet irony of this ploy. Under its Socialist prime minister the Greek government had all but broken ties with Jerusalem in its shameless pursuit of Arab favors. It would be satisfying indeed to manipulate the lecherous old goat into serving Israel.

Rose reached for a fresh bottle of mineral water.

"The torpedo, it does not necessarily solve our problem," Levenger said.

"How so, my friend?"

"Ben, you say we have narrowed the position of the American vessel to an area roughly two kilometers by two kilometers? And I believe that at this site, Leon's underwater wadi is almost four kilometers deep? Well, then, at what exact point within these sixteen cubic kilometers do you propose we fire Mother's torpedo?"

Rose looked to Goren.

"Ephraim is right," Goren said. "We need precise coordinates."

"A minor change in plans," Rose declared. "Instead of stopping the research vessel, we shall permit it to lead us to the target."

"That is risky," Levenger protested. "Very risky. It will give us a very narrow window in which to act."

"Agreed. I am more than willing to entertain alternatives."

Levenger shrugged.

"Ben, your submarine will be in position tomorrow morning? We must tell Ephraim's agent at the earliest opportunity that he is not to impede the Americans until after they locate our *Dakar*." Leon Rose twisted off the cap of the mineral water bottle. "Come, my friends, we have much work still to do."

Clifford Zeman squared the service records that had been faxed from NavOceano, got up from his desk, and walked to the window to gaze down on the traffic streaming along Independence Avenue. What had seemed so straightforward two and a half hours ago was getting thorny.

Months ago, to build support for Bright Shark, he had persuaded his counterpart at CIA to cosponsor it. The mission was such a long shot that they had never formalized the arrangement beyond an exchange of memos agreeing to split the minimal start-up costs and share the data. Zeman had just learned that his Langley partner was taking advantage of the long Memorial Day weekend to fly off on vacation with his family; he wouldn't be back until Tuesday. Until then CIA was willing to support Bright Shark by providing intelligence from the Eastern Med, including Israel, but for now the decisions—and the bills for such extravagances as the A-3 speeding Wendell Trent to Washington—were Zeman's.

Equally worrisome was the situation aboard the research vessel in the Med. Although Zeman would have denied it, there lurked in him a residual streak of sexism that neither his wife, Jeanne, nor their daughter, Nora, nor his talented Number Two at DOE, Ann Davis—strong-willed women all—had quite been able to eradicate. The news that the senior officer aboard *Fanning II* wasn't a him, but rather a her, had not gone down well. Further, this Lieutenant Edna Haddix was not some fast-track Navy hotshot; her previous experience on sensitive missions had been as a junior officer, and this first command would probably also be her last before she went back to pursue a degree in marine geophysics.

Why the hell had she been assigned, Zeman wondered, though of course he knew the answer: on the Navy's list of priorities, searching for traces of *Dakar* ranked just above guarding the PX at Guantanamo Bay. He may have been able to badger CNO into lending DOE deep-sea research vehicles, but that didn't mean the A-Team went along with them.

There was a knock at the door.

"Yes."

Ann Davis stuck her head in and said, "We've just secured a secure patch to the Med."

Zeman grabbed a clipboard and hurried through the door.

"Carol, I'll be down in communications," he said to his secretary. Then he turned to Davis. "What took so long?"

"Authorization. They had to chase down someone who started his weekend early. And then their bean counters got into the act . . . it seems they want to bill out that relay plane at six thousand dollars an hour."

Zeman snorted. "Is that with or without tax?"

"Mr. Da Silva is going to be thrilled," Davis said, referring to DOE's own chief bean-counter.

"With a little luck, Annie, this operation'll be history before Mr. Da Silva gets a look at the numbers."

As Zeman and Davis approached the communications room, she said, "We've set up one channel for video and one for audio. Lieutenant Haddix had the presence to summarize the search to date on a greatest-hits tape, so I told them to start piping it in. The Navy specialists are looking at it."

"You've spoken to her?"

"Haddix? Yup."

"How'd she seem."

"Pretty capable . . . for a dame."

Zeman, pausing at the door, was unable to suppress his grin. "She knows we're flying some personnel out?"

Davis nodded. "Three of our decontamination experts are on the four-oh-five out of Dulles. They'll also be able to help out with security. I've had Trent ticketed on the same flight."

"When does that get them aboard the *Fanning*?"

She studied her watch and did a quick computation. "Twenty-four hours from now. That's five P.M., local."

"Too slow. Annie, call in some more chits and see what military transports are headed for Europe."

"Poor Mr. Da Silva."

"Poor Zeman and Davis," he said. "We're undoubtedly spending next year's merit raises."

As Davis headed for her office, Zeman entered the communications room.

One of the twenty-seven-inch monitors in the room was displaying streaky images of wreckage.

"Is that the best you can do on the picture?" asked Zeman.

"Yes, sir," a communications specialist replied. "They've got a balky transmitter board they'll troubleshoot later."

Zeman turned to the submarine specialist from NIS. "What do you think, son?"

"Hard to say, sir. We had one big piece that might be pressure-hull plating. The lieutenant says there's better stuff coming up."

"Is she continuing the search?"

"Yes, I am."

Zeman reflexively turned to the side speaker through which a woman's voice emerged.

"That you, Lieutenant Haddix?"

"Yes, sir."

"Cliff Zeman here. Any way we can get a feed of what you're seeing now?"

"Hold on," Haddix replied.

The monitor flicked from a still picture of debris to a real-time view of a phantasmagoric undersea mountainscape. To the left, a jagged vertical face across which something large and heavy had gouged a great gash; below, a sloping ledge on which a giant furrow was clearly visible. Strewn about were ripped chunks of metal.

"Lieutenant, your picture's breaking up again."

"Let me try something," she said. "There. Better?"

"A little."

"One of our techs will try to fix this thing when we're done," Haddix said, "but no guarantees. Mr. Zeman, we're currently flying our sled at one knot at a depth of ten thousand nine hundred feet. We first picked up the debris field a mile and a quarter northwest of our present position, and about sixteen hundred feet below it."

"Haddix," Zeman said, "any estimate on how close you might be to the submarine?"

"Less than a mile, sir."

Zeman took a deep breath and slowly let it out; could they sneak a look before anybody else learned about their discovery?

"Can you give me a time frame?" he asked.

"A couple of hours, give or take," Haddix replied. "When we came through here earlier, we mapped a very prominent outcrop that juts out at about fifty-two hundred feet. If this course holds, it'll put that outcrop between us and our vehicles, and it's going to be dicey keeping the line from snagging. In fact, we may have to position our ship to . . . Oh, Jesus."

"What? What?"

"Sonar's showing that this ledge drops off abruptly in about five hundred feet."

"I'm sorry, Haddix, you'll have to spell it out for me," Zeman said, his eyes never leaving the monitor. Like the others he was transfixed, even though the vehicle was traversing the otherworldly terrain at the speed window shoppers strolled Madison Avenue, and the picture it was sending halfway around the globe was as smeary as a rain-streaked windshield.

"If we don't find the target in the next five hundred feet, it slid off the ledge," she replied. "The bottom's sixteen hundred feet below our present depth, but it won't be there . . . we would've seen something when we were taking core samples at that location. Which leaves us a number of ravines on the way down. And, sir, those figure to be mean mothers to explore."

"Haddix, let's assume it slid over the edge. What sort of time frame would we be talking?"

She thought it through for a few seconds. "Worst case, it'll be days rather than hours. You see, the . . . What?" When Haddix spoke again, she sounded shaken. "Mr. Zeman, Dr. Wolfe's reporting an anomaly in the cable. He's going outside to check it. With your permission I think I should join him."

"By all means."

"It may take a while."

"Take all the time you need," Zeman said. "Meanwhile, can you resume transmitting your taped material?"

The monitor flickered, then started to display a black smudge in the distance that slowly turned into a wet suit.

The submarine specialist from NIS leaned forward. "Vintage gear, sir. See those weight belts? I'd say that model dates back to the late sixties."

Suddenly Haddix, noticeably short of breath, came back on net. "Mr. Zeman? We had an accident . . . the cable started to give."

Zeman turned to the NavOceano specialist, who immediately said, "Where, between the traction unit and the A-frame?"

"Affirmative. The winch operator saw the metal sheathing start to unravel in midair, but he managed to put the brakes on before that section went over the side. He's winding it back onto the drum right now."

The NavOceano specialist turned to Zeman and said, "The vehicles are safe."

"So they can continue their search?"

The NavOceano specialist shook his head. "Not from what I've been hearing here, sir. If you were working a shallower depth, yes, but it sounds like your target's lower. As soon as you expose the damaged section again, you subject it to fifteen thousand pounds of tension. If the outer armor's badly damaged, it won't last an hour. Lieutenant Haddix, this is Chris again. You still got your video?"

"Affirmative."

The NavOceano specialist rubbed his jaw. "Mr. Zeman, you've got two options. The recommended procedure is to replace the cable, or at least three miles of it."

"Time frame?"

"Assuming my brass'll make one available to you, figure your transit time from San Diego to Crete, then add two days. I'd say you'd be up and running sometime Wednesday or Thursday."

Zeman's face tightened in frustration.

"Option two is a field splice. That's considerably quicker. You get a team from Reliance—the company that fabricated this cable—and you scramble those guys today, maybe you'll be back on line as soon as Sunday."

"How safe is a field splice?"

"Let me put it this way, sir. If someone like Marullo or Gioia was doing the job, I'd personally go down in a submersible attached to the other end."

"Will you set that up for me? Any problems with authorization or finances, Miss Davis will sign off on it."

As the NavOceano specialist hurried from the room, Zeman turned and said, "Lieutenant, are you certain it was an accident?"

The question gave Haddix pause. Finally, she said, "Negative, sir. That was just my preliminary assessment. It may have been premature."

Zeman scowled. "You better go back outside and take a closer look. You might also ascertain which crew members were in the immediate vicinity of the traction unit at the time, and get statements from them."

"Yes, sir."

Fifteen minutes later, her voice grim, Haddix said, "Sabotage, sir. We spooled the cable back on the drum and inspected it. Someone cut through a bunch of the steel strands, probably with some sort of carbide blade."

Zeman ran a hand through his hair, trying to sort the possibilities.

"And Mr. Zeman? I'm afraid we can probably rule out an act of random revenge by some disgruntled member of the ship's crew, or even Dr. Wolfe's party."

"How's that?"

"I've been going over this afternoon's log. We were operating at twelve thousand four hundred feet until an hour ago. Then we climbed fifteen hundred feet. That means the cut section of cable was underwater until after I ordered the van cleared."

Damn it, Zeman thought, so much for a quick and quiet peek inside *Dakar*—someone had managed to penetrate the operation in, what, three hours? The leak couldn't have been at DOE; not enough time. Suitland? Highly unlikely. He cast his eye down the list on his clipboard. There were currently forty-seven people on *Fanning II:* three Navy, twenty-six civilians in Wolfe's party, the rest ship's crew. Their nationalities ranged from American to Israeli to French to Greek to the Cabo Verdean cooks and mess attendants.

"Haddix, how much security can you muster until our agents arrive?"

"I've declared the research area—that's the afterdeck and the fantail—off limits. I've got enough men at the moment to make it stick. But there's no way to sanitize the ship, unless you replace the entire crew."

"That's not a move I want to entertain right now," Zeman replied. "There's no way to do it quietly, and I'm still hoping we can finish our mission without attracting a lot of attention."

"Sir, I should tell you I've confined one person to quarters."

"Kahane, the graduate student from Israel."

"Yes. He wasn't too thrilled about it," she said.

"That can't be helped. I've been analyzing your manifest for more than an hour, and no one else seems to have the slightest reason for preventing us from finding the *Dakar.*"

"I agree, sir."

Zeman sighed. "I do have one bit of decent news to pass along. We've vetted Dr. Wolfe and three of the people in his party: Heppel, Leonard; Reuss, Joseph; McConkey, Billy Ray. In addition, we've cleared Nichols, William, the captain of the ship. I hope to have another batch identified as friend or foe by twenty hundred, Zulu."

"Yes, sir."

"Haddix, it appears we're going to be talking at each other a lot over the next few days. Since this isn't a Navy operation, why don't you call me Cliff."

"I roger that."

"May I call you Edna?"

An almost imperceptible hesitation, and then she said, "I'd prefer 'E.J.' or 'Haddix.' "

"Okay, Haddix."

JERUSALEM

1413 Zulu/5:13 p.m. local time

As the three men got up from the table and filed out of the safe room deep beneath the Old City, Ben Goren remembered to turn off the lights before locking the door.

The solemnity of their parting handshakes was due partly to the gravity of their predicament and partly to the fatigue that came from improvising complex scenarios.

Assessing risk had been easy; one miscalculation, and the ensuing national crisis would far overshadow their personal disgrace. Choreographing a safe passage through the political minefields had been harder. Ultimately, for the clockwork scheme they had settled upon to work, key cabinet ministers would have to approve several unpalatable actions. But why raise the dilemma until they knew that the scheme was logistically viable?

In this respect the upcoming weekend was a welcome ally. While the rest of the government sat home wishing the *intifada* would vanish like a bad dream at sunrise, Leon Rose would try to establish a back channel to Mother to request an urgent meeting. Since Rose's porcine figure was readily identifiable well beyond Israel's borders, Ephraim Levenger would play go-between; the Mossad analyst was taking a flight north that evening to position himself should Mother agree to the rendezvous. Meanwhile, Ben Goren would translate the data expected from the agent aboard the American research vessel into a battle plan.

Levenger and Goren turned and headed to the northwest. Rose glanced at his watch and grimaced. It was well past four, which meant the highway to Tel Aviv would be clotted with traffic. He sighed and hurried back toward the restaurant off Habad Street.

50,000 FEET OVER MITCHELL, SOUTH DAKOTA
1432 Zulu/9:32 a.m. local time

It never took long for the women in Wendell Trent's life to notice that he had two dramatically different modes of sleep. Comfortably tucked between sheets, he retreated into an oblivion that even World War III might not disturb. But when catnapping, the slightest sensory stimulus—a change in the ambient sound pattern, a subtle alteration of motion or speed—would bring him instantly awake. The latter trait, common among submariners, was born of the need to grab sleep when it was available, yet be able to come out of it and, within a heartbeat, lock on to the task at hand.

Trent's eyes sprang open. Location, the cramped rumble seat of an A-3; destination, Andrews Air Force Base; clothing, alien, a flight suit borrowed back at McChord. But what had roused him? And then he had it: the plane had slowed to subsonic speed and was losing altitude.

The pilot was craning his neck to look below and to port.

Trent peered down and saw the Air Force KC-135 tanker that they were dropping to meet.

The pilot, sensing his passenger stir, tapped his own helmet.

Trent flicked on his intercom.

"Sir, we are descending to twenty-seven thousand to fill her up," the pilot said. "Care for a cup of joe?"

"No, thanks. You know the old saying . . . sleep when you can."

"Yes, sir. I'll give a holler just this side of Andrews."

Trent turned off his intercom. A midair refueling was like good ballet, a dazzling mix of grace and precision; but having gawked through his share of them, he scrunched deeper into his seat and closed his eyes again.

LOD, ISRAEL

1518 Zulu/6:18 P.M. local time

From his station next to a courtesy phone Ephraim Levenger sighed and studied the departures board once more. He really needn't have, for the diminishing chaos in the normally packed terminal of Ben-Gurion Airport was the surest sign that the number of flights still to arrive or depart that evening were down to a handful. He checked his watch again. Leon Rose would have called by now if Mother refused to meet. But if Leon was unable to get through to Mother, as was probably the case, the rendezvous would have to be pushed back a minimum of sixteen hours—the death knell for a plan that was already tenuous.

Activity now in front of the customs area; several charter-bus representatives were stubbing out cigarettes, checking clipboards, and readying placards. Must be the American charter flight that developed engine trouble at Gatwick, the Mossad analyst thought, shaking his head wryly at how much worthless intelligence he'd effortlessly accumulated during his long wait.

A chime sounded on the loudspeaker system, followed by an announcement that the flight to Rome was now in final boarding.

The door from customs slid open. Several middle-aged couples shuffled out on travel-stiffened legs, their knit shirts and khaki pants crumpled from having been worn across seven time zones. One man paused, removed the lens cap from the camera slung around his neck, and fired off several frames. May you have a wonderful visit, my friend, Levenger prayed; and when you go back home, convince your relatives and friends that the American TV networks are painting a false image of us, that our streets are safe and free of tear gas. Since the beginning of the *intifada* the previous winter, Israel's vital tourist trade had dropped precipitously. Levenger blamed this on the West's sensationalistic and biased coverage of the insurrection. If Israeli troops wounded a masked rock-flinger, there would surely be photographs of the writhing young Arab; yet why did they never report the incontestable fact that more Palestinians were suffering death and torture at the hands of their own than from Israeli troops?

The trickle of bedraggled Americans emerging from customs grew into a stream.

Another chime: "Will Yair Klein come to a courtesy phone . . . Mr. Yair—"

Levenger snatched up the receiver and said, "This is Yair Klein."

"One moment, please."

Several clicks as the call was patched, and then Leon Rose came on the line. "Istanbul, tomorrow morning. He arrives on the LOT flight due in at zero-nine-four-five. Is there still a flight to Athens tonight?"

"No."

"Very well, arrange a charter. Be on the first Turkish Air flight to Istanbul in the morning."

"Understood."

"Call me tonight for the exact rendezvous point. Shalom."

Levenger banged down the receiver and started threading his way through the throng of dazed tourists toward the office of the air charter service covertly financed by Mossad.

WASHINGTON, D.C.

1713 Zulu/1:13 P.M. local time

Wendell Trent sat on the couch in Clifford Zeman's office, intently studying videotaped images of the debris found by Edna Haddix at the bottom of the Hellencian Trench. Zeman was due back momentarily from a command lunch with one of the politicians to whom he answered, the chairman of a key Senate oversight subcommittee on nuclear proliferation. In the meantime Trent was pressing ahead with a briefing that had begun upon his arrival at Andrews Air Force Base some forty-five minutes earlier. Waiting for him on the apron was Ann Davis, with both a driver and an update that had consumed most of the drive into Washington.

Three DOE agents versed in decontamination procedures, in case NavOceano's two deep-sea vehicles came into contact with radioactive cargo, were currently on an Air Force transport bound for Athens; they would land shortly after midnight, local time, and be aboard *Fanning II* in time for breakfast. The cable manufacturer, Reliance, was scrambling a technician from New Jersey and another from San Diego; at least one of them would be at work field-splicing the damaged cable by tomorrow afternoon.

But Davis had admitted that Zeman and she were no closer to unraveling the motivation behind the sabotage. It could conceivably have been an act of revenge carried out by a disgruntled researcher or crewman. More likely it had been performed on behalf of the only party with a plausible reason for keeping *Dakar* from prying eyes: Israel. Yet no matter how that nation had managed to react so quickly to the discovery of the debris, its attempt to sidetrack the search seemed an exercise in futility. Trent would soon join Haddix, and *Bert* and *Ernie* would be ready to resume operations shortly thereafter. Barring some extraordinary action like a naval showdown on the high seas, surely the secrets from two decades ago could not escape scrutiny much longer.

At DOE headquarters Davis had set Trent up in Zeman's office, then headed off to arrange a replacement for the passport he had left sitting in a desk drawer back in Seattle. She was also trying to expedite the transfer of the Bright Shark archives from NIS. And Davis was walking through a cash advance requisition so Trent could augment the fisherman's outfit on his back with clothing, toiletries, and a carry-on bag. "Wish me luck," she had said wearily. "If Mr. Da Silva's in a good mood, you might get enough for a spree at K mart."

Trent paused the videotape several times to scrutinize the electronic stills of the wet suit with the Star of David insignia. *Dakar;* he was sure of it. With vehicles like *Bert* and *Ernie* back in the late 1960s, he thought enviously, who knows what we might have found? But just as quickly he recalled one of Zeman's trademark aphorisms: "If my aunt had wheels, she'd be a teacart."

Suddenly, another deeply buried fragment from the past threatened to bubble up out of his memory. Trent knew better than to chase after the thought, so he switched off the VCR, finished the sandwich Davis had thoughtfully ordered him from a neighborhood delicatessen, and picked up the latest issue of an angler's magazine from the coffee table.

He was reading the cover story, on the monstrous thirty-pound-plus salmon that return to the River Tana in Norway to spawn, when Zeman came through the door.

"Wendell," he said, motioning Trent to remain seated. "Sorry about breaking up your weekend with Erica."

Trent smiled and held up the magazine. "That's okay, Cliff, I've plotted my revenge. I'm flying her to the River Tana, calling the trip a follow-up on *Dakar,* and putting it on my expense account."

"Fine by me, though to get you reimbursed I'll probably end up facing a Manslaughter One." Seeing Trent's puzzled expression, Zeman added, "Our accountant, Mr. Da Silva, throws nickels around like they were manhole covers."

"This Da Silva sounds like Rambo with a calculator. He's got you spooked, he's got Ann Davis spooked . . . the only guy I've ever heard of who can do that. What's his secret?"

"You don't want to know." Zeman hung up his jacket and plopped into an armchair across from Trent. "Annie's brought you up to speed? Good. Thoughts? Questions?"

"You personally were not surprised at what this mud boat stumbled across."

"No," Zeman replied. "It's something we've been working on for about seven months. I received a call last winter from a friend over at Justice. I'd met her during the course of a Congressional probe into how Pakistan's obtaining enriched uranium for its Kanupp facilities. She was now working on Irangate, part of the team trying to keep the investigation going despite Meese. They had just interrogated an investment banker whose name kept turning up on wiretaps. She thought one of his depositions might be of interest.

"It turns out this gentleman was one of the prime financial conduits between that retired Air Force tight-ass and Nir, the Israeli arms dealer who fronted the shipments to Tehran. Wendell, this investment banker definitely did not want to do time . . . he was willing to give up anybody, including his firstborn.

"The transcript my friend sent over dealt with a conversation the banker claims took place at a dinner party in Tel Aviv in February of '74 or '75. A member of the Israeli cabinet got pretty drunk. Seems his youngest brother would have turned thirty that day, except he died in a terrible submarine accident in the late sixties."

"*Dakar,*" Trent said. "They only had three other boats at the time, and I don't remember hearing of a second one sinking."

"Neither do our computers," Zeman agreed. "Anyway, accord-

ing to the banker, the drunken minister started ranting about how
Jerusalem had panicked because the missing sub was, and I quote,
'carrying supplies for Dimona.' The minister charged his government with launching a cover-up that probably doomed his brother
and everyone else on board. He claimed the Israeli navy was ordered to search the wrong area, even though they knew where the
distress signals were actually coming from."

"Which was west of Crete?"

Zeman nodded.

Trent whistled. "No way the Israeli navy could have inadvertently blown *Dakar*'s position by that much. But tell me, what made
you believe the stoolie's story?"

"Two things. First, the banker said the reason he remembered
the evening so clearly was that after about ten minutes, three men
appeared at the door and hustled the drunken cabinet minister
away. They were weight-lifter types wearing badly tailored suits."

Trent made a face: "Shin Bet."

"More to the point, I managed to obtain a copy of *Dakar*'s manifest. One of her officers was born in February of '45. The man had
three brothers. The oldest held a cabinet post under Yitzhak Rabin,
who was Israel's premier in '75 . . . the year the dead officer
would've turned thirty."

"Bingo. But if you knew this last winter, how come it's taken so
long to mount a search?"

Zeman grunted. "On this department's budget?"

"I'd have thought that Bart would find the money somewhere,"
Trent said, referring to the deputy director of DOE to whom
Zeman reported.

"Think again. Hell, I had to lobby CIA aboard as a cosponsor
just to convince Bart this was a lead worth pursuing. Then Langley
balked at the cost of a full expedition . . . they insisted we piggy-
back onto someone else's. As you can imagine, NavOceano has
little interest in that part of the Med. Luckily, though, civilian scientists do. I finally tracked down a tectonics expert from the Gillette
Institute of Oceanography who wanted to take core samples of the

Hellencian Trench just west of Crete. It took me two tries, but I finally persuaded CNO to lend that gentleman a pair of unmanned probes."

Trent shook his head in admiration. "That's one reason why I could never hold a desk job. How the hell did you learn that kind of patience?"

"I didn't. I go out at night and kick stray cats."

Trent smiled. "This scientist from Gillette . . ."

"Rick Wolfe."

"Is Wolfe reporting to you?"

"No. He had no idea the vehicles came with strings attached. The expedition is currently under the command of Lieutenant Edna Haddix, an eighteen-hundred ticketed to NavOceano."

"Edna? Do parents still name their daughters that?"

"Evidently, and she's a bit sensitive about it," Zeman said, recalling the end of his last conversation with her. "As you might suspect, she's never found herself in quite this position before."

"Her security sucked," Trent pointed out. "Research ships are notorious targets for foreign data-gathering operations. I'd be surprised if at least one of the crew isn't in someone's pocket."

"It's not totally her fault," Zeman grudgingly conceded. "Apparently, her brief was so short you could fit it on the back of a cereal box."

Trent sighed. "Same old Navy. I guess you're right . . . usually, on-board snoops are thirty-buck-a-day amateurs, paid to just look and listen. In fact, I've never heard of any engaging in active sabotage until now."

"Until now no research ship has stumbled across a find like *Dakar*," Zeman said. "What a time to have a woman in command."

"So my mission, should I choose to accept it, is help Edna Haddix locate the submarine, then look inside for a smoking gun."

"Correct . . . up to a point," Zeman replied. "This operation is being conducted by DOE, so she'll report to you. You should also know that at this late date, we scarcely require additional corroboration that Israel possesses a nuclear capability. But we would definitely like proof of who its suppliers were back in the late sixties, when Dimona was coming on line. And if it turns out to be Norway, that'll give us some leverage on Oslo when—"

Just then, Zeman's phone rang.

He got up, crossed to his desk, and answered it. "Zeman. Oh. Right. Hold on a second, okay?" Cupping the mouthpiece, he rolled his eyes and said, "I have to take this."

"Want me to leave?"

Zeman shook his head, so Trent retrieved the fishing magazine.

Zeman was still on the phone when Ann Davis entered the office carrying a bulging red Top Security folder, a smaller white envelope, and a batch of triplicate forms. She sat down on the couch next to Trent and handed him the smaller white envelope: "Here's your advance. Sign these receipts, and don't spend it all in one place."

As Trent took the pen from her, he asked, "How much did Mr. Da Silva okay?"

"Two thousand five hundred dollars."

"Well, aren't you the miracle worker. Where do they sell Armani suits in this town?"

"Lots of places . . . but then you won't have enough left over for underwear. Your new passport should be ready within the hour. Here, this folder's the Bright Shark files. You need to sign these security clearances too."

Trent had just opened the red folder and pulled out a sheaf of summaries when Zeman hung up and reclaimed his seat. "I see the files finally came," he said. "Let's wrap this up and give you as much time as possible with them."

"I won't need more than an hour," Trent said, skimming the sheet in his hand. "What are my travel arrangements?"

"An Air Force transport straight to Soudha Bay, one of the NATO bases on Crete," Davis replied. "It leaves Andrews at six."

"No sweat," Trent said. "I think all that's left to discuss are the rules of engagement."

"Just three," Zeman said. "First, *Dakar* is a warship, and remains

the sovereign property of Israel. It is technically illegal to go inside
her, so don't leave any traces. Second, this is not a military operation. In the highly unlikely event that you or your crew is con-
fronted by armed forces of another nation, you are not to resist.
Third, should there be further acts of sabotage directed against the
mission, you are not to take the law into your own hands like, like"
—Zeman scowled—"Annie, what the hell's the name of that underwater superhero, the guy from NUMB?"

"Dirk Pitt," Davis said with a grin. "And he's from NUMA."

"You are not to play Dirk Pitt. Any questions?"

Trent was about to say no when he spotted a phrase in the summary before him that completed a memory circuit: "Actually, yes.
I'd forgotten that *Dakar* underwent extensive modifications. Back
in the early seventies, just before I made captain, I was on a Sub
Dev One flyaway when I met a Brit who . . ."

Noticing the blank look on Ann Davis's face, he backtracked.
"Sub Dev One's the Navy's Submarine Development Group One
in San Diego. One of their tasks is coming up with better ways of
rescuing men from disabled boats. As part of the process they stage
a periodic drill called a flyaway. They load you and the DSRVE—
your rescue sub—onto a C-124 and fly you to a simulated underwater emergency.

"The year I was there, we held a joint exercise with the Royal
Navy in the North Atlantic. If I remember correctly, they had an
Oberon-class boat parked on the bottom, in about seven hundred
feet of water. In any event, we spent two or three days in Ports-
mouth afterward, debriefing. That's when I found out this senior
British observer had supervised the refitting of *Dakar*."

Zeman and Davis exchanged quick glances.

Trent held up a sheet of paper. "Something was at the back of my
mind a little while ago, but it didn't click until I saw this passage
about the boat gaining twenty feet in mods. Damn, what was his
name . . . Victor, Victor Collins or Victor Cowens, something like
that. One night he hinted the changes may have contributed to the
accident. It was in a pub, where a bunch of us were swapping disas-

ter stories. I must've mentioned something about helping to search for the Israeli boat, because he said he had known the sub about as well as anybody alive. I think he either served on it, or a sister ship, toward the end of World War II. And, of course, he had been asked to oversee the mods on *Dakar*.

"Naturally, I tried to pump him for details. It wasn't much use. He kept pretty mum . . . state secrets and all that, my good chap. Looking back now, I'd say Victor was having a jolly good time at my expense.

"But he had a very interesting take on the Israeli claim that their boat disappeared while practicing crash dives. He was silent for a few seconds. Then he said, with great scorn, 'If you or any other sane submariner were to look at the plans, you would never consent to take her out to sea, much less practice crash dives.' "

"You remember his last name as Collins or Cowens?" asked Davis.

"Something like that. I think he was a captain when I met him in the early seventies. Wonder if he's still alive."

Davis turned to Zeman. "Worth a couple of calls?"

Zeman nodded. "Even if this Victor's not around anymore, maybe we can persuade the Admiralty to let us look at the blueprints of the mods. Wendell has time to detour to London. It doesn't sound like they'll finish splicing the cable until sometime Sunday. Son, is there anything else you need right now?"

"An office where I can go through this file," Trent said. Then he looked at his watch, made a quick calculation, and added, "One with a phone. I want to make sure Erica got home okay."

"You got it," Davis said, standing. "Follow me."

Trent gathered up the papers, then said to Zeman, "Mind if I borrow your magazine?"

"Keep it. Jeanne and I fished the River Tana three summers ago."

"Worth the trip?"

Zeman nodded.

"Then I better start saving my pennies." Trent rose from the couch. "By the way, Cliff, combat pay on this assignment, right?"

Zeman laughed. "Just be thankful I'm not charging *you*. Hell, half my staff would kill for the privilege of an all-expense-paid week in the lovely Med."

ATHENS

1737 Zulu/8:37 P.M. local time

Striding across the lobby of Athens International Airport, Ephraim Levenger was too preoccupied to notice the flicker of recognition in the eyes of a young man just entering the building.

The young man, attired in T-shirt and sweatpants, was a junior political attaché at the U.S. Embassy. Job title notwithstanding, he addressed most of his reports not to the Mideast Desk of the State Department, but rather to the Mideast Desk of the Central Intelligence Agency out at Langley.

And now his mind raced with questions. Why was Ephraim Levenger, a deskbound Mossad officer known for his analyses of Arab terrorist groups, entering a country that had severed relations with Israel? And traveling without so much as an overnight bag?

The young man paused to look up at the arrivals board, a move that, not coincidentally, enabled him to surreptitiously watch the Israeli hurry out of the lobby and climb into a cab.

So Levenger was here on his own, he thought, and not in an official capacity.

Under normal circumstances the young man would have tailed the Mossad analyst. But his fiancée would be arriving soon on an Air France flight from Paris, where she had stopped to visit friends en route from Minneapolis. He assuaged his conscience with a rationalization that was almost Zen: had he not come here to fetch her, he would not have chanced upon the Israeli. The young man decided to further square pleasure with business by swinging past the embassy on his way home and cabling Langley a report of the sighting. The long Memorial Day weekend had begun, which meant that in all likelihood the message would lie unread until Tuesday; but Gloria would sure get a kick out of seeing him in action.

THE EASTERN MED
2047 Zulu/11:47 p.m. local time

The afterdeck of *Fanning II,* flanked by a quartet of floodlight-topped stanchions, was brightly illuminated only when *Bert* and *Ernie* were working down below. On this night the vehicles were safely back on board, and the yammering diesel that powered the traction unit silent, but the lights continued to blaze for reasons of security.

Edna Haddix had confined most of the personnel aboard the ship to the forward areas. When she announced the curb at dinner, the men of *Fanning II* had merely carried on with the serious business of eating; they rarely ventured back to the afterdeck anyway. But as she feared, the ban did not go over well with Rick Wolfe's party. Several senior members argued vehemently that with Ariel Kahane under virtual cabin arrest, they should be free to go about their business; while they awaited the cable technicians, for instance, there were other vital maintenance steps to perform. Haddix knew this to be true. But she felt she had no choice; perhaps tomorrow, when the DOE team arrived and when Zeman's office forwarded several more names that had passed scrutiny, she would be able to ease the restriction.

Until then her resources were laughably thin: Each watch consisted of one vouchsafed sentry up on the bridge and one down here.

Haddix was finishing the first of two back-to-back watches on the afterdeck. Although bone weary, she wanted Lieutenant (j.g.) Parkhill to be well rested and sharp when he relieved her.

Relentlessly prowling from control van to fantail and back again —less to search the shadows for saboteurs than merely to stay awake—Haddix continued to second-guess her responses to the day's events. Why hadn't she moved faster to black out the video feed before all those people could glimpse the Star of David on the wet suit? Why hadn't she secured the afterdeck better in the hour during which the cable was cut? Was she correct in linking GIO intern Kahane to the cable, or had it been personal dislike heightened by an unconscious religious bias? God, she thought, the worst part of this watch was not the fatigue or the loneliness, it was the boredom that forced her thoughts inward.

She stopped at the winch operator's van, hefted the thermos, and poured herself another cup of coffee, her third of the night.

She was going to be a wreck tomorrow. And although Cliff Zeman back in Washington obviously thought the mission would be a snap once the cable was spliced, Haddix knew better. The rugged ravines into which the submarine had most likely skidded would not yield their secrets easily.

WASHINGTON, D.C.

2330 Zulu/7:30 P.M. local time

The long weekend was officially under way and now, at twilight, an uncharacteristic quiet had settled over the capital. By morning the city would bustle with tourists bent on spending their Memorial Day holiday queuing at various historical sites; but for the moment the streets were virtually deserted, those who lived and worked here having begun their exodus several hours earlier.

Clifford Zeman, though, was still in his office, scrunched in his reading chair, catching up with the paperwork generated on this hectic day. Next to him on the floor were two growing stacks. The first contained an assortment of hastily scribbled notes on Bright Shark that he would shortly enter into his mission log. The second consisted of departmental memos and, more important, intelligence flashes on Israel that had begun to flow in response to his request to Langley.

Time yet for two fingers of bourbon, neat? No, not until he cleared the memos and flashes.

With a sigh Zeman picked up the stack. He quickly worked through it, consigning most to either the file cabinets or the shredder. One of the last sheets was a copy of a CIA report, from a political attaché in Athens, on his unexpected sighting of a high Mossad officer at the airport. Zeman pondered the flimsy for several moments. If he asked the other intelligence agencies for help in monitoring similar anomalies in the travel patterns of Israeli officials, that request would be known in Jerusalem within a few hours. Yet the sabotage of the underwater cable suggested Bright Shark was already compromised. Reasoning that he stood to gain more than he could lose, Zeman went to his desk, booted up his laptop computer, and drafted a query, the printout of which he walked down the hall to the communications room.

On his return he poured himself his liquid reward. Then he returned to his computer and began the Bright Shark mission log.

After the setback with the fiber-optic cable, things were starting to look cheerier. Ann Davis had not only located the British submariner, a man named Victor Cowling, but also arranged for him to be at the Admiralty offices in Whitehall the next morning. Wendell Trent was now somewhere over the Atlantic en route to London, and his meeting with Cowling, before continuing on to Crete. If all went well, he would reach *Fanning II* by breakfast time Sunday. And later that same day he and Edna Haddix would relaunch the search for *Dakar.*

There was a knock on Zeman's door, which was ajar.

"Yes."

"Good evening, Mr. Zeman," said a tall, crisply dressed man in his early thirties who entered clutching several sheets of paper in one hand.

Zeman's heart sank. "Mr. Eugene Da Silva," he said. "Your devotion to duty is commendable, but how come you're not taking full advantage of the long weekend?"

"Well, I was all set to leave at five-thirty—my wife had made plans for a wonderful barbecue—but then the telex started chattering. And you know what they say about telexes."

"No news is good news?"

"Exactly. And vice versa. Is this an inconvenient time, Mr. Zeman, or might I impose on you for just a little bit?"

Zeman forced himself to smile. "Certainly, Mr. Da Silva. Come on in and have a seat."

The departmental business manager crossed to the couch and carefully hitched his pants before sitting.

"So," Zeman said. "What can I do for you?"

"Well, I really hate to bother a busy man like you, Mr. Zeman," Da Silva said, his eyes fixed on the coffee table in front of him. "Especially at this time of night. I was looking for Ms. Davis, but I believe she's gone for the weekend."

More likely just hiding in the bathroom until you leave the building, Zeman thought.

"Anyway, it's about these telexes." The business manager raised the papers in his hand and slowly shook his head. "Irregular, most irregular."

"What are they, Mr. Da Silva?"

"Vendor invoices for expenses charged to a nonexistent account and authorized by you or by Ms. Davis."

"Really?"

"Yes." Da Silva held up a sheet. "Account four naught naught three naught eight-slant-OBS. I've checked our books carefully. Mr. Zeman, I must inform you that we have no such account."

"That's because the paperwork hasn't reached you yet. Bright Shark is a joint DOE-CIA operation that started running this morning and will most likely conclude this weekend—"

"Excuse me, sir," Da Silva interrupted, "but if it is a joint operation, how is it that we seem to be receiving all the bills?"

"Like I said, Mr. Da Silva, the paperwork hasn't cleared yet. In addition, the operation is extremely sensitive, and I was hoping to keep it tightly compartmented until it was over."

The business manager shot Zeman a baleful look. "I would have thought that after four years in this department, my record of preserving confidentiality was beyond reproach. Evidently not. But that's not the real issue, Mr. Zeman. The real issue is the nature of these expenses." Da Silva began to read from the first telex. "The United States Air Force, one thousand six hundred and fourteen dollars for the use of a UH-1 helicopter in Washington State. . . ."

"I had to pull in a special agent who was on vacation in a national park," Zeman said, reaching for his bourbon. "Join me in a drink?"

"Oh, thank you, but I couldn't," the business manager replied. "I live out in Rockville, and you know the traffic at this time of night. A drink or two, I might not make it home in one piece."

Would any jury in the world convict me if I were to pour half this bottle down your geek throat, Zeman wondered, dreading what he suspected was still to come.

Da Silva did not disappoint. "The United States Navy," he continued. "Nine thousand two hundred sixty-two dollars for transporting a passenger from McChord Air Force Base, Washington, to Andrews Air Force Base, Maryland. Really, Mr. Zeman, I find that outrageous! Why do you think we have commercial airlines in this country?"

"Speed was of the essence, Mr. Da Silva," Zeman said, praying that the charge for the midair refueling had not yet turned up. "I had to have my man here by early afternoon for a briefing so that he could get to Europe by morning. But now that you mention it, that bill does sound high, very high. You might want to double-check with the Navy to see if they didn't misplace a decimal point."

"You can set your clock by the fact that I will," the business manager replied grimly. "Speaking of Europe, we also received the following invoices. From the United States Air Force, three passengers from Washington, D.C., to Athens by military transport. From Olympic Airways, one passenger from New York to Athens. And from TWA, one passenger from San Diego to Athens. Do the directives I issue mean nothing to you, sir?"

"I beg your pardon?"

"It is the stated policy of the United States Government that all personnel traveling overseas on official business must fly on an approved American carrier. I have pointed this out in an annual memo that I issue every year." The business manager paused, then said in a voice dripping with sarcasm, "This special agent you pulled out of some forest in Washington State at such great expense . . . I suppose he's flying to Europe first class?"

"Afraid not. The last British Airways Concorde of the day was booked solid."

Eugene Da Silva shot to his feet. "Mr. Zeman, I must say that I find your attitude rude, insulting, and most unprofessional. Furthermore, I regret to inform you that you leave me no option but to bring these invoices up with the deputy director on Tuesday morning."

"As you choose, Mr. Da Silva, as you choose," Zeman said wearily. "Try to remember a couple of things, though. First, it ain't your money."

"But I am empowered to guard it."

"Guard it against misuse, yes . . . hoard it, no. Which brings me to my second point: I am authorized to use my budget in the defense of this nation's security. Which is precisely what I'm doing. It may appear wasteful to you, but I assure you the money's not being squandered. Go home, Mr. Da Silva. Enjoy your barbecue."

The business manager wavered, not sure of whether he should prolong the argument. Finally, he stalked past Zeman.

"Good night, Mr. Da Silva."

There was no reply.

Zeman shrugged, got up, and refilled his tumbler.

DAY TWO:
28 MAY 1988

Just before dawn a low-pressure front, propelled by winds gusting to Force Six, had rushed in from the northwest. Now solid clouds gray as wet slate hung low in the sky and the seas, glassy smooth the previous day, writhed in a confusion of whitecaps. *Fanning II* slipped and yawed in six-foot swells as it strove to maintain station.

Edna Haddix, knees flexed to keep her balance, stood under a running shower. She was in willful violation of the ship's rule on conserving fresh water—use it only to wet and to rinse, since the research vessel lacked desalinization equipment—but at the moment she didn't give a damn; the hot spray was soaking away the drowsiness left by just four hours sleep.

Had it been even that much?

Alone on the afterdeck during the midnight-to-four, pacing to keep warm in the freshening wind, Haddix had continued picking at her misery as if it were a scab. How could she have been so careless about security? Then again, why had Suitland been so cavalier about her briefing? And what was Clifford Zeman's problem—why was he taking so long to vet her a few more bodies?

In those still watches of the night, her questions unanswered, her self-esteem sapped by the tortuous mental gymnastics, she had allowed herself to be mugged by self-pity. Naval performance ratings no longer mattered much to her; in three months she would be out of uniform and back at Scripps. But it rankled to be dealt a short hand. Especially if the cards had been stacked in part because this 1800 wore skirts.

Haddix had worked herself into a foul humor by the time she was relieved by Lieutenant (j.g.) Parkhill. Nor surprisingly, she had lain wide eyed in her bunk for the better part of an hour, despite her deep fatigue. When sleep finally came, it was troubled and short-lived. And on being roused by her travel alarm she had immediately phoned the bridge, only to have her sense of abandonment reinforced. There were no overnight signals from Washington, which meant Zeman had not certified anyone else as secure.

Haddix reached out and turned off the shower.

The hell with it, she thought. It'd soon be the headache of that DOE wonderboy whom Zeman was parachuting in to clean up after her.

She toweled herself dry, slipped into her robe, then returned to her cabin and quickly dressed. Swinging by Rick Wolfe's cabin, she found the monitor linked to the control van still on—though all it displayed at the moment was the computer-generated navigational chart—but no sign of the scientist.

Haddix descended a deck and made her way to the mess.

On a normal morning the room would be clearing out by now. Today, though, it was filled with crew members with nothing better to do than speculate on the mystifying events of the past twenty hours. The chatter petered out when she ducked her head into the room.

Wolfe wasn't there either. The expressions on the faces of the men staring back at her ranged from curious to anxious to openly hostile. Should she should say something to ease the tension? Probably. Trouble was, what could she tell them that wasn't classified?

"Anyone seen Rick?"

"I think maybe he is aft," Roland Vigneron volunteered.

"Thanks, Rollie." Haddix rather self-consciously crossed to the hot-water urn and made herself a mug of instant coffee. As she carried it from the galley, the conversations resumed behind her.

She high-stepped through the two watertight hatches to the afterdeck and spotted her other j.g., Kabelo, sitting atop a fifty-five gallon oil drum off to one side, swaying to the inaudible beat of his Walkman.

He waved and pushed up one earpiece.

"Everything quiet, Jeff?"

"Affirmative, E.J."

"Seen Rick around?"

"You might try the van," he replied, tugging the earpiece back in place.

Haddix held the coffee mug carefully and navigated the rolling afterdeck to the control van some thirty feet away.

The overhead track lights were on. Rick Wolfe, hunched over the chart table, looked up as she entered and said, "Morning. Rough night?"

"More short than rough."

He gestured at the stack of rolled-up paper in front of him. "Our sonar plots from the last couple of days. I thought I'd use the downtime to work up a morphological cross-section of the prime search areas. Hope you don't mind me being in here."

"Of course not."

"Look," Wolfe said, "I want to apologize for yester—"

"I'm the one who owes the apology."

"Let me finish, damn it." Wolfe scratched his unshaven chin. "Once you produced the papers, I was out of line challenging your authority."

"And I should have been less—less officious about taking command. I guess we're both new at this kind of thing."

Wolfe laughed. "And at finding sunken subs too. But we'll manage."

Haddix stepped to the chart table and studied the three-dimensional sketch he was preparing.

"Here's the ledge with the skid marks," he said. "I've been trying to scope the ravines between it and the bottom. So far there are three that seem large enough to swallow a sub."

Haddix frowned. "Looks like it's going to be hand-to-hand combat."

Forty minutes later Billy Ray McConkey's voice squawked over the intercom: "Van, Bridge here."

Haddix replied, "Go ahead, Cowboy."

"Yo, Navy, cavalry's riding into Dodge City. And in style too."

"How's that?"

"Aw, don't make me spoil the surprise."

Haddix grabbed a walkie-talkie, followed Wolfe from the van, and hurried to the starboard railing, where Kabelo was peering into the distance.

"Over there," the j.g. said.

She followed his outstretched arm out over the roiling gray sea. Some four miles off, just below the horizon, she spotted a flaming orange smudge disappearing behind a swell. But the white rooster-tail it flung up lingered, serving as a marker.

"Is that what I think it is?" asked Wolfe.

The object rematerialized for an instant, then dropped from view again.

Haddix nodded. "A Cigarette racer, making about twenty knots."

"DOE has a damned generous budget," Wolfe said.

Haddix raised the walkie-talkie. "Cowboy, you in radio contact with them?"

"Roger that."

"Get me a head count, please."

"One head count coming up."

Fanning II slid up to the top of a ten-foot wave. Just before the research vessel began dipping into the trough, Haddix, Wolfe, and Kabelo spotted the approaching boat hanging in midair, entire belly exposed, like an orange salmon battling upstream.

"I rented a Cigarette once, off the Keys," Haddix mused. "Talk about your boy-toys. The seas were calm, but it was like being strapped to a dozen jackhammers. Those poor guys are going to need kidney transplants."

"Navy, Bridge," McConkey interrupted. "We got three DOE agents coming aboard, and one cable splicer."

"Well, make my day," Haddix said. "Rick, that sub's going to be ours by lunchtime Monday."

ISTANBUL

0733 Zulu/10:33 A.M. local time

Ephraim Levenger eyed the chaos in the lanes to his left and thought, thank God I am driving against the traffic. The westbound half of the Bosporus Bridge, the sole manmade link between Europe and Asia pending the completion of the new span to the north, was bumper to bumper with cars and buses and lorries inching into Istanbul. The exhaust fumes spewed by the trapped vehicles rose into an already sullen sky. Who would have thought they had such a rush hour on a Saturday? Or was there perhaps some big festival in town?

The Mossad analyst checked the rearview mirror of his hired car, trying to remember those long-ago instructions on how to elude a tail.

A black Citroën had fallen in behind him back at Yeşilköy Airport. Every time he speeded up, it speeded up; every time he switched lanes, it switched lanes; every time he slowed, it slowed. Only when Levenger had driven past the Istanbul exits and turned onto the access ramp to the bridge did the Citroën disappear from view.

But had he merely been passed along to another tail? The only vehicle in his immediate wake was a fiery red Alfa-Romeo roadster, a car which even the most thick-headed novice would judge unsuitable for surveillance.

The Israeli permitted himself a rueful smile. Field work was for the young, or at least those with the unfrayed nerves of youth. He himself had been away from it since the mid-1970s, when he'd joined in the long but ultimately successful stalk of those who had butchered Israel's athletes at the Munich Olympics. Luckily, Levenger thought, age had its compensations. Perhaps I have grown too easily rattled by phantoms in the rearview mirror; yet that same sense of anxiety—all right, fear—was an essential component of statecraft. Without it, what diplomat or warrior would ever back down, would ever exchange pride for lives and the chance to fight another day?

Down below he could see ferryboats gliding across the strait that separated two continents.

First exit off the bridge, Leon Rose had said last night when Levenger telephoned from his hotel near the Athens airport.

Levenger eased the car into the right-hand lane, turned onto the ramp, came to a stop at the bottom of the ramp, and consulted the rearview again.

The red Alfa-Romeo was no longer behind him.

Take the road north, toward the Black Sea, Rose had said.

Levenger checked the traffic, then made a left turn.

Did Leon Rose know anxiety or fear? Maybe not, mused Levenger. Of Israel's military leaders Ariel Sharon's reputation was the most fearsome because he courted fame as other men courted women. In fact, compared to Rose, Sharon was a moderate. A long-ago phrase—the Law of the Hammer—flitted into Levenger's mind. He had heard it, on one of his periodic visits to Langley, from a deputy director of CIA sardonically describing the chaos in Lebanon. The Law of the Hammer: *Give a child a hammer, and everything becomes a nail.* The conceit also aptly summed up Leon Rose. Who else could have dreamed up this audacious scheme, much less persuaded such normally cautious men as Ben Goren and himself to commit to it?

Several hours earlier, Rose and Ben Goren had finally established a communications link with the Israeli agent aboard the American research vessel and ascertained that the underwater terrain was indeed favorable to their operation. *Dakar* was resting directly beneath a large overhanging abutment. The abutment, in turn, lay slightly below 1,600 meters, or within the range of the experimental Soviet deep-diving torpedo. In anticipation of receiving the torpedo Goren had contacted the Israeli submarine *Sabra*, in the midst of a priority run to Cape Town, just south of the Canaries and ordered it to head back north at flank speed. But what

if Goren could not manage to hamstring the American ship for
another three or four days? Or what if he, Levenger, could not
convince Mother to give Israel the deep-diving torpedo? What if
the operation fell apart at the hinges—would Leon Rose be able to
recognize defeat and raise the white flag? Levenger thought he
knew the answer to the last question, and he didn't like it.

Up ahead, the sign for the Paşabahçe exit. The Israeli took it and
headed west to the second crossroad. There he turned right, at the
same time consulting his trip odometer; drive precisely 4.6 kilometers from the intersection, Rose had said, then park on the right-
hand shoulder with the front passenger-side door left open.

The road proved to be a lane-and-a-half-wide dirt track so badly
eroded that, even at thirty kilometers per hour, the car kept bot-
toming out. Levenger was glad the car was rented, and not his own.

The rendezvous site had been well chosen. It was on the crest of a
hill and offered clear sight-lines of the road in both directions and
of the empty fields that fell away on either side.

Levenger shut off the engine and got out of the car. The stillness
was absolute. He went around to open the passenger-side door,
then retrieved the *International Herald Tribune* he had purchased at
Yeşilköy. There was a shade tree a short way up the road. He
walked over, leaned against the base, and opened the paper.

The lead story, datelined Helsinki, speculated about the agenda
of the imminent Moscow Summit. Normally, the Mossad official
would have sifted through it with keen interest to gauge whether
the carefully nuanced diplomatic language squared with the intelligence from his agents in the U.S. and USSR. Their reports predicted that increased emigration of Soviet Jews would not be a
major item; that the American president would only utter symbolic
pieties, as in his Helsinki speech the previous day, for fear of inviting a lecture denouncing Israel's hard-nosed response to the *intifada.* But today Levenger found it devilishly difficult to concentrate.

Damn these stress symptoms, he thought. Damn Rose for what
he did twenty years ago, the unauthorized actions that have led to

the current predicament. And damn the American oceanographers for stumbling across *Dakar.*

With a sigh Levenger refolded the newspaper, laid it at the base of the tree, and lowered himself onto it.

Five minutes later he tensed.

A vehicle was approaching from the north.

He caught a momentary glimpse of it atop the crest of the hill to his right and scowled: false alarm.

The battered pickup truck groaned and clattered closer. As it passed, the Turkish farmer and his wife, both riding in the cab, stared openly at this foreigner sitting beneath a tree, as did the two teenaged boys in the truck's open bed.

Then the Israeli spotted the youngest member of the family, a doe-eyed girl of about four. She was clutching her oldest brother's knee with her right hand and waving shyly with her left.

Levenger waved back.

But when the truck disappeared from view, he went back to fretting. What if Mother couldn't get out of the Soviet Union? Or missed a connecting flight? Or what if Rose had gotten the rendezvous site wrong? In an attempt to stanch his rising anxiety—all right, fear—he willed himself to think about nothing.

Gradually, his breathing grew shallow, his neck muscles unbunched.

Now a plume of dust from the south, the direction of the airport. The vehicle had to be negotiating the washboard road at a breakneck sixty-five kilometers per hour, he thought, standing for a better look.

White Peugeot; single occupant; male; not slowing . . .

As the Peugeot roared past, kicking pebbles in its wake, the driver glanced at neither the car parked on the shoulder, its passenger-side front door open, nor the man standing beside it.

Levenger turned to track the Peugeot.

Two hundred meters away, at the crest of the next hill, its brake lights suddenly winked.

The driver executed a fast U-turn, sped back, and slewed the car to a stop on the far shoulder, directly opposite the Israeli.

Levenger, his adrenaline racing and his breath catching, peered at a full-faced man in his late forties.

The driver stared back for several moments. Finally he switched off the ignition, opened the door, and with some difficulty climbed from the car.

In keeping with Rose's description the gaunt-framed man stood almost two meters tall. As he started across the road his right shoulder dipped, like that of a sailor on a tossing deck, to accommodate the severe limp caused by a withered right leg.

Levenger let out his breath, all doubt dispelled.

Though the man was dressed in civilian clothes, it was Mother: Lieutenant General Pavel Chesnokov, Second Directorate, *Glavnoe Razvedyvatelnoe Upravlenie*—the Soviet military intelligence agency known as GRU.

As Ephraim Levenger's car receded to the south, Pavel Chesnokov climbed back into his rented white Peugeot. His eyes flicked to the nylon carrying case on the passenger seat, then his watch. He and the Israeli had talked for nearly an hour. Chesnokov had to start back to Yeşilköy in fifteen minutes if he was to make the LOT flight to Warsaw and there connect with Aeroflot to Moscow. Meanwhile, GRU's Istanbul station chief, or *residentura,* was waiting in the communications room of the Soviet embassy on the other side of the Bosporus, monitoring an agreed-upon frequency for a message to relay to Chesnokov's adjutant back at the Aquarium, the agency headquarters near Moscow's Khodinka Airport.

The general recognized the feeling of lightheadedness that swept over him. It was his normal first-phase reaction to deadline pressure, a period when his mind strove to make order out of chaos, and would quickly fade. Chesnokov trusted his ability to make correct decisions. So did the Soviet High Command, which had repeatedly promoted him, the Sinai incident notwithstanding.

The Sinai incident: what a mixed kettle that was still proving to be.

In the spring of 1967 Chesnokov, then a rising young Army lieutenant colonel with two good legs, had been posted to Egypt. Ostensibly, he was tasked as a training advisor to Gamal Abdul Nasser's light artillery forces. In fact, he commanded an experimental surface-to-air missile battery (which NATO later designated as "Spandrel"); Moscow sensed armed conflict with Israel nearing, and wanted combat data on its newly developed system.

That May, Egypt deployed 100,000 men and some 1,000 battle tanks in the Sinai. With them went a number of SAM units—including Chesnokov's—to support the armored columns that Nasser planned to send eastward into Israel.

But Egyptian intelligence fatally underestimated the enemy's air force. Even had all the surface-to-air missiles proved as devastatingly accurate as the Spandrels, Israel's warplanes would still have ruled the skies over the Sinai. By the fourth morning of the Six-Day War, Chesnokov's battery resembled a punch-drunk boxer. Shuttled from position to position by the ever more panicky Egyptian leaders, the men were running on little more than nervous energy.

To this day the GRU general could still remember his last orders and the despair, fear, and pain that had followed.

Word had come that counterattacking Israeli tanks under the command of Ariel Sharon had been observed dashing west toward Suez. Chesnokov was to outrace the forward elements to the Mitla Pass and employ the Spandrels against Sharon's air support. Chesnokov now knew that had he reached the pass, he would most likely have died there; it was already turning into a bottleneck fatally clogged by the retreating Egyptian Sixth Division.

Instead, three of his support vehicles, denied even the routine maintenance demanded by desert operations, gave out on a mountain track forty kilometers short of their destination.

Repairs were out of the question.

So was help.

Shortly after eleven A.M. on Friday, June 9, as the searing heat of the Sinai neared its zenith, Chesnokov had ordered the precious Spandrel launcher and remaining missiles dragged into a gully—the *arabi* called it a wadi—that ran alongside the track. His men had just begun to cover the launcher with tarpaulin, and to rig one wall of sand with explosive charges, when the silence was broken by the thin drone of a single-engine Israeli reconnaissance plane.

In less than ten minutes four light armored vehicles assigned to protect Sharon's right flank arrived on the scene.

The third mortar round fired by the Israelis exploded some seven meters to Chesnokov's right and instantly rendered him unconscious.

Not until later did the pain come: unspeakable waves that jolted him awake, madly gibbering for another morphine reprieve. Chesnokov had remained in a drugged delirium for the better part of a week, during which time he was evacuated to a military hospital back in Israel.

There, upon reflection, he decided that his career was as shattered as his leg—until his interrogation by the man who commanded the unit that had captured him, an Israeli colonel named Leon Rose.

When Chesnokov was strong enough to be moved, he was repatriated through the offices of the International Red Cross. He arrived back in the Soviet Union bearing a proposal from Rose that could only be termed bizarre, but he dutifully channeled it to the High Command. Even more bizarre, the offer was conditionally accepted by Premier Leonid Brezhnev himself. Chesnokov would never have known of that decision had he not been chosen—at Leon Rose's insistence, he soon learned—to close the deal.

In September of 1967 Chesnokov was flown to a private sanatorium in Switzerland. The orthopedic specialists there were better, as was access to Westerners. It took four days for him and Rose to hammer out the details, and another two for an Israeli naval officer to coordinate delivery schedules with a captain of the Soviet Navy.

Moscow rewarded Chesnokov for a job well done with a transfer from the Army, where his crippled leg weighed against him, to

GRU. There, his aptitude for intelligence work caught the attention of Peter Ivashutin, then already ascending toward command of that organization.

Over the decades Chesnokov and Rose had kept in sporadic contact. The two men found a metals trader in London willing to serve as a cutout in exchange for advanced production figures on gold from the Soviet Union, courtesy of Chesnokov, and from South Africa, courtesy of Rose. At covert reunions in cities like Geneva and Vienna, the Russian and the Israeli swapped war stories and bemoaned the latest follies of their respective political leaders. Never had either revealed a state secret to the other, never had either requested anything of the other.

Until yesterday.

The general consulted his watch again. Ten minutes left. Had it truly been less than a day since London relayed Rose's urgent request for a talk?

Chesnokov remembered being possessed by a chilling sense of foreboding while waiting for a secure line to be established; still, he had been unprepared for the Israeli's stunning news. The implications of the American research ship's discovery were sufficiently grave to risk this journey to Istanbul. The meeting with Levenger had done nothing to ease his mind. As outlined by the Mossad official, Leon Rose's clockwork plan of battle, which had already been initiated, was tenable only if the attacking submarine carried the proper ordnance—and only if a dizzying number of variables fell into place in precisely the right way.

It was decision time, Chesnokov thought.

First things first: Could he deliver an experimental deep-diving antisubmarine torpedo?

Ordinarily, no; the High Command would take quick notice of a GRU officer requesting a naval weapon. But these were no ordinary times. The High Command was preoccupied with planning the Army's retreat from Afghanistan and with suppressing the secessionist uprisings in the southern republics. To cap it off, the marshals, including his own boss, were engrossed in preparations for the Soviet-American summit scheduled to commence in Moscow the next day. Turmoil bred opportunity. Chesnokov was able to fly to Istanbul because he hadn't had to seek the approval of the GRU head. Similarly, for the moment his old comrade Deputy Admiral Boris Patolichev—who twenty years earlier had dealt with the Israeli named Goren in Switzerland—held provisional authority over experimental weapons. Would Boris Alekseyevich share his view that *Dakar* was history which must not be allowed to surface?

Chesnokov had checked the disposition of the torpedo requested by Leon Rose. The news was both good and bad. Two of the wire-guided weapons had been loaded aboard the Soviet Navy's prototype Mike-class nuclear submarine *Komsomolets* for field-testing on the Barents Sea range. Unfortunately, the weapons could not be fired. Shortly before leaving port *Komsomolets* had been suddenly ordered to race into the North Atlantic to tail an American carrier transiting from Norfolk to the Mediterranean; in the confusion the electronic firing control box had been left behind. Still, if Boris Alekseyevich agreed, that and other logistical problems could be overcome, for from its present position *Komsomolets* needed half a day at most to reach the rendezvous point suggested by the Israeli.

Question two: Should Chesnokov deliver the torpedo?

There were four compelling arguments against doing so.

First, transferring a classified weapon to a nation with which the Soviet Union refused diplomatic relations would be properly construed as treason.

Second, the Israelis might well open up the torpedo and share its technology with the Americans.

Third, the operation Rose proposed, even if successful, would by necessity involve several dozen men in two countries and the crews of two submarines, and thus remain highly vulnerable to exposure.

Finally, the secret that would be protected had been approved by Brezhnev, who was long dead, as were his successors Andropov and Chernenko; the current regime could rightly argue innocence.

On the other hand, there was one compelling argument for supporting Rose: The mere revelation that the Soviet Union had con-

ducted business with Israel in late 1967—and the exact nature of
that business—might jeopardize Moscow's influence with the Arab
states for the foreseeable future, not to mention further inflame
fundamentalist passions in the Soviet republics of the south, which
were predominantly Islamic.

End game, Chesnokov thought, and I cannot win. But there is
one course that holds out the promise of not losing.

He reached over to unzip the carrying case.

The previous afternoon, based on preliminary information from
Rose, the general had prepared a contingency plan that was now
locked in his office safe. Nothing in Levenger's update demanded
that the plan be altered.

The laptop computer nestled inside the case looked like a
Toshiba 1000, and indeed could perform enough tasks to convince
Western airport security inspectors that it was not a bomb. The
tasks were rudimentary, though, for the technicians at the Aquarium had used most of the machine's internal space to cram in a
scrambler and a miniaturized burst transmitter.

The general swiveled up the screen of the laptop, toggled two
switches to establish the link, typed two words, and pressed the F1
key. Then he lowered the screen and rezipped the case.

I am in the West, Chesnokov mused. Should I remain in its
safety? No. I must make the request of Boris Alekseyevich in person. Besides, I am doing this not for myself, but for *Rodina,* for the
Motherland. Therefore, I must return to the Motherland to answer
for my actions in person.

Wendell Trent looked from the sketch he was completing back to the faded blueprints, then broke the silence. "I don't get it. Eighteen months and several million pounds for those mods? *Dakar* was more seaworthy entering Portsmouth than when she left."

"Precisely." Victor Cowling, a beefy retired naval commander in his sixties, set down his styrofoam cup and lit another cigarette. "You can see why the Israelis were anxious that these plans be held in the strictest confidence."

The two men were in a cramped, windowless chart room adjacent to the records section deep in the Admiralty Building in Whitehall. Trent, now eight hours removed from his native time zone, had stumbled off the JFK-Heathrow red-eye, grabbed a shower at the airport, and then cabbed into London for his ten o'clock appointment. Cowling, looking none too chipper himself, had arrived several minutes late. The officer groused about unexpectedly heavy traffic encountered while driving down from his pensioner's cottage in Harwich, but his pallor and slightly unkempt air led Trent to suspect that the real reason was a bad night resulting from unexpectedly heavy quantities of Scotch consumed.

After picking up coffee, tea, and biscuits in the canteen the two men had presented themselves at the records section. The blueprints were already pulled and a room waiting.

Trent instantly saw that much of the dry-dock work performed at Portsmouth consisted of retrofitting. The submarine, a T-class patrol boat, had been launched near the end of World War II. When purchased from the Royal Navy by Israel, it had seen almost a quarter century of service and was thus in sore need of new wiring, piping, and air-filtration systems; a pair of modern diesel engines; and up-to-date navigational and communications instruments.

The structural modifications were equally extensive, but their contradictory nature perplexed Trent.

Seen from the side, the submarine consisted of the forward torpedo room at the bow; next the operations area, clustered around the conning tower; then crew quarters and galley; and finally, toward the stern, the engine room and aft torpedo room. Oxygen, water, and fuel were stored in bilge tanks that ringed the vessel.

Assuming the Israelis had wanted to convert the submarine into a cargo carrier, then stretching its twin hulls by twenty feet made sense, as did adding an unusually wide airlock that accessed the forward torpedo room. Made sense, that is, if the twenty feet had been used to enlarge the torpedo room into a more capacious hold.

Yet according to the blueprints, the footage had been tacked onto the submarine's stern, behind the engine room. Trent saw that in addition, the aft torpedo room had been gutted and the tubes sealed. Crammed into this now sizable space were several large tanks suspiciously marked WATER and OXYGEN that were connected by a network of new pipes and valves to external ports. Surrounding the tanks were extra banks of batteries that would virtually double the time the boat could cruise beneath the surface. Coupled with the enlarged fuel tanks under the operations area and crew quarters, *Dakar* was by Trent's quick computation fully capable of stealthily sailing from Israel into the North Atlantic and back without need of a refuel.

The renovations had also made *Dakar* decidedly more uncomfortable for the sailors manning it. In the crew quarters all nonstructural walls and partitions had been dismantled and replaced by stacks of aluminum bunks. The new configuration, Trent thought, was like the cabin of a commercial jetliner; in less than an hour the lightweight bunks could be stripped down and stored, leaving a vast open area. But why create the hold amidships, rather than forward, where the new and unusually wide airlock was located?

Jet lag, the stuffy air in the cramped room, and Cowling's inexplicable insistence that he sketch rather than photocopy the prints were dulling Trent's concentration. He stood and began to pace around the table.

"You look somewhat out of pocket, old chap," Cowling said. "I should have thought these prints would merely confirm what you Yanks had already guessed."

"Yes and no. We thought she had been reconfigured into a pure cargo carrier. These plans indicate otherwise . . . or they were camouflaging something."

Cowling rubbed his chin. "This may be talking out of school, but their liaison officer, chap by the name of Goren, did give a rationale once. Seems our Hebraic friends were forming an elite commando unit. Primarily airborne, which is not surprising, given the short distances between Israel and her immediate enemies. But according to Goren, they also desired a covert alternative for projecting the unit. You can't get much more covert than *Dakar*."

Plausible, Trent thought. Manned by a skeleton crew, the submarine depicted in the blueprints was capable of transporting at least a platoon of elite soldiers. That might account for the new life-support reserves of water and oxygen in the aft torpedo room. On the other hand the Israelis could just as easily have pumped the tanks full of such contraband as heavy water.

Equally troubling was the fact that the weight redistribution made the submarine dangerously stern heavy. Cowling had been correct those many years ago at that pub in Portsmouth: with such a dramatic loss of underwater stability not even the most suicidal captain would dare practice crash dives in *Dakar*.

"How could the Israeli captain go out to sea in that boat?" asked Trent. "Look, I don't mean to insult you . . ."

"No offense taken," Cowling said. "We pointed out the design deficiencies time and time again. But they were the clients, weren't they? Though I don't mind telling you we all let out a discreet sigh of relief when she cleared harbor."

Trent sat down again and sipped his coffee, which had gone cold. He made a face. "If I were the Israeli Navy, I'd have court-martialed the guys who came up with this design. Hell, according to these prints they didn't even move the bulkheads around, much less add one at the stern to support the extra twenty feet."

"We specifically challenged them on that," Cowling said, rummaging through a folder. "Goren presented us with a set of calculations showing that the existing bulkheads were sufficient to handle the added stress. Those figures presumed smooth sailing, milk runs, if you will. So we said, what about combat maneuvers . . . sudden dives, sharp turns, that sort of thing? He was all winks and smiles. 'Combat? Whom would we, a peace-loving nation, fight?' In the end he gave us this and said, end of discussion."

Cowling pulled out a sheaf of papers and offered it to Trent.

The document was a waiver signed by ranking officials of the Israeli Defense Ministry. It released the British Navy and all its subcontractors of liability in the event *Dakar* sustained hull damage attributable to insufficient structural support.

"Good thing we had that. After she went down in '68, we never heard a cross word from Tel Aviv," Cowling said. He paused, then added, "It's rude of me to ask, but you've found her, haven't you?"

"Maybe," Trent said. "I'm not trying to be coy with you, Commander. Yes, we did come across evidence of a sunken submarine, but we have yet to confirm its identity. When we do, and if it is *Dakar,* we will of course immediately notify Israel."

Cowling cocked his head as he mulled over the implications of Trent's overly precise disclaimer, then grinned. "Right. And you wanted to review these prints so that you can properly identify the ship in the event the fish have chewed off all insignias and numbers."

Trent grinned back. "Am I in for any surprises down there?"

Cowling regarded the blueprints. "Structurally, no. As to whatever our Hebraic friends were carrying on board, I don't know quite what you expect to find, do I?"

"Nothing," Trent replied, turning to gather his things. "We have no plans to board and explore a sovereign warship."

Cowling continued to gaze at the blueprints for several moments, then began to roll up the sheets. "Funny how the past has a way of resurfacing," he said. "You know, Trent, it wasn't our ship, wasn't our crew who were lost, but I think about *Dakar* from time to time. Were we wrong not to have insisted on more thorough mods? Unless it's classified, I should be happy to receive news of her condition."

"I'm sure that can be arranged."

"Join me for a pint?"

Trent checked his watch. "Ordinarily I'd make the time, but I'm due out at Heathrow in less than an hour. Commander, I really appreciate your coming all the way in for this, especially on a weekend."

"Nonsense," Cowling replied. "Since I went on pension, every day is a Saturday . . . glad for a chance to break out of the rut. Off to the Med, are you?"

Trent nodded.

"I envy you. Nice time of the year down there."

THE EASTERN MED

0926 Zulu/12:26 p.m. local time

Rick Wolfe passed his tray of dirty luncheon dishes over the counter to the Cabo Verdean steward. He turned to the platter of fresh fruit to his left, dug out an orange, then left the mess hall and went outside.

The seas were still high, but the clouds had begun to thin.

Fanning II's afterdeck throbbed with a level of general activity unseen since the ship took on equipment and replenished its stores in Athens. The arriving DOE team had brought a list of a half dozen more members of the GIO team who had been vetted. Happily, these included chief mechanic Eldon Gary and several of his crew, who were preparing to begin the time-consuming job of un-spooling the damaged cable.

Denny Flanagan, the first Reliance technician to make it out, stood by the traction unit, a coffee mug in one hand. He saw Wolfe approaching and waved.

"How's it going, Denny?"

"Doctor says I'll live."

"In case you haven't eaten, they're about to close down the mess."

Flanagan winced. "No way, José. The ride out here fucked up my digestive system. Permanently, I think."

"How's the cable?"

"I haven't seen the cut yet," Flanagan replied. "Eldon's getting ready to lop off a hundred feet for me to splice with. Haddix says the fiber-optic's okay."

Wolfe nodded. "We got clean pictures from the vehicles the whole time we were hauling them up."

"Then it should be a piece of cake. That fiber-optic's sitting under two layers of armoring. Each layer is twenty-five strands of wire, braided together. If your guy didn't hack into the fiber-optic itself, he couldn't have cut through more than a third of the strands. I'm guessing I have maybe fifteen to twenty splices to do, tops."

"How much damaged wire do you have to strip away?"

"To be safe, an average of fifty feet on either side of the cut. Some of the new strands'll be longer, some shorter. If I don't stagger my solders, all your stress is going to come at two points. Then it's one bad move and good-bye, vehicle."

Wolfe did a quick computation in his head. "Hell, that's almost half a mile of wire you'll be replacing."

"You got it, good buddy. That's why I'm hoping the other tech gets here soon. Hey, listen, I've been looking for your lieutenant. What depth were you guys operating at, what's the max around here, and what is it directly below us?"

"The max is about twelve thousand five hundred feet, and we were flying at ten nine when we, uh, we sustained the damage."

Even a day later Wolfe was still having trouble accepting the fact that there was a saboteur aboard his ship. "We've moved a bit to the east since then. That means we've cleared the canyon. I'd say there's about five thousand feet under us right now. Why?"

"It'd be better to move back out over deep water," Flanagan said. "I need all the deck space I can get. You guys don't have a take-up spool, so the best place to store the excess cable is over the side. We have to unspool almost eleven thousand feet to get at the cut. If we pay it out in shallow water, I guarantee you it'll foul itself on the bottom."

"Sounds good to me," Wolfe said. "You better let me run it by Haddix, though."

"What's the scoop on her?"

"What do you mean?"

"Not too shabby to look at, but Jesus, a real bitch on wheels."

Wolfe, trying to keep his voice even, said, "Fatigue . . . the way I figure it, she's caught six hours sleep, tops, the last couple of days."

"Right." Flanagan smiled skeptically. "Hey, listen, the sooner you get her to sign off on my plan, the sooner I get to work."

Where had Haddix gone?

Wolfe crossed to the control van and unlocked the door. The van was empty. He picked up the phone and dialed her cabin. No answer. He was about to leave when he thought to call the bridge.

"Yo, McConkey here."

"Cowboy, this is Wolfe. You seen E.J. around?"

"I'm looking at her. Want me to wake her?"

"No. I'll come up."

She had crashed in a bosun's chair set up to overlook the afterdeck some forty feet below. Haddix's sleep was so deep that it seemed her breathing had stopped. At that moment the sun finally broke through the scattering clouds, bathing the aft quarter of the bridge in radiant light. Not a muscle on her face twitched.

I should let her rest, Wolfe thought. Flanagan's request was sim-

ple enough. Yet he was not commanding the search; was there some
critical reason for *Fanning II* to hold station? Wolfe had no way of
knowing.

He reached out and gently shook her shoulder until he saw eye
movement beneath the lids.

Haddix frowned, then came painfully awake. "Oh, hell, I drifted
off. Everything okay?"

"Yup. But something's come up that needs your approval."

Haddix massaged her eye sockets as Wolfe quickly filled her in.
Finally she lowered her hands, blinked a few times, and said, "Let's
do it. Did Flanagan tell you how long it's going to take?"

"No," Wolfe said. "But it doesn't sound quick."

"If Kahane was sending signals at regular intervals, the Israelis
must be getting antsy by now. But I'm sure Zeman would rather
have us in later than not at all." She turned her attention across the
bridge and said, "Cowboy, could I trouble you for some coffee?"

Before McConkey could respond, Wolfe said, "Eldon and Flanagan have things under control down there, and I got a full six hours
last night. Why don't you go recover from that double shift you
pulled?"

"Best idea I've heard since this thing started." Haddix struggled
out of the chair. "Wake me if there are any signals from Zeman?"

"Promise."

Starting for the stairs, she paused before the television monitor
that Wolfe's techs had installed above the chart table so that images
could be piped to those on the bridge. At the moment the screen
was displaying a computer-generated navigational chart.

"Can't wait until this thing starts showing more interesting pictures again," she said.

"E.J.? You're doing good."

She turned and, shielding her eyes against the bright glare, threw
Wolfe a sleepy smile. "Thanks, Rick. 'Night."

BALACLAVA, USSR

0939 Zulu/12:39 P.M. local time

Not much more than half a league from Tennyson's famed "valley of Death," into which charged the British commander Lord Cardigan and his doomed Light Brigade, on a hill above a picturesque bay rimmed by distinctive red and ocher rocks, stood a series of bleak gray apartment houses. Hastily thrown up in the early 1960s after Admiral Sergei Gorskov strong-armed Premier Nikita Khrushchev into a crash program to expand the Soviet Union's Black Sea Fleet, the flats helped house the flood of naval personnel then descending on the Crimean Peninsula.

As always, rank had its privileges. High officers were billeted nearest Fleet headquarters in Sevastopol. Their most trusted subordinates lived on the outskirts of that city; the next echelon had to commute from slightly farther out, and so on, with the most junior officers living as far away as Balaclava, sixteen kilometers to the south.

Now, with the Black Sea Fleet grown to 350 surface vessels and thirty submarines, there were modern quarters within easy reach of the sprawling bases for all its officers. Surplus apartments, like those in Balaclava, had been turned over to noncommissioned specialists and technicians, the unappreciated backbone of the Fleet. Although the cinderblock units on Gagarin Street in Balaclava had been neither patched nor painted in a quarter of a century—maintenance not being a strength of the Soviet military—they were nevertheless much coveted.

For instance, Yuri Tikhonov, a torpedo systems engineer, had not endeared himself to his colleagues at the Admiral Nakhimov submarine base when he won the rights to Apartment 301 in Building H, Block Eight. Yes, Yuri Andreevich was capable at his job. But he was only in his late twenties; he had never gone to sea, and probably never would; and his behavior toward senior officers was famously, shamelessly obsequious, learned no doubt at the fancy technical college from which he had graduated.

In fact, Tikhonov had not lobbied for the apartment. Unbeknownst to him, an uncle high in the Politburo had pulled the necessary strings. When Tikhonov discovered the truth, at his mother's fiftieth birthday party, he had almost given it back. Then he had faced facts. His family of three, with a fourth on the way, had already outgrown their single medium-sized room with a sleeping alcove. But were he to put his name back on the waiting list, Nadya, he, their daughter, and the new baby would most likely spend the next four years sharing a one-bedroom apartment with another family. In the final analysis the animosity of jealous colleagues had seemed preferable.

It was early afternoon. The yells of neighborhood children drifted in through windows opened wide on this hot day, but they did not disturb the sound sleep of Tikhonov, who had recently come off duty.

In the late 1980s a significant portion of the Soviet military had quietly redrawn schedules so that specialists and technicians were responsible for splitting two watches per day, each lasting twelve hours. Commanders were quick to acknowledge the undesirability of such an arrangement—performance fell off dramatically at the end of each watch—but the party line attributed this "need for temporary sacrifices" to two factors. First, there was the rapidly increasing sophistication of Soviet military technology, which required even the most skilled technicians to undergo periodic retraining. And second, there was the considerable slack left by the brave comrades fighting in Afghanistan.

The rank-and-file accepted the latter explanation, albeit with cynicism; since 1983 the *Afgantsy* were judged less brave than unlucky for having been chosen. The first explanation was met with outright derision. The truth was that in an era when the Soviet Union's non-Caucasian citizens—the Moslems and Asians who made up the majority of the republics east of the Urals—were increasingly agitating for autonomy, the High Command in Moscow no longer trusted them in sensitive support positions. Hence, labor shortages; and hence, twelve-hour watches.

There was a knock at Yuri Tikhonov's door.

He rolled over, drew the sheet higher over his head, and waited for his wife to answer it.

The knock was repeated, louder this time.

Tikhonov twitched as he started to emerge from his dreamless sleep. Where the blazes was Nadya? Was today Saturday? Yes, which meant she was in the park with the little one.

"Wait," he called out. "I am coming."

Tikhonov rolled out of bed, started across the room, then remembered to go back and tug on a pair of boxer shorts.

The man at the door wore the uniform of a GRU lieutenant.

Tikhonov was too groggy to panic.

"Systems engineer Yuri Andreevich Tikhonov? You are to gather clothing for one week and come with me." The officer pushed past the stupefied Tikhonov and into the apartment. "Quickly, comrade. Where is your duffel bag?"

"I, uh, our neighbors went on vacation. They borrowed it."

The officer spotted a string bag near the stove. "You dress. I will pack. Where are your clothes?"

Tikhonov finally regained his wits. "Am I being punished?"

"No, comrade," the officer replied. At least he didn't think so; the orders had come from the Aquarium on the emergency channel reserved for urgent business, not the arrest of a trivial technician. "Now hurry."

As the officer threw open drawers and started to jam underwear into the string bag, Tikhonov pulled his military jumpsuit down from a peg.

"No, Comrade . . . the orders are for civilian clothes. Where do you keep your trousers? And the toiletry kit?"

By the time Tikhonov had climbed into T-shirt and jeans, and finished lacing his workboots, the GRU officer was waiting impatiently by the door.

"Now what are you doing, Comrade?"

Tikhonov had crossed to a bookshelf and grabbed a pencil and pad of paper. "My wife, she will worry. . . ."

"No notes."

"Please. Nadya is carrying our second child. I will tell her only that it is a secret emergency preparedness drill. She is accustomed to those, and therefore will ask no questions of others."

The GRU officer hesitated, then nodded.

Tikhonov scribbled two sentences, placed the pad on the dining table, and followed the officer from the apartment.

In the back of the Tundra, Yuri Tikhonov came alert. The general utility vehicle, which much resembled the American World War II jeep that served as its template, was beginning to slow even though the Nakhimov submarine base lay an additional five kilometers down the highway into Sevastopol.

To the technician's surprise the driver turned into the Red Navy aerodrome. They are flying me to another base, he thought. That's odd; the other bases all have full complements of torpedo systems engineers. Tikhonov tried to remember if there had been any recent scuttlebutt about some hushed-up disaster up in the Kola Peninsula or on Sakhalin, out east beyond Siberia. Nothing came to mind.

The Tundra was waved through the gates and continued past the administration complex to the airstrip, where it came to a stop alongside a low concrete building.

Thirty-five meters away a pilot and a group of senior officers stood in the shade of a MiG-31 from whose swept-back wings dangled detachable fuel pods. Tikhonov began gnawing his lower lip. He had been on planes before, the military transports to and from deep-water exercises at the seemingly bottomless Lake Baikal, but never a fighter-interceptor, much less one fitted to fly extremely long ranges. Shit, he thought, it's Sakhalin for me. Then he recognized one of the men and his breath caught. It was his base commander; what could be urgent enough to bring that alcoholic party hack out in public, in full uniform, on a Saturday?

"Come," the GRU officer said.

Tikhonov hopped from the Tundra and followed him into the low concrete building.

The changing room for pilots was immediately to their right.

The GRU officer said, "What size are you?"

"Uh, fifty-six."

The GRU officer spoke with the grizzled old quartermaster behind the counter.

The quartermaster disappeared into a side room, then returned with two pressure suits. Taking Tikhonov's measure, he seemed to weigh them in his hands before placing the smaller one on the counter.

It was still too big.

Tikhonov tugged at sleeves that covered his fingers and looked forlornly to the quartermaster, who shrugged.

"Come, they are waiting," the GRU officer said, handing over a flight helmet.

Tikhonov felt like a month-old puppy who had yet to grow into its skin as he waddled back out onto the tarmac. The suit was a heat sump and the helmet, which he carried with both hands, weighed a ton.

The technician glanced at the MiG-31 and felt his anxiety rise even more. While he was dressing, a light truck had pulled up alongside it. Crewmen were transferring two large metal cases from the truck's open bed into the belly of the jet. Each case, Tikhonov knew, contained a firing-control unit and tools for the new deep-diving antisubmarine torpedo; since when had that experimental weapon been declared operational?

The senior officers were all looking at him.

Now his base commander was stepping forward, a broad smile creasing his weathered face.

As Tikhonov's right hand went up in a salute, his helmet tipped and a pair of gloves fell to the ground.

"Yuri Andreevich," the base commander intoned, "you have been chosen for a most demanding mission because you are the best we have. I am confident you will bring honor to *Rodina,* to the Nakhimov submarine base, and to yourself."

Tikhonov forced himself to return the man's earnest gaze. It was difficult because of the sweat running into his eyes, and because he could see the other officers restlessly shifting their weight, wishing only to get out of the hot sun.

"These are your transit orders," the base commander continued, melodramatically flourishing an envelope before passing it to the pilot of the MiG-31. "Classified, of course. You will receive a full mission briefing at the appropriate time."

The man paused, as if to rehearse his next words, then unexpectedly drew himself fully erect and shot his right arm up. "Yuri Andreevich Tamarov, we salute you!"

Tikhonov reflexively proclaimed, "I serve the Soviet Union!" and returned the salute, but his heart was racing. They didn't want him, they wanted sonar specialist Alexei Tamarov. . . . And then he remembered the metal boxes containing the torpedo gear. No, he was the right man; it was the drink-addled base commander who had blurted out the wrong name.

Tikhonov retrieved his gloves and waddled over to the boarding ladder on the left side of the plane.

"It is easier if you put the hat on now, Comrade," the pilot said with a tight smile.

Tikhonov began to pull on the helmet. Its dark visor banged down, blotting out most of his view.

"Relax, Comrade," the pilot said, reaching over to slide the visor back up. "Take your time, and do not hyperventilate. I do not want to stop to resuscitate you, mouth to mouth, at fifteen thousand meters."

Tikhonov dragged himself up the ladder and lurched into the narrow compartment at the rear that was designed to carry the electronics/weapons officer.

A crewman who had followed him leaned into the cockpit and began attaching the life-support systems.

Tikhonov was drawing on his gloves when he saw the pilot's head emerge. "Comrade, am I permitted to ask our destination?"

The pilot shot him a warning glance, then climbed into his seat. He quickly ran through his preflight checks, radioed the tower for clearance, lowered the cockpit canopy, and began taxiing the fighter toward the end of the runway.

"Is your seat belt secure, Comrade?" the pilot asked over the intercom.

"Yes."

"Then hold tight."

Tikhonov looked around for something to grab. Seeing only levers and knobs marked with indecipherable acronyms, he grasped his right glove with his left and began kneading it.

The MiG-31 pivoted into takeoff position and came to a stop.

Suddenly, the whine of its twin Tumansky engines deepened.

The pilot popped the brakes and the jet lurched forward.

Tikhonov tried to relax. He shouldn't have.

Without warning the nose of the MiG-31 tilted skyward like a roller-coaster on its initial climb, and then the pilot boosted power. The jet bolted forward with a 60,000-pound punch that seemed to drive Tikhonov's stomach into his vertebrae.

The steep ascent angle was giving him vertigo, so he closed his eyes.

It took the pilot ten minutes to reach altitude and set a south-westerly course across the Black Sea. Now, facing a boring three-and-a-half-hour run, he wondered if he had been too hard on his passenger. There was no need for the sarcasm, nor for that show-offish climb. The poor guy, who obviously had no clue as to his mission, had handled it gamely, all things considered.

Checking to see his radio transmitter was off, the pilot said into the intercom, "Comrade, you asked about our destination. Here is a hint."

The pilot hummed the opening bars of an American song. Then, realizing it was unlikely that a mere submarine technician would recognize it, he sang the words: " 'From the halls of Montezuma to the shores of Tripoli . . .' Does that tell you something, Comrade? Comrade?"

He received no answer because Yuri Tikhonov was fast asleep.

ATHENS

1006 Zulu/1:06 P.M. local time

Adonis Thomopoulos, Jr., was daydreaming about his pending assignation with Kristin as he neared Syntagma Square. When the delivery van in front of him slowed without warning, he let out a mild oath, whipped his Mercedes around the van—and stabbed the brakes.

The car rocked to a halt inches from two quivering tourists who had quite naturally expected oncoming motorists to obey a red light, even in Greece.

At forty-six "Junior," as all called him, was licensed to operate a car, but he did it poorly and only on Saturday afternoons. Born into a wealthy mercantile family, he had been chauffeured through his Athenian childhood and his Swiss boarding-school days. And now, as a deputy of intelligence for the ruling Panhellenic Socialist Movement, or Pasok, he was entitled to a chauffeured Mercedes around the clock.

But Saturday afternoon was playtime, and Junior had discovered some years back that his libido was dampened by the thought of a driver waiting outside. Rather than concentrate on the woman in whose arms he lay, he would worry about how long to remain with her: too short a time, and the driver might think him overeager; too long, and the driver might think him impotent. Therefore, on Saturdays he took the wheel himself. The privacy had the added benefit of giving him time to get fully in the mood for fleshly pleasures, a process that seemed to require more effort with each passing year.

The light changed. He began to negotiate Syntagma Square, thankful that the midday traffic was thinning.

Junior's never-ending quest for approval, even from his chauffeur, helped explain how he came to end up an official in Pasok, a leftist party devoted to toppling the oligarchy—including the Thomopoulos clan—that had long dominated Greece.

Despite wretched grades at his Swiss boarding school, he had persuaded Adonis senior to buy him into one of the most prestigious universities on the Continent so that he might prepare for a career as an art dealer. It hadn't taken Junior's fellow students at the Sorbonne long to tag him with the new and crueler nickname of "Lesser" (as in "Adonis the Lesser"), for the young man spent his waking hours not in studies but in panting pursuit of long-legged Northern European beauties. In fact, during Junior's six years at the school, his female classmates invented a game known as "The Lesser Evil." Its goal was simple: see how many four-star restaurants, nightclubs, winter weekends at Chamonix, and spring weekends at Cap d'Antibes they could wheedle out of the playboy before they had to sleep with him. The winner was an American, a rangy blonde from Santa Fe, who dated Junior for five weeks solid, capped off by spring break in a villa in Marrakesh, without allowing him near her bed.

Had Junior graduated close to schedule, his father might well have bankrolled him to an art gallery on Míkonos or some other tourist-trap island in the south. Instead, he was still in Paris in May of 1968, and had the misfortune to wander into one of the calamitous government crackdowns on protesting students.

Blinded by tear gas and desperately nauseous, he threw up in precisely the wrong place. The grizzled paratrooper from Marseilles who received the young Greek's four-star lunch full in the face returned the kindness with the butt of his rifle. When Junior woke up in the filthy cell where he would remain incommunicado for four days, he had a concussion, no front teeth, and a broken nose. His

gold Rolex and his wallet, containing some 5,000 francs, were gone.
So was his reflexive respect for uniformed authority.

Adonis senior had not been amused. When Junior recovered
from his plastic and oral surgeries, he was yanked out of the Sorbonne without a degree, taken off allowance, put to work in the
family firm, and forced to marry the shrewish daughter of a shipping magnate.

The in-laws treated him like the dim bulb he was. So did his
father, who time and again refused his pleas for promotion. Junior
learned to drown his bitterness in mistresses.

Until, that is, August of 1976, when he accompanied the leggy art
student whom he was then wooing to a Pasok rally.

It was a classic case of an empty political vessel suddenly filled to
overflowing. By evening's end Junior had been mesmerized by featured speaker Andreas Papandreou's passionate call for a new,
populist-governed Greece. Two days later he wrote a letter, on the
stationery of the family firm, volunteering his services as a party
organizer. The Socialists were rightly startled. Was this some bizarre attempt at infiltration by the far right? Covert checks were
quickly conducted; no, the young man was genuinely disaffected.
He was also genuinely inept, but surely some post could be created
for one whose name carried such great propaganda value. Could,
and was; early the following year Pasok scored a sizable political
coup by appointing Adonis Thomopoulos, Jr., as paid advisor in the
field of visual arts and antiquities.

Junior was immediately disinherited by Adonis senior. His wife
was immediately disinherited by her father. But the estrangements
were not terminal. In 1981, shortly after Andreas Papandreou was
swept into office, Junior summarily won appointment to the board
of directors of the family firm, and he, his wife, and their children
were welcome again at his in-laws' Sunday dinners.

Since then Junior had been shuffled unprotestingly through a succession of medium-profile, low-responsibility slots. The pay could
have been better, but the perks were outstanding. For instance his
current posting, as third-ranking deputy of Pasok's intelligence

forces, carried with it a complimentary beach-side bungalow out in Vouliagméni. That was where he had installed Kristin, a statuesque free-lance illustrator met on a business trip to Oslo a year earlier, and where he was now headed.

The midday traffic was thinning as Junior pointed the Mercedes down toward the waterfront. Directly ahead loomed a sight that never failed to provoke a scowl: the gray ranks of imperialist warships swinging at anchor in Piraeus harbor. Would the prime minister never make good on his promise to revoke the port privileges of the hated U.S. Sixth Fleet?

Reaching the coastal highway, he turned left, in the direction of Cape Soúnion. At first the road was lined with forlorn rows of apartment buildings abandoned before completion. The government-controlled press blamed it on a rocky economy. Junior, who had served two years in the Finance Ministry, knew better. Were Pasok ever to lose control, Greece's jails would burst with contractors who had gorged at the public trough in return for thirty-percent kickbacks.

Gradually, beyond the airport and beyond Ellinikó, the concrete husks to his right gave way to sandy beaches. Out of habit Junior slowed to mentally undress the bikinied young things taking the sun or frolicking in the limpid waters. He felt himself stir. But Kristin— possessed of small but exquisitely sensitive breasts, alabaster legs that ended above his navel, and a mouth that could teach a Turkish rug merchant lessons in greed—his Kristin was more desirable than anything he now beheld. Junior stepped on the gas.

At last he saw the cluster of moored yachts announcing that the Astir Palace's beach bungalows were close at hand. He swung into the parking lot and clumsily squeezed the Mercedes into a spot at the far end. After ascertaining that his erection was not too blatant, Junior climbed from the car and started down the crescent-shaped beach.

Kristin's bungalow was at the far end.

Ten meters from it he glanced at his watch. Mustn't be early; timing was vital if they were to play their roles well. Good, he was slightly late. Then he casually scanned the beach. Good, no one was looking his way.

Junior stepped onto the small, semienclosed porch, knocked on the door, and called out, "Mailman."

Inside, footsteps.

Kristin was wearing high heels today.

Junior's heart quickened. Sometimes she would answer the door as a Scandinavian peasant girl, dressed in only earmuffs and knee socks; other times as a Moslem temptress, wearing but a black veil; still others as a suburban American housewife, draped in Saran Wrap. But today she was his favorite, a German: she would have on high heels and the metal-studded black leather push-up bra he had purchased by mail order from California.

He quickly unzipped his fly and bent forward to fumble out his hardened penis.

As the door swung open he said, "Special deliv—"

The words died in his throat. Instead of Kristin it was a mousy man of about thirty-five who readjusted his wire-rimmed glasses in amazement at the sight before him.

"Puzanov! Where—where is Kristin?"

"You mean Tatyana? On my orders she cancels your rendezvous of today." Dimitri Puzanov, GRU's Athens station chief, smiled thinly, then gestured impatiently at the Greek's rapidly shriveling member. "You will please return that to its place, we have much to discuss and too little time."

Junior stuffed himself back into his trousers and hurried after the Soviet agent. "This is highly irregular. I protest."

Puzanov continued to the living room and settled into an armchair. "A matter comes up suddenly. Kostos is in hospital, Agamemnon is at conference in Brussels. So you are acting chief of intelligence, no?"

Junior went to the bar to fetch the ouzo. "Kristin is one of yours? She is not Norwegian?"

"Junior, we discuss later, okay?"

"No, not okay. Why do you do this to me? You cannot blackmail me, my wife knows about Kristin."

Puzanov snorted. "If I have choice, I am not here with you. You are not worth trouble to blackmail. You leak secrets like open sewer. Tatyana is just to make sure Kostos and Agamemnon, they do not hide information from us."

Junior poured ouzo and water into a tumbler and downed half the drink in one gulp. "I don't believe it. My Kristin, spying on me?"

"No, she fucks you for love," Puzanov said with thinly veiled exasperation. "Junior, if you do not sit down and listen, I will order Tatyana on morning flight to Moscow."

Adonis Thomopoulos, Jr., quickly sat down and listened.

LONDON

1022 Zulu/11:22 a.m. local time

Wendell Trent's eyes sprang open, then blinked shut as he averted his face from the strong, shadowless midday sun. He knew that he was stretched across the backseat of a cab bound for Heathrow Airport; the slight pressure on his chest was Cliff Zeman's fishing magazine, opened to an article he had been reading when he dozed off. What had awakened him? And then he had it: the metronomic beat of a turn signal, combined with the slowing of the taxi.

But if they had reached Heathrow, why no jet sounds, only the dull whine of motorway traffic? And why was his view out the left-side window of leafy treetops rather than concrete terminals?

Trent was pulling himself up for a better look when he caught the cabby studying him in the rearview mirror. Their gazes locked, and then the other man looked away.

The cab was angling to the left, heading for an emergency stop some one hundred yards ahead on the A4.

"What's the problem?" asked Trent, raising his voice to be heard through the Plexiglas partition. "Why are we stopping here?"

"The, uh, the motor looks a bit hot. Might be a bum gauge, but better safe than sorry, eh, guv'ner? Don't worry, I'll have you on your flight."

The cabby's nervous voice and taut posture prompted Trent to look past him.

The narrow lay-by, now only seventy-five yards away, was blocked by a dark van flanked by two men in blue windbreakers.

Trent reflexively turned and looked out the rear window.

Three hundred yards behind them a Rover sedan, its left-turn signal blinking, was also slowing and angling toward the lay-by.

Trent swiveled around again—the men in windbreakers were moving to meet the approaching cab—and barked, "Keep going!"

By way of response the cabby raised his right hand to the small cash window in the Plexiglas partition.

In it was a pistol.

"Stay calm!" the cabby shouted. "No one wants you hurt!"

Fifty yards to the lay-by now, and one of the men in windbreakers, as if sensing something amiss, was running forward while fumbling for something under his jacket.

Trent saw that the cabby was having an awkward time both steering and keeping the pistol pointed through the opening. Further, the small size of the cash window severely restricted the man's field of fire. It had been years since Trent's last refresher course in unarmed combat, and longer still since his athletic prime. Was his body up to the challenge? Did he have a choice? Surreptitiously gathering his legs under him, Trent swung his attention from the barrel of the gun to the rearview mirror. The wide-eyed cabby was staring back at him, but sooner or later the man would have to return his attention to the road.

Like now.

Trent suddenly twisted off the seat, grabbing the cabby's gun hand as he fell.

The pistol went off.

The bullet thudded harmlessly into the leatherette upholstery above Trent, who hit the floor without relaxing his death grip on the gun hand. His momentum corkscrewed the cabby half out of his seat and jerked his head back against the Plexiglas partition, hard, but the man still clung to the pistol. Trent rocked forward and upward and drove the cabby's wrist against the far edge of the opening—a raw scream as bones shattered—and then he twisted back again with enough force to wrench shoulder from socket.

As the cabby lost consciousness, the falling pistol glanced off Trent's face, opening a cut on his left cheek.

Outside, incoherent yells as the out-of-control cab careened into the lay-by.

Trent felt a sickening thud atop the front left fender and sensed rather than saw a shape hurtle onto the windshield. But before he could scramble off the floor, the cab rammed the back of the van with an impact that catapulted him face first into the back of the driver's seat.

A horn began to blare.

Trent was bathed in the clammy sweat of mild shock. He tried to clear his head and take stock. Injuries: blood, but only a slow drip, probably from his nose; pain in right shoulder, but it felt like a bruise rather than a break. Enemy disposition: cabby, out of action; man in windbreaker reaching for his gun, out of action; second man in windbreaker—and whoever was in the trailing Rover—still active.

The horn blared on and on and on.

Trent took several deep breaths, then pushed up on the backseat until he could peer out the rear window.

The second man was to the right of the cab, sprawled stomach down on the cement divider that separated the lay-by from the motorway; he seemed stunned but unhurt. The Rover was a couple of hundred yards away and closing fast; through its windshield Trent could see two silhouettes.

Three against one, he thought. He could probably handle the man on the divider, but not the two in the Rover. Trent glanced at the cabby's pistol on the floor. The prospects of shooting his way clear were at best slim; his experience with guns consisted of the Navy's mandatory practice-range sessions, the most recent some four years ago, just before his resignation. No, his only chance was the van—but even if the key was in the ignition, he would never be able to outrun the approaching sedan.

And then Trent noticed, beneath the clamorous horn, the rhythmic chatter of metal striking metal. Where was it coming from? The cab's engine compartment . . .

He turned and looked through the Plexiglas partition. It was a scene right out of an action movie. A curtain of steam billowed from the cab's ruptured radiator; the man who had been reaching for his gun was stretched across the shattered windshield; the cabby was slumped against the steering wheel, his chest resting on the horn. Trent ignored the carnage and searched out the dashboard gauges. They were still registering, which meant the engine was still running.

Trent grabbed his overnight bag, threw open the right-side door, and lunged from the cab. Regaining his balance, he wrenched open the driver's door and wrestled the cabby's inert body off the steering wheel.

Suddenly, the horn fell silent.

The man on the divider reacted with a startled yell.

Trent ignored him as he leaned into the driver's compartment and shoved the automatic-shift lever into reverse.

The cab heaved backward with a groan of metal but wouldn't budge—it seemed riveted in place.

Trent hoisted the cabby's foot onto the gas pedal. The engine whined in protest, the clatter of bent fan blade against engine housing growing with alarming intensity, but still the vehicle refused to move.

The man on the divider was struggling to his feet and the Rover was barreling into the lay-by.

Trent finally saw the problem: the cab's bumper had hooked under the van's.

He hopped onto the back of the van and started jumping up and down.

Now, through the steam, he could see the Rover slewing to a stop, its doors flying open and its two occupants jumping out.

Just then the van's bumper rose high enough for the cab to break free. As it started back down the lay-by, the man sprawled across its windshield slid onto the hood and then tumbled onto the pavement.

The cab was still gaining speed as it plowed into the Rover.

Trent grabbed his bag, wheeled, and scrambled into the van. The keys were in the ignition. He kicked the engine to life, shifted into gear, and checked the wing mirror. The oncoming traffic was swerving to the right, to avoid the chaos in the lay-by, so he quickly accelerated into the clear lane ahead.

Once back on the A4, and once his heartbeat had slowed to a mere gallop, Trent looked at himself in the rearview. In all his years as a rough-and-ready submariner he had been involved in one fight, at a Yokohama gin mill while on leave. Now, less than a day into a simple mission for a civilian agency, he resembled one of Mike Tyson's sparring partners. Blood still seeped from his nose and from the nick on his cheek. His nose looked swollen; he'd probably have at least one black eye by morning. The ironic grin spreading across his face only increased the pain.

No airport security guard in the world would allow him to board a plane looking like that. He unzipped his overnight bag and pulled out the first garment his fingers encountered. It was a T-shirt. He spat on it several times and began to wipe away some of the blood. It was almost eleven-thirty; how far was he from Heathrow? And would he have time to both reach the airport and call Zeman before his flight took off? Trent threw the crimson-stained T-shirt onto the passenger seat and stomped down on the gas pedal.

HELSINKI

■▬■▬■▬■▬■▬■▬■▬■▬■▬■▬■

1231 Zulu/3:31 P.M. local time

"**M**r. Secretary, how good to see you again."

The American secretary of state forced a wan smile.

"Did you have a pleasant flight over?" asked the U.S. ambassador to Finland.

"Tolerable," the secretary replied. Actually, it had been a living hell. Drained by a week wasted on the failed Panamanian negotiations—State had been unable to persuade strongman Manuel Antonio Noriega to relinquish his office in exchange for quashing the federal drug-running indictments against him—the secretary had been looking forward to sleeping his way from Washington to Helsinki. Instead, he had spent most of the long hop across the Atlantic staring at the cabin ceiling and cursing the damned note in his pocket. "You know those Air Force planes."

"Indeed," the ambassador replied. "The President asked that you join him as soon as you arrived. He's up in the library, taking a brief on his Moscow itinerary."

The two men climbed the stairs to the second story.

The secretary continued to ponder the wisdom of giving the note to the Old Man. Noriega had hand-addressed the envelope to the President, and crashed a reception at the Papal Nuncio in Panama City to deliver it to the CIA station chief. The fact that Langley still associated with the strongman, while the rest of the government was working to end his odious reign, infuriated the secretary. Yet the director of Central Intelligence must have been nervous about the note. Instead of transmitting it directly to the White House, Langley had forwarded it to State.

The secretary was not a man to read other people's mail. Neither was the Vice President of the United States, in whom he had confided the unorthodox receipt of the Noriega letter. After agonizing deliberation both men had set aside their scruples—and soon wished they hadn't. It would be derelict not to inform the Old Man of the communication, the secretary thought, but if I do, I'll probably have to provide the translation too.

Outside the library the U.S. Air Force officer carrying the Football, the black attaché case containing the portable coding device for launching America's nuclear arsenal, sat in an armchair reading a paperback technothriller.

One of the Secret Service agents saw the secretary approaching and knocked lightly on the library door, then opened it.

As the secretary made his way into the crowded room, he nodded to the national security adviser, a burly black man, and to the diminutive White House chief of staff.

The Old Man was seated on a sofa, eyes closed, brows knit in furious concentration.

Across from him the only female in the room, a woman in her late forties, slowly and distinctly pronounced the words *"Rodilsya, ne toropilsya."*

"Ro . . . rodilsya, ne toropilsya."

"Rodilsya, ne toropilsya," she repeated.

The Old Man opened his eyes. *"Rodilsya, ne toropilsya."*

"Almost, Mr. President. It's really more of an 'eel' sound: *Rodeel-sya, ne toro-peel-sya."*

"Rodilsya, ne toropilsya."

"Perfect! I still can't believe how you can pick up Russian phrases so quickly."

The Old Man beamed. "Well, it's a darn sight easier than some of the dialogue they used to hand me in Hollywood. 'Listen, Chuck, if you and your chums aren't back in camp by chowtime, I'm calling in the cavalry.' "

The others in the room laughed politely.

The Old Man spotted his secretary of state. "Good of you to join us, Mr. Secretary. How was the flight?"

"Fine, Mr. President."

"That's swell." The Old Man picked up a candy bowl and offered it to his language instructor. "Any urgent matters of state?"

"No, sir," the secretary replied.

"There better not be, with all of us over here." The Old Man winked broadly, then turned to the woman beside him. "Margaret, I believe you know the secretary? Margaret here is helping us prepare a surprise for tomorrow. The other day somebody showed me an article about the last summit. The article said our young Russian friend was sick and tired of hearing me say *'Doveryai, no proveryai'* . . . 'Trust, but verify.' Well, fair enough, though if you'll excuse me for saying so, how can anyone take offense at those words of wisdom?"

He paused to pick out several green jelly-beans from the candy bowl, then gestured to the coffee table, on which lay a leather-bound copy of the Jessamyn West novel *Friendly Persuasion.* "When Margaret learned about the gift we're taking to Moscow, she suggested an old Russian proverb, *'Rodilsya, ne toropilsya'* . . . 'It is born, but it cannot be hurried.' "

"That's, uh, that's very eloquent, sir," the secretary said.

The Old Man rose from the sofa and clasped the woman's hand. "Thank you again, Margaret. You've been such a patient teacher. Just say a little prayer for me tomorrow, won't you? I'd feel awfully foolish flubbing your wonderful lines."

"Oh, you won't, Mr. President. You'll knock them dead."

As she left the room, a junior aide approached the Old Man. "Sir, we have your briefing tape racked up."

"What's the running time?"

"About twenty minutes, sir."

"Oh, all right." The Old Man sank back into the sofa. "But give me the remote-control thingamajig, in case I want to fast-forward."

The secretary of state caught the national security adviser's eye, then tilted his head toward the door.

The national security adviser nodded.

"Mr. President," the secretary said, "would you mind if I excused myself? It was a pretty rough flight over."

"I told you, you should have come over with us on Air Force One. Not a single bad ride in seven and a half years. You know, that might be the thing I miss the most, come January." The Old Man smiled ruefully. "See you at dinner?"

"Of course, sir."

The national security adviser was waiting when the secretary of state emerged from the library. The two men repaired to an empty study down the corridor.

"What is it?" said the national security adviser.

"You know that Noriega went before the Panamanian parliament to denounce our offer of amnesty. He also back-channeled this."

The national security adviser studied the envelope for several seconds, saw that the seal had been broken, and opened it.

The note was written in large, bold strokes on the strongman's official stationery:

Señor Presidente: Chupe mis huevos. Noriega.

"My Spanish is kind of rusty," the national security adviser said, "but I sure do catch the drift."

"So. Now what?"

"If we show this to the Old Man, he'll probably send in the Marines by dawn."

The secretary nodded glumly.

"Anyone else read this?" asked the national security adviser, handing back the note.

"The Vice President."

"And?"

"Never saw him so mad. Swore like a Texan for a change, not some old shoe from Andover. Hell, if he were sitting in the Oval Office, even he'd send in the Marines at dawn. But we both vote for the burn bag. If you concur, that is."

" 'Concur' is putting it mildly. You shouldn't have opened it, but I'm glad you did. Anything else going on Stateside?"

The secretary shook his head. "Quiet as a church mouse. For want of a better phrase, the world seems to be at peace."

"Good. This is not the weekend for unexpected mischief."

The national security adviser returned to the library.

The videotaped briefing on the President's Moscow itinerary was playing on a large-screen monitor; over footage of a shop-lined street the announcer intoned, ". . . pedestrian mall known as the Arbat . . ."

The Old Man raised the remote-control wand, dimmed the sound, and said, "Looks pretty civilized there."

"Sir, it's the most fashionable street in Moscow," a junior aide volunteered.

"Is it safe? To walk around, I mean?"

"Yes, sir. The crime rate in Moscow is surprisingly—"

"No. I mean for me to walk around."

"Mr. President," the White House chief of staff interjected with alarm, "the security logistics would be a nightmare."

"Well, you know, I was talking to Mike before I left, just checking in to see how the rehabilitation was going, and he had an interesting thought. Remember how our young Russian friend left his limousine last year and walked into the crowds? And how the networks just ate it up? Well, Mike said, 'Mr. President, turnabout's fair play.' Look at those people there. Heck, I'm probably safer there than I am on the streets of New York."

The chief of staff did not join in the chorus of chuckles. Once his boss got a notion in his head, there was no stopping him; damn it, he thought, the Old Man was intent on glad-handing his way up and down the Arbat, with or without security coverage. He jotted down a note to give the head of the Secret Service detail advance warning.

The Old Man punched the sound level back up.

". . . on the following day, which is Monday, Mr. President, you are scheduled to have a late breakfast with senior members of the American embassy."

The picture of Spaso House dissolved to a long-range shot of a brooding stone building that had seen better days: "Then, you will journey across the Moscow River to meet with Soviet dissidents at the historic Danilov Monastery. There—"

The Old Man unexpectedly cut the sound again. "That monastery . . . have I been there before?"

The others in the room glanced at each other in total bafflement, but remained silent.

"I know that I know that name."

Suddenly, the national security adviser made the connection. "Sir, you do. The American journalist whom the Soviets accused of spying."

The Old Man grinned with unaffected delight. "I knew it. You know, boys, when you've been in public life as long as I have, well, if there's one thing you learn, that's how to remember names. Poor guy. Didn't I call his wife?"

"Yes, Mr. President. And you had them to the White House after his safe release."

"Russians framed him, didn't they?"

"Yes, sir. He was lured to a covert drop up in the Lenin Hills. KGB agents were waiting."

The Old Man made a face. "Dirty pool, if you ask me. Say, maybe I should work that into one of the speeches I have to give in Moscow . . . something about, oh, I don't know, freedom of expression, First Amendment rights, that sort of thing. We could script it so it seems like an ad lib." He paused to work his tongue around a chunk of candy caught between two teeth.

His aides exchanged worried glances.

Finally, the national security adviser said, "Sir, perhaps it'd be best not to raise the subject. The Soviets sincerely believe the documents they confiscated contained information that could compromise their national security."

"But we already have nuclear bombs," the Old Man said with a straight face. "Hell, they stole the formula from us, didn't they?"

When the polite laughter subsided, the national security adviser said, "Mr. President, the journalist was apprehended receiving newspapers printed in the city of Frunze."

The Old Man affected a wry smile. "Well, I guess we should have

sent the Kremlin a subscription to the *Des Moines Register.*
Could've saved us all a lot of grief."

"Sir, a more appropriate analogy would be Los Alamos or
Livermore. The local papers in those towns are monitored by KGB
for soft intelligence . . . stories on prominent visiting scientists,
upcoming lectures, even social events where laboratory personnel
might be approached and recruited. Frunze happens to be an important Soviet research center, so we read their papers too."

The Old Man's hand froze over the candy bowl. "You mean that
journalist guy was actually a spy? He was working for the CIA?"

"Mr. President, I can assure you categorically that he was not on
CIA's payroll."

"You had me scared there for a minute," the Old Man said as he
fished out several more sweets. "Damn shame about that, though.
It's just the sort of thing we need to catch our young Russian friend
off guard."

He popped two jelly beans into his mouth, pointed the remote-
control wand at the screen again, and returned to his briefing.

WEYERS CAVE, VIRGINIA
1357 Zulu/9:57 A.M. local time

Jeanne Zeman heard her daughter come into the kitchen from
the back deck. Nora let the screen door bang sharply behind her
and said, "Mom, can you get Dad off the phone?"

Jeanne turned off the blender. "Why, were you expecting a call
on the secure line?"

"Oh, come on, Mom. He missed dinner last night, and he still
hasn't said more than five words to Jake and Mr. and Mrs. Levy.
That's pretty antisocial, don't you think?"

"Yup."

Nora's face clenched into a pout. "Well, it's not fair. This was supposed to be a family weekend."

"Oh? How about last year? Weren't you supposed to be here on your father's birthday, rather than San Diego?"

"But that was different. The bank was counting on me to crunch the numbers on that buy-out."

Jeanne suddenly experienced a disconcerting sense of déjà vu. Having survived her two children's passage through teenhood, she had naturally expected them to have forever outgrown the whiny self-absorption so characteristic of those dark ages. Yet here was Nora, in her late twenties, already sounding like a character from that infuriatingly smug new television show, *thirtysomething.* What accounted for its popularity—was it required viewing for young bankers? Jeanne looked at her daughter and said, "I can't wait until you have children."

"But, Mom, what will the Levys think?"

"They'll think your father is more important than he really is." She reached out and brushed Nora's cheek. "I've got to go check the grille. Be a sport, finish this gazpacho for me. And if your brother doesn't show up in the next five minutes, I'm sure Jake'll be happy to serve as bartender."

Jeanne stepped out onto the deck, where a pair of chickens was roasting over a low flame. Some thirty yards away, on the other side of the vegetable garden, her husband sat against the base of a tree, the STU III scrambler phone by his side. He had arrived with the unit the previous evening and been on it nonstop until two A.M., and then again this morning since seven, when he had been wakened by the first of Ann Davis's calls. Nearly three decades of marriage had taught Jeanne how to gauge the severity of the professional crises in her husband's life. On a scale of ten, she thought, lifting the grille cover, this one rated an eleven.

Cliff Zeman would have scored it a twelve.

"I appreciate that he's away from his desk," he said into the phone, trying to keep his voice civil. "But you just finished telling me he's the only person authorized to sign off on my request."

"Affirmative, sir."

"Look, son, do you want me to have him paged? Or call every restaurant and bar within ten miles of the Pentagon?"

"Uh, no sir. It's just that, well . . ." The ensign was obviously trying to protect his superior. And what could that man be doing on this fine morning: Jogging? Sleeping off a hangover? Coaching a Little League game? Trysting? "Sir, could you give me ten minutes to track him down?"

"I don't have ten minutes," Zeman said.

"Then five minutes? I'll call you back in five minutes, promise."

"Thank you, but I'll hold."

Zeman glanced at his watch. Damn it, he thought, Wendell Trent had gotten through to Ann Davis two hours earlier, just before flying out of London, and proper security at Athens airport still hadn't been nailed down. Coaxing decisions out of the military bureaucracy was a Herculean task at the best of times; obtaining prompt action at the start of a lazy holiday weekend was like running a marathon in molasses. Yet Trent remained at risk. On short notice someone had sent three cars and five men against him in England. They undoubtedly had the resources to try again in Greece—and much more time to prepare.

If there was a bright side to the past twelve hours, it was that no further trouble had befallen the research vessel. Edna Haddix seemed to have reestablished control, but he'd rest easier when Trent was finally aboard. He shook his head ruefully. Nora would have teased him mercilessly if she'd been privy to the thought that had just passed through his mind. But Zeman felt confident that he was no chauvinist, that he would feel the same apprehensions if the 1800 running a dicey operation happened to be a man.

He saw his wife turning the chickens on the grille and waved to her.

"Want a drink?" Jeanne called across the yard.

"That'd be much appreciated."

"The usual?"

Zeman thought about the day and night ahead of him and said, regretfully, "No, better make it an orange juice or iced tea."

TRIPOLI

1417 Zulu/4:17 P.M. local time

As the pilot raised the canopy of the MiG-31, the heat that surged into the cockpit made Yuri Tikhonov's head swim. The torpedo technician was known back at the Admiral Nakhimov submarine base for habitually being the last man out of the sauna, and for working uncomplainingly through the spell of hundred-degree days that baked the Crimean Peninsula every August. But this—this was hell on earth. And then, as Tikhonov pried off the flight helmet, an even more disorienting sensation: above the whine of jet engines he could hear a *muezzin*'s call to prayer ululating from loudspeakers around the air base.

A jeep and a light truck were headed toward the plane.

"I hate the days here," the pilot said as he rose from his seat and stretched. "You do nothing but drink water like a camel. I hate the nights too. They are cooler, but we never leave the base because it is the only place where you can get vodka."

"Do you fly here often?"

"Worse than that, my friend. I was posted here as an advisor. One whole year watching our Libyan allies grind fine jets into junk. The *arabi* cannot fly them, they cannot maintain them." He turned and winked at Tikhonov. "But better Tripoli than Kabul, no?"

Down below, a member of the ground crew released the boarding-ladder handle.

"Come," the pilot said as he swung his foot over the side. "Too long in this sun, and you become as stupid as the *arabi*."

By the time Tikhonov climbed down, crewmen were already unloading the two cases from the belly of the MiG-31. The pavement seemed to sear the soles of his feet, even through the boots.

The pilot was a few yards off, sharing a joke with the driver of the light truck.

"How far is it to the submarine base?" asked Tikhonov.

The pilot shrugged. Then, taking pity on his passenger, he spoke briefly with the driver. "The submarine base is way over in Ras El-Hilal, Comrade, but that is not where your crates are going."

He turned and pointed across the tarmac.

Tikhonov felt his gorge rise. The plane being fueled was the two-seat version of the YAK-36. To the uninitiated it looked like any other military jet. But Tikhonov knew its underbelly contained a series of ports that allowed the pilot to execute helicopterlike vertical takeoffs and landings. The Soviet Navy had developed the YAK-36 for one reason: to fly to and from its aircraft carriers.

"You are to depart in fifteen minutes," the pilot said.

"Comrade, am I permitted to go inside?"

"Of course," the pilot replied. "You must be thirsty."

"No, suddenly I have need of the bathroom."

THE EASTERN MED

1504 Zulu/6:04 p.m. local time

Billy Ray McConkey poked his head into *Fanning II*'s lounge. The curtains were drawn and some dozen of his shipmates were sprawled about on the chairs and built-in banquettes. They were lethargically staring at the television on which the *Dirty Harry* videotape was playing yet again.

Clint Eastwood stalked down a San Francisco street through the mist from a broken fire hydrant and approached the wounded bank robber. As the actor lifted his pistol and squinted down its barrel, McConkey rasped, in perfect sync: "I know what you're thinking. Did he fire six shots, or only five? Well, to tell you the truth, in all this excitement I kind of lost track myself. But this being a forty-four Magnum, the most powerful handgun in the world . . ."

Ezra Schell, one of *Ernie*'s flyers, said, "Hey, Cowboy. You grubbed down yet?"

McConkey replied with a belch.

"What're they serving tonight?"

"Steak."

"How was it?"

"Fucker tasted like it died of old age."

"You would know," muttered navigator Leonard Heppel.

"Yo, Mister Brie-and-Chablis, who asked you?" McConkey spotted Roland Vigneron, the owlish French electronic specialist, across the room. "Rollie . . . didn't I tell you we shoulda sweet-talked our way aboard that launch? Hell, we'd be in Crete right now, scoring Greek pussy, instead of—"

"Knock it off, Cowboy, we're watching a movie," Heppel said.

"What's the matter, you trying to pick up tips on how to act like a man? Well hear this, pardner: Harry Callahan don't eat quiche." McConkey made a rude noise, then turned to leave.

"Cowboy, wait." Vigneron had gotten out of his seat and was making his way toward the door.

Out in the corridor McConkey said, "You ought to stay and watch my man Clint, *mon ami.* He's all-American. Pay attention, you can be too."

Vigneron narrowed his eyes and gravely intoned, " 'Go ahead, punk, make my day.' No, Cowboy, I have seen this film, and all the other Dirty Harrys, too many times already. Tell me, what do you plan to do?"

"Right now? Fix me a Jack D. and catch some fresh air. Come on, I'll buy you one. We'll go watch that poor sonuvabitch Flanagan work on the cable."

Vigneron hesitated.

"Something the matter?"

"I am not yet cleared to be on the afterdeck."

"Oh, right." McConkey shook his head. "What a crock of shit. Here you are, knocking yourself out to patch that goddamned transmitter, and you're still grounded."

"Maybe they wait to see if I am successful," Vigneron said puckishly.

"Nah. Haddix's more fucked up than my spinster aunt in Waco, and the numbnuts in Washington and Paree—no offense, Rollie—by the time they get their acts together, we're back on the beach."

"I am permitted up top, Cowboy," Vigneron said. "Perhaps we have the drinks there?"

"Sure. Look, why don't you grab a couple of glasses and some of that Frog water—the kind without the bubbles—and I'll go fetch the bourbon."

McConkey took the companionway down a deck, then detoured to the head. There were two men in it. One of the freshly arrived DOE security agents was leaning against the wall, keeping an eye on Ariel Kahane as the young Israeli stood at a urinal.

McConkey stepped up to the other one and said, "Yo, Mr. Surgeon."

Kahane continued to stare at the graffiti on the wall.

"Made any fresh incisions lately?"

Kahane glanced over. "You are not amusing, Cowboy."

The young man's calm response curbed McConkey from making another wisecrack. Instead, he said, "Hey kid, they treating you okay?"

"Yes, thank you." Kahane flushed, rinsed his hands, and, trailed by his DOE watchdog, left the room.

■　■　■

"It was the damnedest thing, Rollie." McConkey took another sip of his drink as he tried to sort out his thoughts.

He and Vigneron were up on Steel Beach, the roof of the bridge that was the highest point on *Fanning II*'s superstructure. To the west the sun, as if drained by its day-long game of hide-and-seek with the clouds, was now a pale yellow as it began to inch toward the horizon. In this most peaceful time of the day the wind had died and the seas were calming. The only activity in all they surveyed was on the afterdeck fifty feet below. There, Flanagan and several helpers continued the tedious task of splicing cable.

Finally, McConkey said, "This is going to sound kinda weird, but you know what his attitude reminded me of? Saint Sebastian."

Vigneron's eyes twinkled with amusement. "You mean now they tie his hands and stick him with arrows?"

"No, I'm serious, Rollie. I mean, here's Kahane, just taking a leak, but he has this dignity—this dignity of a martyr."

"Perhaps the cable, Ari does not do it."

McConkey shook his head. "It's been more'n twenty-four hours, and nothing else's gone wrong. But you know, that's one of the things that don't compute. Why would anybody cut the cable in the first place? Why don't we just put this mud boat into port and make the repairs . . . why is the beach air-mailing in specialists? Who gives a fuck whether or not we find the Jewish boat that diving suit came off of?"

Vigneron shrugged. "I just wish they hurry, so we are done with it. The repairs, how do they go?"

"Flanagan's boasting we'll be on line by tomorrow morning. He's good, and he's working his nuts off, but fat chance. Even if the second tech turned up right now, I'd say we're looking at sometime Monday."

"This second tech, he comes when?"

McConkey took another sip. "Last I heard, tomorrow A.M."

"Look, your nemesis." Vigneron pointed downward. Edna Haddix and Rick Wolfe had emerged from the ship and were crossing the afterdeck toward Flanagan.

McConkey made a sour face.

Vigneron laughed. "You are still mad because she says no."

"Nah. Anyway, she looks like the kind that don't push back, know what I mean?"

ATHENS

1532 Zulu/6:32 P.M. local time

The immigration officer at Athens International Airport studied the fresh bruises on Wendell Trent's face for several moments, but stamped the passport without comment.

Trent hiked his overnight bag onto one shoulder and strode toward the baggage claim area. He was feeling almost human again; on the flight from London he had found three adjacent empty seats in the back and stretched across them for a luxurious nap. If only sleep had refreshed his memory as well. During his hurried preboarding call to Washington he had been unable to tell Ann Davis much about the assailants other than that the cabdriver seemed more Mediterranean than British. That should narrow the suspects down to several hundred thousand, he thought glumly. There must be something else, some other clue. . . .

Passengers were beginning to congregate around the baggage carousels. Trent swerved around them and got in line at one of the customs counters. According to Davis a Navy driver would meet him on the other side of the customs exit and take him down the road to Hellenikon Air Base, where a Navy plane was waiting to fly him down to Crete. With luck he would be there by nine P.M. and aboard *Fanning II* first thing in the morning.

"Papa! Papa!" The teenaged girl in front of Trent leaned to her left and started waving madly.

He followed her gaze. Some one hundred feet to his left an open passageway ran at an oblique angle out to the lobby, in which a man was waving back. In the crowd that surrounded him, Trent noticed a detail of young men wearing the uniform of the U.S. Navy Shore Patrol; some poor sailor was about to step into a world of grief.

The customs inspector nodded to the teenaged girl, who collected her bags and hurried toward the exit.

Trent stepped forward and handed over his declaration form.

The inspector glanced at it. "Please, what is the nature of your trip?"

"I'm here on official business for the government of the United States."

"You have no luggage?"

"Just this," Trent said, hefting his overnight bag.

"Kindly open it."

Trent set the bag on the counter and unzipped it.

The inspector rummaged through the contents for thirty seconds. Then he looked past the far end of the counter and shrugged.

Trent saw he was signaling to three men seated around a long metal table that had been set up against the wall. Now, as the men stood, one of them began gesturing to the table.

The inspector said, "You will go over there, please?"

"Is something wrong?"

"You will go to that table, please? At once?"

Trent rezipped his bag and started toward the men. Could this be related to the cab? Could the London police have determined his identity and tracked him to the Athens flight? He glanced at his watch and factored in the time zones. No, not in less than four hours.

The two younger men by the table carried themselves with the nonchalance of weight lifters. The leader, who was in his mid-forties, had the sullen air of a leashed ferret.

"Put the bag here," the leader said.

Trent set it on the table, which was bare save for a round glass amber ashtray almost as big as a Frisbee.

"You are in a fight aboard the plane?"

"What? Oh, my face. No, I slipped in the shower this morning."

"Papers."

"Excuse me," Trent said. "Who are you, and what's this all about."

"I am Adonis Thomopoulos, Jr. I am the deputy director of intelligence for the Panhellenic Socialist Movement. Your papers."

"Listen, Adonis, I am here on behalf of my government. Do you tell me what's going on, or do I call my embassy?"

Junior's eyes narrowed. He had spent the past few hours silently cursing Dimitri Puzanov for treating him like a common secretary: Junior, I want your agents on Crete to do this; Junior, I want you to personally do that. Now he damned the GRU agent for also imposing strict ground rules on the airport assignment. Find some pretext for detaining the American at least thirty-six hours, Puzanov had said, but do not harm him, we cannot afford a diplomatic incident. Junior was sorely tempted to disobey. This insolent American who stood before him needed to be taught some respect, and Junior could see that his boys were itching to add a few more scars to the bastard's face. Instead, he said, "We have reason to believe that you enter Greece with contraband items."

Trent was more baffled by the Greek's patent animosity than by the unexpected accusation. He forced a smile. "Well, we should be able to clear that up quickly. Let me open up my bag. . . ."

"That is not necessary," Junior replied. "How much money do you carry?"

"I'm not sure," Trent said. "A couple hundred dollars in cash, maybe, the rest in traveler's checks."

"Your wallet."

Trent handed it over, his mind racing at full throttle. First the cab, now this—surely related, but he couldn't imagine anyone having the clout and the reach to scramble an attack team in London, then bring in the Greek government less than five hours later. He sneaked a glance past Junior's two muscleboys. Just around the corner and down the passageway a Navy driver was waiting for him.

How to get word out? Or, if push came to shove, could he make it that far? Doubtful.

Junior finished counting the bills in the American's wallet a second time. One hundred eight-seven U.S. dollars, plus forty-three British pounds; not even close to the $500 limit imposed on incoming tourists. Damn, he would have to take this one into a back room and plant some hashish on him. Junior was handing back the wallet when a more cunning solution presented itself.

"Your watch," he said. "What is the brand?"

"Rolex."

"Rolex is very expensive. How much it costs?"

"I really don't remember."

"Then you show me the sales receipt, please."

"Hey, I bought this eight, nine years ago in Geneva," Trent said. "You keep your sales receipts that long?"

Junior's mouth twisted into a smirk. "It is illegal to smuggle valuable items into my country. I think we go to headquarters and continue the interrogation there."

"Wait." Trent glanced around the large, gymnasiumlike room. "If I haven't cleared customs, I haven't technically entered Greece, right?"

Junior frowned, then said, warily, "That is correct."

Trent unbuckled his Rolex and placed it on the table. "Then I will not enter Greece with any item of value. May I go now?"

Junior was flabbergasted. What sort of fool would walk away from a $2,000 watch? He became aware, from the hush descending over the room, that several nearby customs inspectors, and the passengers waiting before them, were raptly watching the scene between the American and himself. Then he noticed one of his own men covetously eyeing the abandoned Rolex. Was there nothing he could do to detain this cunning son of a bitch?

Trent picked up his bag and started to sidle around the two muscleboys. It was perhaps twenty feet to the passageway, and then another seventy-five feet to the lobby. . . .

"Wait," Junior cried triumphantly. "Arrest him!"

Trent turned slowly. "You have a law against being an American?"

"The charge is attempting to bribe a representative of the Hellenic Republic! And the evidence is the watch!"

Trent sensed the two muscleboys behind him tensing for action. He could take on one, but not both—not without a diversion. And then he spotted the large glass ashtray on the table. He looked at his inquisitor and said, in a firm voice, "I demand the right to call my embassy."

"Not now," Junior sneered. "Maybe later, if you answer my questions."

Trent abruptly wheeled to face the roomful of waiting passengers and yelled, "Someone call the U.S. Embassy and tell them Wendell—"

One of the muscleboys cut Trent off by looping an arm around his throat and rabbit-punching him in the kidney. As Trent's knees buckled, the man let go. Trent slumped to the floor, still clutching his bag, and loudly gasped for air. Careful, he told himself, don't overdo it. . . .

"I think you go with us, yes?" asked Junior cheerfully.

Trent nodded mutely, then clutched the edge of the table with his free hand and laboriously pulled himself semierect.

Over the dead silence in the customs area, faint sounds of a ruckus in the lobby.

"You Americans . . . all bluff and bluster." Junior chuckled. He would dine out on this episode for months to come.

The large glass ashtray was inches from Trent's hand.

He cupped his palm around it and, with all the force he could summon, propelled it toward Junior. The ashtray rocketed down the metal table top like a giant shuffleboard disc, flew off the far end, and smote Junior's privates with a gelatinous squish that made bystanders wince.

The nearest muscleboy was transfixed by the sight of his boss keeling over in slow motion; he never saw the American whirling out of his crouch, much less the overnight bag that Trent swung into the side of his head.

The second man had managed to snap his mouth shut and was groping for his holster when Trent blitzed into him like a sack-hungry linebacker. Trent kept his legs churning, driving the man backward until he sandwiched him against the wall.

Now, all across the customs area, startled shouts rang out.

Trent disentangled himself from the now semiconscious young man, wheeled around the corner, and started down the passageway, accelerating with every stride.

The only person between him and the lobby was a terrified airport security guard, a rail-thin man in his fifties unarmed except for a nightstick in one quivering hand.

"Move!" bellowed Trent.

The guard emitted a high-pitched squeal and brandished his nightstick, swordlike, at the approaching American.

Sorry, old man, Trent thought as he lowered his shoulder.

The guard flew back ten feet and skidded another fifteen.

Trent hurdled his prostrate form, sprinted the last few yards into the lobby—and pulled up short.

Most of the people in the waiting area were sprawled on the floor. The reason: Six U.S. shore patrolmen and a dozen Greek policemen were facing each other with drawn guns.

"You Trent?"

Trent whirled and spotted the chief petty officer in charge of the American detail, a black man in his late twenties. "You got that right, Chief."

"We seem to have us a problem. At this point in time a clean getaway looks kind of dubious."

A senior Greek policeman spoke up. "I warn you again, give us your guns."

The chief petty officer shook his head. "Fight's over, guy. We don't want in anymore." He shifted his gaze to Trent. "Seems you can't go inside customs from this side, but we heard you yelling for help, so—"

The Greek policeman barked an order to his men, then wheeled and rushed into the customs area.

The chief petty officer's name tag read COOKSON.

"Chief, I was supposed to be met by a driver. You seen him around?"

"You're looking at him. Jesus, friend, they sent a whole detail to pick you up because they thought something heavy might be going down, but this is like over the top, you know?"

"Sorry about that. Look, uh, you think it might be diplomatic to lower your guns?"

"Think they'll lower theirs?"

Trent glanced around. In addition to the policeman already surrounding them, more were converging from various parts of the lobby. "Chief, can you get us out of here without wrecking NATO?"

"You know, that's exactly the problem I've been working on."

The senior Greek policeman returned from the customs area supporting a doubled-over Adonis Thomopoulos, Jr.

Junior had blood in his eyes but pain in his voice. "Arrest all the bastards!"

The policeman leaned down and whispered in his ear.

Junior tried to straighten but thought better of it. Cocking his head to look at Cookson, he wheezed, "You are in charge here? Well, we have no quarrel with you. But this one, he is not one of your sailors, he is our prisoner. So you leave him to us, no?"

"Sorry, sir, actually he does happen to be one of ours."

"What! His passport says—"

"Bogus, sir," Cookson replied with barely suppressed outrage. "Do the papers say 'Wendell Trent'? Well, sir, not only is this sorry individual a deserter from the United States Navy, but I guess we can add forgery to the charges."

He turned to the senior policeman. "Sir, I apologize for the misunderstanding. We know this man to be dangerous, which is why we wanted to go in there . . . to help subdue him. Navy wants Chief Petty Officer Otis Redding here for desertion. I therefore claim jurisdiction pursuant to the relevant sections of the treaty that governs relationships between our two nations. My orders are to transport him to Hellenikon and slap him in the brig. Should you wish to press civil charges, he will of course be made available to you."

The Greek policeman stroked his chin. He was about to speak when Junior grabbed his arm and pulled him to the side. Though whispered, their argument was explosive. Thirty seconds later the policeman pulled away and issued a command. His men reluctantly lowered the barrels of their weapons.

"Jackie, the cuffs," Cookson ordered.

One of the seamen clapped handcuffs over Trent's wrist.

Cookson drew himself to attention and saluted the policeman: "Thank you, sir. Again, my personal apologies for this incident. It shouldn't have happened. Okay, men, let's move this scumbag out of here, on the double!"

The detail hustled Trent wordlessly through the lobby and into the back of a waiting jeep.

As the vehicle pulled from the curb, Cookson turned and said, "Hope you don't mind, friend, but I aim to leave those cuffs on till we're safely inside Hellenikon."

"Hey, Chief, who'm I to second-guess someone who's working on a no-hitter? Just tell me this: Where'd you come up with that stuff back there?"

Cookson's poker face dissolved into a grin that betrayed his youth. "Right out my ass, that's where! Waaa-hooo!" He exuberantly punched the air, then recomposed himself. "Yo, friend, they do that to your face in there?"

"No. That's from London, this morning."

"What is it that makes you such a popular mother?"

Trent shrugged. "That's what I've been asking myself all day. I never thought life at the Department of Energy could get so exciting."

"And that squinched-over dude back there . . . who was he?"

"He said he was Greek intelligence."

Cookson whistled. "Hey, Hal, punch up a secure frequency and pass the handset back, will you? The brass wanted to know if we ran into any problems. This ought to start the beehive buzzing."

"What do you mean?"

"You, friend, are a civilian who Navy has agreed to transport to a mud boat stationed off Crete. Yours truly was all set to ride shotgun, and I got to tell you, I was looking forward to it. Crete's the only place to be for a homeboy."

Trent shot him a questioning look.

"They don't get many blacks down there, so no one makes a big deal of us," Cookson explained. "Not like here in Athens. But if a lot of heavy political shit's about to go down, my guess is, Navy doesn't want you overnighting at Soudha Bay, Navy doesn't want you in one of its patrol boats tomorrow morning. My guess is, Navy's about to give you deluxe service, beach to ship and door to door."

JERUSALEM

1610 Zulu/7:10 p.m. local time

Ephraim Levenger hurried down the dim tunnel beneath the Old City to the safe room and barged through the door without knocking.

The only person seated at the card table was Leon Rose. He was playing solitaire.

"Well?"

"Mother called three hours ago," Rose replied, continuing with his game. "His friend Patolichev has agreed."

"Wonderful news!"

"Better than that we just received from your man aboard the American vessel."

Levenger grew very still.

"Before our submarine arrives in position to relay messages, your man takes it upon himself to stop the Americans. He cuts the cable which holds the two underwater machines."

"What!"

"Yes. Quite a Rambo, that one." Rose looked up and unexpectedly smiled. "Relax, my friend. Luckily for us, he did not sever the cable. And the time it takes the Americans to make repairs will work to our advantage. Even if the rendezvous and the transfer of the torpedo go well, Ben tells me our submarine cannot reach the eastern Med for another seventy-two hours, at a minimum. In fact, we shall have to order your man to delay the Americans further . . . although in not quite such dramatic fashion next time."

Levenger took off his jacket and sank into a chair across from Rose. "I am sorry to be late. I missed the connecting flight, and then I had to go get the reports from London."

"So. What is the damage there?"

"One agent has a broken pelvis and leg, another severe injuries to the chest and shoulder. Both cars must be written off."

Rose shook his head. "Why not just have them wear signs that say, WE WORK FOR MOSSAD?"

"London assures me the site was sanitized," Levenger said defensively. "There will be no clues pointing back to us."

"I'm sure not, Ephraim. Forgive me. But this American, what is his name . . ."

"Wendell Trent."

"Wendell Trent escaped the trap? By himself?"

Levenger nodded.

"Maybe we can convert Wendell Trent to Judaism. Then you can recruit him."

"Very funny. Were they able to detain him in Athens?"

"I have not yet heard." Rose glanced at his watch. "The flight from London landed less than half an hour ago. I expect Mother to call again at ten."

Levenger began to gnaw his fingernails.

"By the way, Ephraim, your man aboard the research vessel reports that the Americans have detained a suspect in connection with the cut cable. An Israeli graduate student. It is always *cherchez le juif,* eh?" Rose snorted and tossed the cards aside. "What did you think of Mother?"

"Tough. Smart. Probably a good chess player, as so many Russians are. Perhaps bitter. About his leg, I mean."

"There you are wrong. What makes Mother bitter is the mediocrities who run his country. This new one, Mother considers him promising, but he says the Kremlin bureaucracy makes even our cabinet seem intelligent."

Levenger's mouth curled in a wry smile. "Where is Ben?"

"At his office, trying to smooth some ruffled feathers. The submarine he chooses to rendezvous with the Soviets, the *Sabra,* was en route to Cape Town on a priority run for the Ministry of Science and Technology. Some people over there heard about the change in itinerary. They are very upset that their delivery will be late, and threaten to raise a stink."

"How did they learn this on the Sabbath?" asked Levenger in consternation. "And from whom? Leon, what you are telling me is, we have a leak."

"No, we do not. Have you forgotten in which country we live? Israel. Home of the brave, home of the free . . . home of the yenta. Ben assures me he can contain the situation. In any event, secrecy shall not be an issue after tomorrow."

Levenger shifted uneasily in his chair. "I am still not sure we should bring it up so soon. Perhaps Ben can—"

"Ben Goren can stretch his authority no more. He has already ordered *Sabra* to divert and take on a Soviet torpedo. But he cannot order the captain to fire it. He has already ordered *Rahav* to station itself near the American vessel and relay transmissions from your agent on board. But he cannot order that submarine, or any other ship in Israel's navy, to forcibly remove the Americans. Those remain political decisions."

"Perhaps Trent has been stopped in Athens," Levenger said.

"Perhaps my agent should permanently sabotage the American vessel."

"Then another will come. And if that one fails, yet another. Tell me, Ephraim, what is it that you fear about telling the cabinet?"

"What shall we tell them?"

Rose looked down at the card table. A puckish smile flitted across his face. "The truth . . . or at least ninety percent of it. And, we shall tell them no lies."

"There will be many questions," Levenger protested. "Perhaps someone will guess the ten percent we omit."

"Ephraim. Unlike Ben and myself, you did not participate in the original negotiations with Mother."

"Correct."

"What was your reaction when we first outlined to you *Dakar*'s primary mission? Can you remember?"

"Shock. Not at the mission, but at the fact that it failed. Sorrow, overwhelming sorrow, at the loss of life. And I suppose pride, because we had the courage to try."

Rose nodded. "Did you think, at the time we told you, that there might be yet another cargo aboard the submarine?"

Levenger shook his head.

"Neither did the cabinet officials who approved the operation twenty years ago. Nor will those who shall hear about it for the first time tomorrow. Ephraim, nobody can guess the secret we seek to protect. It can only be revealed if we fail to bury *Dakar*."

"I have seen exactly these baskets in Athens. We will look like a pair of peasants, carrying them aboard the airplane."

Demetra Stathoplos laughed at her husband's grousing. "Poor Yanni. Do you want me to carry them the rest of the way?"

"No."

"They were not exactly the same baskets," she said. "These are much better crafted."

"Because the Cretans have nothing better to do on their tourist trap of an island. Cretans. Did you know that sounds like an English word for morons?"

"My, but won't you be an amusing dinner partner tonight."

"Yes, I will. The four of us will be eating, not shopping."

Demetra Stathoplos laughed again. The sun had dipped below the buildings to the west. She peered through the softening light at the nearest street signs, then turned left and led her husband up a narrow lane that climbed to the stately villas above the harbor. The reason the couple had cut short their stay aboard *Fanning II* by a day was that they had arranged to spend the weekend with old friends who lived in this picturesque port town on the northwest coast of Crete.

It took only a few minutes to reach their destination.

The Stathoploses had no sooner gotten inside the gate when the door of the villa sprang open and their host came hurrying down the walk in a state of high agitation.

"Toli! What is the matter?"

"I have been telling them you would be back hours ago. . . ."

"Telling whom?"

"Two men from Pasok."

"I gave at the office," Yannis said acerbically.

"No, no, they are from the intelligence unit."

At that moment two men in their late twenties emerged from the villa. The taller one said, "Dr. Yannis Stathoplos? I am Constantine, and my partner is named Mavros. We want to ask you and Mrs. Stathoplos some questions about what you witnessed aboard the American research ship."

"What we witnessed? You mean, the depravity, the debauchery, the ax murder?"

"Please, sir," Demetra implored with a straight face. "We tried to warn them that making fun of our prime minister's mistress was rude and possibly illegal."

"Silence! This is not a matter for jokes! It has come to our attention that the Americans are analyzing rocks of the Mesozoic Age for hydrocarbon content."

" 'Analyzing rocks of the Mesozoic Age for hydrocarbon content,' " Demetra repeated with mock awe. "Yanni, it is comforting to know our security is guarded by such learned gentlemen."

Constantine flushed and took a step forward.

Yannis dropped the baskets he was carrying and edged between the Pasok agent and his wife. "On what authority do you come to question us at this hour?"

"Emergency decree number seventy-one," Mavros, the smaller agent, responded officiously. "The integrity of the nation's natural resources is at stake. It is your duty as citizens to cooperate."

"Are there no Turkish saboteurs to chase?" asked Demetra. "Are there no butchers who cheat housewives to—"

"What my wife means is, surely this can wait," Yannis interrupted, hoping to defuse the situation. The fingers with which Demetra clutched his arm were rigid, not from fear but from anger. "We will be back in Athens on Monday. At that time we will gladly submit a detailed report of our expedition."

Constantine shook his head. "We have our orders."

"Tell me, do you boys know the difference between Mesozoic and *mezedes*?" snapped Demetra, referring to the traditional snacks served in *tavernas*. "And kindly inform us what you believe a hydrocarbon to be."

"Silence, woman!" Constantine brandished an envelope. "This authorizes me to conduct the interrogation. Here, if you prefer, or we can all drive to our headquarters in Iráklion."

Yannis accepted the envelope and opened it. Turning to catch the last of the available light, the Stathoploses read the two-page document, then looked at each other.

"Very well," Yannis said.

As the group headed inside, Demetra murmured to her host, "Toli, I am sorry."

Toli shrugged and continued to finger his string of worry beads.

THE EASTERN MED
1749 Zulu/8:49 P.M. local time

Liz Trimble's heart sank when she saw the ace dropping onto the discard pile. It was the third one her normally disciplined, normally unbeatable opponent had thrown away in less than two minutes. She sneaked a quick peek over the top of her cards at Navy.

Edna Haddix was contemplating the Formica table top with unseeing eyes.

Trimble felt awful. The two women weren't exactly friends, but they had fallen into the habit of playing gin every evening after dinner. On reflection, Trimble realized, it was less for the actual pleasures of the game than for the respite it afforded them from the frat-house atmosphere that pervaded this and most other ships. They usually played in the lounge or the mess hall. But tonight, with so many members of the scientific party treating Haddix like Captain Queeg, they had wordlessly retreated to the sanctuary of Haddix's cabin.

Trimble regarded the ace for several more moments. The young

GIO intern had never met a woman with Haddix's self-confidence. It was a trait she wanted for herself—but not if the price was that now being paid by Navy, whose shell seemed to be hardening dangerously. Would tomorrow morning ever arrive, and with it that DOE troubleshooter? And would he be strong enough to lift the unfair load from Haddix's shoulders?

"Your play, Liz."

Trimble reluctantly picked up the card and said, "Gin."

"Good for you. You caught me with forty, fifty-eight, sixty-four." Haddix laid down a fistful of unmatched cards and consulted the score sheet. "That closes me out in games one and two, and you're working on a schneid in column three. Your deal."

"Sure you still feel like playing?"

Haddix flashed a tired smile. "Win your Cokes back while you can, kiddo."

Trimble gathered the cards and began to shuffle.

The phone rang.

"Haddix here. . . . Say again? I'll be damned. What's wind speed and wave height . . . are they going to be able to land directly on the afterdeck?" Haddix listened for another several seconds, then said, "Look, I'm on my way. Start clearing the afterdeck, and you better launch the Zodiac, just in case."

She slammed down the receiver: "Mr. Wendell Trent of DOE. He and the second cable tech are coming in by chopper, ETA fifteen minutes."

"And you were bitching about how this mission didn't rate."

Haddix bent to retrieve her shoes. "Whatever they think is on that sub, I sure hope it's there."

"Too bad this DOE guy's first name isn't John."

"How's that?"

"If he turns out to be a real dweeb, we could've called him John Doe."

Haddix flung one of her Reeboks at Trimble, then joined her in laughter.

■ ■ ■

First Wendell Trent spotted a glow no brighter than a dying ember just beyond the subtle line where black sky converged with inky sea. Then, as the Sea Stallion clattered nearer, *Fanning II* materialized on this side of the horizon and started to dominate the ocean. Its immensity was an optical illusion; the shimmering aureole that radiated from the research vessel was a byproduct of the blazing banks of high-intensity lights on its afterdeck.

"Damn. Looks like Buccaneer Night on a Caribbean cruise ship," Chief Petty Officer Cookson said.

"How's that?"

Cookson pointed to the towering A-frame tilting out from the fantail. "With a gallows like that, who needs to walk the plank?"

A flight crewman tapped Trent on the shoulder. "You guys are in luck. We think we can drop you right on deck."

As the helicopter continued its descent, Trent began to make out details. Scattered about the afterdeck were clusters of what looked to be modular cargo containers that had been painted an electric shade of blue. Men were working in the center of the afterdeck, wrestling a slack cable to one side. Two deep-sea research vehicles were parked near the fantail. And immediately behind the superstructure several men were launching an inflatable black Zodiac chase boat over the port side.

Glenn Marullo, the Reliance technician who had flown out with them from Athens, craned his neck to study the scene.

"What do you think?" asked Trent.

"All we need is time and elbow grease," Marullo said. "I spoke to Flanagan about the cable just before we took off, and he said there was no hidden damage. He thinks we can get you back on line Monday morning latest."

Trent turned to Cookson. "Where're you headed after you drop us off, Chief? Crete?"

"Sure am," Cookson replied with a grin. "And I made the time for some R and R. Swapped watches with some buddies. . . . I get to hang out at Soudha Bay until Wednesday."

The Sea Stallion kept closing on *Fanning II*. Now Trent could see people assembling on the various decks of the superstructure. Must be the ship's crew and the members of Wolfe's party who had yet to be cleared by security, he thought.

Overhead, the pitch of the rotors changed. The helicopter was steadying into a hover in a patch of sky painted a harsh metallic white by the lights below.

The flight crewman slid open the cargo door, flooding the cabin with unexpectedly chilly night air. He tossed out a grounding wire to diffuse static electricity, then unfastened the sling: "Who's first?"

Trent pointed at Marullo.

"Me?"

"Sure," Trent said. "How else am I going to know if the winch works?"

Marullo flipped him a finger, then picked up his bag and crossed to the sling. As the flight crewman strapped him in, the technician closed his eyes and crossed himself.

"Remember, relax," the flight crewman shouted.

Marullo was still nodding when he was abruptly jerked out of the cabin. For a moment he was a vivid silhouette suspended in midair —his cry of surprise lost in the rotor wash, his legs reflexively bicycling—and then he disappeared from view.

Trent and Cookson leaned over the edge and squinted into the glare.

The sling was descending smoothly toward a party waiting some one hundred feet beneath them, in the middle of the afterdeck.

Trent pushed himself back into the cabin and hitched his overnight bag across one shoulder. Then he picked up a case that Zeman had managed to borrow from NavOceano; inside was a pressure-sealed gamma-ray detector that would allow them to gauge just how brightly their sunken shark glowed. "Thanks again for everything, Chief."

"My pleasure."

"How much more time you got on your hitch?"

"Oh, I don't know. Maybe six months and four days?"

The flight crewman began winching the sling back up.

"It doesn't sound like you're reupping," Trent said.

Cookson shook his head.

"Navy's loss," Trent said softly.

Cookson smiled and held up a fist. Trent clenched his right hand, gently banged knuckles with the chief petty officer, and turned toward the open cargo door.

Of the eighty or so music cassettes in the control van, exactly three contained classical works. One of these, suggested by Rick Wolfe at Trent's request, now played on the sound system. Having within the past thirty hours survived six flights and two fights, and done his best to put *Fanning II*'s jittery crew at ease, Trent had understandably craved something calming.

So it was to the strains of Telemann flute sonatas that he had reviewed the complete set of videotape and laser-disc images sent up by *Bert* and *Ernie*. Judging from the debris trail, the vessel down below could only be a submarine. And judging from the macabre wet suit, as well as the absence from U.S. Navy archives of any other submarine reported sunk in this area, it could only be *Dakar*. Yet though the target lay tantalizingly close at hand—within a half mile of the last work site—the chart drawn by Haddix and Wolfe suggested that it was resting in extremely inhospitable terrain beneath a treacherous overhanging abutment.

Trent sipped his coffee, then turned to Haddix and said, "Lieutenant, when do you think the cable will be back on line?"

"Flanagan's estimating sometime tomorrow afternoon."

"Do you agree with him?"

"What?"

"I said, do you agree with his estimate? Techs are notorious for telling you what you want to hear."

Haddix flushed, in part because of Trent's tone and in part because he was right. Suddenly, the frustrations that had been mounting for more than a day came to a head; before she could stop herself, she said, "Well, then, why don't you ask him yourself?"

"Because you're the eighteen-hundred in command of the sled

and the ROV," he replied evenly. "I may know a fair amount about boomers, but as far as I'm concerned, those vehicles are as exotic as a space shuttle. That's why I'm relying on your expertise, Lieutenant, as well as Doc's."

"Aye, aye . . . sir!" she snapped sarcastically. "I hope I won't disappoint you again, like I did with my lax security."

Rick Wolfe cleared his throat. "Look, maybe we should take a break."

"That's okay, Doc." Trent turned back to Haddix. "Stop being so damned defensive, will you? You had a three-hundred-foot ship to secure, and only Doc and two j.g.'s to help out. No one's blaming you for the cable."

"That's not the impression I got from Zeman."

"Zeman's sitting on the beach, six thousand miles away. Some things, you have to be there." Trent wasn't trying to be diplomatic; in fact, since coming aboard he had come to disagree with his boss's rather negative long-distance assessment of Haddix. For one, she was conspicuously more attractive than any 1800 had the right to be, and her ring fingers, Trent couldn't help but notice, were conspicuously free of jewelry. True, Haddix was prickly—her characterization of the remainder of their mission as "hand-to-hand combat" seemed fully in character—but she seemed to know the research vehicles inside out. What he still needed to ascertain was her operational mind-set. If she was flexible, she would be a clear asset; if she turned out to be rigid, a definite liability.

After a few moments Haddix said, "Sorry. I was out of line."

"You're being defensive again," Trent replied. "Look, if the three of us can't be frank with each other, let off steam when we have to, that Israeli boat's going to stay unfound."

She nodded, then asked a question that took him by surprise. "What did you play in college?"

"Lacrosse. Why?"

"I thought it'd be a team sport. You know, I used to laugh when I heard guys say the most valuable thing they learned from playing games was teamwork. Maybe I should've tried out for Little League, like my father wanted me to."

Trent smiled. "The main thing I learned was, win at any cost. It's taken me half my life to unlearn it. Look, you guys are probably more tired than me. Why don't we finish up in the morning?"

"I'm okay," Haddix said. "Rick?"

"Ditto," Wolfe replied.

"Then let's do it." Trent moved back to the chart table. "So how do we go about finding *Dakar*?"

Haddix tapped the chart with a finger. "Rick and I both recommend returning to our last position, which is here. We're pretty sure our target slid off the ledge, but it should have left a trail. More debris, gouges in rocks, that sort of thing."

"Agreed," Trent said. "Worst-case scenario: It left no trail. Then what?"

"That depends. Are you the kind who dips his toe in the pool, or do you jump right in?" She pointed to Wolfe's sketch of three U-shaped ravines that lay below the ledge. "This one, Ravine A, affords the safest access . . . we can keep our line well clear of the abutment. These two over here are another story. We could easily foul the line if we have to explore them."

"Assume we have to. How do we do it?"

"We begin by standing off here, well west of the abutment," she replied. "We drop the vehicles straight down until they're at the depth of the ravine. Then we scoot *Ernie* due east across to the wall . . . and we pray. You have to decide before we launch the vehicles, though. If we go for B or C, we need extra cable on *Ernie,* just in case."

As Trent studied the chart, Haddix thought she knew what his decision would be. In his few hours aboard it had become apparent that he was no Geiger-counter-wielding dweeb, even though the darkening bruises on his face gave him the comical appearance of a clever raccoon. But despite Trent's disclaimer about no longer wanting to win at any cost, Haddix guessed that his submariner's bravado would surface, that he would want to begin with one of the more treacherous ravines.

Trent straightened and stretched his neck. "You two know the terrain. I don't. It's your call."

It was Haddix's turn to be caught off guard. She looked to Wolfe and, when he nodded, said, "Let's go for Ravine B first."

"Done."

The three of them pushed away from the chart table.

Trent turned to Haddix. "Lieutenant, how much time do you need to set up the robots?"

"Rick's team began checking out everything—cameras, lights, sensors—as soon as we brought them back on board. Everything should be finished by early afternoon, except maybe that radiation detector you brought aboard. Actually, Rick, didn't Len and Ezra start on the interface already?"

"Yes," Wolfe said. "Mounting it on *Ernie*'s no problem, it's setting up the software. Damn, I wish the paperwork on Rollie would come through. He could probably do it in a couple of hours. By the way, Trent, the ship carries a store of low-yield explosives. Do you want some stowed aboard *Ernie,* in case we need to blast our way in?"

"Thanks, but our rules of engagement prohibit forcible entry. Anyway, I doubt we'll need them. *Dakar* must have imploded pretty violently to have thrown off hatch covers and sections of pressure-hull plating." Trent hesitated, then said, "Doc, would you mind if I have a moment alone with the lieutenant?"

"Of course not," Wolfe replied. "There's beer in the lounge, and if you're hungry, Edson can rustle something up for you."

The prospect of food appealed to Trent, who had eaten only a candy bar, cadged from Cookson, since breakfast. "You guys run a midnight mess?"

"Sure do."

"I can hold out until then."

When Wolfe left the van, Trent said to Haddix, "I didn't mean to come down on you so hard about when the cable would be ready."

"That's okay. We've both had a rough thirty-six hours. Anyway, you were right. I'll give you my own estimate first thing in the morning."

"Thanks. I also wanted to say that it can't be pleasant for you to have someone parachute in and assume command, especially since you were doing just fine without me. But I meant what I said earlier . . . you and Doc are going to have to tell me what to do every step of the way, and what not to do."

Haddix nodded. "Can I ask you something?"

"Sure."

"The next two days are going to be real tough, especially for people who've never worked together. You said 'be frank,' so I will. What's your major concern about me?"

Trent thought it over for several moments. "Somebody doesn't want us to find *Dakar*. So far they've cut the cable and tried twice to stop me from boarding this ship. I'd be surprised if they didn't start to play rougher. Lieutenant, my guess is you've never seen action. I worry that if it hits the fan, you might freeze."

"Fair enough," she said.

"Now it's my turn . . . what's your major concern about me?"

"That under pressure," Haddix replied, "you'll revert to being a submariner, that you'll push my vehicles until they're scrap metal."

"Warning noted," he said.

THE WESTERN MED

"**A**ny change?"

"It is getting worse, Comrade Captain," replied the chief meteorologist of the Soviet helicopter cruiser *Moskva.*

"Damn it." The captain resumed stalking the darkened bridge. It had not been a good day, and now the weather several hundred miles to the west was threatening to turn the mission suddenly thrust upon him into a calamity.

Shortly before noon *Moskva,* on extended patrol duty in the Med, had been steaming east below Minorca, one of the islands of the Balearic chain. Then new orders had come through: Immediately turn and retrace your course west at flank speed. The reason had not become apparent until dusk, when a YAK-36 out of Tripoli hovered down onto the afterdeck to deposit a befuddled torpedo technician. According to the eyes-only papers the man carried, he and the two crates accompanying him were to be helicoptered to a postmidnight rendezvous out in the Atlantic, well beyond Gibraltar.

Folly, thought the captain. A helo-to-ship transfer on open waters was risky enough in broad daylight; he had been instructed to wait until the middle of the night, to take advantage of a narrow window when the skies would be free of American spy satellites. Further, the rendezvous coordinates were an impossible distance away for a Ka-25 helicopter. Even with drop tanks that nearly doubled its range, the craft might not be able to load enough fuel to return. Finally, there was a weak storm sweeping out of the Atlantic toward the Continent. Poor visibility and sloppy conditions could only increase the time on site, and thus drain still more of the precious fuel reserve.

The captain scanned the pitch-black sea. Out there, invisible to the naked eye—but not to his radar and sonar—were a growing number of NATO surveillance vessels trying to make sense of *Moskva*'s mad dash to the west.

He continued aft and gazed down on the afterdeck. Under banks of mercury vapor lamps, crews were readying the first trio of Ka-25's for the training drill he had unexpectedly ordered. One lone helo taking off at this unholy hour would surely attract NATO's full attention; but if most of *Moskva*'s complement of twenty went on nighttime maneuvers, with each craft landing at least once to refuel, then perhaps the rendezvous helo might slip away in the confusion. Just to be safe the rendezvous helo was being fitted with drop tanks down in one of the belowdeck docks, out of sight of prying eyes.

Somehow, he needed to further tilt the odds. One possibility was loading on even more fuel. Another was shortening the distance the pilot would have to fly. Still another was forgetting about a direct helo-to-ship transfer.

Without turning, the captain said to his adjutant, "Nikolai, do you remember the rescue operation we ran in the Caspian three years ago? When we wedged an extra fuel bladder inside the cabin?"

"Yes, sir. A YAK-25, and this one has a larger cabin."

"But this one has to carry two heavy crates as well as three men, and if it is late to the rendezvous . . . Run the numbers on it. I want to know how the extra fuel affects speed and range, and the latest possible launch time."

"Yes, sir."

The captain glanced over to the gauges. *Moskva* was still plowing westward at thirty knots. "Also, assume we will maintain this speed and heading after the launch. Project our position in fifteen-minute intervals. I want to know how close we can come to Gibraltar."

"Aye, aye, sir!"

As his adjutant hurried over to the chart table, the captain picked up the telephone and dialed the officer in charge of belowdeck operations. "We must lighten the rendezvous helo. Strip it of all armaments."

"Yes, Comrade Captain. Anything else?"
"Where is the torpedo technician?"
"Sir, he is in the crew quarters, sleeping."
"Wake him and find out if he swims."

DAY THREE:

29 MAY 1988

Clifford Zeman pushed through the door and strode into the lobby of the DOE building. At this hour on a holiday weekend it was like entering a mausoleum. The bored guard behind the security counter glanced up from his newspaper, quickly straightened his tie, and placed the logbook on the counter. "Evening, sir."

Zeman flashed his ID card and signed in. He was surprised to note that Ann Davis, who had arrived at the building shortly after dawn, was still upstairs. When she had called Weyers Cave in early afternoon to inform him of Wendell Trent's safe arrival aboard *Fanning II,* Davis was still planning to take her young daughter out to her rented beach house. The fact that she hadn't did little to ease Zeman's conscience.

On the long drive back from his country house he had found himself questioning the merits of continuing with the operation. The sabotage; the calling in of chits from departments and agencies all across the capital; the mounting bills that would soon transfigure Eugene Da Silva into RoboAccountant; the two attacks on Trent— were all these worth it just to scratch a twenty-year-old itch? Or was Bright Shark turning into a grudge match against those who seemed prepared to match Zeman move for move, and dollar for dollar, to preserve *Dakar*'s secrets?

He got off the elevator and headed down the corridor. The door to Ann Davis's office, which was adjacent to his, stood open, and through it he could see lights, hear music playing softly on her CD player, and smell the aroma of freshly brewed coffee.

Davis, in T-shirt and Bermuda shorts, was sprawled on the carpeting amid stacks of files and flimsies.

"Annie. I thought you were taking Sarah down to the shore."

"Tomorrow morning." She let out a tired laugh and waved the flimsies in her hand. "I guess I'm just a sucker for mysteries."

"Is Sarah with Steve?" he asked, referring to her ex-husband.

"No. He's out in Colorado on business. I got my folks to sit."

"I know you were looking forward to the weekend. I'm sorry."

"Don't be," Davis replied. "Barb and Hal, the couple I'm sharing the house with? I found out they invited one of his bachelor buddies to the dinner I'm missing tonight. Just for little old me."

"Aren't you being hasty? He may be a terrific fellow."

"Come on, Cliff, I get enough of that from my folks." She struggled upright and propped herself against the side of a filing cabinet. "Ask me what Mr. Right does."

Zeman went over to the coffee machine. He poured himself a mug, peeked at her, then sighed. "Oh, all right. What does he do."

"GAO.* He's one of their Eugene Da Silvas."

Zeman laughed so hard that he sloshed hot coffee on himself.

"You going to keep playing Cool Hand Luke, or you want me to bring you up to speed?"

"Please," he said, settling into a chair opposite her.

"Trent reports that both cable technicians are now working on the cable. They hope to resume the search noon Monday, their time." Davis consulted her watch. "That's thirty-four hours from now."

"I thought they were going back on line Sunday afternoon."

"They had to revise the estimate," she replied. "I'll give you the rest chronologically, starting with London. The cab was reported stolen about two hours before the attack. They found it by the side of the highway, right where Trent said. They had to cart it away on a flatbed, it was so smashed up. Sounds like our guy put up one hell of a fight . . . he thinks there were five perps, at least two of whom were wounded."

*GAO: *General Accounting Office.*

"Any leads," Zeman asked.

"The police lab report on the cab won't be ready until sometime late tomorrow. My guess is, it'll amount to zip. They seem like real pros. Cleaned up the site, made off with their wounded."

"What's your read, Annie?"

"Obviously an intelligence operation. Trent got a fair look at one perp, the cabdriver. Dark hair, deep tan, Mediterranean features. I've asked Langley for their mug shots of Mossad agents working out of London. Just to be safe I also requested known Norwegian agents. When the shots come through, we'll pipe them to Trent." She paused for a moment. "If it wasn't one of those two services, we're in more trouble than we think."

Zeman grunted. "Who did it worries me less than how they knew to go after Trent. When did we decide he should stop in London en route to Athens . . . about three P.M.? You personally booked his ticket under an assumed name, and by then Haddix had the ship buttoned up. Where the hell's the leak coming from?"

Davis stood and headed for the coffee maker. "Factor in Athens, and it gets even weirder," she said. "The ringleader at the airport was one Adonis Thomopoulos. Fancy title: deputy director, Pasok intelligence, but our sources say he's such a stiff, he makes candidate Dukakis look witty. It appears Thomopoulos went after Trent on his own authority. We're trying to find out why."

"Strange bedfellows," Zeman mused. "It's my understanding that Greece severed diplomatic relations with Israel some time ago."

"Correct. I told you it gets weirder, Cliff."

He sipped his coffee. "That flimsy I saw last night, about the Mossad official in Athens. Perhaps we ought to follow up on that."

"False alarm," Davis said. "The man was Ephraim Levenger, head of one of their Arab desks. Thanks to your APB we're being copied on all raw traffic on Israeli movements. Someone in the Istanbul embassy observed Levenger flying out of Yeşilköy late Saturday morning. I'd say our friend was just transiting Athens to do business in Turkey. We have confirmation he was back in Jerusalem by late afternoon."

"Jerusalem-Istanbul-Jerusalem in less than a day. What could that have been about? The Israelis aren't very friendly with the Turks either." Zeman studied the carpet as if it would yield up clues or inspiration. "Annie, what time was he sighted in Athens?"

Davis returned to the flimsies and plucked one from the pile. "About eight-thirty P.M. Friday, their time. Why?"

"If your analysis is correct, it might be helpful to know whether he could have continued on to Istanbul the same night."

"I'll check the airline schedules," she said, jotting a note. "You know, if he didn't get there until the next morning, he wouldn't have had much time to do business. In fact, I wonder if he even left the airport. Why don't I ask for all cable traffic from Istanbul?"

"Fine. It's a long shot," Zeman conceded, "but we don't have that many straws to clutch at. Anything out of Israel?"

"No unusual military alerts. The cabinet meets in about five and a half hours, but it's just the regular Sunday session. One interesting item from Langley, though." She hesitated. "You know, Cliff, our friends across the river are being pretty damned cooperative."

"Then take advantage. It sure as hell won't last."

Davis grunted in agreement. "Anyway, they picked up a tickle out of Haifa. A sub called *Sabra,* a modified Agosta-class, left last week on a priority run down to South Africa."

"Any word on the manifest?"

"Langley thinks it may be a missile guidance system. I queried Navy, who've been picking up *Sabra*'s traces all the way across the Med and then south as far as the Canaries." She retrieved another flimsy. "But about five hours ago, they heard her turning back north, toward Gibraltar."

"Will Navy keep reporting her movements?"

"If she heads back into the Med, and if she reports in with COM-

SUBGRU Eight.* Otherwise, no way we're going to convince NIS to mount a special search."

Zeman nodded and took another sip of coffee. "Anyway, even if Israel's contemplating an attack on *Fanning*—and I can't believe they are—they wouldn't need to recall a sub all the way from the Atlantic. They've got ample resources closer at hand." He sighed, then said, "Annie, are we overanalyzing the situation?"

"Maybe, maybe not. Listen, why don't we do a little role playing? You're Israel, and your goal is to protect *Dakar.* What're your options?"

"Diplomatic protest," Zeman said.

"Ineffective, and it would take too long."

"Sink the *Fanning.*"

She rubbed her chin. "There'd be hell to pay, and it wouldn't accomplish much unless—"

"Unless I had some way to get rid of *Dakar* for good! That's the key, Annie . . . they must think they have a way to do that. The cut cable, the attacks on Trent, those can be interpreted as delaying actions. But how do you get at something lying at twelve thousand five hundred feet? Could *Sabra* be carrying some secret weapon?"

Davis jotted another note.

"Damn this long weekend," Zeman said. "We'll be lucky to get answers from across the river before Wednesday. How are things aboard *Fanning*? Were any more of the science party vetted?"

"Affirmative. Nine new names came through, and I sent along eight."

He looked at her questioningly.

"The ninth was Ariel Kahane, the graduate student," she explained. "Turns out he's a dual national—Israeli and American—and according to security, he's clean."

*COMSUBGRU 8: *The traffic control center set up in Naples, Italy, to coordinate the movements of all military vessels in the Mediterranean that belong to NATO members and to Israel.*

Zeman winced. "And we denied the young man due process. Neither Trent nor Haddix knows this yet?"

"Correct. I thought it should be your call."

He nodded. Even if Kahane were immediately released, he might have sufficient grievance to interest an attorney. The best way to protect Haddix, who had ordered the young man confined, and Trent, who now headed the mission, would be to withhold this new information and shoulder the consequences himself; in White House parlance he would provide them with "plausible deniability."

"The ship has been trouble free since Kahane was locked up," Zeman observed. "This may be unfair to Kahane, but at this particular juncture I'm reluctant to tempt the gods. Anything else?"

"One more thing. I took the liberty of calling a friend over at NavOceano. Haddix is more capable than you think."

"I'll keep that in mind. And thanks for not oinking. Now why don't you go home?"

Davis tapped her clipboard. "The moment I get out these queries."

THE ATLANTIC

0207 Zulu/2:07 A.M. local time

Even at its periscope depth of seventeen meters the Israeli submarine *Sabra* was buffeted by enough turbulence to make drinking beverages difficult. The storm up top is bad—just like this half-assed mission, thought Dov Halevy, the commander of the fifty-two-man boat, a French-built Agosta-class that had been extensively modified after delivery at Israel's Elat shipyards. *Sabra*'s maximum submerged speed had been boosted five knots by way of a closed-cycle oxygenation system, and a hatch to allow underwater cargo transfers had been cut into the forward torpedo room.

The submarine had been on a priority mission to Cape Town when the baffling new orders came through. Halevy knew the South Africans were anticipating his cargo, the inertial guidance system for an Israeli Jericho-2B that would be cloned for the intermediate-range missile under development at their Waenhuiskrans complex. Similarly, the nuclear jockeys at Dimona were anxious to receive the enriched uranium he was to carry home.

Adding to the captain's unease was the sketchiness of his new directive. Like any good driver Halevy hated surprises, but the boys in Jerusalem were truly playing this one close to the vest. Proceed to latitude 33° 27′ 51″ north, longitude 8° 47′ 23″ west—a desolate stretch of the Atlantic far from any shipping lane—arriving no later than 0130 Zulu on Sunday, the orders had read; wait at periscope depth for a non-Israeli submarine, with which you will rendezvous at 0220 Zulu; take on an unspecified cargo from the other boat, as well as one or possibly two foreign nationals; then make for the island of Crete with all due speed. Further instructions would be transmitted at 1500 Zulu on Monday.

Halevy stepped back from the periscope, there being nothing to see except black waves and black sky, and massaged the back of his neck. Try as he might, he could not fit a frame around the puzzle of his new mission.

"Sonar," he said. "Anything?"

"Negative, sir."

Sabra had reached the rendezvous, which was near a seamount rising out of the southern reaches of the Iberian Abyssal Plain, shortly before midnight. Arriving early had proved beneficial. To precisely position his boat Halevy was forced to paint the seamount with sporadic *pings* of his short-range sonar—a breach of security he would not have condoned under normal circumstances.

Since then the submarine had been lurking at periscope depth with all nonessential systems shut down, all listening devices on passive modes. Nothing. Halevy checked his watch. Less than ten minutes to the scheduled rendezvous; the other boat would be late.

"Comrade Captain, I must again protest my orders. It is against regulations for you to operate without a political officer."

The captain of the Soviet submarine *Komsomolets* turned from Nikolai Krestnikov in an effort to hide his amusement. The wiry, bespectacled Krestnikov—his nuclear-powered attack boat's *zampolit,* or Communist party officer—looked absurd in a wet suit.

"Nikolai Petrovich, you are correct, as usual. But I do not bend regulations lightly. Three officers aboard possess reasonable fluency in English. There is me. There is the ship's surgeon, who is responsible for the well-being of ninety-four men. And there is you. I have no choice but to assign you to this mission . . . one that is, as you know, most vital to *Rodina.*" The captain paused, then decided to dig the knife deeper. "Besides, who better to gather data on another nation's submarine? Not to mention protect an impressionable young Soviet technician from, from . . . what were your words, 'filthy Zionist scum'?"

"As you wish, Comrade Captain. But it is my duty to inform you I plan to file a formal protest the instant we return to Polyarnyy."

"That is certainly your privilege. Now, perhaps, you will be so good as to join your comrades in the forward pressure chamber."

The captain watched Krestnikov leave the wardroom. Although there could be no argument about the correctness of the decision, Krestnikov could in fact make much trouble at cruise's end. The captain sighed. Perhaps the *zampolit* would die first of an overload of bile; a member of the rabidly anti-Semitic movement Pamyat, he was about to spend as many as five days locked in a claustrophobic diesel boat with some fifty hardened Jews. And anyway, the crew of *Komsomolets* would breathe freer without that officious little bastard aboard.

The wardroom telephone rang.

"Sir?" It was his XO. "The helo from *Moskva.* ETA seven minutes."

"Is the *Amerikanskii* satellite gone?"

"Yes, sir."

"Very well. Take her up."

"Aye, aye, Comrade Captain."

"Any further contact with the Israeli boat?"

"Negative, sir. They remain at heading zero-eight-zero, range six hundred meters."

The captain permitted himself a grin. The Israeli submarine had tried to creep in quietly just before midnight; but in groping about for the seamount it had used its sonar as promiscuously as a panicky bat. This he knew because he had arrived at the rendezvous even earlier and rigged for silent running. Since settling in the Israeli skipper had been listening in vain for traces of *Komsomolets.* That man's puzzlement was about to end; he was about to hear something that would make him soil his pants.

"Frol, make sure the chase boats are ready to launch. I'm on my way." The captain replaced the receiver, grabbed his foul weather gear, and started for the door.

"Captain! I have a contact!" blurted *Sabra's* sonar man. "Bearing two-eight-one! He comes from nowhere!"

Dov Halevy swiveled the periscope: "Range."

"S-s-six hundred meters," the stunned youth answered.

"Time."

"Oh-two-eighteen," his executive officer replied.

So the other one is punctual after all, and he also likes to play games, Halevy thought, his adrenaline surge subsiding. Well, let's solve our first mystery and see what flag he flies.

Several seconds later he detected a patch of roiling sea where the waves did not roil. Yes, a submarine was surfacing there, broadside to his own boat. He pressed into the eyepiece skirt, trying to make out the telltale silhouette of its sail and afterfin. Halevy's eyes suddenly widened. The inky form was that of a Russian fast-attack boat, NATO designation "Mike-class," and it was still rising, rising like glistening black death itself; the Soviet submarine must be all of

120 meters, he calculated, or nearly double the length of his own *Sabra*. . . .

The Soviet Ka-25 helicopter, having flown almost four hours from the cruiser *Moskva* to this desolate sector of wind-whipped ocean, was circling at a height of seventy-five meters when the copilot spotted a signal lamp flashing to port.

"Break radio silence," the pilot ordered. "Find out the surface conditions, and how they wish to handle the drop."

A few moments later, the copilot reported, "Wind speed thirty knots, waves two to two-point-five meters. We cannot lower him directly aboard the sub. They are putting out inflatables."

The captain nodded. "Do you think our passenger will let go of the line?"

"Perhaps."

The captain grunted and eyed his fuel gauge. "Damn. I hate to drop down to the deck, but it will save us time. That way you can kick him out the door if you have to."

"Agreed," the copilot said as he unbuckled his harness.

Back in the unheated cabin, torpedo specialist Yuri Tikhonov was both sweating freely inside his heat-retentive wet suit and shivering uncontrollably from the memory of a colleague at the Nakhimov base. Several years earlier the man had been flown out to correct a problem aboard a destroyer in the Crimean. The helo-to-ship transfer—carried out under optimal conditions, in broad daylight on a calm day—had ended in an accident that left his colleague paralyzed from the neck down. And now they proposed to land him on a submarine in the dead of night, while an Atlantic storm raged?

The pitch of the overhead rotors changed.

The copilot made his way into the cabin from the cockpit.

Tikhonov felt his guts tighten another notch.

"Give me a hand with your things," the copilot bellowed over the din.

The two men began moving the torpedo specialist's crates, each of which was swaddled in a flotation bag and rigged with a battery-operated stroboscopic light, to the starboard-side door.

"We drop these first," the copilot said. "There will be men in the water to retrieve them, and you as well."

"Me?" said Tikhonov, his face, if possible, turning even whiter. "You are dropping me into the ocean?"

"It is the safest way in this storm, Comrade," the copilot replied. He wanted to calm the badly frightened technician, but it was difficult to sound reassuring when he had to shout merely to be heard. "Jump feet first. Cross your arms over your chest, like this, and try to maintain good posture. Understood?"

Tikhonov nodded.

"When you hit the water, you will sink down perhaps two meters. Do not panic. I repeat, do not panic . . . you will come up again because your body is naturally buoyant. In fact, more quickly if you relax. And trust yourself to the men in the water. Let the divers do their work, and they will have you aboard a raft before you know it. Understood?"

Tikhonov nodded again.

The copilot doused the cabin lights and wrestled the door open. Cold wind and rain gusted into the cabin.

Tikhonov squinted out but saw only blackness.

The Ka-25 continued to descend.

And then its lights picked up the submarine, and Tikhonov's jaw fell. The enormous size of the boat, the distinctive squared-off sail and podless afterfin; it could only be *Komsomolets*.

As the helo swung to the east, Tikhonov saw two clusters of dim lights bobbing in the water. Those would be divers aboard the inflatable rafts from the submarine.

The pitch of the rotors changed again as the Ka-25 settled into a hover and began inching downward.

Now, the jittery white finger of *Komsomolets*'s bridge searchlight stabbed the waters directly below the helo, creating an oval that rhythmically dilated and contracted with the waves.

The copilot aimed a signal lamp at the inflatables and blinked a quick message. In response six frogmen, three from each raft, rolled into the water.

"Here," the copilot shouted, handing the lamp to Tikhonov. "Aim it directly below us. We do not want to crush our comrades."

Tikhonov nodded. Then he glimpsed something out of the corner of his eye that almost caused him to drop the lamp.

Farther east, almost a kilometer from *Komsomolets,* the chaotic Atlantic was parting to reveal a second surfacing submarine.

Komsomolets was wallowing so badly that its captain had to brace himself as he operated the bridge searchlight atop the sail. With one hand he angled the wildly pitching beam upward and acquired *Sabra.*

"We will never get that torpedo across in these seas," he shouted to his XO. "Signal the other boat to open a channel on VHF. Have Sparks patch me in as soon as we have a link. Then get me a Met update . . . perhaps this system will pass through earlier than dawn. And find out when the next *Amerikanskii* satellite appears."

"Very good, Comrade Captain."

The Soviet captain deflected the beam from the Israeli boat, which was slowly starting to close with *Komsomolets,* back to the sector in which the helicopter would be jettisoning its cargo.

While the two boxes were being manhandled aboard the inflatables, a pair of divers had returned to the dancing oval of light directly under the Ka-25 and were anxiously craning their faces upward.

"It is your turn," the copilot said, positioning Yuri Tikhonov by the door. "You remember my instructions? You must relax."

The torpedo specialist nodded dumbly as he stared down at the white, rotor-washed waters five meters below.

"Good luck, Comrade!" the copilot shouted.

At least he is not my base commander, Tikhonov found himself thinking as he crossed his arms over his chest; that drunken fool would babble on about the glories of risking life and limb for *Rodina. . . .*

He felt a gentle, almost fatherly pressure on his back, and then the floorboards were giving way to . . . nothing.

Plummeting through the shockingly cold air, Tikhonov reflexively squinched his eyes shut and started to draw a deep breath—but the Atlantic caught him with his mouth still open. As he plunged below the surface he began flailing his arms and legs. Nothing seemed to curb the momentum that carried him deeper and deeper into the curiously warm sea.

I am dead, he thought.

Just when his half-filled lungs were ready to combust, just when the brine he had ingested was about to make him gag, Tikhonov felt himself stabilizing. And then floating upward. He forced his eyes open and saw, almost within reach, the dancing oval of light.

Tikhonov broke surface with an explosive gasp. Almost immediately, a wave slapped over him, setting off a painful spasm of coughing.

Then strong arms were encircling him, forcing his shoulders back until he faced the sky, and a voice was saying, "Relax, Comrade. Relax. I have you. You are safe."

Overhead, through the rain, he dimly saw the copilot in the door of the Ka-25. The man waved, and then the helicopter quickly rose and banked into the night.

"Can you tread water, Comrade?" shouted the diver.

"Yes."

"Good. Two minutes, and the boat will be here. I am releasing you now."

Tikhonov and the two divers bobbed in the water until one of the inflatables could complete its cautious approach. It took tugs from above and pushes from below to get him over the gunwale and into the raft.

By the time the divers were aboard, Tikhonov had regained enough strength to push himself into a sitting position. The inflatable, powered by a twenty-five-horsepower outboard attached to its transom, lay roughly 200 meters from *Komsomolets,* which was directly upwind, and 500 meters from the foreign submarine, which was downwind. Someone threw a blanket over him. It was spray-sodden and clammy, but at least it dulled the wind's sharp bite.

The man at the wheel of the inflatable was having a terrible time maneuvering in the heavy seas. A wave struck them broadside, the icy water sluicing calf high across the floorboards, but the raft remained afloat and upright.

Now, above the storm, Tikhonov could hear the outboard rev up. The inflatable steadied as it gained speed. Shelter and warmth were near, he thought; at last they were heading for a submarine.

The wrong submarine.

Stunned, Tikhonov glanced to starboard. It was no mistake; the second inflatable was keeping pace slightly aft.

Up ahead, the foreign submarine began to turn broadside to the approaching inflatable.

Now the man at the wheel was glancing about, as if trying to gauge the wild waves around him; and then, as the raft was overtaken by a big curler and rode up its face, he twisted the throttle full forward.

They caught the wave and surged ahead as if flung from a slingshot.

The inflatable was just seconds away from the foreign submarine when Tikhonov heard the engine die. Rather than veer off, though, the man at the wheel maintained his collision course.

Tikhonov desperately wanted to shout a warning, but he could find no words, his mind suddenly emptied by the sinister metal hull that was growing to fill his vision.

"Our Met agrees with yours," Dov Halevy said into the radiotelephone, thankful that the *Komsomolets* captain spoke English. The Israeli was standing on the exposed bridge atop *Sabra*'s sail. "The front will not pass through until dawn. However, I do not agree that we should wait."

Down below he saw the first Russian inflatable shoot out of the darkness, skitter up the side of his hull, and beach itself squarely within the area painted by *Sabra*'s searchlight. Several of his men, rigged in safety lines, rushed forward to secure it before the next swell hit.

"What's that?" Halevy cupped the receiver closer to his ear. "I said, I do not think we need to wait. Tell me, please, this torpedo we are to take aboard, it is five three-three millimeters? Yes. Does it have an attach point? And what is the gross weight in air, and the weight in water? . . . Four-zero kilos in water? Very good. Captain, I believe I have a solution to our problem. We make the transfer underwater. Yes, that is correct. Listen, perhaps we continue our discussion just below the surface, on UQC frequency? Agreed. In fifteen minutes, then. Out."

Halevy turned to his XO. "Assemble the divers. Alert the handlers that we use the belly hatch and winch . . . we are taking on a fish. And take us to periscope depth the moment all hands are safely aboard."

Down below, his men were pushing the Russian inflatable back into the water. Remaining aboard *Sabra*: one man and one medium-sized container. As Halevy looked on, his mind shifted to another issue. What our technical boys wouldn't give for a firsthand look at a Mike-class attack boat, he thought. The hull, said to be titanium; the electronic sensors, and their deployment; the screws, said to be reduced-cavitation. And he knew just how to conduct such an inspection undetected.

Continuing to scan the darkness for the second Russian raft, Halevy wiped the rain from his face and reached for the intercom.

Komsomolets's captain signed off his UQC conversation with *Sabra* and said to an aide, "Instruct the divers to ready themselves, and have Zhenya report to my cabin."

Then he turned to his XO. "The Israeli says his men are specially trained in underwater transfers. It seems his boat has some sort of belly hatch. We have agreed to stand off nose-to-nose with one-five-zero meters of horizontal separation and two-zero meters of vertical separation. They will submerge to four-zero meters. Take us down to two-zero meters, then paint them with our sonar to finalize the positioning."

"Yes, Comrade Captain."

The captain left the control room and hurried down two decks to the electronics storeroom. He unlocked a cabinet and took out a pressurized Panasonic camcorder, a cassette of super high-grade videotape, and an experimental SIT face mask that amplified low-light images. The Israelis would be preoccupied with the torpedo. Whatever footage his most able diver, Zhenya, could sneak of the other boat's load in/load out capabilities—the size of the hatch, the lift-weight of the winch—would be of immense interest to the naval analysts back in Polyarnyy.

Forty meters below the Atlantic *Sabra*'s belly hatch slowly swung open. The divers who began to emerge wore wet suits, fins, scuba tanks, and weight belts, but their bulky helmets were decidedly not standard issue. The helmets, which boasted SIT visors, had been developed by the technical boys to allow nightwork close to the surface without the giveaway use of lights.

The first diver out clamped a strobe to one of the hatch doors.

The next four divers dragged tethers from which trailed spheres that were roughly two feet in diameter. Each of these ten-kilogram buoyancy metal floats was counterbalanced with precisely the same amount of lead weights attached to a quick-release line.

The sixth and last diver to leave *Sabra* held a Sony camcorder.

The group formed up and began pushing the quartet of metal floats toward the Soviet behemoth that lay above them in the seamless black void. Halfway there, the diver with the camcorder peeled off to starboard.

The Soviet work party had set up a strobe alongside *Komsomolets*'s opened Number Five torpedo door. Because their masks were not SIT-enhanced, the divers had on their underwater lamps —and were thus startled when the Israelis materialized without warning.

The Israeli leader shielded his visor and gestured to the lamps.

Reluctantly—for the odd helmets with blue Stars of David stenciled on them deserved closer scrutiny—the Soviet divers lowered
their beams.

One of the Israelis tugged his metal float up toward the open
torpedo door.

The turbulence generated by the topside wave action extended
down to this depth; the slippery hull of the submarine rhythmically
lifted and dropped a meter at a time while the lighter-weight diver
rose and fell through a two-meter cycle.

The head of the Soviet team swam up alongside the Israeli and
trained his lamp on the torpedo door, from which a warhead ex-
truded slightly.

The warhead's smooth, dark metal was broken by a tip loop, a
nipplelike protrusion at its very crown.

The Israeli treaded water as he located the snap-hook at the end
of the float's tether. Though he synchronized his bobs with the
boat's as best he could, it still took him three tries to fasten the
snap-hook onto the tip loop.

Backing off several meters, the diver reached for the float's
quick-release line and freed it. As the counterbalancing lead
weights fell toward the sea floor, the float climbed until its tether
was taut against the unyielding mass of the torpedo.

A second Israeli approached, snap-hooked his float to a loop in
the first tether, and quick-released its lead weights.

There was now a twenty-kilogram lift on the nose of the torpedo
that matched half the weapon's weight in water; the two remaining
floats were to be deployed at the tail.

The Israeli leader unbuckled several CO_2-activated neoprene
balloons from his web belt—insurance flotation in case the Russian
fish proved slightly heavier than stated—and then signaled his team
to proceed.

Two of his men slowly slid the torpedo almost free of the flooded
tube so that a third could clip his float to the tail.

Just as the fourth and final float was about to be fastened, the
boat bucked—spilling the torpedo out of the tube.

It began to descend.

The Israeli holding the last float, as well as two alert Soviet divers, managed to grab on to the sinking fish, but it continued toward the ocean floor.

The Israeli leader caught up with them, clipped a neoprene balloon to the nose tether, and popped the CO_2 cartridge.

The torpedo continued to sink.

Several other divers caught up with the fish and lent their muscle, but to no avail.

The Israeli leader fastened a second balloon and popped its cartridge.

The torpedo continued to sink.

Three balloons left, but they were fast approaching the red zone for scuba gear, the Israeli leader realized as he desperately clicked home a third balloon and popped.

Still sinking, but at a slower rate now.

How could that Russian idiot not know the actual weight of the fish? Swallowing his fury, the Israeli leader attached and inflated his next-to-last balloon.

The torpedo stopped descending.

The Israeli diver who had been caught holding both fish and float, his muscles on fire, drew the tether down and rammed the snaphook home.

One by one the divers holding the torpedo cautiously let go.

Buoyed by two floats at each end and four balloons at the nose, it remained suspended at a slightly bow-up angle.

Almost as an afterthought the Israeli leader coupled a strobe to one of the forward floats. He signaled his team to start back toward *Sabra,* then turned to salute the Soviet divers, who had followed the fish down.

His ploy didn't work; the Soviets, who were already assuming flanking positions, clearly meant to accompany their torpedo all the way across.

An unprofessionally thick stream of bubbles escaped from the Israeli leader's mouthpiece, the product of his disappointed sigh.

■ ■ ■

Carefully keeping his distance from the bobbing *Sabra,* Zhenya
trained his Panasonic camcorder upward into the Israeli boat's
open belly hatch. Inside a pressure chamber cut through the double
hulls of the forward torpedo room lay a pulley system no doubt
powered by a high-torque winch. Nothing special in the way of
technology, but at least he had not been required to take undue
risks to obtain this footage. The Soviet diver exposed the last of the
tape. He checked his air gauge and was pleased to note that he was
right on schedule. Securing the camcorder strap around his wrist, he
started for *Komsomolets.*

Zhenya had used the experimental SIT mask on other occasions,
but still felt uncomfortable with it. The thickly coated lens made
depth perception difficult; objects tended to suddenly loom out of
the gloomy gray background.

Up ahead now, strobing flashes that were growing brighter.

Zhenya had been instructed to give the Israelis a wide berth,
which meant he could pass them anywhere but from below, where
his rising air bubbles might be spotted. He decided to go above
them. The SIT mask was disorienting but operationally valuable, he
realized; they will never see me unless I stray too low and come
within the range of that flash.

Drawing abreast of the approaching divers, he stopped to gawk
down at the surrealistic image that materialized and vanished with
each blink of the strobe: six of his mates and five Israelis, looking
like nothing less than a herd of giant seahorses, were majestically
convoying a bouquet of dark and light balloons from which trailed a
slightly canted torpedo. Zhenya cursed himself for having shot all
the tape; this was a scene more arresting than any to be found in a
fairy tale.

Zhenya turned and resumed swimming.

He had gotten no more than five meters when he pulled up short
again, heart thudding in mortal terror. There was something out
there directly in front of him, something belching bubbles of quick-
silver.

It was another diver—Israeli, and as shaken as he.

The two men treaded water for several moments. Then, the Israeli tilted his head to study the Panasonic strapped to Zhenya's wrist. Zhenya looked down and saw that the camcorder strapped to the other diver's wrist was a Sony.

Finally, the Israeli threw Zhenya a jaunty salute.

Zhenya, not knowing what else to do, returned it. Then, skirting the other diver, he continued back toward *Komsomolets.*

Dov Halevy stood by the chart table in *Sabra's* control room watching his navigator recheck the plotted course. Crete was one damned long run from his present position west of Gib, yet Ben Goren wanted him there yesterday. The mission obviously involved the fish he had just taken aboard. But why was it so special, and at what target might he fire it? Halevy had already been assured by Menachem, his weapons officer, that the Russian torpedo was not nuclear tipped. Then why not call upon one of the other three boats in Israel's submarine fleet, which also carried conventional torpedoes and were much nearer the Greek island to boot?

He glanced at the shorter of the two Russians, the interpreter, who was shuffling about the control room, making mental notes on *Sabra's* electronic gear. Decent enough English—language would not be a barrier—but a bit of a priss. Krestnikov apparently had a phobia about germs, for upon touching a person or an object, even glancingly, he would unconsciously knead that hand, as if to cleanse it. And when Halevy had tried to sound him out about the torpedo, the man had reacted like a Hasid served a fresh-broiled rock lobster.

"Captain, the hatch is secured and the cargo is stowed."

"Good," Halevy said. "Set course to zero-seven-two. All ahead two thirds."

"Aye, aye, sir. Set course to zero-seven-two, all ahead two thirds."

As *Sabra's* diesel engines throbbed to life, Halevy looked from his watch to the chart. It was now 0409 Zulu on Sunday. If he pushed his modified diesels to the maximum and could maintain an average speed of twenty-three knots, he should arrive at his destination at approximately 1700 Zulu on Tuesday, or roughly sixty-one hours from now.

THE EASTERN MED
0336 Zulu/6:36 A.M. local time

Wendell Trent, his body clock still set to a time zone ten hours removed, drifted out of a light sleep several seconds before the knock on the door of his cabin.

"Come on in."

It was Edna Haddix, anger and disbelief rippling across her tired features. "We've had another security breach. The fresh water's contaminated."

"How?"

"We're not sure yet. I'm on my way down below."

"Right. Join you in a minute." He rolled out of the bunk, threw on some clothes, and hustled down the companionway to the bowels of *Fanning II.*

Trent passed through the surprisingly well-lit engine room, astrum with the vibrations of heavy machinery, to a forward compartment. Gathered around the tanks holding the ship's potable water were Haddix; Rick Wolfe; the DOE security agent who had been guarding the engine room since midnight; the mud boat's captain, Bill Nichols; the Cabo Verdean cook; the chief engineer; and the first assistant engineer, who was drawing a sample from the tank.

"What happened?" asked Trent.

"Edson noticed it first," Haddix replied, motioning to the cook. "While preparing breakfast."

"When I turn on the cold water, it looks funny and smells bad, like it comes from the washing machine," the cook said. "Sometimes, the ship's pipes, they are not the best, so I allow the water to run. It is not getting better, so I call Chief."

The water flowing from the tank was blanketed by a thin layer of froth. The first assistant engineer finished filling a glass jar and handed it to the chief engineer, who raised it to a light.

The others could see small particles swimming about.

The chief engineer sniffed the water.

"Ammonia," he said in a heavy voice. "Bleach. Detergent, not all of it dissolved. This crap's unpotable."

"All of it?"

The chief engineer nodded glumly. "When the level falls below a quarter, the tanks feed into each other unless we manually override the system. And the bitch of it is, we don't have the equipment to filter what's in here."

Haddix turned to Captain Nichols. "Bill, how much time do you need to take on fresh water in Crete and return to station?"

Nichols ran a hand through his hair. "We're probably talking Soudha Bay, which means about six, seven hours each way—"

"Negative," Trent interrupted. "Crete's out. The security clowns waiting for me at Athens airport were obviously trying to stop this mission. If we put into port, the Greeks can bottle us up indefinitely in customs. We're better off requesting Navy to ship out some water . . . it'll compromise what's left of our security, but at least we can keep going. Lieutenant, what's our head count?"

Haddix answered, "Forty-seven, plus you, the two techs, the three DOE agents . . . that makes fifty-three."

"Minimum rations in this heat must be at least two to three gallons per man per day. Figure in the mess hall, and—"

Suddenly, the chief engineer spoke up. "Edson, did you run the hot water this morning?"

The cook shook his head. "I have no dirty dishes."

The chief engineer wheeled, hurried to one of the hot-water tanks, and shut first its intake valve and then its outlet valve. "The galley tank feeds on demand," he explained. "It doesn't take in water until you use some." He fetched a clean jar and twisted open the drain cock.

The water that trickled out looked clear.

The chief engineer sniffed it. Then, glancing at the others, he raised the jar to his lips and took a dainty sip. "I've tasted better, but it's okay. Will five hundred gallons help you out?"

"Affirmative," Trent replied. "Good thinking, Chief. Skipper, how's our supply of soda and beer?"

"Decent enough," Captain Nichols said. "And we still have several cases of Evian and juices."

"We'd better secure those."

"Right." Captain Nichols went aft to use the engine-room phone.

"Trent, a lot of us have beer and soda stashed in our cabins," Haddix said.

"Morale's going to be enough of a problem without confiscating personal stores," Trent replied. "Five hundred gallons should see us through the next couple of days if they're properly rationed. Edson, what's the situation on things like cold cuts?"

"Fine, sir. But I do not need the fresh water so much. I can cook some things almost like usual. Chief, do you remember when we have the engine trouble in the North Sea maybe five years ago? And we go on the short rations for two days?"

The chief engineer smiled. "Absolutely. We were caught in a winter gale that kept our supply ship from reaching us. Edson found ways to feed us."

"Any way to get to this tank from outside this room?" asked Trent.

"Negative."

Trent turned to the DOE agent. "I want the engine-room security watch doubled. Chief, do you recommend we drain the tank now, or draw only what we need?"

"Draw what we need. That way, fewer containers to wash."

Trent nodded. "That leaves us with the problem of who did this, how, and with what. Are the freshwater tanks easy to access?"

"Yes and no. The intake hatch's up on the afterdeck. You had a crew working on the vehicles through the night, right? Well, no one could have monkeyed with the hatch without being spotted." The chief engineer looked at the DOE agent. "Anybody come down here?"

"Negative. Not since midnight."

The chief engineer shrugged. "Those are your two obvious points of access. The tanks are also vented by pipes that open on the quarterdeck, but those have one-way valves to keep seawater from sloshing in. You can't jimmy the valves without some know-how and some serious tools that make a whole lot of noise."

"We'd better check them out anyway."

Haddix was already starting for the door. "On the way," she said, "I'll show you where they got the stuff to dump in."

The padlock on the storeroom door at the back of the ship's laundry had been forced.

"Are we going to play FBI and dust for prints?" asked Haddix.

Trent shot her a sardonic look so she removed the broken lock and opened the door.

The storeroom was empty.

"Bill, how much cleaning supplies did we have on hand?"

"More than enough to foul twelve thousand gallons of water, I'm afraid."

The party continued up to the main deck and went outside.

The sun had already burned off the morning haze and the breezes were light; it was going to be a hot day.

"The intake hatch's right in back of that van," Captain Nichols said, pointing to a cargo container on the port side of the afterdeck that served as a shelter for the traction-unit crew. Next to it stood a light stanchion and a television camera that beamed images of the winch to the control van. Trent instantly realized that no saboteur would have chosen this site, probably the best lit and most heavily trafficked on the mud boat, to do his dirty work.

Captain Nichols led them up the port-side ladder to the quarterdeck and knelt next to a large circular housing. "Here's where the main vent comes up," he said, examining the nuts that held the unit to the deck. "You can't get at the one-way valve without removing this. These nuts haven't been touched since the last time we painted the deck. The stuff couldn't have been dumped through this vent."

"Over here."

The others turned to Haddix, who was kneeling by a thin sealed pipe several yards forward.

She lightly wiped two fingers across the deck, then examined them. "Soap powder. What's this pipe for?"

"Damn, why didn't I think of that?" said Captain Nichols, hurrying to her side. "We use it to take soundings of the main water tank, to gauge how much we've got left. Chief?"

The chief engineer reached into his overalls for a wrench.

Captain Nichols freed the metal cap of the pipe, ran a forefinger around the inner lip, and withdrew it. His finger was now coated with white powder.

Trent looked around. The nearest light was twenty feet away, above a watertight door. After two A.M. the saboteur could have worked here as long as necessary with full confidence that he would be undisturbed.

Haddix stood and slapped the detergent off her hands. "Well, we have all the answers, except who did it."

"It was a pretty nice piece of improvisation," Trent said grudgingly. He was lounging in one of the swivel chairs in the control van, idly playing with a headphone-and-mike set.

Haddix nodded. "Lucky he didn't think of it sooner. Thirty-six hours earlier we probably would have had to put in to port. Damn, I wish I knew who it was."

"Someone who wasn't expecting to be forced to act. Think about it. He must have spent a good minute sawing the cable, when Black

& Decker probably sells some pocket-sized gizmo that can cut clean through it in half that time. Would've been adios to the vehicles too."

"But why now? We're still more than a day from going back on line. What did he hope to gain?"

"Maybe the guy doesn't like to take showers," Trent grumped. "Hope everybody's got a supply of deodorants. I'm more worried about what Edson can whip up, and how the crew'll react to it."

"What the hell," she said. "Nothing like a little food mutiny to cap off a peaceful research expedition."

The intercom squawked to life. "Van, Bridge."

"Trent here. Go ahead, Bridge."

"Just received a radio message for you from C. Zeman."

"Is it in code?"

"Negative. Want us to run it down?"

"No, just read it."

"Message reads, 'Concur with both suggestions,' end of message."

"Thanks much, Bridge." Trent double-clicked the Talk button and swiveled around to face Haddix again. "How many names on that list?"

"Twenty-six," she replied, holding up a sheet. "Trent . . . what if it's someone who's already been vetted?"

"Hush your mouth and trust the system. Lieutenant, why don't you go assemble the crew. It'll be easier for me to tell our friend."

She shook her head. "Thanks, but I did it, so I should be the one to undo it. I'll let you play warden."

They left the van and went forward into the ship.

Trent began rounding up those aboard who still lacked clearances to inform them they would henceforth be confined to quarters; the mess crew would be allowed out to prepare meals, but they would have to do so under surveillance.

Meanwhile, Haddix took the companionway down a deck and made her way to the forward port cabins.

A DOE agent was camped outside one of the doors.

"Neal, isn't it?" she said. "We're canceling this guard duty. Would you go to the lounge and see if Trent needs help?"

As he left, Haddix knocked on the door.

It took Ariel Kahane a half minute to open it; he wore only skivvies, and his young face was puffy with sleep.

"May I come in?"

Kahane stepped back to let her enter.

"Ari, I owe you an apology. I acted hastily in confining you to quarters, and my suspicions were unfounded. You're free to move about the ship without restrictions."

The Israeli graduate student scratched his rumpled hair. "Lieutenant Haddix, why this new decision of yours, please?"

"Two reasons," she replied. "One, we just got word that Washington does not consider you a security risk. Two, there's been another act of sabotage aboard the ship."

"Oh?"

"Someone contaminated our fresh water with soap, bleach, and ammonia."

"Oy."

"Exactly. Look, I should also tell you that after we get back to the beach, you have the right to protest your treatment. If you choose to do so, I'll understand."

Kahane was silent for several moments. "That, I must think over. Perhaps I will, perhaps not. Please answer me this, though: From the first, you do not like me very much. Why is this?"

Haddix found it uncomfortable to meet his gaze, but she made herself do it. "I guess that's a fair question. It's probably a cultural difference. I don't mean between Americans and Israelis, I mean between Navy and civilians. You ask questions all the time. That's what good students do—I'm sure that's how I was back in grad school—but sometimes, aboard a ship, it can be misinterpreted."

"I know," he said, breaking into a hesitant smile. "Cowboy, once he tells me the famous Navy motto, Loose lips sink ships. I am stupid not to take it to heart."

"Not really. You're not Navy, you're training to be a scientist. Again, my apologies."

"I accept them. Thank you very much, Lieutenant Haddix."

JERUSALEM

0725 Zulu/10:25 A.M. local time

Leon Rose and five other officials of Israel's coalition government sat in numb silence around the long hardwood table in the sun-dappled cabinet room of the Knesset building, home to that nation's parliament. The empty seats separating them attested that this was not the regularly scheduled Sunday session of the full body; indeed, at Rose's request, only select ministers had been allowed to attend his presentation. Now, the briefing finished, the questions long answered, one of the Labor ministers still wept softly into a handkerchief. The others, Rose noted, hid their distress more successfully, but were as profoundly shaken.

Finally, the minister of industry and trade, a hard-line member of Likud, opened his folder and again leafed through the photocopies documenting Rose's bombshell revelation. The prime ministerial authorization for opening back-channel talks with the Soviet Union, dated August of 1967, was there for all to read. So, too, were a series of memos from later that same year in which Tel Aviv's negotiators, Rose and Ben Goren of the Israeli Navy, reported their progress. Looking back, the mission that had ended with *Dakar's* loss was as appallingly misguided as the current American president's covert *contra* operations. Looking ahead, the solution proposed by Rose was just plain appalling. Yet what alternative did Israel have? Public exposure of *Dakar's* cargo would ignite a firestorm of worldwide condemnation that would have been damaging in the best of times; today, in the midst of the *intifada* crisis, it could prove fatal.

The minister of industry and trade didn't care much for Rose, his bitter rival for the archconservative vote; but this was clearly a time to rise above partisan politics. He cleared his throat and said, "Mr. Prime Minister, I move we instruct our ambassador to the United States to file a formal protest over the sovereignty issue."

The prime minister's eyes darted nervously about the table. "I, uh, do we have the right to entertain a motion? Have we a quorum present in this room?"

The minister of industry and trade's face turned a frightening red. "You want a quorum? You want I should go drag in a few more ears to hear Leon's story? You want this on the TV news in every country in the world before you even sit down to lunch?"

"Oh, calm down," the prime minister snapped. "I only want to make sure we do not needlessly compound our problems. There is a motion on the floor."

"Second the motion."

"Discussion?" asked the prime minister. "No? All in favor?"

There were six "ayes."

"Mr. Prime Minister," continued the minister of industry and trade, "I further move we authorize the captain of *Sabra* to fire the Russian torpedo at Leon's discretion."

"Second."

"Discussion?" asked the prime minister.

"To bury the *Dakar* like that, it is a desecration," said the minister who had been weeping.

After several moments of silence the prime minister asked for a vote.

Again, there were six "ayes."

"Finally, Mr. Prime Minister," said the minister of industry and trade, "I move we authorize Leon Rose to deploy military units as he sees fit in support of *Sabra* . . . with the proviso that unnecessary force shall not be used against the American vessel."

"Second."

"Discussion? All in favor?"

There were five "ayes," with Leon Rose modestly abstaining.

The prime minister let out a loud sigh. "We are through?"

"One moment," Rose said. He picked up the nearest telephone and dialed a number: "Ephraim, are there reporters in the corridor? How many? Thank you."

Rose surveyed the ashen faces around the table. "Gentlemen, I propose we take several minutes to compose ourselves before meeting the press."

Several others nodded mutely.

"And perhaps you would start passing the folders back to me?"

WASHINGTON, D.C.

0812 Zulu/4:12 A.M. local time

The communications clerk manning the lobster shift at DOE, his nose buried in a thick paperback, frowned when one of the line printers in the room whined into life. At this hour of the morning? He marked his place, stretched, and crossed to the printer. The incoming cable was brief. He ripped it from the machine and held it over the IN basket, whose contents he usually distributed at six A.M., just before the first workaholics began arriving. Then he spotted one of the messages left by the previous watch: *Deliver all traffic for Zeman/A. Davis ASAP.* A futile exercise, he reckoned, for surely they had gone home, but it gave him an excuse to visit the candy machine on the way back.

Much to the clerk's surprise the door to Clifford Zeman's office was open and the lights on.

Zeman was asleep on his couch. Any thought the clerk entertained of quietly dropping off the cable vanished as he surveyed the files and flimsies strewn about the room; the man would never know that another had arrived.

"Mr. Zeman?" he said hesitantly.

Zeman opened his eyes.

"This just came in."

"Thank you, son." With a wince Zeman pulled himself upright and accepted the sheet.

"Uh, would you like me to make a coffee run for you?"

"That'd be much appreciated. Black, please."

Zeman saw that the cable, forwarded by Langley, was a copy of a flash from its Jerusalem station. He looked at his watch—he'd been dozing about three hours, which meant Trent had resolved the water crisis aboard *Fanning II*—then turned back to the cable.

According to the CIA report the Israeli cabinet had been halfway through its regular Sunday morning meeting when all members save for six were asked to leave the room. The unscheduled recess eventually stretched to almost a full hour. When the doors at last opened, those who emerged appeared unusually somber. They also refused comment on what had transpired until one minister allowed that the group had been analyzing "a sensitive new initiative to deal with the *intifada*."

Right, and my aunt's a teacart, Zeman thought; he was willing to lay seven-to-five that the agenda had been *Dakar*.

He studied the names of the six attending the closed session. Only one surprised him: Leon Rose. Since when had that Arab-baiting redneck bullied his way back into the innermost circle of Israeli government?

Zeman was skimming the last two paragraphs when a sentence caught his eye: "After the cabinet adjourned, Gen. Rose was observed leaving with an individual tentatively identified as one Ephraim Levenger of Mossad." Well, well, Zeman thought, if it isn't our very own Mr. Frequent Flyer. For a deskbound analyst Levenger sure got around; eighteen hours after returning from a fast round-trip to Istanbul, there he was, conferring with Leon Rose.

When the communications clerk returned with a styrofoam cup of coffee, he found Zeman seated at his laptop computer, furiously pecking out two cables. Both were addressed to CIA. The first asked for additional HUMINT, or station reports, on the unusual meeting of the Israeli cabinet. The second asked for permission to go across the river to read Langley's dossier on Leon Rose.

ATHENS

0845 Zulu/11:45 A.M. local time

"**H**e is just entering the building," an aide said, hanging up the telephone.

One of the men in the cabinet room looked at his watch and made a coarse remark about the insatiable ardor of young women, adding, "We better have an oxygen tank ready for the P.M."

The others, all members of Pasok's innermost circle, laughed appreciatively.

Normally, Adonis Thomopoulos, Jr., would have joined in. But Junior was exhausted from a mostly sleepless night nursing his throbbing groin and from his morning-long strategy session with Dimitri Puzanov. The Athens GRU *residentura* had drilled him mercilessly for this emergency meeting, anticipating possible objections and tailoring rebuttals to play on the prime minister's almost pathological hatred of Americans. It had reminded Junior of the turgid seminar in philosophy he had once taken back at the Sorbonne; unfortunately, Puzanov was not a senile fool like Monsieur le Professeur Mauroy, nor would it be prudent to fail this upcoming test.

The door opened to admit the prime minister of Greece. The balding septuagenarian looked terribly drawn, as he had since the opposition press revealed that he had deserted his wife of four decades for a buxom blonde less than half his age.

"I am sorry to be late," he said as he led the others to the conference table. "What is this about? Why are we convening on a Sunday? Who called this meeting?"

The others turned to face Junior.

The foreign minister coughed politely. "Mr. Prime Minister, we are summoned here by the deputy director of intelligence. Alas, Junior refuses to share his reasons. He insists that we wait for your arrival."

The prime minister beamed. Young Thomopoulos was a simpleton, but at least he knew to respect authority, which was more than could be said for some in the room. "Well, I am here. What is so urgent as to tear us from our Sunday pleasures?"

Several ministers suppressed knowing smirks.

Junior's mouth went suddenly dry. Get a grip on yourself, he thought; Puzanov has rehearsed you well, and the evidence will speak for itself. "Mr. Prime Minister, I have shocking news. There is an American boat that enters our waters under the guise of furthering science. My department has developed incontrovertible proof that the so-called researchers aboard this boat are in fact secretly employed by ONYXX."

The prime minister—an economist by training, a socialist by temperament, and a conspiracist at heart—reddened at the very mention of the hard-bargaining American petroleum giant.

"They do not seek knowledge per se," Junior continued. "They seek rocks containing a high hydrocarbon content. Such rocks, Mr. Prime Minister, would constitute evidence of substantial oil deposits. It appears that operating in broad daylight and without shame, even as we sit here, the Americans have succeeded."

The prime minister's jaw dropped. "You say you have proof?"

"Yes, sir. It is all here in these." Junior handed a batch of folders to an aide, who began to distribute them. "The top document is a report from our bureau in Crete. The behavior of the American boat has been the subject of provocative rumors circulating among the local fishermen. Our agents located two Greek nationals who were aboard the boat as observers for nearly a week. This couple was interviewed last night. They report that the expedition is uneventful until Friday. Then, suddenly, there is much excitement on board."

"For what reason?"

Junior permitted himself a rueful smile. "They cannot say for certain, sir. But it appears that a launch comes to remove them from the boat . . . a full day ahead of schedule."

The prime minister's jowls began to quiver. "How many times do I have to say it: the Americans are as trustworthy as a starving Turk! All the years I spent teaching there, I was forced to witness it firsthand. The greed, the venality, the arrogance. Junior, this couple, they are reliable sources?"

"Yes, sir. He is a marine geologist. And if I may respectfully direct your attention to the next document?"

All around the table the ministers turned to Junior's artfully vague report on his airport run-in with Wendell Trent.

"Yesterday afternoon I received a call from our ever-vigilant agents about a suspicious passenger arriving from America." Junior hesitated; the next part required considerable finesse. "A case of petty smuggling, it turns out. Yet rather than pay a fine, this man, whose name is Wendell Trent, flees the customs area, badly injuring two of my agents in the process. And who should await him in the lobby but a platoon of heavily armed American sailors?"

Surprised murmurs swept the room.

"They claim that Trent is a deserter from the Navy. They claim that they are taking him to the brig at their Hellenikon base. They claim that he will be made available to us to answer charges of smuggling and unlawful assault. Instead, it appears that the U.S. Navy flies Trent directly to the American geological boat."

Junior paused melodramatically before delivering the coup de grace. "Mr. Prime Minister, I have since ascertained that this man is not a deserter from the U.S. Navy. In fact, Wendell Trent is an operative of the U.S. Department of Energy."

It was the prime minister who finally broke the stunned silence to ask, "Where is this American vessel?"

"It is west of Crete," Junior replied. "The exact location appears in the next report."

As one, the others around the table began shuffling through their folders.

A few moments later the minister of justice said, "Mr. Prime Minister, I believe Junior is to be commended for, uh, for his zeal. But if the Americans have succeeded in locating petroleum reserves, it is only to our benefit."

"What do you mean?" growled the prime minister suspiciously.

"The United States recognizes the two-hundred-mile limit on mineral rights. This vessel—the *Fanning II*—according to the report, it is some forty miles offshore. Any oil they find at that location belongs to us."

Junior had to tauten his neck muscles to keep from grinning; Puzanov had not only foreseen this argument, but also fed him a response. "If I may be so bold, Mr. Minister?"

"What is it, Junior?" the minister of justice replied with irritation.

"The next document."

The others turned to a map of the waters off western Crete.

"The Americans, you will note, are over a particularly deep section of the Hellencian Trench," Junior said. "Our countrymen who were so rudely asked to leave the boat report that the so-called scientists are removing rock samples from almost three miles down."

"So?"

"Mr. Minister, I took the liberty of consulting with experts at the university. The question I put to them is, why does an oil company spend great amounts of money to explore at depths where they cannot drill? There is only one plausible answer. The Americans must be mapping the lower reaches of an immense dome-shaped formation known as"—Junior stopped to consult his notes, then turned to the prime minister—"The formation is known as an 'anticline.' Sir, where there is an anticline, under it may lie a fabulous reserve of petroleum. It becomes a simple matter of locating the oil-bearing layer and tracing it landward."

The prime minister instantly leapt to the conclusion Dimitri Puzanov had desired. "Priceless knowledge! If ONYXX alone knows of this information, the bastards will bid low for exploration rights, they will offer only miserly royalty rates. That explains why they rid themselves of our observers—to protect their data. Once again the Americans seek to victimize Greece by cheating us of what is rightfully ours!"

"It appears so," Junior agreed, fueling the prime minister's rage. "Revenues that will surely run into the hundreds of millions, perhaps even billions. Sir, I submit the perfidy of the Americans is sufficient grounds to revoke their exploration permit. I further submit it is our patriotic duty to order them to withdraw beyond our two-hundred-mile limit at once."

"My thoughts exactly, Junior!" The prime minister leaned forward eagerly and fixed his minister of justice with eyes as fiery as an avenging angel's. "What Thomopoulos proposes is legal, is it not?"

The minister of justice began kneading his brows in a bid for time. The prime minister, to whom he owed his high appointive office, hadn't seemed so animated since the scandal had engulfed him. On the other hand, Junior had produced more xenophobic bluster than persuasive evidence. While suspicion alone might serve to temporarily force the American vessel from Greece's waters, he, the minister of justice, dreaded the inevitable repercussions from such an ill-founded eviction. Still, what irreparable harm could it cause? At worst the foreign minister would issue an apology.

The minister, acutely aware that all eyes were on him, said, "Junior's reasoning has technical merit. We—"

"Well, then, by God, we should teach those conniving Americans a lesson," the prime minister thundered. "How precisely is this accomplished?"

Last chance to counsel reason, the minister of justice thought. Then, with a mental shrug, he replied, "Our Foreign Office must notify the U.S. State Department that the permit is revoked, as well as set a deadline for the vessel's departure."

"I so move," the minister of culture exclaimed. "Let's give those thieves two hours to pack and leave!"

"That is a bit precipitous, Madam Minister," the minister of justice said. "It will take two hours just to draw up the necessary papers. May I suggest twenty-four?"

"Done."

"I second the motion."

The prime minister rubbed his hands with relish. "All those in favor?"

As the voting members raised their hands, several glanced at Adonis Thomopoulos, Jr., with newfound respect.

Junior, his acute physical discomfort forgotten, basked in the unexpected glory like a kitten bringing home its first dead sparrow. But he also found himself wishing the meeting would soon end. Puzanov was waiting out at the beach cabana. For once the Russian would have to swallow his pride and praise him for a job well done.

MOSCOW

1051 Zulu/1:51 P.M. local time

The skies above Vnukovo Airport, normally clotted with planes, now belonged to a single white-and-blue Boeing 707 with the flag of the United States of America emblazoned on its tail. The jet was banking into its final approach. Gathered by the terminal to greet the passengers aboard Air Force One were ranking officials of the Soviet Union, an honor guard, a military band, and a battalion of international journalists. To enhance the images and stories that the press corps would soon be dispatching around the world, the welcoming crowd had been fattened with photogenic schoolchildren and ordinary Muscovites bused out from the capital, as well as cadres of lesser government officials.

Among this last group was a tall, gaunt lieutenant general from the Aquarium.

Pavel Chesnokov sneaked a glance at his watch. Exactly on time, he noted. The American president was to set foot on Soviet soil at two P.M., and it would take another nine minutes for his plane to land and taxi to the apron; for the ground crew to position the debarking ladder; for those in the cabin to collect themselves. If only all of life's endeavors could be so precisely regimented.

He returned his attention to Air Force One and watched it touch down.

The *squirp* of tires meeting tarmac seemed to cue those with roles in the impending ceremonies to stir themselves into action.

Chesnokov's bad leg ached from having stood for too long, but he felt otherwise fine. In fact, since hearing the news six hours earlier that the torpedo was safely aboard the Israeli submarine, he had found within himself a curious peace. In his spectral world the moral ambiguity of intelligence work tended to team with the fatalism for which Russians were renowned to prematurely rust the soul. But now that the GRU general's role in the mission was over except for monitoring the developments in Greece, he felt liberated by two certainties. First, the weapon transfer that he and Boris Alekseyevich Patolichev had engineered could not remain hidden for long. From this followed the second certainty, that their careers were over. It was of some consolation that whatever the punishment meted out by the High Command, he and his old naval ally knew that they had done the right thing.

The 707 swung off the runway and lumbered toward the apron. There, the honor guard commander looked over his men one last time as members of the military band, unsure of such alien tunes as "Hail to the Chief" and "The Star-Spangled Banner," reviewed their sheet music. Off to one side a fleet of limousines stuttered to life; they would ferry the dignitaries from the airport west into Moscow, where the young Soviet president awaited his aging American counterpart.

Air Force One inched to a stop some fifty meters from Chesnokov. The whine of its engines slowly died. The ground crew rushed forward to jockey the debarking ladder into position. Another work detail began unrolling a red carpet. Collecting the young girl chosen to bear a bouquet of freshly cut flowers, the welcoming troika—the figurehead Soviet prime minister, the influential foreign minister, the Kremlin's longtime ambassador to Washington—started toward the plane.

Chesnokov, recalling the list of Americans aboard the jet, suddenly realized that he beheld a terrorist's dream. He glanced up to the roof of the terminal. The sharpshooters peering over the edge were the only security visible, but he knew the entire airport perimeter was ringed by forces whose arsenal included the latest model SAMs, and the skies above patrolled by fighter jets and attack helicopters. Impressive, yet meaningless. One lone zealot, crouching anywhere within a radius of three kilometers and firing a single high-yield mortar round accurate to forty meters, could all but decapitate both superpowers. Nor was the risk theoretical; before the Mathias Rust incident, had the Soviet Air Force ever dreamed that a demented West German teenager could pilot a single-engine Cessna through the entirety of its vaunted air defense system and land in Red Square itself?

An enigmatic grin creased Chesnokov's face as his thoughts shifted mercurially. Marinka's sleeping dust, how he wished it were real rather than merely the wile of a deliciously evil temptress of Russian folklore. Chesnokov was no superstitious peasant, but he sought out and studied *stariny,* the fables through which myths were passed down. With Marinka's magical powder he could render all the important decision-makers within his reach comatose for the next fifty-eight hours, until the Israeli submarine reached its destination. Striking a deal with the devil would be worth it—assuming, of course, the experimental torpedo worked as well as Boris Alekseyevich promised, and the Soviet technician fired it as accurately as he had been trained.

At last Air Force One's door swung open.

Several seconds later the President of the United States hesitantly emerged from the shadowy recesses of the cabin.

The waiting crowd burst into applause.

The President, who appeared surprisingly spry for a man of his years, blinked several times in the strong sunlight. He waved his right arm in acknowledgment, then glanced back at his wife.

Chesnokov was tall enough to have an unimpeded view of the plane. But as he continued to clap, he found himself craning forward, as if to better satisfy his sudden, irrational curiosity about the American woman. Could this one possibly be as imperious, as opinionated, as frivolous a clothesmonger, as Russia's modern-day Marinka, the justly reviled wife of the young Soviet leader?

THE EASTERN MED

1429 Zulu/5:29 P.M. local time

The two doors to *Fanning II*'s dining room were still closed. Taped across them were identical signs handwritten in Magic Marker:

NEEDED!
Volunteers to take dinner trays to those
confined to quarters. Thanks for your help.
(signed) *Wendell Trent*

"Do I look like a fucking Domino's pizza truck?" groused Billy Ray McConkey from the front of one line.

"No, but you smell like one," Leonard Heppel said.

"Get a life, Big Len. Better yet, get me something to drink. It don't even have to be cold."

"Amen," Heppel replied. "I wonder if the pharaohs had a similar incentive system . . . finish the pyramid first, then we'll give you water."

"This dude Trent, he makes old Haddix look like a wimp."

"Amen again. Listen, you going to take a tray down to Rollie, or you want me to do it?"

"I'll go," McConkey replied. "I might as well take mine down, too, and eat with him. Poor sonuvabitch could probably stand some cheering up. By the time his people and ours get it together, Haddix'll be having hot flashes."

Just then a mess attendant opened the door.

McConkey went in, threw paper plates and plastic utensils onto two trays, and pushed them down the rail. Breakfast had consisted of eggs and cold cereal, and lunch sandwiches and potato chips; what would dinner bring? He studied the contents of the steam-table trays. The food appeared normal: smothered pork chops or baked scrod, french fries or baked potatoes, broccoli or succotash. On a nearby table was arrayed the usual assortment of cold cuts and cheeses, large bowls of salad greens and fresh fruits, and a dessert that appeared to be strawberry shortcake.

Spotting the Cabo Verdean cook, McConkey said, "Yo, Edson. This crap safe to eat?"

"Yes, Cowboy."

McConkey used a spatula to probe the scrod. "I don't know. This fish sure do look awfully white, like it's been sitting in Clorox or something."

"No, Cowboy. Clorox makes the fish meat go gray."

"Really?"

The cook shrugged.

McConkey gestured to the other dishes. "You telling me the water supply's okay? I know you can't cook this other crap without water."

"The water is tainted, that is for certain, all but a little of it. But I do not use good water to cook, I use seawater. It is easier . . . I do not have to use so many salts." Suddenly, the cook giggled. "Cowboy, be sure you take the pork chops. That is where I put the saltpeter tonight."

"Hearty har-har," McConkey said as he began loading up a plate. Then he remembered the dessert. "Yo. What about that there shortcake? Seawater too?"

"No, Cowboy. This cruise, I cannot give away the fruit cocktail. So we open up all the cans and we drain the syrup to use for the dessert. The shortcake is very tasty tonight."

"That'll be a change," McConkey muttered.

"Hey, Cowboy, stop bitching and move it," someone barked from the rear of the line.

"Hold your damn horses," McConkey replied. "Edson, last question. I see the coffee urn over there's showing full, and it's showing hot. Mind telling me what's inside?"

"No, Cowboy. It is filled with the Pepsi-Cola, the kind that is not no-caffeine."

"Well, I'll be goddamned," McConkey said, breaking into a broad smile. "Hot cola. You finally got something right."

WASHINGTON, D.C.

1518 Zulu/11:18 A.M. local time

The Israeli ambassador, clearly unmollified by the low-key reaction to his charges, studied with distaste the man in whose office he was seated. In part he was chagrined to be dealing with so junior an official as this young deputy undersecretary of state. More to the point, where did the American foreign service keep finding such lightweights? Was there a secret farm for cultivating a breed rich in manners and glib profundities, yet utterly lacking in sweat glands and common sense? Was there a secret campus for tutoring the importance of horn-rimmed glasses and dark three-piece suits? Or were such mealy-mouthed fools in reality cloned from the preserved tissues of John Foster Dulles?

The ambassador said, "I cannot emphasize enough that this matter poses a grave threat to the special friendship between our nations. At the risk of repeating myself, I must remind you that the submarine *Dakar* is the sovereign property of Israel. The remains aboard it are those of military heroes. My government feels certain that this American research vessel acts in all innocence, unaware of the significance of what it is about to disturb. Still, it must not be allowed to proceed. Should we fail to obtain satisfaction through diplomatic channels, I am authorized to state that Israel shall use whatever measures it deems necessary to protect the sanctity of its dead. Surely, sir, you appreciate my government's sensitivity on that issue?"

"Yes, Mr. Ambassador, I do," replied J. Marshall Mear III, although in fact he didn't. Mear was sorely tempted to mention the USS *Liberty,* the unarmed, noncombatant U.S. Navy surveillance ship that had been in international waters when it was unmercifully shelled for six consecutive hours by Israel during the Six-Day War of 1967; in the wake of that attack Tel Aviv had demonstrated precious little remorse for killing thirty-eight American sailors. But Mear was too well schooled to raise such an undiplomatic issue. Nor was it his place to do so; he was merely pulling watch duty on what had been, until ninety minutes ago, a typically somnolent holiday weekend.

The ambassador stood.

Mear also got up and escorted his visitor toward the door.

The ambassador decided to try, one last time, to impress upon this young deputy the gravity of the situation. He said slowly and distinctly, as if to a retarded child, "Sir, I expect you will promptly convey my government's concerns to the secretary himself?"

"Mr. Ambassador, you have my assurances that I will immediately investigate the matters we've discussed, and consult with the secretary as necessary."

The ambassador suppressed a scowl, shook hands, and left.

Mear returned to his desk and retrieved a file that had arrived in his office minutes before the ambassador. He had requested it in response to an earlier protest, this from an envoy of the Greek government. Yes: incredible as it seemed, two separate countries were up in arms over the activities of the same American-flagged ship, a research vessel named *Fanning II.* According to Athens the scientists aboard were exploring for oil without a permit. According to Tel Aviv they were about to desecrate an Israeli tomb of sorts. Who the devil was running this expedition, Indiana Jones? A dark thought flitted through Mear's mind; could this operation bear the prints of an intelligence agency like NIS or CIA? He took a deep breath, turned the page—and breathed easier.

According to the State Department form *Fanning II* was under charter to the Gillette Institute of Oceanography in Mystic, Connecticut.

Mear reviewed his options. Ordinarily he would just buck the two protests up the command chain. This weekend, though, most of State's water walkers were with the presidential party in Moscow. He could easily enough raise a superior. But disturbing someone trying to concentrate on the summit, particularly for guidance on a low-priority flap like this, felt like a bad career move. His other course of action was to use the watch officer's inherent authority to negotiate the withdrawal of the research vessel.

Fifteen minutes and three phone calls later Mear was congratulating himself for having taken the initiative. When he had finally reached the GIO director, the man seemed astonished that one of his institute's scientific expeditions could be causing such a controversy. He had agreed to contact the ship, ask it to evacuate the area, and telephone back a confirmation within the hour.

The young deputy undersecretary looked at his watch and uttered a mild curse. It was too late to call his wife, who was already on her way in from Bethesda. Thinking that his schedule would be light, they had made plans to go jogging on the Mall during his lunch hour. Now, unless the GIO director acted quickly, Sheila would have to settle for some yogurt and salad in the Foggy Bottom cafeteria.

The phone rang.

Let it be the guy from GIO, Mear thought.

As he waited for his call to be answered, Clifford Zeman glanced around the windowless cubicle, down the hall from Langley's archives, in which he had been closeted since nine A.M. Spread out on the desk was the CIA dossier on Leon Rose. Patriot or opportunist; military genius or militaristic madman? After two solid hours of reading Zeman still didn't know.

And then he came suddenly alert: "Good morning, Mr. Mear. This is Clifford Zeman over at DOE . . . that's right, the Department of Energy. Yes, well, I'm an assistant director of intelligence, and I'm calling in regard to that ship in the Med. Would you be so kind as to background me? . . . What's that? Yes, I can assure you it concerns DOE."

As Zeman listened, his blood pressure started to rise. As if the hostile forces trying to disrupt Bright Shark weren't enough, the operation was now also under attack by another arm of the U.S. government. Zeman fought down the host of unanswerable questions vying for his attention and began to map a way to neutralize State before it could bring its bureaucratic firepower to bear on him.

Finally, at the conclusion of Mear's brief, Zeman said, "Your department's concerns are well taken, Mr. Mear, and I share them. Unfortunately, I do not share your view that the ship should weigh anchor and leave. It is currently operating under the auspices of DOE. That fact renders the Greek protest moot . . . *Fanning II* is no longer engaged in geological research, and thus has every right to remain in international waters. Further, the Israeli protest comes as a complete surprise. To the best of my knowledge the crew has not located any sunken vessel, much less disturbed such a vessel."

Mear's next question posed a problem. Should Zeman give an answer that was technically true, but a bit of a stretch? How badly did he want *Dakar*? Pretty badly: "No, sir, I am not at liberty to reveal my ship's current mission. It's an interagency operation, with need-to-know clearance. . . . The other agencies? Yes, that I am permitted to tell you. CIA and NavOceano . . . the Naval Oceanographic Office."

Zeman listened for several moments, then felt a great weight lift; Mear was starting to waffle. "Documentation? Of course we have it, Mr. Mear. . . . Yes, I'd be glad to copy you, but it might take a while. I'm calling you from Virginia, where I have a country house. . . . Unh-hunh, Weyers Cave. . . . Oh, you know the town? Yes, it does have many charms. As I was saying, I'll try to track down my deputy. If I can't, I'll have to drive in and go through her files myself . . . By five o'clock? I certainly hope so, Mr. Mear."

Terry Searfoss nervously paced the fifteenth green of Quaker Ridge Country Club in Scarsdale, New York. A deftly struck seven-iron shot had positioned his ball safely on the green, but the twelve-foot birdie putt now facing him was sharply downhill and complicated by a big left-to-right break. A touring pro would have found it demanding. Searfoss, a low-handicap golfer despite a clumsy putting stroke, found it absolutely unhinging. He could aim slightly left and strike the putt firmly in an attempt to negate the break; but if the ball missed the cup, it would speed at least six feet past. Or he could aim well left, tap the putt gently, and hope the slope would curve the ball down toward the cup; but how far left, and how gently?

His host in the member-guest tournament, having surveyed the putt from the across the green, walked up to the hole and held his club above a spot a good four feet to its left.

"That much break?" asked Searfoss.

His host nodded.

"I was thinking of maybe trying to ram it in."

"I wouldn't."

Searfoss took two practice strokes, stepped up to the ball, and aimed where directed. Soft hands, he told himself, soft hands. Putter back, putter forward, the feathery *click* of steel meeting Surlyn, and the ball was on its way.

Oh, hell, he instantly thought, I hit it too far left and too softly.

But as the putt started to die, gravity went to work; the ball refused to stop, tailing farther to the right with each revolution.

"Be there, be there . . ."

The ball trickled down to the very lip of the cup, hesitated two beats, then surrendered and toppled in.

Searfoss flung up both arms in exultation.

"Better grab it before it decides to come out again," his partner joked. "Nice putt."

Searfoss retrieved the ball, then went over to his bag to wait for the others to hole out. Not only did the birdie give his team a shot at one of the prizes, but it also placed him on the brink of a personal best. One of the perks of his position—vice president of shipping and logistics for ONYXX—was the chance to cement relationships with clients and vendors while playing the world's best courses. Of these Quaker Ridge was among the toughest. Though this was his ninth round here, he had never come close to breaking eighty. Defying superstition, Searfoss pulled out his scorecard and readded the numbers. He and his partner had begun their round on the seventeenth because this tournament was a shotgun, in which play started simultaneously from every tee on the course. With one hole to go Searfoss had taken seventy-three strokes. The sixteenth was a monster four-par, but he could hack it up pretty bad and still come home under eighty.

"Turning pro soon?" It was his partner.

"Might, if I could drop more rainbows like that."

As the foursome moved to the next tee, they spotted one of the clubhouse assistants speeding toward them in a golf cart.

"This the Parter group? Great, I've been driving all over looking for you. Is there a Mr. Searfoss here?"

"I'm Terry Searfoss."

"You have a phone call back at the clubhouse. A Mr. Harris Knox. He says it's urgent."

Harris Knox was chief counsel for ONYXX. The first thought that flashed through Searfoss's mind was a hostile takeover bid; in an age when anyone carrying a gold card seemed to have sufficient credit to float junk bonds, even a *Fortune* 500 giant like his company was vulnerable. Just as quickly he realized that he wasn't high enough on the management chart to rate such a call. In fact there could be only one emergency that could require his immediate attention: Somewhere in the world an ONYXX supertanker was spilling oil.

Suddenly numbed by the prospect of imminent doom, Searfoss climbed into the cart.

When the caddy finished strapping his clubs onto the back, the clubhouse assistant popped the brake and started down the path. "How you hitting them today, sir?"

"What? Oh, okay, I guess," Searfoss replied. He was desperately trying to recall the specifics of the Friday situation report, which he had last reviewed shortly before leaving the office that night. Two tankers in the Persian Gulf, under the protection of the U.S. Navy; three transiting the Atlantic; one taking on crude in Anchorage, Alaska . . .

Fifteen minutes later Searfoss stood on the clubhouse veranda quenching his anger with an iced tea. The legal department had called not to alert him to some maritime catastrophe, but to get his approval on transferring a charter contract from an oceanographic institute to a government agency. Goddamned Washington bureaucrats; to them everything was top priority, even some diddly-squat paperwork that could easily have waited until Tuesday.

Golfers were streaming off the course.

Searfoss consulted his scorecard again. Would he ever again have such an opportunity to break eighty on Quaker Ridge? He set down his drink and started past the practice green toward the pro shop. Surely they'd give him a cart and let him complete his round by playing the sixteenth. If he had to, he'd show them his scorecard. They'd understand.

J. Marshall Mear III stared at the fax sheets as if they were soiled underwear. This DOE character was trying to play him for a chump. When they first spoke in late morning, Zeman had intimated that the research vessel was already operating under DOE jurisdiction. Mear, while patiently waiting for documentation through the long afternoon, had been forced to fend off both the Greek and Israeli ambassadors, each of whom had called twice.

Now, Mear felt the rage of the betrayed. The papers on his desk clearly showed that *Fanning II*'s charter hadn't been transferred from GIO to DOE until an hour ago.

He glanced at his watch. In less than an hour he and his wife were due at a cookout. But he would have to meet her there, for he still had to notify the two diplomats. Worse yet, no matter how skillfully Mear crafted his cables, they would provoke displeasure in Athens and Jerusalem—which would all too soon translate into his boss's displeasure.

He reached for the phone to call Sheila. At that moment he vowed to take revenge on Zeman, who probably thought he was being cute with his devious little games. By the time Mear finished documenting the man's unethical conduct and filing interagency protests, that DOE bastard would learn a lesson or two about bureaucratic infighting.

THE WESTERN MED

Zampolit Nikolai Krestnikov, who had never before sailed on a diesel submarine, naturally blamed *Sabra*'s cramped quarters and its inelegant food on the international Zionist conspiracy. Grumbling to himself, he made his way up the passageway until he came to the area that served as the mess.

Torpedo specialist Yuri Tikhonov was still at one of the tables, nursing a mug of tea as he patiently chatted with the Israeli cook. This man, Krestnikov had ascertained, spoke a few rudimentary words of Russian; his grandmother had been born in Kiev.

Krestnikov coughed menacingly.

"Ah, Comrade," Tikhonov said. "Come join us."

The *zampolit* was about to unleash a retort that the Israeli cook would not be able to understand when Dov Halevy appeared.

"There you are, Krestnikov. And Yuri too." The Israeli captain turned to Tikhonov and said, "Did you sleep well?"

When Krestnikov translated, Tikhonov smiled sheepishly and said, *"Da."*

"Good. How about we go up to the torpedo room? I want Yuri to have a look about. That way, if there is a problem, we have plenty of time to solve it."

Tikhonov waited for the *zampolit* to translate.

Instead, Krestnikov curtly motioned the torpedo specialist to follow.

Halevy led the way forward. "The sun sets in ninety minutes," he said over his shoulder. "We will surface shortly thereafter to recharge the batteries and ventilate the boat."

"What is position now, please?" asked Krestnikov.

"Just south of Alborán. A Spanish island halfway between—"

"Yes, I know," Krestnikov interrupted.

Halevy silently rolled his eyes toward the ceiling as he pushed through the watertight hatch to the torpedo room.

The tail of the torpedo from *Komsomolets* was visible through the open door of *Sabra*'s Number Two tube. The two flotation bags containing the fire control boxes, both still zipped tight, lay atop the unmarked crates that contained the disassembled Israeli Jericho-2B inertial guidance system.

At Halevy's gesture Tikhonov squeezed past, inspected the fish, and said, "A good fit. It is compatible."

Krestnikov, who was studying the crates and wishing that he possessed X-ray vision, looked up and translated.

"Yes," Halevy agreed. "No liner needed . . . both are five-three-threes."

Tikhonov inspected the bulkhead penetrator in the center of the tube door, through which he would pass a lead from his fire control box, and smiled.

"It is okay?" asked Halevy.

This time Tikhonov required no translation; he flashed the captain a thumbs-up, then knelt and opened the nearest flotation bag. He drew out a wire and jacked it into the bulkhead penetrator. It fit perfectly.

"I am led to believe this fish is classified as experimental," Halevy said.

"No comment," Krestnikov replied.

"Has it been fired successfully?"

"Of course."

"Has Yuri fired it before?"

When Krestnikov translated, Tikhonov shook his head.

"Then how will he know that it works?"

When Krestnikov translated, Tikhonov wrestled the firing control box free of the flotation bag and toggled several switches. Lights began to blink as the mechanism initiated a self-test.

"No, no," Halevy said. "I mean, how does he know if all the

connections are correct? How does he know the torpedo will not detonate while still in the tube?"

When Krestnikov translated, Tikhonov replied with a shrug.

HAIFA

2013 Zulu/11:13 P.M. local time

Leon Rose's operation had been accorded a generous command post, a suite of offices at the Haifa Naval Station. In Rose's room a large, acetate-overlaid map of the Mediterranean had been tacked to one wall. A silhouette of a ship had been drawn off the western tip of Crete: *Fanning II.* There were also two lines, in crimson grease pencil, that would eventually converge on the American research vessel. The first, representing *Sabra,* extended from Gibraltar to east of Cartagena, on Spain's Costa Brava. The second, representing an Israeli naval task force that was forming, extended west from Haifa. Rose glanced at a clock. The task force—comprised of a Sa'ar-class corvette and three Dabur-class coastal patrol boats— would sail at dawn on Monday, refuel en route that evening, and arrive in position at dusk on Tuesday.

Ephraim Levenger entered the room muttering to himself.

"What is it, Ephraim?"

"The merchants of Crete . . . gonifs, each and every one of them."

Rose suppressed a grin. "Are not your agents pretending to be filmmakers? Are not filmmakers the world over famous for their disdain of budgetary restraints?"

"I can justify the Gulfstream that takes them there," Levenger replied. "I can justify the lavish hotel, even for a backup operation. It is a necessary part of the team's legend. But two thousand five

hundred American dollars per day to charter a helicopter? And
though we provide our own crew, we must still pay their pilot two
hundred dollars per air hour? Leon, not even an Israeli union has
such chutzpah."

"Money well spent even if the team ends up with nothing to do
but enjoy the sights," Rose said. "Consider the price if our operation fails. Tell me, my friend, is the chopper big enough should we
need to evacuate your agent aboard the American boat?"

Levenger nodded. "They have a Super Frelon available. It has
enough seats, and our pilot is familiar with it."

"Good. Have you settled on the size of the team?"

"Yes, Leon. We will send seven. A two-man Air Force crew to fly
the Gulfstream, four Mossad agents to portray the filmmakers, and
an Air Force helicopter pilot. They leave Lod at dawn and arrive in
Iráklion by midmorning. The Gulfstream remains there while the
others go by helicopter to the western end of the island. They will
spend the rest of tomorrow, and all of Tuesday, flying up and down
the coast, pretending to scout locations."

Levenger walked around Rose to the left-hand side of the map,
studied the line that showed *Sabra*'s progress, and said, "What is
her ETA?"

"Forty-six hours. Were you able to locate the proper videocassette equipment and the other unit, the one for laser discs?"

"It was not easy," Levenger groused. "Especially the Beta-format machines. It seems they are used mainly for commercial pur-
poses. Forgive me, Leon, but I still say you are being excessive."

"Perhaps. But let us say the Americans discover *Dakar*'s secrets.
How do they prove it to the world? According to your agent on the
ship the evidence can only be on videotape and laser disc. Do you
propose we simply remain aboard and use their equipment?"

"Why not?"

"They take time to review," Rose replied. "If the sudden silence
from the American ship does not alert Washington, the detonation
of Mother's torpedo surely will. Sound travels through water five
times faster than through air. That means the explosion will be

heard by the American listening station on Crete in forty seconds, and the one on Malta in nine minutes."

"Perhaps they will ignore it," Levenger said.

Rose smiled. "Ephraim, my friend, would you ignore something that makes your ears bleed? I fear Mother's warhead will inflict pain all across the Med . . . and quickly attract unwelcome attention. Ben calculates the first aircraft may reach the area within twenty minutes, depending on the weather."

Levenger shrugged, then returned his attention to the map. "*Sabra* requires forty-six more hours? She will not make it in time. We shall have to employ force."

The Mossad analyst had been despondent since midday, when his agent last transmitted a report. Fouling the research vessel's tanks had not produced the desired results. Not only were the Americans remaining on station despite a critical shortage of potable water, but his agent was also part of a large group subsequently confined to quarters. The man's remote taps were still operative, for all the good that did; the American technicians had begun intensive preparations on the ROV—including the installation of a sophisticated radiation detector—which meant they planned on resuming the search the following day. Adding to Levenger's distress was the news from Washington that Israel's formal protest, along with Greece's, had fallen on deaf ears at the U.S. State Department.

"Courage, Ephraim," Rose said. "We are still waiting to hear from our friends in America. The bureaucrats there are quick to listen to influential legislators. If the lawmakers whom AIPAC* is trying to reach agree to help us, that accursed boat will be gone by Tuesday morning."

"Why not tomorrow?"

"It is a holiday there. Something called Memorial Day, to honor their war dead. Offices are closed."

Levenger made a rude noise and slumped into an armchair.

*AIPAC: *American-Israeli Political Affairs Committee.*

Rose was still at the map when Ben Goren returned from the communications room, where he had been in signals with *Rahav*, the Israeli submarine currently shadowing the American research vessel.

"All is set," Goren announced. "The captain suggests how to buy us at least another half a day, perhaps more. The tactic, it is quite ingenious, really. He is under orders to wait until as late as possible, until the Americans actually sight *Dakar*."

"When might that be?" asked Rose. "Ephraim, can your agent give us a rough estimate?"

"I will ask." Levenger stood and headed for the communications room.

Rose picked up a grease pencil and wrote *2300/Tue—Sabra ETA* next to *Fanning II's* position. "Ben, how far must we move the research vessel from the blast site, and how long will that take?"

"The experts say fifteen, twenty kilometers, which is an hour's sail," Goren replied. "Do we care about their underwater vehicles?"

"Why?"

"If those vehicles are in operation, they will be at three thousand meters or more. It takes two hours to retrieve them from such a depth."

Rose massaged his jowls. "Let us say for now we will not damage the underwater vehicles. Fewer repercussions that way. So. Two hours to raise them, one hour to sail from the blast site."

He wrote *2000/Tue—Boarding Party* above his previous note, then *1200/Mon—Americans Operational*.

"Let us hope the Americans are overly optimistic, as usual," Rose said dryly. "If not, and if our lawmaker friends are unable to help, they will have almost thirty-two hours before I can make my move. You say *Rahav* can delay them half a day? Then the question becomes, how much time do they need to get inside *Dakar*?"

"Leon, that is beyond my competence."

Rose stared at the map several moments more before returning to his desk and slumping into a chair. He reflexively picked up a sandwich. Taking a bite, he scowled and put it aside. "You know, Ben, these offices are just what we need, but I rather miss the Jerusalem safe room."

"Oh?"

"Yes. All that walking to and from our meetings, I think I was starting to lose weight."

DAY FOUR:
30 MAY 1988

Each Greek cabinet member arriving for the hastily convened meeting in the office of their prime minister was handed a copy of an overnight cable from Athens's ambassador to the United States. Washington had rejected the formal protest over the illegal activities of the American research vessel off Crete. Further, through legal chicanery the U.S. government itself had taken over the ship's charter, and intended to continue operating the pirate boat in Greek waters until its unspecified task was completed.

An aide crossed the spacious office to the man staring out a window and whispered, "Sir, they are all here."

The prime minister remained for a few moments more with his back to the others. The doctors had warned him that anger placed a dangerous strain on his weakened heart. Yet rage, as he was rediscovering, also focused the mind, also purified the soul. Through the miasma of smog left by the morning rush hour he noticed a small crowd forming on Syntagma Square, in front of the Memorial to the Unknown Soldier. Those would be skimpily clad tourists readying their cameras for the changing of the Evzone Guards. Poor Greece, he thought; the cradle of Western civilization, and now we are reduced to a colorful photo opportunity for foreign tourists, a doormat for foreign bullies. Well, no more, by God, no more.

He finally turned and glared at his minister of justice. "Can the Americans get away with this travesty? Just by altering a few papers?"

"I am afraid they can, sir."

"I would expect this of the Japanese," the prime minister said, moving from the window. "Government and big business, in blatant cooperation. But the U.S. Department of Energy performing ONYXX's bidding? Washington usually prefers to maintain the illusion that it is not merely the lapdog of the capitalist barons. Junior, have we any intelligence on this matter yet?"

"We do not, Mr. Prime Minister." Adonis Thomopoulos, Jr., began to sweat. Summoned unexpectedly, he had been unable to reach his mentor, GRU *residentura* Dimitri Puzanov, for guidance.

The prime minister clasped his hands behind his back and began a measured stroll around his ornate desk. By law he had to call parliamentary elections within the next twelve months. Pasok's popularity stood at a seven-year low in the polls; might this be an opportunity to start reversing that trend? The prime minister looked over to Junior and said, "This research ship, is it armed?"

"No, sir. It is a civilian vessel."

"Good. Then our navy will have no trouble escorting it from our waters. With force, if necessary."

"Bravo!" exclaimed Junior.

The minister of justice blanched. "Sir, I—"

"It is time we show the Americans we are not their serfs," the prime minister continued, his eyes dampening with righteousness. "Besides, the exercise will be good for the morale of our sailors. Notify Admiral Karageorgis. Tell him I expect a plan of battle by noon, and I expect that accursed boat gone by morning."

The minister of justice persisted. "Mr. Prime Minister, I frankly question the legality of your proposed action."

"The legality of my action? The Americans play tricks with pieces of paper, and you dare question the legality of my action? Am I not the prime minister?"

"Yes, sir."

"Have I not the constitutional duty to defend the territorial integrity of our homeland?"

"Yes, sir."

The prime minister abruptly turned and stalked back to the window.

The others stood about awkwardly for a few seconds, then began to file from the room.

Once outside, Junior went off in search of a phone. Surely by this hour Puzanov would have arrived at the Soviet embassy, and surely he would chortle over this latest development.

Several ministers deemed the prime minister's hawkish actions worthy of further discussion at a nearby *ouzeri*. Their colleague from justice begged off joining them, pleading an urgent meeting. Instead, he hurried back to his office; perhaps he could help contain the fallout from the P.M.'s ill-advised posturing by back-channeling a warning to the Americans.

THE EASTERN MED

0819 Zulu/11:19 A.M. local time

Blue skies, hot sun, lazy zephyrs edged with the tang of brine; the Med as it ought to be, thought Edna Haddix as she contentedly jumped rope in time with the uptempo rock cassette filling her Walkman headphones. She had spent the morning cobbling together three watches from the personnel who had been vetted, as well as helping Rick Wolfe's techs set up the two underwater vehicles. Alone now on Steel Beach, atop *Fanning II*'s bridge, she was working out for the first time since Thursday, driving away the fatigue that had claimed her entire body, luxuriating in the sweat that spilled down her face and drenched her leotard.

Down below, the afterdeck teemed with work crews.

Bert and *Ernie* were parked by the port rail, surrounded by techs. Several were running checks on the sled's various systems. Others were debugging the modifications recently performed on its little sidekick, which included installing the electronic still camera that had previously been aboard the sled as well as the newly arrived gamma ray detector.

The most radical reconfiguration, though, had been designed to improve *Ernie's* chances of not only gaining entry to the sunken Israeli submarine, but also exploring its interior. Wolfe had pointed out that if *Dakar* lay in a ravine, its hull probably rested at an awkward angle. The ROV was normally trimmed to maintain a horizontal attitude; unlike an airplane its nose never rose when it ascended or dipped when it descended and its flanks never tilted when it turned. After consulting with engineers at NavOceano the techs had made two changes to dramatically alter *Ernie's* dynamics. First, the lead ballast plates that kept the ROV dead level were shifted from the bottom of the vehicle to the top, raising its center of gravity. Second, to take advantage of the resulting instability, *Ernie's* controls had been modified so that its flyer could control each thruster separately; for instance, by down-thrusting on the starboard side while up-thrusting on the port side, the vehicle would tilt to starboard. Haddix reckoned the new commands would take some getting used to, but the payoff would be a quantum gain in maneuverability.

In the middle of the afterdeck Glenn Marullo of Reliance was finishing the last of the splices while Denny Flanagan closely inspected the team's previous handiwork; the three thousand–plus meters of undamaged cable still dangling below them would be back on board by 1245 hours. And over on the starboard side two mechanics were tuning the large traction-unit diesel; its yammer, insistent enough to penetrate Haddix's headphones from thirty-five yards away, came as a welcome relief after almost three days of silence.

In fact, the only sour note was the balky microwave transmitter, which had gone altogether dead; Rollie Vigneron said the unit could only be resuscitated with a replacement board.

It's a pity that Zeman won't be able to share the pictures from the ocean floor, Haddix thought, because we're going to find that sucker. If not today, then by dinnertime tomorrow, latest. Even allowing for the treacherous overhanging abutment that sat between *Fanning II* and the Israeli submarine, *Dakar* was just too close at hand to elude little *Ernie*'s probing eye for longer than a day.

The next song on Haddix's tape was a golden oldie to which her parents had courted. Twirling the rope faster, she picked up the furious beat of "At the Hop" and launched into a sustained spell of cross-handed speed-work that Muhammad Ali would have admired.

Finally, her calves screaming in protest, she dropped the rope and grabbed her Evian bottle. If the water crisis worsened, she would contribute the almost full case that remained in her cabin to the ship's stores, but until then, by God, they were hers to enjoy.

One exercise left. She slipped off her headphones, walked over to the nearest railing, and knelt with her back to it. Then, hooking both ankles over the middle rail, she did two quick sets of push-ups, twenty-five per set.

A shower was definitely in order but definitely out of the question. Haddix ambled around the perimeter of the deck, mopping herself with a towel. The glassy blue waters looked even more inviting than usual; perhaps she could talk Liz Trimble, or one of the guys, into buddy-systeming a quick dip before lunch.

Reaching the front of Steel Beach, she stopped short. Down on the fo'c'sle a solitary man in gym shorts was performing aerobics amid the litter of hatches, windlasses, and anchor chains.

Mr. Wendell Trent, DOE troubleshooter. After thirty-six hours of working with him Haddix felt no closer to rationalizing the contradictory elements of his nature. Two kids he seemed to adore, an ex-wife with whom his relations seemed decidedly civilized, and a willingness to travel to the ends of the earth to hook a salmon; this much she had gathered over dinner. That plus the fact he continued to address her by rank, rather than as "E.J." or "Navy," as did everyone else aboard. Yet Trent was, if possible, even more goal oriented than she. He masked it well—with patience, with banter, neither of which she could quite carry off—but subject him to pressure, as when they had discovered the water contaminated, and his command presence was unmistakable. Which brought Haddix back to her major reservation: If things got sticky would Trent react like a macho submariner, and unthinkingly jeopardize both crew and vehicles in an attempt to complete his mission?

She retraced her steps across the roof, stowed her gear in her knapsack, and climbed down.

Captain Nichols was on the bridge.

"Lieutenant Thumper," he said.

She laughed. "Was I that loud?"

He nodded. "Good thing Cowboy wasn't up here. With his imagination, we'd have had to revive him with smelling salts."

"I was only jumping rope."

"Right."

"Really," Haddix protested, laughing again. She glanced at the monitor above the chart table that carried the feed from the van. The navigation display had been replaced by a test pattern; evidently, the techs were still checking out the underwater cameras. "Bill, what's our current position?"

"About six miles northwest of the last search site."

"That's half an hour's sail, right? Good. It'll take us at least that long to hook up the vehicles and run a final debug. Why don't you get under way as soon as the cable's on deck?"

"Aye, aye, ma'am."

"Are we going to be as lucky with the weather?"

"I'm afraid not, Navy," Captain Nichols replied. "That series of storm fronts is still coming our way from the west. Sicily's reporting five- to six-foot seas."

"Damn. We can handle that, but anything heavier, and it starts to get dicey."

"Want me to have the noon Met run down to you?"

"No, thanks," she said. "I'll come up after lunch."

Haddix descended another deck, hesitated, then stepped forward onto the fo'c'sle.

"Hi."

Trent's momentum carried him through another jumping jack before he could drop his arms and turn. The bruises on his face, she noted, were beginning to take on Technicolor hues.

"Steel Beach is better for exercising," she said. "Nothing to bang your arms against."

"I started to go up, but you were already there."

"When?"

"When you were jumping rope. I didn't want to crowd you."

For a split second Haddix found herself inexplicably flustered.

"I'm a firm believer in the adage No pain, no gain," Trent continued, "but not the one about Misery loves company."

A smile played around the edges of her mouth.

He leaned down to pick up his Pepsi. "Lieutenant . . . Lieutenant, do you ever go by your first name?"

She snorted. "Would you want to be called Edna? It's not even a family name, so I don't know what my folks could've been thinking of."

He took another sip. "Edna J. Haddix. What's the *J* for?"

"It's in my files."

"Your files are in Washington."

Haddix hesitated, then said, "Jones."

"Now, that sounds like a family name."

"Wrong. My mother's favorite actress won an Oscar two days before I was born. Shirley Jones . . . from *Oklahoma!* and *Elmer Gantry* to Ma Partridge." Haddix smiled ruefully, then said, "Actually, I just stopped by to tell you we're resuming our watches at noon. It looks like we'll be back in the water no later than fourteen hundred."

"How long's it going to take to get the vehicles to depth?"

"About two hours. And the same amount of time to stabilize the DP.* *Bert* pendulums a lot on the way down. We have to wait out those cycles, then send up enough true data for the computers that control the bow and stern thrusters."

*DP: *Dynamic Positioning system.*

"That puts us at eighteen hundred."

"Give or take. Look, I'll catch you later," she said, turning away.

"Jonesy?"

Haddix frowned, but let the nickname pass unchallenged.

"I assume you weren't planning on taking a shower?"

"I've been known to lighten my hair," she allowed, "but not with Clorox."

"I was thinking about how inviting the water looks. Since everybody else seems to be busy, and since we're both kind of grungy . . ."

Haddix rehitched her knapsack. "Why, Wendell Trent. Are you asking me for a date?"

"I guess I am, aren't I? But you'll have a whole boatload of chaperons."

"And a seaful of sharks. I accept anyway."

"Sharks?"

"Yup," Haddix said. "They're attracted by the kitchen scraps Edson throws over the side."

"Oh."

"Still want that date?"

Trent took another sip of soda as he tried to recall whether any man-eating species lived in the Med. Or was she merely pulling his leg? Finally he said, "Pick you up in five minutes?"

"Perfect. I'll go rig the Jacob's ladder."

Leon Rose sat by a scrambler phone in a secure room of the Haifa Naval Station. Six minutes earlier he had received a call from his private back channel to the Soviet Union, the metals trader in London: Mother needed to talk—immediately. Now, a circuitous linkup was being forged over the web of wires that made mockery of national borders and natural boundaries. Only some sixteen hundred miles separated Moscow and Haifa, but Chesnokov's call would shunt through four automatic relays, and cross the Atlantic twice, before reaching Rose.

The scrambler phone buzzed.

Rose picked it up and said, "Hello, Pavel."

"Leon. Is bad trouble in Athens. Prime minister of Greece orders his navy against *Amerikanskii* boat."

"What?"

"Yes. My *residentura* in Athens just calls. He is surprised by development also."

"This is not good, my friend," Rose said. "If the Greek Navy attacks the research vessel, the U.S. Sixth Fleet may intervene."

"Yes. I have plan to put pressure on prime minister, but I want to check with you first, please."

"No, Pavel, I leave it in your capable hands. Do whatever you think is necessary."

"Okay, Leon."

"Is there anything I can do to help?"

"You have way to put pressure on prime minister also?"

"Actually, perhaps I might." Rose hesitated before adding, "How are you holding up? Emotionally, I mean."

"Okay. Is hard. My family will suffer."

"Not so much if we are successful, my friend. Nor will you. Your leaders will understand and appreciate your sacrifice."

There was a brief silence. Then Chesnokov said, "I pray you are correct. What is latest news about *Sabra,* please?"

"She is running slightly behind schedule. You have been monitoring the storms in the Med? They are the cause of the slippage. But do not worry, Pavel. As I told you, we have a way to further delay the Americans. And *Sabra* shall make it there, and she shall deliver your warhead, and our problems shall be gone."

"Okay, Leon."

"We will talk again at eighteen hundred Zulu?"

"Agreed. But if news comes from Athens earlier, I call."

"I shall be here, my friend."

Rose broke the connection and thought back to a Mossad file that had crossed his desk some months back. At the time it had been amusing in the way that derogatory gossip about one's enemies usually was. An Israeli source in Washington reported that a U.S. Justice Department probe into illicit arms trade had accidentally turned up information highly embarrassing to the regime in Athens. Had the Americans already used it against the Greeks? If not, did Mossad possess a copy of the source documents? And if so, could Ephraim Levenger dispatch it to Athens in a way that would suggest the blackmail was being attempted by Washington? A long shot, Rose knew, but low risk and worth trying. He dialed Levenger's number.

1253 Zulu/8:53 A.M. local time

Ann Davis put down her pen, lowered the volume of her CD player, and studied the figure in shirtsleeves slouched in her office doorway. After a few moments she said, "You look like hell."

"I've felt better," Clifford Zeman conceded. "Though I must say, at least no one would mistake me for the house special at the Lobster Pot."

"Yeah, I kind of overdid it at the beach yesterday," she said, glancing down at her sunburned arms.

"Thanks for coming in, Annie. That's another one I owe you." Zeman straightened and headed for her coffee maker.

"Judging by the files you left, I should've been here yesterday too. Your last cable was time-stamped five-thirty this morning."

He filled a mug and wearily slumped into a chair. "The experts say the older you get, the less sleep you need."

"Is it true?"

Zeman shook his head. "Luckily, I was still here when the flash arrived from Athens. It never fails . . . a contingency that cannot be anticipated, in this case an aging politician who imagines himself to be young again. Has CNO responded to my query?"

"No, but we've heard from just about everybody else in town," she replied, holding up a sheaf of messages. "Not even nine on a holiday morning, and look at this. Too bad Congress isn't in session . . . you could've taken care of most of these with a single visit."

Zeman riffled through the slips. Davis wasn't kidding; two members of the Senate, nine members of the House, and two influential Washington attorneys were all demanding immediate audiences. He placed the slips back on her desk, squared the stack, and said, "I didn't hear a word on the radio this morning about one of our nuclear plants scramming, which leaves us with Bright Shark. Whatever's aboard that submarine, Jerusalem surely wants us stopped.

Seven Democrats, four Republicans . . . I suppose we should be grateful that they have yet to tap any of our oversight committee members."

"The day is young," Davis pointed out. "Bet you a dollar one of them calls by noon."

"No bet," he replied glumly. "Thank God it's Memorial Day. It affords me an excuse to duck everybody until tomorrow. By then, with luck, Trent'll have had his look-see."

She pulled out one of the slips and held it up. "I don't think that'll work with this senator."

"Him?" said Zeman derisively. "Gary Hart could date those Dallas Cowboy cheerleaders—all of them on the same night—and still have more credibility. Our friend the senator can't lace his own shoes, much less cause us trouble."

"Wrong, Cliff. Remember when our esteemed deputy director went skiing in Aspen last Easter? One guess who Bart and the missus shared a chalet with."

Zeman winced.

"They were both at Harvard in the late fifties, and roomed together for two years," Davis continued. "This senator can cause trouble with a capital *T*."

"Bart doesn't return from Tokyo until tomorrow afternoon," he protested. "Surely nothing can happen before then."

She consulted her clipboard. "You could guarantee that with a preemptive strike. I took the liberty of punching up Bart's itinerary. He's being picked up from his hotel in Tokyo at nine A.M. their time, which is ten hours from now. If we can keep the senator from telephoning or telexing before seven P.M., our time, Bart'll either be in transit or in the air until he lands at National noon tomorrow."

"Annie, Annie, does a day go by when you fail to dazzle me? Where in the world did you come by your deviousness?"

"I was the fifth child of seven. Want me to get back to the senator and set up a meeting?"

"Please. Now perhaps we can turn our attention to where it belongs? Will CNO give us protection against the Greeks? Or will he take one look at my memo and politely suggest I offer it to the author who writes that Turk Spit series?"

"Dirk Pitt," she corrected, picking up the two pages Zeman had slid under her door before his brief trip home. "Probably the latter, I'm afraid. I don't think it's a matter of what *Dakar* was or was not carrying . . . we still haven't even established that there's a submarine down there."

Zeman sighed and sipped his coffee.

Davis skimmed the sheets again. Working with a patience that would have pleased Le Carré's fictional spymaster, George Smiley, her boss had combined his homework on Leon Rose, done across the river at Langley, with morsels gleaned from two days' worth of traffic from CIA and NIS.

Item: Langley's dossier on Leon Rose contained a lengthy entry dated September 1967. It concerned a serendipitous gift from Israel to its friends in Washington, namely two Spandrels—prototype Soviet surface-to-air missiles—captured in the Six-Day War. An Egyptian unit, led by a Soviet advisor, had been wielding the SAMs against Israeli jets in the Sinai when it was ambushed by troops under the command of Rose, then an army lieutenant colonel. Although the missile launcher was destroyed in the fighting, the pair of intact Spandrels had helped Pentagon designers to fit American warplanes with effective countermeasures. The Soviet advisor, severely injured in the firefight, recovered and was later repatriated. His name: Pavel Chesnokov.

Item: CIA's Istanbul station reported that on Saturday morning, at roughly the hour Mossad analyst Ephraim Levenger began his journey back to Tel Aviv, a Soviet military intelligence officer was sighted at Yeşilköy Airport boarding a flight to Warsaw. His name: Pavel Chesnokov, now a high officer in GRU.

Item: Naval Intelligence reported, in separate flashes, two events that became provocative when viewed together. On Saturday afternoon the Soviet helicopter cruiser *Moskva* unexpectedly began making flank speed west across the Med toward Gibraltar, only to stop around midnight to commence unorthodox nighttime exercises; the last Ka-25 hadn't straggled home until 0540 Zulu. And at about that time, shortly after dawn on Sunday, the Israeli submarine *Sabra,* believed to have broken off a run to Cape Town, was detected slipping back through Gibraltar from the Atlantic; yet COMSUBGRU 8 had no record of the vessel's presence in the Med.

Davis looked up. "It's a shame we don't have anything concrete, because this is one wild scenario," she said. "Twenty years ago Rose gets the goods on Chesnokov. Now he's blackmailing Chesnokov into transferring something from a Soviet ship to one of his submarines. But hell, Cliff, the Israelis don't need Soviet technology to take care of *Fanning.* Unless—unless it's some new toy that can finish off *Dakar*? But if they lifted it out to *Sabra* by chopper, how big could the damn thing be, and what can it do that a torpedo can't?"

"I've asked NIS for input on the types of weapons carried by Soviet helicopter cruisers like *Moskva,*" Zeman said. "Also, I've asked NSA to check whether any birds might have photographed the Gibraltar area Saturday night–Sunday morning."

"Some more bills to quicken Mr. Da Silva's heart," Davis observed dryly.

"That's the least of our concerns. In fact, our biggest headache at the moment is the Greeks. Why the hell are they so riled? If only there were some way I could send a signal that this affair has nothing to do with them. . . ."

"Isn't there?"

"I'm afraid that after yesterday, I'm non grata at State."

"So forget State," she said. "Why not simply explain the situation to Athens in a note on DOE stationery?"

Zeman regarded her with alarm. "And burn CIA's source inside the Greek cabinet? Langley would have my you-know-whats for that."

"Cliff, sometimes I think you're too honorable to be in this game," Davis replied, a devilish smile stealing across her face. "Pretend you don't know that they're about to sic their navy on our boat. Make it an apology for the diplomatic unpleasantness of yesterday . . . we should have informed you immediately of our sudden mission, we'll be finished by Tuesday latest, blah blah blah."

"And what might our sudden mission be? What business could DOE have in that part of the world?"

Davis thought for half a minute, then said, "How's this? DOE has been tracking a freighter that's carrying nuclear wastes from a Middle Eastern nation, which must remain nameless, to a disposal site in West Africa. The freighter was passing southwest of Crete when it ran into a storm. According to our intelligence, several drums were swept overboard. So we borrowed a research vessel with the necessary deep-diving robots to see if the information was accurate, and if so, to retrieve the nuclear wastes and thus protect the good citizens of Crete. Sorry for the secrecy, but we didn't want to cause undue panic, blah blah blah."

"Annie, that's positively brilliant . . . though if that's the way the fifth child of seven's mind works, I think Jeanne and I are fortunate to have stopped at two. I'd better go write that note right away."

As Zeman started to get up, Davis's phone rang.

"Yes? Oh, hello, Senator," she said, motioning him to stay. "I'm Ann Davis, Mr. Zeman's deputy. . . . Yes, I have your message right in front of me. I'm sure he'd be more than glad to meet with you, sir. Yes, today."

Davis scribbled a name and turned the slip toward Zeman; it was their deputy director's friend from the Senate. "No, he hasn't called in yet, but I expect to hear from him within the hour. I believe he's driving in from his country house. . . . I see. Well, sir, if Mr. Zeman has made plans, I know he'd gladly change them to accommodate your schedule, although later in the day would probably be better. . . . Six-thirty sounds perfect. May I brief him on the subject of your meeting? . . . Yes, I understand. No offense taken. Senator, will you be coming here, or would you prefer him to come to the Dirksen Building? . . . Oh. I see. Could you give me that address?"

She repeated it back to him, then said, "Senator, where can we reach you to confirm the meeting? . . . Fine. Either Mr. Zeman or I will call your office by noon. . . . Yes. You're welcome, sir."

Davis broke into a broad grin as she hung up the phone. "We're in luck. He's out in his hometown, getting ready to serve as grand marshal of the Memorial Day parade. He says he can't get back to Washington much before five."

"And by seven Bart will be in the air," Zeman said, sharing her delight. "If the senator won't tell you what he wants to discuss, it's safe to assume the subject is Bright Shark. I must admit I find it peculiar that he should be stepping into this affair. His specialty is banking . . . I don't recall him demonstrating much previous interest or expertise in foreign-policy issues."

"I'll call up his last couple of financial disclosure statements," Davis said, referring to the list of major campaign contributions required of all federal legislators. "Another odd thing is, he doesn't want you going to his office. You're to meet at one of his clubs, the Century, over by Dupont Circle."

"Damn it. I'll have to go home to pick up a jacket and tie."

"Cliff, this operation's giving off very bad vibes. The inferences you've drawn, the phone calls from all the senators and congressmen . . . something's not adding up. Would the Kremlin actually authorize transferring weapons to a sworn enemy, especially in the middle of a summit meeting? And when the Israeli protest to State was shot down, why didn't they appeal it upward, instead of sending their supporters after a DOE bureaucrat? It's almost as if whatever is happening is happening outside of channels. Way outside."

Zeman nodded. "My thoughts exactly. It does possess the disquieting texture of a rogue operation. Have we any way of checking whether Ollie North has cousins in Tel Aviv and Moscow?"

"Excuse me, Mr. Zeman?"

They both turned to the open door, where a communications clerk stood with a cable in his hand.

Zeman beckoned him in.

"Did you know we're the only ones on the floor?" the clerk said as he handed over the sheet. "Some way to spend a gorgeous holiday, hunh?"

Zeman scanned the cable, then slowly shook his head. "London, replying to my request for an interview with Commander Cowling. It appears my suspicions were correct . . . who else could have alerted the cabdriver that Trent was ready to leave for the airport?"

"He admitted it?"

"No. It seems Commander Cowling never handed back the blueprints spelling out *Dakar*'s mods. Nor did he return home after his meeting with Trent. And when MI-Five, which is also looking for him, searched his house yesterday, they found his diaries, financial records, and other documents missing."

"Jesus."

"Annie, we'd better communicate this to Trent earliest. If Cowling has been double-agenting for Israel all this time, those plans he shared with us might be tainted as well."

THE EASTERN MED
1448 Zulu/5:48 p.m. local time

Nine hundred meters above a slowly rising sea one of the Mossad agents aboard a chartered SA-321 Super Frelon helicopter refocused his binoculars, then switched on his intercom. "There is a ship at two o'clock."

The others in the cabin pivoted to look.

"Yes, the *Fanning II*," the team leader said. "See that yellow A-frame at the stern, and the bright blue cargo containers?"

"Do you wish to overfly it?" the pilot asked.

"Rachel, do we need to come closer?"

"I am checking," another agent replied. She hefted a Nikon

rigged with a monstrous 1000-mm lens and sighted through it. "Ahhh, very nice. No, we are close enough. But perhaps we can come around a bit so I can capture it in profile?"

"Agreed," the team leader said. "Keep your distance, though. Also, after we pass the ship, continue on your course until we are well clear of their radar. Our orders are to raise no suspicions."

"Understood," the pilot said, gently banking the helicopter to port.

"Van, Bridge."

Leonard Heppel reached over the navigator's console in *Fanning II*'s van and flicked the intercom switch. "Van here."

"Tell Trent we have a visitor. A chopper to the west, at an altitude of three thousand feet."

"Hold on a sec." Heppel swiveled around. "Trent, did you catch that?"

Wendell Trent, seated at the *Bert* engineering station in the rear corner, was deep in conversation with Rick Wolfe. He looked over and said, "Catch what, Len?"

"Bridge says we got a chopper to the west."

Trent instantly thought of Cliff Zeman's warning about a possible visit from the Greek Navy. "Military or civilian?"

Heppel consulted the bridge, then said, "Civilian."

Trent sank back in relief. "Ask them to keep an eye on it. I want to know if it starts to circle us."

"Roger."

Trent took a moment to survey the van. As forsaken as a classroom in summer since he had come aboard, it was now primed for business. Under the spectral red glow of the night-operation lights, the four-to-eight watch sat manning the various stations; the images filling the banks of monitors were live from the cameras aboard *Bert* and *Ernie*, which had been relaunched on schedule; and one of Heppel's endless supply of New Age tapes—or was it actually the same cassette, playing time and again?—droned softly in the background.

"I guess we ought to get back to the lesson, Doc," Trent said to Wolfe.

"Right. Pan to port."

Trent hesitated, then keyboarded a command into the computer.

The pan-and-tilt camera aboard *Bert* began to pivot—but to starboard.

"Damn."

"Give it time," Wolfe said. "It'll come. Ready? Give me a pan-and-tilt to port. . . . Good. Now go to the forward-looking . . . Good. Switch to *Ernie,* good, now give me its pan-and-tilt and show me what's to starboard . . . that's right. Now zoom, now electronic still . . ."

Trent pressed the red button at the right of the console and captured an image that would later be stored on the laser disc.

"Terrific," Wolfe said. "But remember to call out the frame number."

Trent looked at the counter. "Four-two-nine."

Denny Flanagan, one of the Reliance technicians pressed into service as a data processor, dutifully logged the frame number and the time of exposure.

The sled and its sidekick had been transmitting since reaching 10,000 feet some two hours earlier, but the images were only of water and the occasional fish that swam past the cameras. Until the DP program acquired sufficient data—and until *Ernie's* flyers gained sufficient practice with the ROV's reconfigured controls—navigator Heppel was keeping *Fanning II* a respectful distance from the craggy walls of the Hellencian Trench. Haddix had taken advantage of the downtime by having Wolfe teach Trent the rudiments of running the *Bert* engineering station.

Just then, Heppel called out, "Trent? Bridge says the chopper's continuing to the southwest."

"Good. Ask them to track it on radar for a while, though. I want to make sure we're not being reconned."

"Roger that," Heppel replied.

Wolfe, who was pleased with Trent's progress, leaned over and said, "You're catching on pretty fast. Let's take a break. Sure you don't want me to write you a crib sheet?"

Trent shook his head. "The starboard and port moves on the pan-and-tilt are the only things still giving me trouble. Anyway, Doc, when we go inside *Dakar,* one of you pros is going to be occupying this chair."

Wolfe excused himself and headed forward to consult with Haddix, who was taking her turn practicing with *Ernie.*

Trent stood to stretch. Funny how the van seemed both familiar and alien, he mused. As a submariner he was accustomed to painstakingly exact teamwork carried out in close quarters. The difference lay not in the unfamiliar video gear that surrounded him, but a sense of inadequacy unfelt since his days as a j.g. By the time he'd made XO, Trent knew every aspect of every job aboard a submarine. Here, though the operation was under his command, he was its most inexperienced, and hence weakest, link. Might he inadvertently jeopardize *Ernie* by ordering it to perform a maneuver it couldn't? If so, would Jonesy or Doc or any of the others have the gumption to call him off?

Probably, Trent thought, as long as fatigue didn't dull their judgment. That was the risk inherent in the clever new watch schedule.

Even though the other two navigators had been vetted, the continuing manpower shortage had forced Jonesy to press into service an uncomfortably large number of young, untested players. To compensate either she or Doc, plus at least one other unflappable veteran, would anchor each watch.

The twelve-to-four was keyed by Wolfe as watch officer/*Bert* engineer and Billy Ray McConkey as sonarman. Kerry McMahon was the navigator, Sam Lippman and Ezra Schell flew the sled and the ROV, and Reliance tech Denny Flanagan was the data processor on this watch, as well as the first two hours of the next.

Trent was watch officer/*Bert* engineer on the four-to-eight, but the real expertise belonged to Haddix, flying *Ernie,* and navigator Len Heppel. J.g. Kabelo manned sonar, GIO intern Liz Trimble

flew the sled, and halfway through the watch Glenn Marullo replaced Flanagan as data processor.

The eight-to-twelve was keyed around Haddix, this time serving
as watch officer /*Bert* engineer, and Wolfe, now flying the ROV. Joe
Reuss was the navigator, j.g. Parkhill flew the sled, the rehabilitated
Ari Kahane manned sonar, and Marullo continued as data processor.

Trent realized that the longer the search took, the greater the
strain befalling Jonesy and Doc, both of whom would be pulling
two watches out of every three. What the hell was happening back
on the beach? Instead of transmitting additional names that had
been cleared, Zeman seemed to be sending only bad news, like the
warning about Cowling's data. Had his boss decided to take the
long weekend off? Trent knew he was being unfair; Zeman and
Ann Davis were undoubtedly pressing as hard as he was. Yet since
boarding *Fanning II* Trent had been plagued by a growing despair
familiar to any athlete who has ever squared off against a superior
opponent.

The door to the van swung open, letting in a pattern of rapidly
alternating sunlight and shade—the first of the fronts was coming
through, Trent thought—as well as Glenn Marullo, ready to relieve
his colleague Flanagan.

"What's it doing out there?" asked Flanagan, rising from his seat.

"Hail the size of golf balls."

"Your ass," Flanagan retorted. "What's for dinner?"

"Filet mignon, baked potatoes, succotash, and ice cream."

"Really?"

"No. It's your favorite . . . peanut butter and jelly sandwiches."

"Marullo, if I'd have known your dorky ass was going to be on
this boat, I'd've demanded combat pay." As Flanagan left the van
he handed over the clipboard and said, "Here. Try not to screw
up."

Marullo headed over to the *Bert* engineering station.

"Filet mignon or peanut butter and jelly?" asked Trent.

"Meat."

"You don't sound thrilled."

"Come on, the way that guy cooks them is a crime," Marullo said. "All that grease and fat . . . you'd think a boat this size would have one of those electric barbecue things, the smokeless kind that you can use indoors?"

"Ever been on a mud boat that had one?"

"No, but last year my wife and I took one of those Cruises to Nowhere? They had one."

"Hey, Jonesy," Trent called out. "Mr. Marullo is expressing dissatisfaction with the cuisine."

Haddix slowly swiveled around in her chair. "I agree with Mr. Marullo. Edson tends to cook as if he's never heard of cholesterol. Mr. Marullo, how would some sushi sound?"

"Are you serious? You know how to make it?"

"Sure do. I've even got a supply of sticky rice and dried seaweed in my cabin."

"Oh, boy," Marullo said eagerly.

"You catch the fish, I'll make the sushi."

Marullo's face fell.

Jonesy seemed to be feeling a bit friskier, Trent thought. That first night she had reminded him of his former wife during the weekend that Kath sweated out the results of a biopsy. Just as the discovery that the tumor was benign had lifted the weight off Kath's shoulders, he supposed, his assumption of command was in many ways a relief to Jonesy. Whatever the reason, he found her new-found cheer most becoming.

"Yo, Navy," navigator Heppel said. "DP's telling me she's ready to rock and roll."

"Hot damn," Haddix replied. "How far are we from our last site?"

"About half a mile."

"Let's go do it."

Heppel nodded, then began keying in instructions. Rick Wolfe slid over to supervise Liz Trimble's flying of *Bert.* J.g. Kabelo set down his can of soda and turned to the sonar charts.

At that moment Trent saw the van and its occupants through fresh eyes. Beneath a marked informality that grated against his submariner's sensibilities, this jury-rigged team seemed surprisingly well integrated and sure of its tasks. Because it was well prepped, he decided. Suddenly, several of his doubts disappeared. Doc would be able to handle the pressure, and Jonesy, arguably the steelier of the two, was a real trouper. If we can just locate *Dakar* before minds, muscles, and stamina are sapped, mused Trent, we just might pull this one off.

ATHENS

1502 Zulu/6:02 P.M. local time

The prime minister of Greece gazed down on the capital from the bedroom balcony of his villa in the exclusive suburb of Kifissia. The heat of the day still shimmered over the city, but he reflexively drew his silk dressing gown more tightly around his body. Over a long and combative life in academia and politics he had survived ostracism, betrayal, even jail. Never, though, could he remember feeling so confused and broken as at this very moment.

A half hour earlier his daily nap had been interrupted by the arrival of a priority packet messengered up from the office.

The packet contained three items.

The first was an apologetic letter faxed by an official of the U.S. Department of Energy to Greece's Foreign Ministry. The letter concerned the American research vessel in the waters off Crete; evidently, it was there to investigate reports that several containers of nuclear waste materials had been swept off a passing freighter. According to an attached note from one of the prime minister's aides, Greek experts thought the claim highly plausible.

Yet if the research vessel's mission was legitimate, how to explain the two manila envelopes, left unopened because each was marked PERSONAL AND CONFIDENTIAL, that were also in the packet?

One bore an ominous return address typed in English: "Friends of *Fanning II.*" Its contents consisted of a half-dozen pages taken from a confidential interrogation conducted by the U.S. Department of Justice. The subject's name had been blacked out, but the prime minister knew it to be a certain Saudi arms merchant hoping to escape prosecution for his role in the Iran-*contra* affair. The arms merchant named five high Pasok officials who he claimed were cashing in on the Iran-Iraq war by illicitly selling weapons to both combatants. In addition, he described how the profits were being laundered through a bank owned by one of the prime minister's protégés.

This ham-handed threat bore the odor of the CIA. But why were those thugs working at cross-purposes with the American Department of Energy? Yet the prime minister knew that it didn't matter; for if the devastatingly accurate allegations in the deposition became public, Pasok's seven-year experiment to reshape Greek society would end the next time his nation went to the ballot box.

Equally perplexing was the second manila envelope. No return address was needed; its contemptible contents could only have come from Moscow. The note inside was written in correct but stilted Greek: "The Navy of Greece must engage in no maneuvers within 200 kilometers of the island of Crete before 1200 hours, Wednesday, 01 June 1988. Failure to comply results in the immediate release of enclosed to all newspapers."

Enclosed were three black-and-white glossies of the prime minister's statuesque lover. Taken with a long-distance lens, they showed her in the backyard of the villa, sunbathing in the nude. The photographs were titillating—actually, they rather flattered her—but posed little political danger. Since he had deserted his wife for a young mistress, all of Greece had taken sides on his personal life. What worried the prime minister was the crassness of the approach. Athens and Moscow enjoyed cordial relations. Why had the Soviets not come to him openly, rather than attempt this blackmail? Worse yet, were he to defy them, what might they do next? And why in the world were their goals in this matter the same as the Americans'?

The prime minister heard a knock. He stepped in off the balcony and said, "Yes?"

"Darling, are you all right?" It was the woman whose photographs lay on his desk. She sounded surprised that his bedroom door was locked.

"Fine, dear," he called out.

After a few moments she said, "Are you getting dressed? We must leave for the reception in twenty minutes."

"I will be ready, dear."

The prime minister slowly toured the room, gathering up photographs and letters and transcript pages and locking them in his wall safe. He glimpsed his ashen face in a mirror. The exhilaration he had felt that morning was now but a taunting aftertaste. How could things have gone so wrong in the space of seven hours? And yet . . .

He decided to sort out options while he showered. But halfway to the bathroom he finally acknowledged to himself that there were no options. With a sigh he detoured to the nightstand and picked up the red telephone, the one linked by dedicated line to his office and monitored around the clock.

When an aide answered, the prime minister said, "Connect me with Admiral Karageorgis. Immediately."

THE EASTERN MED

Displayed on the main monitor at the front of the control van was a phantasmagoric undersea mountainscape dominated by a sloping ledge; the ledge was bisected by a giant furrow, on either side of which were strewn ripped chunks of metal.

"How's my tether, Liz?" asked Edna Haddix from *Ernie*'s console.

"Tether clear, E.J.," Liz Trimble replied. She was flying *Bert* from the seat to Haddix's left.

Haddix consulted the Watchman-sized monitor directly in front of her, which displayed images from *Ernie*'s pan-and-tilt camera, and fiddled with the controls. Eleven thousand feet below, at the other end of the repaired cable, the little ROV responded by gently banking to starboard. She studied the fresh images. "I think we're almost back to where we broke off contact. Show me *Bert*'s forward camera on Monitor Two."

"You got it, Jonesy." Wendell Trent, manning the *Bert* engineering station, switched the feed.

Haddix flicked her eyes up to one of the large monitors overhead. The sled seemed to be yawing slightly to starboard as it was towed forward at a speed of one knot. And the cable was also causing *Bert* to undulate in harmony with *Fanning II* as the research vessel bobbed on a steadily rising sea; the cycles appeared to have increased to three to four feet. "Liz, is your heave getting any worse?"

"Negative, E.J."

"How close are you coming to the deck?"

"Nine meters," Trimble replied.

"Hold it at that or above. And remember, we're about to slow, so look alert."

"Roger."

Haddix quickly marshaled her memories of their previous visit to this site, then said, "Give me a pan to port on *Bert*. There ought to be a big gash somewhere along that wall."

"Panning to port," Trent replied, traversing the camera counter-clockwise.

Suddenly, a welcome gust of cool night air swept through the van; a few members of the eight-to-twelve watch were entering.

"Jonesy, is that it?"

"Affirmative. Sonar . . . distance to end of ledge?"

"One-three-five meters," j.g. Jeff Kabelo called out from the rear of the van.

"What about the scarp?" said Haddix, referring to the abutment sitting a mile down, or almost halfway between the research vessel and the vehicles. "How close is it to our line?"

"Two-seven-zero meters," Kabelo replied.

"Navigator, full stop," Haddix said.

"Roger that," Len Heppel replied, keying in commands to the thrusters and the screws.

"Liz, watch your depth," Haddix said.

"Roger." Trimble prepared herself to winch in cable, for as the ship slowed, the sled would pendulum forward and downward.

Haddix swung little *Ernie* slightly to port and centered the ROV over the ledge—and over the turbulent trail left by the submarine.

Trent felt a tap on his shoulder. It was Rick Wolfe, due to relieve him at eight.

"Need a hand?" asked Wolfe.

"Thanks, Doc, I think I've got it under control."

Over the next five minutes Trent would have regretted his non-chalance had he the time to reflect on it. Responding to a steady stream of commands from Haddix, he intercut continuously be-tween the cameras aboard the two vehicles, captured a batch of electronic stills, and even remembered to pop fresh tapes into the VCRs. Without stopping to take a head count he also felt the van filling up. The sensation came more from drops in temperature as the door opened, and heightened pressure from the bodies crowding in, than any rise in noise level; each new arrival invariably took to gazing mutely at the awesome images on the monitors.

Dakar, it seemed, had not gone quietly to its grave. The scars across the jagged vertical wall to port, the clipped boulders, the depth of the furrow through silt and bedrock, these would bear violent witness to the submarine's last passage until the tectonic plates undergirding this sector of the Med shifted and remolded the Hellencian Trench.

"E.J., coming up on six-zero meters to end of ledge," Kabelo warned from the sonar table.

"I copy, Jeff." She looked up at the main monitor, which displayed the feed from the sled's forward-looking camera, and scowled. The submarine, which was almost 270 feet in length, would be visible if it had remained on the ledge. "Now listen up, everyone," Haddix said. "The target did not remain on the ledge. Keep an eye peeled for clues on which way it might have headed after it slid over the edge. Trent, show me *Ernie's* forward camera on Monitor Four. Sweep the ledge side-to-side with the *Bert's* pan-and-tilt, and keep that on Monitor Two."

"Roger that," Trent replied, reshuffling the feeds.

The dozen or so people cramming the van redoubled their concentration on the images filling the five large monitors.

"Jeff, any chance of a bear trap?" asked Haddix.

"Negative. Next vertical's better'n two-four-zero meters to port, on a heading of one-two-seven."

"Okay, then let's get a better overview. Liz, climb to one-five meters."

"One-five meters," Trimble replied, winching up *Bert's* cable.

Haddix also began to gain altitude with *Ernie.*

Trent could almost feel her impatience; Jonesy wanted nothing more than to dart the self-propelled ROV forward and train a camera over the edge. But little *Ernie* was tethered to the sled, which could go only as fast as momentum carried it.

Now the black void beyond the ledge filled more than half the high-angle shot on the main monitor, now more than three quarters, and now the abyss was scrolling onto the other feeds as well. . . .

The collective hopes of those in the van collapsed like a punctured balloon.

Rather than continuing to cant downward at a steeper angle, the ledge ended in a sheer cliff.

"Jeff, how deep's the drop-off?" asked Haddix in a tight voice.

Kabelo consulted the plotters, then replied, "I'm not showing much of anything for more'n one-eight-zero meters."

Haddix crashed a fist down on the console. Recomposing herself, she turned to her right and said to her navigator, "Len, are we safe here? Good. Then please hold this position."

She got up. walked back to the *Bert* engineering station, and knelt beside Trent and Wolfe. "My guess is, with that much water beneath us, the submarine had to go into a glide. Trent?"

He nodded. "No way to predict its path either. Ripped tanks, blown hatches . . . the damage it took sure would have messed up its hydrodynamics. And don't forget it was extremely stern heavy. Hell, dropping through six, seven hundred feet, it could've stood up and done a loop-de-loop, like a kid's paper glider. I wouldn't be surprised if we found it nose up, with its tail buried in the silt."

"We could lower the vehicles and hunt for traces," Haddix said. "We might even get lucky, but I'd advise against it for three reasons. One, the debris trail may not be that conclusive when you figure in how far the pieces fell. Two, it'll bring us closer to that scarp at fifty-two hundred feet. I'm real nervous about fouling our line. Three, even if we find the submarine, we have to reposition the ship before we can approach it . . . again, to avoid that scarp. Rick?"

"Agreed."

"Jonesy, you propose we reposition the ship first?" said Trent.

"Affirmative."

"How long will that take?"

"Two, two and a half hours, max."

"Done. And you still propose to search Ravine B first?"

Haddix glanced up at Wolfe.

Wolfe nodded. "It appears to be the largest. And as the middle of the three, it's most directly in line with the skid marks on the ledge."

"Sounds good to me," Trent said.

Haddix stood. "Rick, would you mind grabbing *Ernie*? You might as well garage it. I'll get Len and Reuss started on moving us to the new position, and then I need a break before standing my next watch."

"Sure thing, E.J.," Wolfe said.

When the two of them headed up front, Trent switched off the VCRs, there being nothing of value to record until they resumed the search. Then he turned his attention to the paperwork that went with running the *Bert* engineering station: ensuring that the just-recorded cassettes were accurately labeled, the log of those tapes up to date, the electronic stills called up and burned onto the laser disc, the laser disc's frame counter in agreement with the data processor's tally.

Trent was finishing up when he spotted Haddix preparing to leave—through the van's rear hatch, he noted with surprise.

"Jonesy. Wait up."

The temperature had plummeted a good twenty degrees in the four hours since they started their watch. The cold front had brought with it a thick cloud cover and a biting wind; confused whitecaps now danced like ghosts on the dark, glistening waters beyond the brightly lit afterdeck.

Haddix was shivering in her T-shirt and cargo shorts, but she took a series of deep breaths and headed for the stern.

"Where're you going?"

"To see if the guys manning the winch want coffee or hot Pepsi . . . whatever Edson's got in the urn."

Trent tagged along, wishing he had a jacket to offer her.

They took shelter with the crew in one of the utility vans, chatted for several minutes, then started up front.

"You know, your nickname hasn't taken," Haddix said unexpect-edly. "No one else is calling me Jonesy."

"Habit."

"Or is it because they're afraid of me? I guess afraid is the wrong word . . . intimidated by me?"

"I'm not picking up that feeling," he replied. "What brought this on?"

She shrugged. "When I unwind, I never know what'll pop into my head next. Actually, that's not accurate. I . . ." She shrugged again.

He decided not to pursue it. "I should tell you how knocked out I was by your performance in there. If I were rotting in some cell back in Athens, you'd find a way to deliver the goods to Zeman. In fact, I feel kind of like a fifth wheel."

"Why? You did fine."

"Because you carried me. You were running the whole show while you flew *Ernie*. No other flyer has to face that pressure."

"What are eighteen-hundreds for if not to serve?" she said lightly.

"Ever think of becoming an air-traffic controller?"

"Nah. I hear they get migraines all the time."

"How about directing *Monday Night Football*?"

Her giggle surprised him, but not her answer. "Nah. Too tame."

MOSCOW

■▬■▬■▬■▬■▬■▬■▬■▬■▬■▬■▬■

1818 Zulu/9:18 P.M. local time

Edmund Hillary, conqueror of Mount Everest, acknowledged his debt to the Nepalese guide who led him up all 29,028 feet by posing Tenzing Norgay next to him in the historic first photographs taken at the roof of the world. Diplomatic sherpas, though, were expected to sweat the details from backstage. Which was why a White House staffer was loitering in a gloomy passageway off the Kremlin's Chamber of Facets, munching a granola bar as he waited to relay progress reports on the state dinner under way inside.

The day was going well. The Old Man had come across as attentive and sympathetic during his luncheon across the river with Soviet dissidents. The artists and writers selected to attend had seemed surprisingly well mannered and neatly dressed, but then *glasnost* notwithstanding, it was unlikely that the Soviets would have permitted the presence of placard-waving protesters like the rabble infesting every corner of America. Later the Old Man had privately conferred with his young Soviet counterpart and proudly dropped his newly learned Russian proverb three times in slightly more than an hour. Best of all, the two first ladies had managed to tour Moscow together, in the company of an immense press contingent, without scratching each other's eyes out.

Suddenly, the doors to the banquet hall swung open.

Waiters bulky as Olympic shot-putters began wheeling out carts precariously piled with half-empty parfait glasses, pastry trays, and bottles of Georgian sparkling brut.

The White House staffer looked questioningly to his KGB escort.

That man nodded, then snagged an untouched fruit cream parfait from a passing tray.

The White House staffer raised a walkie-talkie to his lips.

■　■　■

Several miles from the Kremlin the American rainmakers not invited to the banquet were finishing their own dinner at Spaso House, the residence of the U.S. ambassador to the Soviet Union.

A discreet knock at the door, and then an aide entered. "Things are winding down. They're clearing the dessert dishes."

The secretary of state consulted his watch. "Right on schedule. Good. The Old Man's got a busy day tomorrow."

The aide was about to leave when the national security adviser said, "Any traffic from Washington?"

"No, sir. We're expecting another advisory in forty minutes, but it seems real quiet in the world tonight."

"May it remain that way for another three days," the secretary of state said softly.

The national security adviser turned to his colleagues and smiled. "I think we deserve a brandy."

"Amen," the White House chief of staff said.

"Brandy, hell," the secretary of state said. "I'll have another martini."

THE CENTRAL MED
2015 Zulu/10:15 p.m. local time

Bundled in foul-weather gear, Dov Halevy stood braced on *Sabra*'s badly pitching bridge, sourly surveying the two-meter seas through which his boat plowed. The Israeli captain had surfaced to recharge the batteries and replenish the fresh-air supply. It was adding to the delays, but he had no choice; his destination was still too distant to cover in one last kamikaze charge. Usually, the Gib-to-Crete passage was a milk run. But Halevy had been ordered to run submerged during daylight hours, and to avoid COMSUBGRU

8's nets. Additionally, the series of fronts sweeping eastward across the Med over the past twenty-four hours had wreaked havoc with his schedule. Time and again, despite the cost to men and machine, he had outraced one storm only to plunge into the back of the next; *Sabra* should have made its current position, due north of the island of Pantelleria, more than three hours ago.

Halevy turned to his XO and shouted, "What is our speed?"

The XO spoke into the intercom, then said, "Seventeen knots."

"Damn! I am going below to check the Met. Perhaps we should do only a fast charge, then try to outrun this system. Shall I send up coffee?"

The XO shook his head.

Halevy climbed down from the bridge, shrugged off the soaked anorak, and asked his meteorologist to update the twelve-hour forecast. Then he started back toward the head.

Passing through the crew quarters, his mood worsened when he spotted one of the Russians snoring peacefully in an uncurtained lower bunk. Krestnikov was not only insufferable, but he had also shown himself to be virulently anti-Semitic. Halevy knew his crew was ready to ram this one into a torpedo tube and fire him away. Would such an act trigger a war with the Soviet Union, he wondered, or would Moscow thank Israel for a job well done?

A few feet farther aft a reading light showed through the drawn curtains of the top bunk. Since the man assigned to it was standing watch on the bridge, Halevy guessed it to be occupied by the second Russian. He hesitated, then gently parted the curtain.

Yuri Tikhonov lowered the magazine in his hands and blushed.

Halevy bit his tongue to keep from laughing. He had heard that in Russia, a heavy punishment befell any comrade caught with a copy of *Playboy*. If so, Yuri would be in for a bad time indeed; piled by his side was a year's supply of capitalistic decadence.

Tikhonov sheepishly tilted the centerfold toward Halevy.

Ah, so he is enamored of the blonde who would feel at home on a milk-producing *kibbutz;* not bad, but the redhead hiking an Alpine trail in only boots and backpack was more to his own taste. The Israeli captain flashed the Soviet technician a wink, then drew the curtains closed.

THE EASTERN MED
2132 Zulu/12:32 A.M. local time

Had the gradients displayed on the large monitors in the control van been four miles higher and knee deep in fresh snow, they would have made a lot of skiers happy. Instead, they lay near the bottom of the Hellencian Trench, at a depth of almost 13,000 feet, and their covering was virgin silt. For ninety minutes j.g. Tom Parkhill and Rick Wolfe had slowly flown *Bert* and *Ernie* across Ravine B, a semicircular indentation in the vertical wall that started some 200 feet below the ledge off which the submarine had skidded. They were almost through meticulously combing an area slightly larger than six football fields, but the cameras had yet to unearth a single manmade object, not even an old tire or discarded soda bottle.

"Uncle," Edna Haddix said from her seat at the *Bert* engineering station, her voice betraying not only frustration but also the weariness that came from standing back-to-back watches. "I give up. Gentlemen, we struck a dry hole. Tom, gain some altitude. Rick, you might as well garage *Ernie*."

"Roger that, E.J."

Haddix glanced up at Wendell Trent. Though not scheduled to be on duty until four o'clock, he had returned to the van to attend the probe of the first ravine.

"Cheer up, Jonesy," he said. "We've narrowed it to Ravine C."

Haddix cocked her head to one side, impressed by Trent's quick grasp of the situation. The prevailing current below was northerly.

Since they had found no trace of debris in Ravine B, it stood to reason that *Dakar* could only lay in Ravine C, to the south.

"Can we go right across, or do we have to back off and make another approach?" he asked.

"We need to move again. If we don't, that scarp comes into play." She called out to navigator Reuss, "Joe, plot us a course to the next ravine south. You'll find the coordinates on the chart Rick drew."

Haddix checked the VCRs, saw that the tapes had almost run out, and popped in fresh cassettes for the next watch.

Just then Wolfe strolled back. "Ravine C?"

Trent nodded.

"ETA?"

"About ninety minutes," Haddix replied.

"Listen, neither of you is scheduled for the midwatch," Wolfe said. "Since half of it'll go to setting up the next position, why don't you both grab some shut-eye?"

"Call as soon as you spot something?" said Haddix.

"Promise."

One hundred and sixty feet forward of the van, down in *Fanning II*'s crew quarters, the occupant of a starboard cabin drew a deep breath. His orders were to hold off calling in help as long as possible. With the first of three ravines empty, and with the control van crew so confident of where to search next, it was time.

Checking to see the door was locked and bolted, he quickly crossed to the boom box sitting on the desk and pried off its battery-compartment lid. Nestled inside was a neatly wound length of extremely thin wire that had a jack at one end and a two-inch plastic disc at the other. He uncoiled the wire, which measured a good twenty-five feet in length, wrapped the jack end twice around a table leg, and plugged it into one of the receptacles in the back of the boom box.

Next he picked up the surprisingly heavy plastic disc—it was in fact a UQC transducer—and felt his anxiety rise. Although he had performed the task at hand almost a dozen times without detection, he reckoned his luck was about to end. The burst from the transducer would scramble the pollywog, the acoustic listening device trailing over the side of the ship, and the sonar plotters. His previous transmissions had come when the underwater vehicles were on deck; consequently, there had been nobody in the van to notice the momentary electronic anomalies. Now, with every console manned, surely someone would spot the spikes. But it couldn't be helped, for this message would be the most critical of all.

He drew open the curtain over the porthole, revealing the pitch blackness outside, unscrewed the porthole lock, and inched open the cover.

The waves were slapping high enough on the hull to spray seafoam into the cabin.

He slipped the plastic disc through the gap, fed out the wire, then lowered the porthole cover and closed the curtain.

For almost sixty hours now the Israeli Naval Ship *Rahav,* a Vickers Type 540 diesel submarine, had been shadowing *Fanning II,* slipping away only to replenish its fresh-air supply. Compared to the typical civilian ship, the American boat sported many more sophisticated listening devices. But these were dedicated to communicating with underwater vehicles and transponders, and sounding the terrain below, rather than scanning for hidden neighbors; thus, unless it was transmitting, *Rahav* could with impunity lurk a mere 1,200 meters east of and fifty meters below the research vessel.

The submarine was suffused with the lethargy common to passive missions. In three days the crew had accomplished little besides hold station in the vicinity of the American boat, relay intermittent messages between the Israeli agent aboard *Fanning II* and Haifa, and otherwise observe strict silence.

Rahav's radio operator suddenly pressed one earpiece tighter and reached for a pencil. He made several quick notations, then turned and said, "Captain? The Americans are moving to a new position. We are to strike before they reach it."

"What is their estimated transit time?"

"Ninety minutes, sir. Do you wish to acknowledge message received and understood?"

"Negative," the captain said, knowing full well that a reply would only double the chances of detection. He turned to his XO. "Alert the divers. Also, I want them to carry more line than they think they need. Haifa has made it most clear that we are not to fail."

WASHINGTON, D.C.
2238 Zulu/6:38 P.M. local time

Clifford Zeman stood under the awning that shaded an exclusive men's shop across the street from the limestone mansion housing the Century Club. Despite a blizzard of cabled replies descending on his office—it being a normal working Monday for the rest of the world, which did not celebrate Memorial Day—he had dutifully driven home, picked up a jacket and tie, and arrived ten minutes early for his meeting with the senator. At precisely six-thirty, when the man had failed to show, Zeman left word with the concierge that he would return shortly. It was far more comfortable in the air-conditioned club than out on the sweltering sidewalk, but, he thought with a smile, Ann Davis had taught this old dog a new trick: Every minute he stalled put Bart that much farther out of reach.

A gun-metal-gray stretch Mercedes limousine with ebony-tinted back windows eased to the curb in front of the club. It bore diplomatic license plates. The car sat idling for several minutes. Finally the driver hopped out and hustled around to open the rear curbside passenger door.

The senator emerged, turned back to ask a question, then nodded and hurried into the club.

Zeman waited until the limousine pulled away and turned the corner. Taking a deep breath, he strolled across the street.

The senator was standing in a corner of the lobby, irritably tapping his foot. He glanced Zeman's way but showed no sign of recognition.

Zeman went to the concierge, who turned and guided him toward the senator.

Early fifties, Zeman gauged. He knew from the financial statements Annie had pulled that the senator, unlike most of his colleagues, came from a resolutely middle-class background. Yet despite his $89,500 salary the man had acquired a taste for two-thousand-dollar suits and pricily overstyled hair. The only thing money seemed unable to buy was a cure for his badly pitted complexion.

"Senator? Cliff Zeman."

"You're late," the senator said, brusquely offering his hand.

"Sorry. I was here earlier, but then I realized I had forgotten to lock my car."

The senator turned to the concierge. "Is the room I reserved ready? Good. Send up some drinks. I'll have my usual. Make it a double." He wheeled and started across the lobby.

The concierge looked to Zeman.

"Is the orange juice freshly squeezed? Then an iced tea, please. No sugar, but I'd like two slices of lemon."

Zeman caught up with the senator, who was impatiently holding the door to a small elevator.

"Come on, friend, I've put in a hell of a day already, and I still have a drop-in to do at one of those damned pass-the-hat barbecues."

Zeman smiled to himself. The files suggested that the man all but tailored his life around such functions, especially those hosted by political action committees—including AIPAC.

They rode up in silence.

When the elevator lurched to a stop, Zeman followed the senator down the corridor to a room that resembled that of a one-star hotel: queen-sized bed, minirefrigerator, imitation-wood desk flanked by two armchairs, scarred bureau, and a wall-mounted, American-made color television that might have been new in 1975.

The senator motioned Zeman to take a seat, then perched himself on the edge of the desk.

"Okay, let's cut to the chase. What's going on off the coast of Crete?"

"I'm sorry?"

The senator frowned, as if searching his mind to make sure he correctly remembered his briefing in the limousine. "Crete. The submarine you're looking for . . . why? What's an Israeli sub got to do with Energy?"

"Mr. Senator, you're placing me in an awkward position. My current assignment is classified. I can neither confirm nor deny that it involves a submarine, or in which part or parts of the world it is taking place."

"Relax, Zeman. I'm cleared for everything this side of the daily code for the Football." He gestured to the telephone. "Go ahead. Call over to FBI and confirm it."

"No need to, sir. I accept your word. But, uh, it's not quite that simple. This is a joint operation that requires written clearances from each of the participating agencies."

The senator's face contracted like a clenched fist. "Listen, friend, I've served on the Hill almost twenty-five years as representative and senator, and I've heard more than my share of bureaucratic bullshit. Your answer doesn't wash with me. Understand?"

"I'm not trying to be evasive. I'd like nothing more than to be of help, but my hands are tied."

The senator sighed heavily. "Listen, what if I get your boss on the horn, and he says it's okay? That should do it, right?"

"Not quite, Mr. Senator. The statute is quite specific. I may only discuss the operation with those holding written clearances from all three of the agencies involved: Energy, CIA, and the Naval Oceanographic Office."

"Christ, I don't believe I'm hearing this." The senator got up, circled the room to calm himself, then took a seat opposite Zeman. "Listen, I've got better things to do, you've got better things to do. Let me save us both some time. I called you down here because I want to make sure that this government does not suffer the humiliation of another foreign-relations fiasco. Do you follow me?"

"I'm afraid I don't, Mr. Senator."

"Late last night, reports of your activities reached me from several sources. And frankly, Zeman, they scare the hell out of me. You know why? Because from where I sit, it looks like your agency may be engaging in an Ollie North–type operation that borders on the criminal."

There was a knock at the door.

The senator scowled and barked, "Come on in."

An attendant bearing a tray entered and placed a double Scotch before the senator and an iced tea before Zeman.

The senator grabbed his glass, took a sip, smacked his lips, then treated himself to another.

Zeman spotted an alarm clock on the nightstand to his right. He glanced at its face, relaxed, and leaned forward to squeeze lemon into his iced tea.

"Let's get on with it, Zeman."

"Mr. Senator, I don't know how to respond except to say that the reports you received are erroneous. No laws have been violated, either international or U.S."

"Where does the buck stop? You?"

"I can't speak for Langley or Navy. At Energy, yes, it stops with me, until my immediate superior returns. Then it becomes his responsibility."

"Where is Bart right now?" the senator asked casually.

"Winding up a fact-finding tour of Asia. He should be back sometime tomorrow."

"I see." The senator hesitated, then said, "Fine, I'll accept your

word that you're obeying the law. But let me be candid . . .
there's another reason why I'm concerned about this matter. I have
it on good authority that your operation is deeply offensive to an
ally with whom we enjoy a most special relationship, namely, Israel.
That what you are seeking is the sovereign property of Israel, and
that in the course of your operation your agents have improperly
detained an Israeli national against his will. These are grave
charges, Zeman."

An embarrassed look crossed Zeman's face. "With all due respect, Mr. Senator, were I to confirm or deny a single element of
what you've just suggested, I would be liable for criminal prosecution under the National Security Act."

The senator studied Zeman for several seconds, then shook his
head. "I expected more sensitivity from you, of all people."

Zeman cocked his head questioningly, though he understood full
well the gist of the remark.

"Some people might construe your operation to be anti-Semitic. I
know better, but still, I would have thought you'd be eager to safe-
guard Israel's interests. With a name like Zeman, I mean."

"I suppose you're right. My paternal grandfather came to America from a town just outside Amsterdam, a town that I believe
sheltered Jews during World War II."

"Dutch, eh?" the senator replied, unflustered by his gaffe. "Good
people. A lot of them live in the southwestern part of my state, out
around Grand Rapids."

"May I address your concerns about Israel?" asked Zeman. "I
think I can do so without violating security. As I'm sure you know,
sir, my section is mandated by Congress to investigate international
transfers of nuclear materials and technology. Now, were we to
look into an affair that involved, say, Italy or Argentina, we
wouldn't expect to be judged anti-Catholic. Were we to investigate
Pakistan or Iraq, we wouldn't expect to be judged anti-Muslim.
Were we to investigate Israel, we wouldn't expect to be labeled
anti-Semitic."

The senator flushed. "That's your answer? Listen, friend, I'm

getting fucking tired of your little by-the-book games. Are you going to tell me exactly what's going down, or do I have to haul your
sorry ass before a subcommittee?"

"That's certainly your prerogative, Mr. Senator."

"God damn it, Zeman, I will personally blow the cover off whatever the fuck it is you're running. I will personally force you to
account for every penny on every line of your goddamned mission
budget. And then I will personally retire you from government service, without pension if I can."

Zeman set down his drink and stood. "Then I await your sub-
poena. Thanks again for the iced tea . . . and I hope I haven't
kept you from your pass-the-hat barbecue."

When the senator heard the door close, he cursed the intractable
bureaucratic bastard and hurled his empty Scotch glass against the
wall. Then he looked at his watch—seven-fourteen P.M., only forty-
five minutes before he was due at the fund-raiser out in Fairfax
County—and reached for the phone. Would Bart's wife be home?
And would she know how to reach him?

THE EASTERN MED

2306 Zulu/2:06 A.M. local time

Wendell Trent's eyes sprang open. Location, the bunk of his
cabin aboard *Fanning II*. What had awakened him? And then he
had it: footsteps in the corridor, rapidly heading his way.

He was switching on the reading light over the bunk when the
knock sounded.

"Come on in."

Rick Wolfe bolted into the room, his face ashen. "Our engines
stopped. We're dead in the water."

"Cause?" asked Trent, hopping out and drawing on his shorts.

"No idea. It just happened about three minutes ago."

"The thrusters. Can we hold station using just those?"

Wolfe shook his head. "The seas are too high. In fact, that's all McMahon's got to back us away from the ravines, and he's having a hell of time."

"Jonesy know?"

"Yes. She's on her way down to the engine room. Meet you there." Wolfe started out the door.

"Doc . . . what about the vehicles?"

"No damage, thank God. We were still establishing position in front of Ravine C. Sam and Ezra are bringing them up above the scarp. Cowboy says they'll be safe there. See you down below."

As Trent tugged on a sweatshirt and stepped into his Nikes, he was suddenly struck by a few lines from a poem first encountered in grade school. Even then they had seemed to him overwrought and hokey, but now Coleridge was proving prophetic: *"God save thee, ancient Mariner!/From fiends, that plague thee thus!"*

And the bitch of it was, Trent thought, he hadn't even killed an albatross.

DAY FIVE:
31 MAY 1988

THE EASTERN MED

"**H**ere they come," Wendell Trent said, raising his voice to be heard above the five-foot seas that slapped high against *Fanning II*'s hull. He crossed the rolling deck to the port-side gangway, stepped over the freeboard onto the Jacob's ladder, and started down into the inflatable Zodiac chase boat.

The small knot of people clustered around the gangway looked toward the superstructure.

Two figures, wearing wet suits and carrying air tanks and fins, were clumsily climbing through the nearest watertight hatch.

Captain Bill Nichols turned back to Rick Wolfe to resume their argument: "I still say we ate a drift net."

Wolfe shook his head. "We've been parked at this site more than ten days. Not one of the local boats we've seen has been big enough to handle a drift net."

"They don't have to be," Captain Nichols insisted. "When one of those damned things breaks loose, it can go for hundreds of miles. Besides, if our screws had hit some submerged object hard enough to stall the engines, I guarantee you someone out here would've heard it. Even over that big diesel of yours."

Unconvinced, Wolfe shrugged and watched the divers approach. Illuminated by the stanchion-mounted floods ringing the afterdeck, each of the black-clad figures radiated multiple spidery shadows; yet, this vision seemed no more disorienting than the past hour, most of which he had spent down in the cavernous engine room.

The ship's first engineer had been on duty when, without warning, the twin propeller shafts started vibrating madly. His reaction had been swift and correct: Declutch the shafts, shut down the engines, and sound the alarm.

The understandable thought leaping to everyone's mind—that

this was yet another act of sabotage—appeared unfounded. The only access to the mammoth diesels was from the engine room. But the security detail, doubled after the contamination of the potable water supply some forty hours earlier, reported no unauthorized visitors.

The chief engineer and his two-man crew immediately began troubleshooting. They unbolted the crankcase housing; the bearings had not seized, nor had any connecting rod been thrown. They barred the engine over; there was no resistance, which isolated the problem to either the shafts or the screws. The engineers worked rapidly and efficiently, but though a mud boat's power plant was uncomplicated, the sheer size of the machinery made the tasks time consuming. Finally, the crew tried to rotate one of the shafts; it was stuck in both directions. The men tried the second shaft; it, too, was frozen.

Captain Nichols declared the screws fouled on a stray fishing net. Three times in the past decade he'd been so victimized, including once in untrafficked seas far above the Arctic Circle.

As a result Edna Haddix and Billy Ray McConkey, two of the six scuba-qualified divers aboard, were now preparing to go underwater to inspect the propellers.

Wolfe stepped forward to grab their air tanks. "The others suiting up?"

Haddix nodded.

Captain Nichols reached down to a row of various-sized underwater work lamps and selected a pair of hand-held units. "Navy, I suggest you go down with these first and just reconnoiter. If we did chew a net, you two won't be able to clear it in one dive, anyway."

"Right, Skipper." Haddix flicked her lamp on and off.

"Take it slow," he continued. "A sea like this, the ship'll be slopping around pretty good. Anything happens to you, I'll be doing paperwork clear into the 1990s."

She smiled.

"And check the fairwaters, okay? If those got bunged up, it may mean we sheared a pin."

Haddix shivered involuntarily; she knew most mud boats didn't bother to carry spares, since replacing a pin usually required the facilities of a shipyard.

"Air tanks are aboard the Zodiac," Wolfe said.

Captain Nichols raised his walkie-talkie. "Engine room, this is Nichols. The divers are ready to go overboard. Chief, are all systems down? Over."

A few seconds later the chief engineer replied, "Confirm all systems down. Navy, Cowboy, have a good trip, hear?"

Captain Nichols turned back to the divers. "Remember, keep an eye on your air supply."

"Aye, aye, Skipper."

Haddix and McConkey double-checked the timer rings on their chronometers, then moved to the gangway.

Trent and two of the ship's able-bodied seamen, or A.B.'s, were down in the Zodiac. The eighteen-foot-long boat was tossing heavily. If it was this rough on the leeward side, Haddix thought, what must it be like out in the open?

"Waitin' ain't going to make it any easier," McConkey said, stepping over the freeboard and gingerly lowering himself down the Jacob's ladder.

As soon as both divers were safely aboard and settled, Trent gunned the Zodiac in a wide arc toward the stern of the ship.

Despite the rough ride Haddix and McConkey managed to strap on their air tanks, with help from the A.B.'s, and tug on their fins. Then they checked that knife sheaths were securely strapped to right calves and drew on their gloves.

"Remember, Cowboy, forty minutes," Haddix called over the surging outboard. "And I don't aim to cut it close either."

"Amen!"

Above them Wolfe, Captain Nichols, and the others were hurrying across *Fanning II*'s brightly lit afterdeck toward the fantail.

Trent throttled back, drifting the Zodiac to a stop some ten yards to port of the fantail; he was staying well clear of the underwater-vehicle cable directly aft of the ship.

Suddenly, eyeing the surly waves buffeting the hull of the research vessel, Haddix fully understood the riskiness of the impending dive. She looked over to McConkey, who seemed uncharacteristically somber. "Under other circumstances a night dip in the Med could be downright romantic," she said. "Even with you, Cowboy."

"Especially with me," McConkey shot back. "Bet you didn't know I can hold my breath for near to four minutes."

"Not surprising, from what I hear about the women you date."

"Aw, Navy, there you go again. Better be nice to me, or I won't shoo away the sharks."

"But then who'd be left to tease you?" she asked.

"Big Len," McConkey muttered.

Haddix leaned over and affectionately punched his shoulder.

Trent, having turned the wheel over to one of the A.B.'s, was making his way back to them. "You guys okay?"

They nodded.

"Listen, I don't want any heroics down there. Got that?"

"Cowboy, what did I tell you about these DOE bureaucrats? Their idea of risk is signing a report they wrote themselves."

"Yeah, but maybe he ain't as dumb as he looks," McConkey noted. "Look who's going in the drink, and who's staying dry."

"Very amusing," Trent said. "Be careful of the cable. We'll put lights over the side once you're down, and we'll hold this station as best we can. Any questions?"

Haddix shook her head. "Ready, Cowboy?"

"Let's do it, Navy."

Perching themselves up on the Zodiac's gunwale, they lowered their masks into position, inserted their mouthpieces, and tested the air flow. Then, clutching their work lamps, Haddix and McConkey nodded to each other and rolled backward into the inky sea.

The water was surprisingly warm.

Haddix stabilized herself, switched on her lamp, and looked around for McConkey.

He was below and to the left, wagging his lamp at her.

She turned and kicked downward. Halfway to the massive

screws, which lay some eight feet below the waterline, she hand-signaled McConkey to take the near, or port, screw, then continued on. Carefully skirting the giant rudder, she swam to a point below the inboard side of the starboard propeller.

Haddix treaded water for several moments while she gauged the rise and fall of the hull. Despite *Fanning II*'s great weight it was arhythmically bobbing through a distance of six feet, not to mention pitching as much as twenty degrees from horizontal. The divers were clearly in danger of getting walloped by the hull. She edged a little closer—and felt the turbulent minicurrents generated by the mud boat's unpredictable gyrations. Damn, she thought, this was going to be like trying to get work done aboard a careening roller-coaster.

Haddix kicked upward and beamed her lamp on the shaft.

Even from five yards away she could see that Captain Nichols was right: they had eaten a net.

She waited until the boat started to lift. Then, raising her left arm as a buffer in case the hull reversed directions without warning, she closed on the shaft.

The wild jumble of strands snarled around it looked as if a three-year-old had gone rummaging in mommy's sewing box, dropped a spool of thread, and tried to reroll it. Unfortunately, the strands were not hair-thin cotton, but rather half-inch-thick polypropylene.

Haddix was reaching up for the shaft when the stern suddenly descended. She took the impact on her left forearm—a hard hit, but not enough to break bones—and felt herself being driven down-ward.

As the stern started up again, she managed to clutch the shaft; as long as I stay moored, she thought, I should be relatively safe.

Only then did she feel a sharp stinging sensation on her forearm.

Haddix shone her beam on it. Blood was curling through a patch of wet suit that had been shredded by barnacles on the hull. Ignor-ing the pain, she clumsily looped her left arm around the shaft and transferred the lamp to her left hand. Then she freed her knife and worked its tip under the topmost strands. No matter how hard she wiggled, it barely budged. That was what Captain Nichols feared most; though the ship had been moving slowly when the screws fouled, even thirty-five rpms were enough to wind the line impossibly tight. The divers would have to hack it away, strand by strand.

Sheathing her knife, Haddix grabbed the nearest loose end.

And frowned.

The blunt-edged propeller blades should have mangled the polyprop—yet the section in her hand was as unfrayed as if sliced with a straight razor. She played the beam around until she located another loose end. It, too, was neatly cut, as was the next, and the next.

Now Haddix noticed something else amiss. A line that had been drifting in the sea for any length of time should have acquired a slimy patina. The polyprop around the shaft seemed factory fresh.

She looked across to the port screw.

Cowboy appeared to be sawing at the shaft with his knife.

Haddix rode the shaft down again and let go when the stern started to ascend. She quickly swam fifteen feet to aft, well outboard of the screw—which could slice her in half on its downward travel—and waited for it to settle back down to her depth. Timing her approach, she closed on the fairwater. The cone covering the end of the shaft looked to be undamaged. But was the giant shear pin under it also okay? They wouldn't know until they started up the engines again.

Haddix consulted the timer ring of her chronometer: twenty-nine minutes of air remaining, so she started for the port screw.

McConkey was awkwardly clinging by one hand to the port shaft, which was just as badly fouled, as he hacked away at the tangled polyprop. Sensing Haddix's light below him, he buried his knife in the knots and held up a cleanly cut end.

Haddix nodded. Then she looked past his hand to the blood oozing from a gash on his right temple. She pointed to the wound and signaled him to surface.

McConkey waved his refusal.

She was about to insist when the hull once more began rushing

down toward her. In self-preservation she grabbed on to the shaft
an arm's length from McConkey.

Now he was pointing his index finger downward, crooking it, and
slowly shaking his head.

What's Cowboy trying to signal? she wondered.

McConkey thought for a moment, then moved his crooked finger
to his mouthpiece and jerked it upwards several times.

Hook, she thought. He was pantomiming a fish hook, to warn her
about snagging her hand on one. But she hadn't come across any
tangled up in the lines on the starboard side—which, Haddix suddenly realized, was precisely Cowboy's point: the absence of hooks
was further confirmation that the polyprop had not come from a
drift net. She nodded that she understood.

McConkey handed over his lamp and gestured for her to illuminate the section he had been cutting. Then, retrieving his knife, he
resumed work.

It took him fifteen minutes to get down to the bottommost
strand.

Haddix, in frustration, blew out a big burst of bubbles.

The shaft was a blackened, lumpy mess; friction from the turning
shaft had fused polypropylene to metal.

McConkey tried to chisel away the melted line.

It was no use.

Haddix checked her chronometer again and tapped his shoulder;
time to surface.

The Zodiac, as defined by the lights lowered over its side, had
been blown some thirty yards to port.

Haddix and McConkey were ascending toward it when she spotted a strange silhouette floating above its lights. She tugged on
McConkey's arm, then continued past the chase boat and directed
her beam upward.

What was a python doing way out here? Or, more correctly, a
nest of pythons?

■ ■ ■

"Over there," one of the A.B.'s aboard the Zodiac shouted.

Trent pivoted and saw two lights bobbing on the waves some sixty yards off *Fanning II*'s port. He waited for the A.B.'s to retrieve the work lamps they had dropped overboard, then gunned the idling outboard and started toward the divers.

Throttling back upwind of them, he turned the wheel over to one of the A.B.'s and moved to the gunwale to help the nearest diver up.

"Here, grab these first," Haddix gasped, holding aloft two long, snakelike lengths of polyprop.

Trent tossed them on the floorboard, then reached down and pulled her into the boat.

"You're hurt," he said, noting the dark ribbons of blood trickling down her left forearm.

"I'm okay. Go look after Cowboy . . . he caught his head against the hull pretty hard."

Trent scuttled over to help haul McConkey aboard. When he played a beam on the diver's lacerated temple, the second A.B. immediately scrambled for the first-aid kit.

"No fracture," McConkey announced, relaxing his grip on several lengths of polyprop. "Slight concussion, but my vision's fine. Shit, I've been bunged up worse in barroom fights."

"It's that bad down there, hunh?" said Trent.

McConkey nodded. " 'Fraid a couple of us might end up in sick bay before we free those screws."

The A.B. returned with the kit and started to clean McConkey's wound.

Trent gave the order to head back to *Fanning II,* then grabbed several gauze pads and made for Haddix. She had unstrapped her air tank and swathed herself in a blanket; the night air was much colder than the water. As Trent approached, she offered up her injured forearm.

"Just the screws fouled, or is there other damage too?" he asked, dabbing at the blood.

"Just the screws, I think. Here, give me that, I can clean myself up. Check out that polyprop we brought back. Some of it's baked onto the shafts . . . it's going to be hand-to-hand combat. Cowboy, how many pieces did you grab?"

"Three," McConkey said. "We probably left more'n a dozen behind."

Trent directed his work-lamp beam at the pile on the floorboard. He picked up a length and stretched out his arms to size it. Then he ran a second length through his arms. "What a coincidence," he announced. "They're both exactly twenty-five feet."

"Yeah," McConkey said. "And they didn't fall off of Zorba's rowboat neither."

"Divers," Haddix said.

"Smart divers," Trent agreed.

By the time Edna Haddix and Billy Ray McConkey received medical attention and entered the control van they had changed into dry clothing and downed a mug each of steaming Pepsi, but their teeth were still chattering.

"God, there's nothing I wouldn't do for a long hot shower," she said.

McConkey, his face as pale as the fresh bandage on his forehead, was too spent to even leer.

Wendell Trent and Rick Wolfe were in the van examining the lengths of polyprop.

"I was telling Doc those bastards showed real ingenuity," Trent said. "With these they could stop us dead without having to go near the sled's cable or, for that matter, the screws. Just take up station amidships, about fifty feet down, then stretch the lines perpendicular to our keel and let go. The polyprop floats upward and gets sucked in by the screws. Release enough lines, some of them are bound to foul."

"They sure as hell didn't swim here from Haifa," Haddix said. "Submarine?"

"Probably." Trent turned to McConkey. "Cowboy, you manned sonar on the twelve o'clock, didn't you? Did you detect anything?"

"Negative. But our gear's not set up for omnidirectional scanning. A fleet of boomers could sneak right up our butt, and we'd never know. Fact is, that boat could've been tailing us for days, from not more'n half a mile away."

"Unlikely," Wolfe said. "Wouldn't its skipper have acted earlier, before we searched the first ravine?"

"Not necessarily."

They all turned to McConkey.

"I just remembered something," he said. "It was near the top of my watch, just after you guys on the eight-to-twelve cleared out. The needles on my plotters went haywire and started drawing sharp spikes. I must've swore or something, because Kerry McMahon over at the navigator's station said his computer was glitching out too. Said the nav screen was all blooey . . . spitting out software code, that sort of thing. Both our systems went back to normal in a couple of seconds, so we didn't bother to troubleshoot. I think he logged it, though."

"So?"

"So, my system detects sound waves, and so does McMahon's . . . the nav screen fixes ship's position based on the pollywog's input from our transponders down there. What I'm suggesting is, we both got momentarily scrambled by some transmission coming from close range."

"How close?" asked Trent.

"Real close. Like, it could've come from the ship itself."

"That would explain how the submarine knew just when to strike," Haddix said, her voice hardening. "It got a signal from someone able to monitor our search . . . which means someone with access to the van. Guys, our saboteur is someone we've already vetted."

Rick Wolfe stood at the chart table in the control van surrounded by the echo sounder plots from the previous two days. The units had been left on, and the continuous-roll paper changed at every watch, even during the pause for cable repairs. After flashing this latest development to the beach, Wendell Trent and Edna Haddix had gone forward to start searching the ship; he had stayed behind to verify McConkey's supposition.

Wolfe found the tube from Sunday's noon watch and unfurled it. As he suspected, the first telltale spike had come at 1220 hours and the second some five minutes later—message, then reply. The anomalies had gone unnoticed because the van had been by and large untended from the previous Friday, when the vehicles were brought up, until yesterday afternoon, when they went back down. Still, to play it safe, the saboteur had craftily timed his (or her) twice-a-day messages: one transmission shortly after noon, when most of the crew was at lunch, and the other shortly after midnight, when most of the crew was in quarters.

Wolfe rolled up the paper and returned the tubes to the cabinet above the table.

"Van, Bridge."

He crossed to the intercom. "Yes, E.J.?"

"Find anything, Rick?" she asked.

"I'm afraid so. Two transmissions and two replies a day."

"Shit. So much for our security . . . the only way we could have made it easier for our friend would have been to broadcast our main monitor feed."

"Are you proceeding as planned?"

"Affirmative. It's probably useless, but we might as well do something while we stand by for Zeman's reply."

"He must be thrilled," Wolfe said. "Want me to help?"

"Negative. Trent and I have things under control. Why don't you see if Cowboy needs a hand."

"Roger."

Wolfe left the van, locking the hatch behind him.

Before going forward to help Billy Ray McConkey and the two cable technicians rig a life raft to serve as a second chase boat, he looked to the fantail.

The Zodiac, manned by flyers Sam Lippman and Ezra Schell, was fifteen yards to port of the stern. Down below, the second team of divers—j.g.'s Tom Parkhill and Jeff Kabelo—were hacksawing away at the tangles of polypropylene line.

The attempt by Trent and Haddix to overcome this latest crisis, Wolfe realized, was severely hampered by the probability that the saboteur had already been cleared by security. To avoid a total shutdown they had used logic—and faith—to place eighteen people above suspicion: themselves and the two j.g.'s; Captain Nichols; those boarding *Fanning II* after the cable was cut, namely the three DOE agents and the men from Reliance; and those working within sight of each other when the last transmission had been made, namely the midnight van watch and the ship's first engineer.

At the moment everyone else aboard was being herded onto the foc's'le while their cabins were combed. Wolfe shared Haddix's pessimism about the chances of turning up a transmitter. Nowadays, such devices could be highly miniaturized and disguised as some altogether different object. Yet the cost of failure promised to be high. *Eighteen of us busting our chops for the next six hours just might manage to unfoul the screws,* he thought, *but then what shape will we be in to resume the hunt for the Israeli submarine?*

Proceeding forward across the afterdeck, Wolfe spotted McConkey, back in a wet suit, with cable technicians Glenn Marullo and Denny Flanagan by the port-side hoist. They were wrestling a sling under a life raft that had been inflated and fitted with a small outboard motor.

"How're you feeling, Cowboy?" asked Wolfe.

"I've been better, Doc."

"You putting her over the side now?"

"Negative," McConkey replied. "Not for another fifteen minutes, when we go relieve the divers."

"You and E.J. are going right back in?"

"Affirmative. Two of the ship's A.B.'s are scuba qualified, but until we nail our mystery sonuvabitch, they're staying high and dry."

"You were right about the transmissions," Wolfe said. "According to the echo sounder charts, two a day."

"Fuck me. And nobody noticed nothing."

"No fault to parcel out, Cowboy. We could have just as easily shut the sonar down, and then there'd be no record."

McConkey rubbed his jaw. "You know, Doc, I've been thinking things over. Seems to me there's really only two possible suspects."

"How's that?"

"Okay, we know it wasn't anyone on the midnight watch, because none of us could've transmitted from inside the van."

Wolfe nodded.

"So the only ones who knew that Ravine B was empty—that what we're searching for more likely than not lies in Ravine C— were the six hands on the eight o'clock." McConkey paused to review the watch roster. "You stayed on for the midnight, so it wasn't you. There was Navy and Parkhill, they're clean. So's Glenn here. That leaves Joe Reuss, the navigator, and Ari Kahane. Doc, neither of them did this thing."

Wolfe mulled it over, then said, "But how could anyone else have known what was going on inside the van?"

"That's the part I haven't figured out," McConkey conceded.

Marullo moved away from the life raft and took several steps toward the van. "What's that up there?"

Wolfe followed the tech's outstretched arm to a bundle of cables that ran overhead from the van to the superstructure.

"The video and intercom feeds up to the bridge and to my cabin," he said, turning away. "Oh, my God . . . Anybody got a walkie-talkie? No, wait, those channels aren't secure. Glenn, go find Trent. Tell him I think the saboteur's been able to track our progress because he's tapped the lines we rigged to the superstructure."

"Sonuvabitch," McConkey said. "Of course. With all the cables running around this mud boat, who'd notice one more?"

Wolfe said, "Cowboy, can you rustle me up a ladder and knife? I'll be over there."

McConkey reached down to unsheathe the knife strapped to his right calf. Then he headed for the workroom at the rear of the superstructure where the ship's crew stored tools.

Wolfe and Flanagan crossed the afterdeck to the van, stopping beneath the opening from which the cables emerged.

McConkey returned with a stepladder and three flashlights.

Wolfe set up the ladder, climbed it, and began cutting through the gaffer's tape bundling the individual cables: "There should be four cables . . . two, three, four."

They followed the bundle across the afterdeck to the superstructure.

There, a pair of cables split off and continued up the exterior wall toward the bridge. The rest of the bundle disappeared through a starboard-side ventilation grill just to the left of the outer watertight hatch.

Wolfe positioned the ladder next to the grill, sliced through the gaffer's tape, and beamed his flashlight on the strands. "Four minus the pair to the bridge, so there should be two left . . . trouble is, I still count four."

Leaving the ladder behind, they traced the bundle through the first ventilation grill and then a second grill set alongside the inner watertight hatch.

Inside the superstructure the bundle was taped across the ceiling of the lateral passageway. There they split again, with two lines headed for an upper deck and two for a lower deck.

"My cabin's up there," Wolfe said grimly. "Looks like our saboteur's bunking below."

McConkey played his flashlight down the companionway. "Well, lookee here. Artful fucker, ain't he?"

The cables had been taped just above the riser. But three fourths of the way to the deck that housed crew quarters and the laundry room, they darted into a small hole drilled into the vertical facing.

"Just above ceiling height," Wolfe said. He clambered down the steps and studied the overhead panels. Each was held by four screws. "We're going to have to pull these. Anyone got a screwdriver?"

"Me," Flanagan said. "And being the tallest, I guess I might as well volunteer."

When he removed the panel, they could see that the cables ran to starboard. To speed things Wolfe told him to pull every third one.

The trio had almost worked their way to the front of the ship when they heard footsteps rapidly approaching from behind. Wolfe turned, saw Trent and Marullo at the head of the corridor, and said, "We've narrowed it down to these four cabins."

Trent scanned the numbers on the doors and pointed to the panel directly above the next-to-last cabin. "I just got off the phone with the beach. Denny, pull this one first. If Zeman's right, our search is over."

WASHINGTON, D.C.

0138 Zulu/9:38 P.M. local time

Clifford Zeman was not one to mourn lost opportunities. Yet, as he waited in the DOE communications room for a reply from Wendell Trent, he couldn't help but curse the fact that the fouling of *Fanning II*'s screws might have been prevented had the Sûreté file in his hand arrived earlier.

To vet the non-Americans aboard the research vessel Zeman had drawn on FBI's data-sharing relationship with foreign police forces and domestic-intelligence agencies. Paris had finally responded with a dossier on Roland Vigneron, one of the electronics specialists on the mission.

A faculty member of the Oceanographic Department of the Université d'Aix-Marseille, Vigneron was a *pied noir:* a Frenchman born in Algeria when that North African nation was still a colony of France. His forebears had settled in the port city of Oran in the late 1800s and founded a shipyard. Though the business grew modestly, it provided sufficient income to send each succeeding generation of children back to France to attend school, to absorb the cultural values of *notre patrie,* and, more often than not, to find a spouse.

In 1948, shortly after Roland Vigneron's birth, control of the firm passed to his father. Vigneron *père,* a marine engineer by training, foresaw that Europe's economic recovery from World War II would inevitably lead to a surge in maritime shipping. Needed were inexpensive modern cargo ships to complement the war-ravaged steamers and cast-off Liberty ships that comprised the merchant fleets of most nations. He had parlayed an aggressive business sense and the availability of cheap local labor to begin building what eventually amounted to an armada of small coastal freighters. So dramatically did the family fortunes improve that the Vignerons would have risen into the ranks of their adopted land's elite had not the Algerians deemed it time to reclaim their country.

France, already waging a losing battle with Ho Chi Minh for control of Indo-China, was not about to willingly grant independence to another jewel in its once-glorious empire. And once Dien Bien Phu fell in 1954, Paris vowed to stamp out the Algerian secessionist movement, no matter what the cost.

As tensions—and violence—escalated, Algeria's privileged *pieds noirs* inevitably became targets. There was a strike at the shipyard. At Paris's request Vigneron *père* resisted the workers' demands. He was still trying to arrange for the evacuation of his family when Algerian radicals planted a crude but powerful bomb in the biweekly delivery of groceries to the Vigneron villa; eleven-year-old Roland was playing in the garden the afternoon the kitchen rocked with an explosion that killed his mother, his eldest sister, and three Algerian servants.

Vigneron *père* insisted on taking his dead back to France for burial. Faced with the probability that Algeria would eventually gain its independence, and that the new government would nationalize most of the businesses owned by *pieds noirs,* he remained in France to start a new life with his four surviving children.

Two months after the double funeral Vigneron *père* accepted an executive position at Ch. de Normandie shipyards in Cherbourg. In addition, surmised the Sûreté dossier, he had acted on his understandable bitterness against Arabs by offering to covertly aid Israel.

For instance, in the mid-1960s Ch. de Normandie won a contract to build seven gunboats for the Israeli Navy. All were finished, but because of politics—specifically, President Georges Pompidou's attempt to placate Arab leaders, and thus maintain France's influence in the Middle East—only two were delivered. Yet on Christmas morning of 1969 the five remaining Sa'ar-class gunboats somehow acquired crew, fuel, and provisions, and broke quarantine by stealing out of Cherbourg harbor. Six days and three thousand miles later, they triumphantly sailed into Haifa.

Naturally, the French intelligence agency suspected Vigneron *père.* Naturally, Vigneron *père* produced an ironclad alibi. In the end, after a three-year investigation, no charges were filed.

Like father, like son? Zeman would have wagered a substantial sum that Roland Vigneron was carrying on the family tradition. Successfully, too: at the moment *Fanning II* was drifting dead in the water, borne northwest at one knot by wind and current.

Damn, he thought; if only the Sûreté dossier hadn't arrived on a holiday; if only the skeleton crew manning FBI communications had forwarded it before late afternoon; if only he hadn't been forced to leave his office to meet with the senator. . . .

"Mr. Zeman?" said the communications specialist. "It's Wendell Trent."

Zeman picked up the receiver.

"Cliff? You were right."

"He admitted it?"

"Negative, but we have confirmation. The science team had rigged lines to pipe the main video and intercom from the van up to the bridge and Wolfe's cabin. Doc found that someone managed to tap into those lines. We traced the tap right into Vigneron's cabin. He even had a minimonitor and VCR squirreled away above one of the ceiling panels."

"A regular electronics whiz, isn't he?" said Zeman tartly. "Small wonder the microwave transmitter didn't work after he finished fiddling with it. Where is Vigneron now?"

"The laundry room, cuffed to a drainpipe. There'll be someone in there with him at all times. The thing that worries me is, he seemed to be reporting in about once every twelve hours. What happens when they don't hear from him at noon?"

Zeman sighed. "If his file had only arrived one hour earlier . . ."

"Then your aunt'd be a teacart," Trent retorted. "Look at the bright side. For the first time we have a fully vetted crew at our disposal."

"My notes show that you were running thin on qualified van personnel. This should help."

"Affirmative. We'll add a couple of bodies to each watch, and switch some duties. But Jonesy and I want to keep the key assignments—ROV flyer, sled engineer—just the way they are."

"It's your call, son," Zeman said. "But watch the fatigue factor."

"Yes, sir."

"What's your timetable?"

"We hope to unfoul the screws by late morning. Assuming the shear pins are okay, we'll be back on site about twelve hundred Zulu."

"Ouch. Any sign of the submarine the divers came from?"

"That's a negative. All we know is, it's not sitting directly below us. I'm going to ask the techs if they can jury-rig some kind of side-scanner capacity onto our depth finders, but I'm not hopeful. Anyway, that boat's only a threat if it decides to target us with a fish. I don't think the Israelis are willing to go that far, or they would have done it already, rather than risk divers on such a dicey mission."

"I hope you're right," Zeman said. "But they might send their divers against you again."

"I doubt it, Cliff. We've got a little mud-boat trick up our sleeve. Any further news on the Greek Navy?"

"Not a peep. I've been calling Suitland every couple of hours. No unusual ship movements. . . . I'm beginning to think Athens gave Langley a bum steer."

"You know, I almost wish the Greeks would try something."

"How's that?"

"First, I'd rather go against them than the Israelis any day. Second, it's an excuse to ask CNO to send in the Sixth Fleet."

Zeman chuckled mirthlessly. "With my luck CNO would agree, and then present Mr. Da Silva with the bill. Anything else we need to discuss?"

"Just this: Cliff, I take back everything I ever said about how boring a desk job is compared to the Navy. Hell, twenty years on attack boats and boomers, I never saw as much action as the last three days."

"We at DOE aim to please," Zeman said lightly. He hesitated, then added, "Wendell, I'm afraid your window is down to a few hours. Our sources in Israel have confirmed that they have some tightly compartmented operation under way. Apparently, it's under the command of Leon Rose . . . he's the one they say is even more militant than Ariel Sharon. When Vigneron misses his next transmission, Rose will most likely suspect the worst. Just remember, this is not a combat mission. I don't care if you're this far from the smoking gun, the safety of your crew and ship is paramount."

"Understood, sir."

THE EASTERN MED
0706 Zulu/9:06 a.m. local time

Dov Halevy, perched on his bunk in the captain's cabin of *Sabra*, read the decoded message from Haifa a second time, then looked up at his XO. "Menachem's guess is pretty good."

The XO nodded.

Menachem was the weapons officer aboard the Israeli submarine.

During the past two nights, while torpedo specialist Yuri Tikhonov and the Jew-hating political officer Krestnikov slept soundly, Menachem had surreptitiously stripped and inspected the Russian fish. The weapon, he told Halevy, was like none he had ever encountered. Its skin seemed to be a titanium-based alloy much like that the superpowers had developed for their pride-of-the-fleet ballistic missile boats. Its innards were protected by the latest deep submergence technologies, such as oil-filled junction boxes in place of conventional pressure housings and extremely dense, cream-colored syntactic foam jammed into every available cranny. Its powerful propulsion system, by Menachem's estimate, could generate speeds approaching sixty knots. And its dual guidance system promised extreme accuracy: in addition to a 3,000-meter-long wire that linked it to a computer in the firing-control box, the fish possessed a sophisticated sonar unit in its nose cone.

The Israeli weapons officer had exposed six rolls of film on the torpedo's various systems and scraped away samples of the fuselage alloy and the syntactic foam. The lab boys back in Haifa would no doubt deliver a learned analysis of the evidence one of these years, but Menachem had concluded that the Russian fish was designed to operate at previously unimaginable depths—a hypothesis now confirmed by Ben Goren.

The newly arrived orders instructed *Sabra* to proceed to specific coordinates off the southwest tip of Crete, to employ its sonar to pinpoint a prominent abutment, and finally to assist Tikhonov in firing the fish at the scarp, which lay a stunning 1,637 meters below the surface.

"I cannot begin to guess the purpose of this mission," the XO said.

"It is more than target practice," Halevy agreed sourly. "Exactly what, you and I shall never know. Something this big, something that involves Russian weapons and Russian personnel, I doubt if even the full cabinet knows."

"Can Yuri's fish actually dive to such a depth?"

Halevy shrugged.

"If so, who needs such a weapon?"

"I think the next generation of ballistic missile boats launched by the Russians and the Americans will be very interesting indeed. They will make that Mike-class we encountered as obsolete as our old *Sabra*. But that is something else you and I shall never know, not while we serve in Israel's navy."

A crewman appeared at the cabin door. "Captain? The chart you requested."

Halevy rose to accept it, then spread the chart across his bunk. According to the last plot *Sabra* was 280 kilometers and seven and a half hours east of Malta. Quickly fixing his rendezvous coordinates, he used calipers to measure the remaining distance to Crete.

"Signal Haifa that our ETA is twenty thirty Zulu," Halevy said.

"Right away," the XO replied, hurrying from the cabin.

MOSCOW

0838 Zulu/11:38 a.m. local time

The national security adviser to the President of the United States purposefully strode east across the Kremlin grounds toward Spassky Gate, which opened onto Red Square. The sun was bright and the skies deep blue and cloudless on this breathtaking midday in Moscow, but he drew no pleasure from the idyllic weather, so preoccupied was he with the unnerving coincidences of the morning.

Fifteen yards behind him the Old Man and the young Soviet president were strolling at the center of an unwieldy group of interpreters and aides. The two leaders seemed to be in an expansive mood. Their just-concluded parley in historic Saint Catherine's Hall had gone smoothly; now, statesmanship concluded, they were also heading for Red Square to joust again in that rather more photogenic sport of pressing the flesh.

The national security adviser reckoned the world's media would hail this, Day Three of the Moscow Summit, as yet another encouraging thaw in the Cold War, or some such glib gibberish. In fact, he thought dourly, presidential tête-à-têtes were truly newsworthy only if one of the men stormed out, for each was carefully programmed to talk at, rather than with, his counterpart, and to ignore any provocative statement uttered by the other.

The same was not true of the lower-level conferences now under way at sites across the city. Though largely ignored by journalists, these were where specialists could speak with utmost candor as they floated trial balloons in areas like defense, trade, and the sciences. Over the past five American administrations they had proven themselves the most productive forums for slowly expanding the common ground between the two nations.

The gravity with which both sides approached such talks was the basis for the national security adviser's current apprehensions, for it appeared that the no-problem summit was springing leaks. Separate sessions had been scheduled that morning to discuss limiting multiple-warhead missiles and revising naval protocols. At each meeting the key Soviet military officials had been replaced at the last minute by subordinates. The bland explanations offered—in one case the flu, in another a wife taken ill, in a third food poisoning—had done little to calm the national security adviser's fears.

He hurried through the thick Kremlin rampart. Massed on the other side of the entranceway was a battalion of cameramen and reporters. Two tried to attract his attention, but he managed to duck them and start across the immense expanse of cobblestone and macadam in the direction of the GUM department store.

The national security adviser's chief aide was waiting off to one side, between Spassky Gate and the Lenin Mausoleum. Spotting his boss, he quickly headed to intercept him.

The national security adviser knew that there were few more vulnerable places in Moscow for a black man—much less a black man with his high-visibility profile—to exchange information than Red Square. The nearest safe room, though, was miles away and time was of the essence. He reached into the left inner breast pocket of his jacket, pressed a button, and prayed that the Secret Service's little electronic toy would successfully jam any parabolic dish or videocamera pointed his way. Then, cupping a hand over his mouth, he said, "Did you get through?"

"Yes, sir," the aide replied, cupping his own mouth. "As of thirty minutes ago, no change in alert status, no unexpected movement of forces."

"Damn," the national security adviser said. "No new rebel offensive in Afghanistan, no riots in the Moslem republics?"

"No, sir."

"I don't like this one bit. If our friends are to be believed, they've got enough heavy hitters on sick call to fill *St. Elsewhere*."

"Langley and DIA* are both working on it, sir."

The national security adviser nodded. "The Old Man's due at the House of Writers in forty-five minutes . . . it's that lunch with Soviet artists. I want an update before we leave for his speech at the university."

"Very good, sir," the aide said, hurrying away.

The national security adviser turned and started back toward Spassky Gate.

The two smiling presidents, having emerged from the Kremlin battlements, were in the midst of an impromptu press conference. *Good,* thought the national security adviser. Journalists sated with pomp tended not to notice sinister circumstances—like the no-show Soviet military conferees.

Suddenly, the young Soviet leader reached down to gather up a little girl and thrust her into the Old Man's arms.

That certainly ought to play well on the seven o'clock news, the national security adviser thought darkly. Unless, that is, I were to

*DIA: *Defense Intelligence Agency.*

inadvertently screw it up. He pulled up short, reached into his
jacket, and deactivated the jammer before it could render the footage unusable.

THE EASTERN MED
0931 Zulu/12:31 P.M. local time

Rain was falling and sea-foam climbing over the rails as a drawn
Edna Haddix emerged from the control van. To her left a group of
crewmen was battening down the Zodiac and the life raft. Over the
past eight hours she and the other five divers had worked two more
forty-minute shifts apiece to hack away most of the polypropylene
snarling *Fanning II*'s screws. The toll had been high. They all bore
assorted lacerations and contusions; in addition, one of the A.B.'s
had sustained a severe concussion, j.g. Jeff Kabelo a fractured arm,
and Billy Ray McConkey a broken hand.

Gingerly pulling the borrowed slicker tight with a bandaged
hand, Haddix steadied herself against the ship's roll and started
across the treacherously slick deck toward the superstructure.

The shafts remained coated with burnt residue—she didn't envy
the shipyard hands who would eventually have to scrape them clean
—but Wendell Trent had persuaded Captain Nichols to test the
screws. The research vessel didn't have to travel very far or very
fast, he had pointed out, merely limp a dozen miles back to site and
hold station until the underwater vehicles finished their mission.
Half an hour earlier the chief engineer had slowly throttled each
screw up to thirty rpms. At that speed one of the shafts exhibited a
noticeable drag. Nevertheless, he had pronounced the mud boat fit
to resume limited operations. Now they were plowing at three

knots through six-foot seas toward Ravine C, which lay some eight miles to the southeast.

Halfway across the deck Haddix was startled by a dull but resonant *crump* from aft of the fantail. Then she identified the sound and grinned. It was Trent's homemade frogman repellent. Mud boats usually carried dynamite to conduct seismic studies. Trent had requisitioned *Fanning II*'s store and transferred the cases to the fantail; there a three-man detail, already nicknamed the Zippo Squad, was lighting and tossing ten sticks per hour into the water at random intervals. The explosives would scarcely discourage the submarine carrying the polyprop-wielding divers, but Trent and Cliff Zeman seemed confident that the boat, presumably Israeli, would not attack an American research vessel. She hoped they were right.

Haddix high-stepped through the two sets of watertight hatches and continued to the mess hall.

The seas had grown heavy enough for the attendants to have deliberately wet the tablecloths to prevent plates and cups from sliding to the floor. She scanned the room. Though lunch was over, it remained crowded with both the van's and the ship's eight-to-twelve watches.

Haddix shrugged off the dripping slicker and approached the table where GIO intern Ariel Kahane sat with three men from the van and one of the A.B.'s.

"Come join us, E.J.," navigator Joe Reuss said. "I think there's still some chow left."

"Thanks, Joe, but I just came in to have a quick word with Ari." She glanced down at the partially eaten sandwich on the young Israeli's plate.

"It is okay, Navy, I am done," Kahane said.

Haddix led him from the mess to the other side of the ship. The lounge was empty. She went in, waited for him to enter, then closed the door behind them.

"It is something bad again," he said nervously.

"No, not at all. I brought you in here because what I have to say is very delicate. You know that we're searching for an Israeli sub." He nodded.

"Trent's decided that as soon as we sight the boat, we're restricting access to the van and shutting down the video and audio feeds to the bridge."

"I understand, Navy. You do not want me to stand my watch."

"Yes, but not for the reasons you think, Ari. No one aboard questions your trustworthiness. The problem is, the beach says you hold dual citizenship."

"Yes. My father is from Chicago, and I was born in Ann Arbor when he returned to America to study for his master's degree."

"Which makes you a U.S. citizen. But you consider Israel your home, and you're a reservist there?"

"Yes," Kahane replied. "Why?"

"If you have intimate knowledge of our operation, you'll be placing yourself in legal jeopardy with one of two nations. As you know, this is now a U.S. government mission. No participant may discuss it without prior authorization. Meanwhile, Israel's taken extraordinary steps to keep us from finding the boat. If we succeed, they'll want to know all about it . . . and if you refuse to tell them, you'll face a lot of pressure, maybe even prosecution. The way Trent and I see it, Ari, your only way out of that bind is to remain ignorant of what we're doing."

Kahane thought it over and said, "I think you are right."

She stood.

"Navy? You are kind to worry about me, and to take the time to explain it. Thank you."

Haddix patted his shoulder, then left the lounge. She had three hours before her next watch. It was not nearly enough to sleep off the debilitating effects of three strenuous dives since midnight, to allow her bruises and cuts to begin mending, but she would take what she could get.

At the foot of the companionway, though, she turned and retraced her steps to the mess.

As usual, Edson had left out a tray of cold cuts. Haddix made a sandwich and, for a quick sugar fix, piled her plate with Oreos. She usually hated to nap on a full stomach; but with a long afternoon— and evening—ahead, she was willing to make an exception.

HAIFA

1156 Zulu/2:56 p.m. local time

Ephraim Levenger and Ben Goren looked up as Leon Rose returned to their command post at the Haifa Naval Station. Rose, who had gone to the communications room to take a secure-line call, seemed uncharacteristically subdued.

"It was Mother?" asked Levenger.

Rose nodded, continued around to his chair, and sat down heavily.

"What news does he send us?"

"Bad news, I am afraid. The Russian admiral who authorized the transfer of the torpedo was taken in for questioning. You knew him, Ben. Boris Patolichev."

Goren turned pale. "The naval captain I met in Switzerland to arrange the rendezvous for *Dakar*? He is the one who gives us the torpedo?"

"Yes. Someone alerted the High Command to the transfer. Pavel says the search for answers has Moscow in chaos . . . a few high-ranking Russian officers even failed to meet with their American counterparts this morning, as scheduled. That, in turn, has made Washington very nervous. Pavel says the Americans are desperate to ascertain why those important men failed to show up. It would all be terribly amusing were not the stakes so high."

Rose leaned forward to study the half-filled pastry tray on his desk. A decade earlier he handled stress with cigarettes; but since giving up smoking he had relied on sweets.

"Have we enough time to carry out the mission?" asked Goren.

Rose nodded. "Pavel says Patolichev knows *Sabra*'s timetable and will hold out until at least late this evening."

"Then he—Mother, that is—he still has time to escape," Levenger said.

"Yes, but he will not. It is a matter of honor. He says his conscience is clear, that although perhaps he acted illegally, he did not betray his precious Motherland. In fact, he will spend the rest of the day at a secure phone, in the event we need something further of him."

Levenger dabbed his forehead with a handkerchief, though the air-conditioned offices were colder than a morgue. Finally, in a tight voice, he said, "Leon, we must act now. Mother might misgauge his friend. What if the Russians learn about *Sabra* in the next hour or two, and start to hunt it? Besides, it is nearly three, and still there is no word from my agent. It is unlike him to be so late with his report unless something is badly wrong."

"And what action do you propose we take, Ephraim?" asked Rose. "Our other ships will not be in position for another four hours."

"*Rahav*. It carries torpedoes, does it not? Can we not cripple the American ship?"

"And I thought that I am the hawkish one in this room," Rose said, picking up his sixth or ninth pastry of the day and biting into it.

"We knew it might come to this," Levenger persisted. "Let us face the facts. Even should Mother's friend remain silent, *Sabra* is still seven hours away. Unless we stop the American ship now, they are sure to find and enter *Dakar*. I say damn the diplomatic repercussions. After all, when *Sabra* arrives, can its captain not sneak in and finish the job with the deep-diving torpedo?"

Rose impassively finished chewing, then gulped down some lukewarm tea and cleared his throat. "It is not diplomatic repercussions that worry me, Ephraim, it is the U.S. Sixth Fleet. Ben, how do you calculate their response time?"

Goren stood and crossed to the large situation map. Since the previous evening the positions of all American naval units within 150 kilometers of Crete had been grease-penciled onto the acetate overlay and updated hourly.

"To cripple the research vessel is not the same as to insure that *Dakar* will never be found. Certainly, *Rahav* can fire a torpedo and escape undetected . . . but if it does, *Sabra*'s mission is doomed." Goren placed his finger below Crete, over the stretch of Med separating the Greek island from eastern Libya. "This American battle group of destroyers can steam up in three hours. If the Americans station so much as one destroyer over the site, I fear not even Dov Halevy can sneak in, much less get off a shot."

Levenger slumped back in his chair. "By the time we are ready to board the research vessel, its entire crew will know the truth, even the kitchen hands. Then what? Believe me, there will be casualties on this operation. Many casualties."

"You worry too much, my friend," Rose said. "Do not forget that the only way those aboard can offer proof to the world is with their videotapes. I assure you, Ephraim, those cassettes shall not be on that vessel when our men leave it."

"Leon's right," Goren said gently. "We gain nothing by acting prematurely."

Levenger sighed loudly.

Rose picked up his half-eaten pastry and regarded it balefully. "God, this is truly awful. It comes from the commissary? Then, Ben, I suggest you consider hiring some Arab bakers," he said, tossing it into the wastebasket.

THE EASTERN MED

"**E**.J., we're starting to come across skid marks and debris."

Edna Haddix groggily blinked her eyes in the darkened cabin and peered at the luminescent hands of the travel alarm to the left of her bunk. The telephone receiver she had reflexively picked up felt like a ten-pound barbell. In a voice husky with sleep she said, "Is it *Dakar?*"

"We're not sure yet," Rick Wolfe replied. "We've only spotted a trail, not the sub."

"Oh."

"Sorry to wake you."

"That's okay, Rick. I have to get up for my watch anyway. Does Trent know?"

"Yes. He's here already."

She hesitated, then said, "Can I ask a dumb question?"

"Sure."

"My clock says it's almost three-thirty . . . but is that A.M. or P.M.?"

Wolfe laughed. "P.M."

"Good. If I felt this shitty after sleeping more than twelve hours, I'd kill myself. Be down in a few minutes."

Haddix replaced the receiver and took several deep breaths in an attempt to come fully awake. Instead of the exhilaration that should accompany hunt's end, she felt only a bruised weariness that was a legacy of her three dives. She summoned her strength and rolled out of the bunk, then crossed to the porthole and drew back the curtain.

The skies were still sullen and a hard rain still lashed the white-capped seas. In the distance she heard a muffled explosion that was courtesy of the Zippo Squad.

Haddix fetched a fresh bottle of Evian from her dwindling cache.

Moving to the cabin sink, she quickly swabbed her face and brushed her teeth, longing all the while for a good, hot shower.

Before heading out to the van Haddix stopped by the mess hall for a mug of something hot. As usual the urn held Pepsi. She spotted the cook in the galley preparing dinner and called out, "Edson, how're we doing on fresh water?"

"We have plenty, Navy. I think maybe it is because we use the plastic plates. Washing the dishes takes much water. I think maybe I tell Captain Nichols we use the plastic plates even when the shortage is over. And I tell Captain Nichols, my men will thank you also."

Two of the Cabo Verdean mess attendants murmured something that sounded to Haddix suspiciously like the Portuguese version of "right on."

Haddix grinned. "The reason I'm asking is, things seem to be heating up in the van. Think we can spare some water to make real coffee?"

"One moment, Navy." Edson beckoned her toward a storage locker at the rear of the galley. "But tell me, what is wrong with the Pepsi? Cowboy, he likes it better. This morning he even puts it on his Froot Loops."

"Hot?" she asked incredulously.

He nodded as he opened the storage locker. Inside stood a mammoth commercial-size electric percolator that could keep a party of fifty in coffee for the rest of the evening. "I fill this and have my men bring it to the van, okay?"

Haddix regarded the machine dubiously. "I don't know . . . that looks like it might short out the whole ship."

Edson giggled. "No problem, Navy. Chief, he has plenty of fuses."

As soon as Haddix entered the control van she was struck by the absence of music; for the sound system to be shut down, things must be getting intense.

She turned to scan the row of large monitors mounted above the forward consoles.

The feeds from *Bert* rose and fell in rhythm with *Fanning II* as the research vessel wallowed on the sloppy seas, for it and the sled were linked by a taut cable. In contrast *Ernie's* images were rock steady, for the semislack tether that connected it to *Bert* also buffered the ROV from the sled's undulations.

Up on the main monitor *Bert's* wide-angle, forward-looking camera showed a smudgy point of light—little *Ernie*—inching across a black background. Since the lights aboard the sled had an effective range of thirty-five yards, Haddix deduced that *Bert's* flyer, Sam Lippman, was forced to keep his distance from the wall of the ravine because of the prominent abutment sitting halfway between the ship and the vehicles. Haddix switched her attention to Monitor Two. It displayed images from *Ernie's* pan-and-tilt camera. At the moment ROV flyer Ezra Schell was maintaining an altitude of fifteen feet above the floor of the ravine, from which height she could clearly make out a deep, broad furrow in the grayish silt, as well as the small chunks of metal that lined it.

After a few moments Haddix headed back to the chart table. Gathered around it were Wendell Trent, Rick Wolfe, and Billy Ray McConkey. Under the dim red night-operation lights McConkey, head and broken hand swathed in bandages, looked like a pop-up monster from a haunted house ride.

"How you feeling, Jonesy?" asked Trent.

"Like I've done back-to-back triathlons." She turned to her diving partner, McConkey. "You okay, good buddy?"

He made a face. "If Crystal Gayle was to walk in here buck naked right now, she'd have nothing to fear from this cowpoke."

Haddix patted him on the back and turned to the sheet on the table, a sketch of Ravine C. As plotted by McConkey from sonar soundings, the giant indentation resembled an upright clamshell.

"Len's currently holding us to the north-northwest, to compensate for drift," Wolfe explained. "We set up *Bert* pretty much in the center of the ravine, right about here, and started mowing the lawn with *Ernie*."

"How far is *Bert* standing off?" she asked.

"Right now, about fifty-five meters. But see how the back wall of the ravine slopes out? The deeper we go, the closer we can approach with the sled." Wolfe pointed to the upper left-hand corner of the sketch, from which a solid red line sliced diagonally toward the center of the ravine. "That's where we first picked up the furrow. We've been following it eastward for about fifteen minutes."

Haddix saw that the vehicles were now roughly halfway down and nearly level with the widest point of the massive indentation.

Wolfe dropped his finger below the red line. Two thirds of the way down the ravine, where its walls started to dramatically narrow, McConkey had drawn a dotted horizontal line. "Cowboy calculates the gradient of the upper field at about seventy degrees. Past this drop-off it increases to ninety degrees."

Haddix groaned. "So unless *Dakar* got hung up on something before it reached the drop-off, it slid to the very bottom, down into this bear trap."

"Looks that way," Trent agreed.

From outside, another blast from the Zippo Squad.

"How much dynamite are we carrying?" she asked.

"Enough to see us through till dawn. Listen, Jonesy, Zeman said your first transmission to Suitland was via Delta cipher. I haven't seen any encoding equipment aboard. How'd you do it?"

"One of Q department's little black boxes. Why?"

"We're moving into the red zone. A lot of what we say to the beach is going to be sensitive."

Haddix nodded. "There's a spare PC in the utility van. If you go get that, I'll set the rest of it up."

"Liz, how's my tether?" asked Haddix from her seat at the ROV station.

Liz Trimble, flying the sled from the station to Haddix's left, looked at her monitor and replied, "E.J., you're nearing maximum reach."

Haddix started to issue the necessary commands. Then she remembered that with Roland Vigneron locked away and manpower back to full strength, they now had a full-time watch officer on duty again. As she started to gain altitude with *Ernie* she said, "Rick, can you reposition us closer to the eastern wall?"

"Roger that," Wolfe replied from the rear of the van. He studied his chart for a moment, then turned to j.g. Kabelo, who despite a broken arm was manning sonar. "Jeff, we need to head south by southeast. Any problems with that scarp?"

"Negative, Doc."

"Len, give us five-zero meters on a heading of one-seven-one."

"Five-zero meters on a heading of one-seven-one," navigator Heppel replied as he keyboarded instructions to *Fanning II*'s screws and thrusters.

The tension in the van immediately lifted. Several of the crew slumped back in their seats; others did quick neck-stretching exercises.

Haddix, whose aches had subsided under mission adrenaline, reached atop the console to retrieve her first mug of fresh coffee in more than two days. Not surprisingly, it had gone cold. For the past twenty minutes, since relieving Ezra Schell, she had continued tracking the furrow eastward across the silted upper field. She had then piloted *Ernie* below the drop-off, and was now approaching the eastern wall at a point just slightly more than one hundred yards above the bottom of the ravine. Soon, she thought, they would find it soon. . . .

As *Fanning II* settled into its new position, the chitchat in the van trailed off.

Haddix turned back to *Ernie*'s controls and coaxed the little ROV farther down the steepening lower field.

"Range to wall, one-zero-zero meters," Kabelo called out.

"One-zero-zero meters," Haddix responded. "What was *Dakar*'s length?"

"Two hundred eighty feet . . . that's eight-seven meters, give or take," Wendell Trent said from his seat at the *Bert* engineering station.

Haddix brought *Ernie*'s nose up to increase the range of its zoom-equipped pan-and-tilt camera. If the submarine lay ahead, it should be coming into view; there was nothing but more furrow. "Damn, it kept going south," she said. "You want some pictures of banged-up rock, or should I continue down?"

"Hold your present course, Jonesy," Trent said. "We might as well document everything."

As the ROV approached the eastern wall, he began firing off a set of electronic stills. The scars left by the submarine as it ricocheted to starboard were amply evident.

". . . nine-seven-five," Trent said to Reliance technician Denny Flanagan, who as data logger was recording the frame numbers. "Nine-seven-six . . ."

"Sonar, range to bottom?" said Haddix, keeping the ROV in its hover.

Just then the Zippo Squad blew off another stick. Kabelo waited for the spike to fade, then replied, "I make it at about nine-zero meters."

Haddix turned to Trimble. "Liz, why don't you start down so Trent can get an overview with your pan-and-tilt. I'll follow you after I get a closer look at that wall. Watch the tether, though . . . don't let it get too taut."

"Roger that, E.J."

"And that back wall's curving out toward us. Don't be shy about asking sonar for your range."

Trimble nodded and began to winch out the cable supporting the sled.

"Okay, Jonesy," Trent said. "On with the show."

Concentrating on the small console monitor carrying the feed from *Ernie*'s forward camera, Haddix banked the ROV to starboard.

This lower portion of the ravine was too steep to hold silt. She

studied the exposed bedrock, which was visibly disturbed, and realized that when the submarine slammed off the wall, it must have
triggered a series of miniavalanches. Suddenly, the hairs on her
nape bristled. Could the landslides have been heavy enough to bury
Dakar?

"Sonar," Liz Trimble called out, "what's my range to the back
wall?"

"Two-five meters and closing . . ."

"Oh, my God," Trent said softly. "Monitor Four, everyone."

Haddix quickly looked above her.

The feed from *Bert*'s pan-and-tilt camera showed that down below, where the ravine ended in a narrow defile, something lay partially covered by rocks and silt; something that was large and dark
—and unmistakably man-made.

WASHINGTON, D.C.

1314 Zulu/9:14 A.M. local time

Too impatient to wait in the DOE communications room for the
sporadic messages relayed from Suitland—Wendell Trent and Edna
Haddix were still in the midst of reconnoitering the second ravine—
Clifford Zeman had returned to his office. Now, standing at a window, he found himself watching several Asian tourists on Independence Avenue. They were taking turns snapping photographs of
each other in front of the entrance to the building. If they knew
who worked here, he thought darkly, they probably wouldn't waste
the film: Welcome to the Department of Energy, where crisis mis-
management is our most important product.

Zeman attributed his grumpiness to the infuriatingly slow progress out in the Med, but in fact it was the product of nearly one

hundred consecutive hours of frantic mental gymnastics, unremitting stress, and bitter reversals. What's more, he knew things would soon get worse. His deputy director was due to land at National Airport at noon, and it wouldn't surprise Zeman if Bart were met at the boarding gate by his old college pal, the senator. How long after that before Bart pulled the plug—the end of the day? Would Trent and Haddix have completed the mission by then?

His intercom buzzed.

"Yes, Carol."

"It's Jeanne, on line three."

Zeman picked up the receiver. "Hi. What's up?"

"Cliff, did you go to London while I was out in Weyers Cave?"

"Of course not!"

"A telegram just came to the house. It's from a cab company over there. You are to call them immediately . . . something about damages to one of their taxis."

There was a knock at his door.

"Hold on a sec, Jeanne." Turning to the door, he said, "Yes."

Zeman's heart sank as Eugene Da Silva entered, a bulging file folder under one arm. He motioned the oddly ashen business manager to take a seat, then resumed his conversation. "There must be some mistake, dear."

"They say they traced you through the subscription label of an angling magazine that was left in the taxi. Cliff, I think it's one of the ones you get."

"Oh, sweet Jesus."

"What is it?"

"I wasn't in London. But one of the men on this operation had to go there, and he borrowed one of my magazines."

"Then you better take down their phone number."

"Not today, dear, not today. Look, I have to run. You'd better not wait dinner on me. Love you."

Zeman replaced the receiver and turned to face the departmental Torquemada.

Eugene Da Silva returned Zeman's gaze for several moments.

Finally, in a subdued voice, he said, "I arrived at my office at seven-thirty this morning. Since then I have done nothing except log the invoices charged against account four naught naught three naught eight-slant-OBS."

He hefted the file folder. "These are most, but not all, of the ones that arrived over the weekend. Several more came in even as I worked. Mr. Zeman, have you any idea how much money you have spent?"

Zeman shook his head.

"The invoices through Sunday afternoon alone total in excess of five hundred twenty thousand dollars. I was also formally notified by ONYXX that you have committed this department to assuming the charter on one of their research vessels, at a cost of some fifty thousand dollars per day. I gather your use of said vessel is not yet concluded?"

"Correct, Mr. Da Silva."

"I see. Then it is safe to project a final sum in the vicinity of one million dollars. Mr. Zeman, I did not come here to question you about your operation, although I fail to grasp what nuclear secrets might lie in the middle of the Mediterranean Sea. I did not come here to chastise you for your disdainful attitude toward taxpayer dollars. I am here to inform you that you leave me with no choice but to bring these exorbitant invoices to the attention of our deputy director."

Da Silva stood. "Accordingly, I have asked his secretary, Ms. Lott, for the earliest possible appointment, which, I believe, is at three P.M. I wanted you to learn of the meeting from me, rather than from the deputy director."

"Understood, Mr. Da Silva. Thank you for the courtesy."

The business manager hesitated. "Perhaps you will find this inappropriate, but may I say that our, uh, unpleasantness of last Friday evening has no bearing on my present course of action? I must admit I was hurt by your refusal to confide in me. Yet even had you briefed me on the mission, these bills . . . I would be derelict to not pursue this matter."

"You have your job to do, Mr. Da Silva. I have mine."

As soon as Da Silva left the office, Zeman picked up his phone and dialed Ann Davis. "Annie, it's going to hit the fan when Bart gets back this afternoon. Call Suitland and get the two of us cleared for their communications room. Tell them we need to be in direct contact with Trent."

"It won't take Bart long to find us," she said.

"I'll take every minute of slack I can get."

"I hear you, Cliff. Want me to lay down a false scent? I can have Carol book us a late lunch at some restaurant across the river. Like three P.M. in Alexandria."

Zeman grinned. "As one of our former presidents once said, 'We could do that . . . but it would be wrong.' No, Annie, sooner or later I've got to face the music. But thanks."

Mr. Zeman seemed to have aged five years in just one weekend, Eugene Da Silva thought as he took the elevator down two floors; the mysterious operation appeared to be taking a heavy toll. Still, that was no excuse for the prodigal expenditures. It was fortunate that his wife had packed him a lunch this morning; he would need every minute between now and his meeting with the deputy director to analyze and summarize the flood of invoices.

The business manager got off the elevator and hurried to his office.

His secretary handed him two message slips. One was from his wife. The other was from the office of a senator. Da Silva knew of the man, of course—a Democrat who represented a midwestern state—but he hadn't the slightest clue as to the reason for the call.

He immediately went to his bookcase and pulled out a thick volume. According to the *Congressional Directory* the senator was a member of neither the DOE oversight committee nor any other body with even peripheral authority over the agency.

Da Silva hung up his jacket, called his wife back, and put the other message aside.

Five minutes later he had resumed entering data into the computer spreadsheet when his secretary buzzed; the senator's office was calling again.

"Mr. Eugene Da Silva?"

"Yes?"

"Kindly hold for the senator."

A farfetched thought ran through Da Silva's mind. In recent years he had heard stories about legislators soliciting reelection funds from bureaucrats. The practice was unethical, and few members of either house would waste their time on a salaried GS-14 like himself. Yet what other business could the senator conceivably have with him?

A few clicks, and a booming voice came over the line: "Hello, Silver? Thanks for returning my call so promptly."

"Uh, you're welcome, sir," Da Silva replied, deciding not to correct the senator.

"Listen, Silver, I've never had the pleasure of meeting you, but I've got a favor to ask."

Da Silva hesitated, then reluctantly said, "Yes, sir?"

"It's come to my attention that somebody over at your shop is running a very—how should I put this?—a very unorthodox operation."

Da Silva reflexively glanced at the stack of invoices chargeable to Mr. Zeman, but remained silent.

After several seconds the senator said, "I suppose my call to you is also unorthodox. But let me be frank . . . my efforts to obtain information through normal channels are being stonewalled. So I asked my staff, Who has his finger on the pulse over there? My people tell me the answer is you, Silver."

"I am flattered, sir, but I—"

"All I'm looking for is a lead or two," the senator continued, "no classified documents or anything like that. Just a little something to initiate a subcommittee hearing. Naturally, what you tell me will be treated with the utmost confidence."

Da Silva, caught between his innate deference and his growing uneasiness, tried again. "Mr. Senator—"

"Since the clock's running, Silver, how about noon today, if you don't have a lunch? One of my senior aides can meet you up here—"

"Mr. Senator, may I say something?"

"Sure, go ahead."

Da Silva took a moment to compose himself. His years in government had taught him a healthy respect for senators and the power they wielded—and an even greater respect for institutional rules. Rules were the bulwark against chaos. Yes, Mr. Zeman had violated departmental procedures. But no matter how serious his transgressions, Mr. Zeman should be held accountable by the department itself, rather than by an outside tribunal. Da Silva's sense of propriety was deeply felt; he only hoped he would be able to adequately convey it to the senator. "Sir, I am afraid I am not at liberty to discuss my department's fiscal matters with anyone outside the department. May I respectfully suggest you make your inquiries to my deputy director?"

There was a lengthy pause before the senator said, "If you're afraid of that prick Zeman, I can protect you from him. Guaranteed."

"Sir?" asked a baffled Da Silva.

"It's a matter of public record. I was a major cosponsor of the whistle-blowing bill. I did it so little people like you can speak your mind freely and without fear of retaliation. You tell me this Zeman character's trying to silence you, I'll have his butt for breakfast."

"Mr. Senator, no one at the department is trying to silence me. There are rules. I obey them. When and if you obtain my deputy director's permission, I shall be happy to meet with you or your staff and discuss any . . ."

Da Silva's voice trailed off because the senator had hung up.

Apparently, Mr. Zeman's tightly compartmented operation was no longer much of a secret. But what was its objective—why in the world was it provoking a senator to mount such an unusual fishing expedition? Da Silva set down the receiver and regarded the invoices. And why in the world was it costing so much? Heck, on that budget Mr. Zeman could almost start a small war.

THE EASTERN MED
1457 Zulu/5:57 P.M. local time

The submarine at the bottom of Ravine C, a full 12,150 feet below *Fanning II*, resembled, in Wendell Trent's words, "one of my son Matty's toys when he was two . . . before he realized plastic breaks when you stomp on it."

It had taken the crew some time to piece together a coherent picture of the boat. The floods arrayed on *Bert* and *Ernie*, though powerful, were nevertheless insufficient to illuminate the entire vessel at one time; the initial reconnaissance pass had been like driving at night on a darkened highway, with only that stretch of pavement within headlight range revealed.

It was unquestionably a World War II–vintage T-class patrol boat. Yet absent exterior markings, there was no way of confirming that this was in fact *Dakar* other than by going inside.

The vessel was basically in one piece, albeit just barely.

The images on the monitors bore terrible witness to the violence of its final dive: dented metal, punctured metal, metal ripped wide open, and, everywhere, large blotches of rust as black as dried blood.

After broadsiding the eastern wall higher up, it had been carried downward by gravity and topography into a V-shaped bear trap at the base of the ravine, some 350 feet above the floor of the Hellencian Trench.

Now, slewed bow first across a severe incline, the submarine resembled a giant black cigar mashed into a funnel filled with dark gray silt. Its bottom and its lower starboard side had dug into the silt to a depth of five feet. The hull was further surrounded by ridges of detritus that had washed down in its wake.

Upon completing one pass around the broken vessel Edna Haddix had tucked the ROV inside the sled's garage and moved back to the *Bert* engineering station. Second only to Roland Vigneron at digitally enhancing the images captured by the electronic still camera now aboard *Ernie,* she was patiently scanning each of the several dozen frames that had been retrieved and permanently stored on the laser disc. Beside her stood Trent, intently watching the images form on Monitor Five and adding details to the rough sketch of *Dakar* he had begun in London.

The first section they had inspected, the tail, was partially severed and lay at an awkward angle to the spine.

The forward seven-eighths of the submarine had slid deeper into the bear trap. It had come to rest diagonally across an impossibly steep one-hundred-degree slope, with a severe list to starboard. The boat would have continued tumbling to the floor of the Trench had it not caught on a large boulder amidships and had its bow not buried itself into the western wall of the bear trap. That awesome impact had gouged out a deep niche in which the bow was now cradled, and pancaked the starboard hull clear back to what remained of the conning tower.

The double hull was breached in a number of places, but Trent and Haddix had thus far identified only three openings sufficiently large to accommodate *Ernie.* Each bore the characteristic inward-curling edges of an implosion. The first gash was atop the stern, where the tail section had split. The second was a ruptured ballast tank on the vessel's exposed port side, one of a series of punctures left by its wild descent down the ravine. The third was at the forward base of the virtually decapitated conning tower.

But gaining access through any of them was easier said than done. The techs had reconfigured *Ernie* to allow the vehicle to execute crude banking maneuvers. Yet the openings in the hull all lay considerably off the vertical and horizontal axes; squirming the ROV through them would require considerable finesse and luck.

Nor would a successful entry necessarily guarantee them a thorough inspection of the interior. *Ernie*'s range was limited by the length of the tether that connected it to *Bert.* Ordinarily, to maximize the little ROV's reach, the sled would snuggle right up to the hull. In this instance, though, the risks were too great. Both Wolfe and Haddix believed the western wall of the bear trap had been structurally weakened when it was rammed by the submarine. Thus, if *Bert* drew too close to the unstable wall and began to pendulum—always a danger in heavy seas—the sled would act as a two-ton wrecking ball that could bring the rock face down on the submarine. Further, in gouging out a sizable chunk of the wall, the boat had left behind a jagged formation that extended out over the hull. This outcrop could easily foul the cable that linked *Bert* with *Fanning II.* For those reasons the sled would have to keep its distance from the submarine, which in turn meant that the ROV would be on an uncomfortably short leash.

"Hey, check this out," Haddix said, keyboarding commands to boost magnification on the latest electronic still.

Outside, another muffled explosion, but by this time those in the van were inured to the Zippo Squad's handiwork.

Trent studied the two circular grooves that lay side by side atop the hull. "Are you calling these up in sequence?"

"Affirmative," Haddix replied. "These are, let's see, about thirty-eight feet forward of the conning tower."

"Those ports weren't on the original boat, and they aren't on Cowling's list of mods. Damn. Remember those other new ports near the stern, the ones feeding into those tanks they added in the aft torpedo room? Why cut two more up front?" Trent scratched his chin. "You know, it's almost as if . . ."

"As if?"

"Ever since Zeman passed on the news about Cowling's disappearing act, I've been suspicious of those blueprints. But this is more than just a little cockeyed. Jonesy, if I didn't know for certain that no T-class was ever reported down within a hundred miles of here, I'd say this isn't *Dakar*."

She glanced up questioningly.

"Take the position of the conning tower. Cowling said they added the twenty feet to the stern, which should place the rear of the conning tower about a hundred and fifty feet forward of the tail. Sure doesn't look it to me. I wish to hell the bow was intact . . . I'd love to get an accurate measurement on this sucker." Trent spotted Rick Wolfe approaching them. "Doc, anything glowing down there?"

Wolfe, who had been checking the computer-stored data from the gamma ray detector aboard *Ernie,* shook his head. "I went over the entire file. Not a blip."

"Maybe you're right, Trent," Haddix said. "Maybe this isn't *Dakar.* Or maybe it is, but everyone guessed wrong on its cargo."

"We won't know until we get inside, will we?"

Wolfe said to Haddix, "How's your review coming?"

"Last nine frames," she replied, turning back to the console. "Our friend Trent has a heavy trigger finger."

Wolfe looked at the latest version of Trent's sketch.

"Here are our possible points of entry, Doc," Trent said. "Three so far. First, atop the stern, aft of the engine room. If those two tanks were installed in there, like the prints indicate, it'd sure shorten our mission. Second, through this ballast tank, which I calculate opens into the crew quarters. Finally, there, by the conning tower. The tightest squeeze of all, and we're really blocked by that outcrop."

"Make that four openings," Haddix said. "Provided we can dislodge one mean rock."

Trent and Wolfe looked up at Monitor Five.

The electronic still she had just enhanced showed another large gash near the bow, deeper down the port hull. The rock to which she referred was an irregularly shaped slab, some two and a half feet across, that tilted across and blocked the lower part of the opening. In addition, the slab was heaped with debris that obstructed even more of the hole: rocks and silt that had tumbled down after the submarine, as well as man-made objects—bottles and cans, broken plates, pots—spilling out from one of the breaches higher up the hull.

Trent began to draw it on his sketch. "Jonesy, how far forward of the conning tower?"

"About forty-five feet."

"It should open into the forward torpedo room, then."

Wolfe studied the echo sounder plot of this portion of the bear trap. "E.J., any shots of that opening from a lower camera angle?"

Haddix zipped through the remaining frames. "Negative, Rick. As I remember it, there were a couple of large boulders that prevented me from dropping *Ernie* any deeper."

"Then let's hope we don't have to make an entry through here."

"How's that, Doc?" said Trent. "Can't we use the arms to move that slab away?"

"Maybe, maybe not. That's not what worries me, though. If *Ernie* can't get any lower, neither can *Bert*. Remember, the tether that links them is buoyant. If the sled has to remain at a higher altitude when we go in with the ROV, the tether'll float up and chafe against the top of the opening. One sharp edge, one wrong move, and we lose *Ernie* inside the hull."

"Warning noted. Jonesy, anything else of interest?"

She shook her head.

"Then let's take it from the top." Trent turned to the extra PC to peck out a brief update to transmit to Cliff Zeman via Haddix's versatile CD player.

Haddix began gathering her notes.

Wolfe knelt beside her. "Somehow, I don't think there'll be any idle watches from here on in."

"Yup," she said, "time for the last roundup."

"We're the only ones who'll be flying *Ernie* for the duration. What say we alternate sorties? It'll keep us both fresher."

"Sounds good to me. You want the next one?"

He nodded.

"Then you'd better tell me how to access the gamma-ray readout, and what to look for on it."

The most accessible opening was the one highest up the nose-down hull, atop the stern just aft of the submarine's engine room. The bare metal that lined the perimeter of the gash had oxidized over two decades, spilling dark ribbons of rusticles down the hull.

Liz Trimble had positioned the sled thirty feet from, and ten feet below, the opening. *Bert*'s forward-camera feed, displayed on the main monitor, was vertiginously disorienting. The seas were still high, and the sled was yo-yoing in rhythm with *Fanning II;* when it reached the top of its travel, the van crew could see most of the elliptical hole, but at the depth of its bob their view was mostly of the silt in which the submarine sat.

Rick Wolfe had positioned little *Ernie* above the opening, with the bow of the boat to his starboard and its tail to port. He started to descend. Under the strengthening beams of the approaching ROV's lights, the rusticles on the hull seemed to magically permute from black to crimson to bright orange.

Haddix pressed the red button at the right of the *Bert* engineering station to shoot another electronic still, then called out the frame number to data processor Glenn Marullo. "Ten-two-two."

"How's my tether, Liz?" asked Wolfe.

"Hold on a sec . . . it's fine, Dr. Wolfe."

"This may be an odd time to say this, Liz, but you don't have to be so formal . . . you can call me Rick."

"Just don't call him late for dinner," Trent added.

A wave of tension-cutting chuckles swept through the van.

"Ten-two-three, ten-two-four," Haddix said.

The breach in the top of the submarine was barely wider than the ROV. To enter it Wolfe needed to nose *Ernie* downward while simultaneously tilting it fifty degrees to port. He used the thrusters to bank the vehicle over as far as it would go—but still couldn't match the entry angle.

Navigator Len Heppel let out a soft curse.

Wolfe studied the situation for a few moments, then extended the ROV's two mechanical arms until he could clamp their pincers onto opposite sides of the opening. The contact knocked loose several clumps of rusticles and sent orange and red specks swirling through the water. Then, using the arms for leverage, Wolfe continued to torque the ROV onto its port side until its angle matched that of the opening.

"Great job, Doc," Trent said.

Wolfe let out a deep breath, then asked, "How's my top clearance?"

"You are good to go."

Wolfe began to bend the arms in as he nudged the throttle and inched *Ernie* forward.

"Ten-two-five," Haddix called out. "Ten-two-six."

All eyes were locked on Monitor Two, which displayed the feed from the ROV's forward camera.

Suddenly, the oppressively black deep-sea environment to which the crew had grown accustomed gave way to a breathtakingly riotous palette of reds and oranges as *Ernie*'s lights illuminated the rust-riddled interior. The view was almost straight down into the aft torpedo room. In the center of the compartment dangled wires and cables that had been ripped loose during the submarine's death plunge; they now weaved eerily in the pressure waves generated by the ROV's entrance.

Off to the left a blind crab turned toward an intruder felt rather than seen, then scuttled away.

"Jonesy, we getting a radiation reading in here?"

Haddix stopped snapping electronic stills and logged her computer over to the gamma-ray data stream. She studied the numbers scrolling across her screen, then replied, "Negative."

Beyond the free-floating tangle of wires and cables, down on the floor of the vessel, sat banks of large storage batteries separated by an aisle.

"Ten-three-one," Haddix called out, firing off another electronic still.

Trent finished counting the batteries and blew out his breath in disgust. "Not nearly as many cells as in the mods. Doc, can you come nine-zero degrees to starboard and give us a look forward?"

"Nine-zero degrees to starboard." Wolfe carefully disengaged the pincers from the hull, descended fully inside the compartment, and waited for the ROV to stabilize. "Liz, how's my tether?"

"Tether clear."

Wolfe slowly skirted several free-floating cables, then pivoted *Ernie* clockwise until it was aligned with the submarine's spine and facing forward.

From the *Bert* engineering station Haddix swiveled the ROV's pan-and-tilt camera down on the bulkhead that separated the tail compartment from the engine room.

"My God," Trent said.

Haddix's former skipper, Jack, had been right. The objects instantly commanding all attention were the rubber-soled boots—a single right and two lefts—lying against the bulkhead, to the right of the closed hatch. The men who had died in them, as well as their clothing, had long since been consumed by fish. Only the boots, made of treated leather, remained, along with a macabre collection of similarly indigestible metal zippers and plastic buttons. These were strewn amid an assortment of tools, cans, and plastic containers that had gravitated to the lowest corner of the bulkhead.

There was, however, nary a tank marked WATER or OXYGEN, nary a pipe or valve leading to the external ports they had spotted atop the hull.

After several moments Trent said, "I make the range to the bulkhead at about twenty feet. Jonesy? Doc? Anyone?"

"Hold on a second, and we'll know exactly," Haddix replied. She hit the red button to take another electronic still, then keyboarded in the code to turn on the laser spot ranger mounted on the bow of the ROV.

A fresh digital readout superimposed itself over the feed from *Ernie*'s forward camera: "7.223 m."

"A little shy of twenty-four feet," Trent muttered. "Jonesy, let's see what the butt camera's showing."

Haddix punched the feed from the ROV's rear-mounted camera up onto one of the large forward monitors.

"Can you aim the spotter back here?" asked Trent.

"That's a negative," she replied. "It's fix positioned."

"I make it to be about half the distance," navigator Heppel ventured. "Three and a half, four meters tops."

Trent consulted his sketch of *Dakar* and scowled. "According to the mods, they added twenty extra feet back here, which should've stretched this compartment to a little over fifty-five feet. We're looking at about thirty-five max . . . the configuration on the original boat."

"How about on the other side of the bulkhead?" asked Haddix. "We know they cut new external ports back here. Could the tanks be in the engine room?"

"Jonesy, no way we're going to fit the vehicle through that hatch."

"We don't have to," she said. "All we have to do is peek inside."

"Which means opening the hatch. Do we have enough power to do that? Look at how it's hinged . . . on this side, so we've got to lift its entire weight."

"Can do," Haddix said confidently. "*Ernie* can undog the wheel unless it's jammed. The engine room's got to be flooded, so there won't be any pressure differential. Finally, the hinges are to starboard . . . the downhill side . . . which means we've got gravity working for us."

Trent hesitated, then nodded. "Okay, let's give it a go. Doc?"

Wolfe angled *Ernie*'s nose downward and flew the ROV toward the white watertight door in the center of the bulkhead. Stenciled on it were the usual warnings but not, alas, the name of the submarine. He stopped the vehicle three feet from the door.

Haddix, staring intently at the forward-camera feed, breathed easier. Pirouetting the ROV to turn the hatch wheel was not as simple as she had implied. Fortunately, they wouldn't have to; the hatch had separated slightly from the bulkhead, no doubt sprung by an implosion or by the submarine's jarring collisions with the walls of the ravine.

Wolfe extended *Ernie*'s mechanical arms, positioned both hands on the hatch wheel at the nine o'clock position, and locked the pincers. Redirecting the thrusters to push up and back, he applied power.

The van crew could sense the ROV straining by the perceptible jiggle in the camera feeds, yet the views remained unchanging.

Wolfe applied more power.

Suddenly, all monitors went to black.

"Shit, what happened?"

"No problem, just a few blown circuit breakers," Haddix announced as she quickly reset them.

The monitors flickered to life as the lights sprang back on.

Wolfe throttled up again.

Still no movement.

He hesitated, then continued increasing the thrust.

"All right, Rick!" exclaimed Trent as the hatch grudgingly lifted free.

The gap grew to four inches, then a foot.

"Rick, you might try angling . . ."

"What the hell . . ."

With throat-catching suddenness a silver blur bulleted out of the blackness beyond the hatch and rushed the camera, blocking out all light as it mushroomed to fill the monitor.

The dancing images took a few seconds to stabilize, for the panicky fish that had collided head on with the camera had been of goodly size. The nervous titters sweeping the van were like those a ghost story might elicit from a campfire audience of seven-year-olds.

Wolfe regathered his wits. Recognizing that he had insufficient aft clearance to move the ROV diagonally—and thus keep it behind the pivoting hatch—he said, "Bear with me."

First, he crabbed *Ernie* to port to increase the leverage of its mechanical arms. Then he applied reverse thrust and slowly drew both arms to the right.

The hatch began to swing open on its hinges.

At the one-third point of the hatch's travel Wolfe stopped. "Any farther and the arms'll be pinned. I think I better release them and try to shove the door over. It may land with a hell of a thud, but I can't see any other way."

"Agreed," Trent said.

Wolfe laboriously pivoted *Ernie* clockwise through almost 180 degrees until the ROV faced the rear of the compartment and the port side of its stern was hard against the inside of the hatch. His view of the mechanical arms was blocked, but he managed to unclench both sets of pincers from the hatch wheel and snake the arms free.

The entire weight of the hatch now rested on the tail of the vehicle.

"Land soft, baby, land soft," Wolfe said, kicking up the power.

The hatch succumbed to the ROV's thrust and continued to swing open. Finally, it fell away, striking the starboard wall hard enough to send a cloud of rust particles swirling about the compartment.

"Outstanding piece of flying, Doc," Trent said with unconcealed relief.

Wolfe leaned back and flexed his neck muscles before bringing *Ernie* back around to face the bulkhead.

As the vehicle descended, Haddix began to shoot electronic stills of the engine room that lay through the open hatchway. "Ten-three-eight. Ten-three-nine . . . Son of a bitch."

In the harsh glare of the lights that penetrated the dark void, it was obvious that the compartment held a pair of diesel engines—period.

Trent slumped against the chart table. "Those mods are absolutely full of shit. Where did they stick the extra twenty feet? And why did they bother cutting dummy ports in the hull?"

"So that from the outside, the boat would conform to the bogus blueprints," Haddix said.

"Yeah." Trent straightened. "Doc, get us out of here. It's time to try our luck farther down."

Having assumed control of *Ernie,* Edna Haddix was maintaining the ROV in a hover off to one side while navigator Joe Reuss and *Bert* flyer Tom Parkhill worked to reposition the sled lower down the hull of the submarine. They were two of the fresh bodies on the rejiggered eight-to-twelve watch, along with Billy Ray McConkey, who despite his injuries was substituting for Ariel Kahane as the sonar man. Rick Wolfe had shifted from flying the ROV back to the *Bert* engineering station, where he was processing electronic stills for Wendell Trent's review, and Liz Trimble had stayed on to take over data-logging duties.

Haddix would attempt to penetrate the submarine through its ruptured port ballast tank.

The problem confronting Reuss and Parkhill was the large boulder supporting the midships of the submarine. To prevent the sled from smashing into the boulder on its downswings, Parkhill needed to keep it well above the opening—thereby exposing the buoyant ROV tether to the sharp edges at the top of the breach. The alternative position, lower down but some twenty feet farther from the boat, would dramatically limit *Ernie*'s range inside the hull.

Parkhill turned and said, "E.J., which part of the boat are you concentrating on?"

"Trent?"

He looked up.

"Positioning *Bert* depends on where we want to search," she said. "I think that would be forward, down toward the bow."

Trent massaged the back of his neck, then nodded. "If the tanks in those damn prints are actually aboard, they won't be aft of the opening. No external ports to service them. You're right . . . we'll do a long-range photo recon of the crew quarters, but concentrate forward."

Parkhill winched out cable until the sled had dropped to within twelve feet of the boulder. Eyes glued to his monitor, he waited out a complete up-and-down cycle, then eased it down another two feet. Finally satisfied that *Bert* would remain clear of the boulder, he said, "All yours, E.J."

"Battle stations," Haddix announced, angling *Ernie* deeper into the ravine.

The bow of the submarine lay downhill, to her port, and its tail uphill, to starboard.

"Ten-five-two, ten-five-three," Wolfe called out from the *Bert* engineering station.

Haddix saw that this gash was larger than the one Wolfe had entered at the stern, but the sundered metal along its edges was considerably more jagged. She banked the vehicle to port to align it with the opening. Piece of cake, she thought; unlike Wolfe she wouldn't have to use the mechanical arms to force the ROV's port flank lower.

"How's my tether, Parkhill?"

"Tether clear."

Haddix nosed *Ernie* a few inches inside, then stopped.

Dead ahead, some three feet past the inner hull, lay several dark rectangles that barred the way. The squatter obstructions to her right filled the lower three quarters of the feed from the ROV's forward camera; running across them were rusted pipes and tubes. The taller unit on the left was covered by a field of grill-like coils oxidized to a flame color by long exposure to seawater.

Trent consulted his sketch and groaned. "Stoves and a refrigerator. We've come in through the back of the galley. Why the hell didn't those things break loose and slide forward?"

Haddix extended the ROV's right arm until it touched one of the stoves, then applied forward thrust.

"No go," she said. "I can't budge it. But I have some room to work with."

"Enough to squeeze past?" asked Trent.

"Give me a moment."

The vehicle's cameras all pointed downward. Haddix backed *Ernie* out of the opening and nosed its bow upward to raise the forward camera.

From this new angle the stoves still dominated the forward-camera feed—yet above them the ROV's lights bounced off the far wall of the galley. Had the top edge of the opening been higher, or had there been more jockeying space between the inner hull and the backs of the appliances, she could have just slanted *Ernie* up over the stoves. The angles here were too acute, though; if she attempted such a maneuver, she would most likely wedge the vehicle in an irretrievable position.

Damn it, what sat above the stoves? "Trent, Cowboy, why would they have set the stoves that far back from the inner hull?"

"Probably to put in shelves or cabinets over them," McConkey said.

"Affirmative, it's shelving," Trent said, consulting his sketch. He peered through the red gloom of the van at the clock on the forward wall. It was nearly nine P.M.—outside, real dusk had also descended—but this was no time to hurry Jonesy.

Haddix continued to stare at her monitor, trying to visualize how to negotiate her vehicle through the tight spaces. "God, I wish we had thought to slap a minicam on the end of each arm," she muttered. "This is going to be like trying to wrestle a grand piano out of a New York tenement. Any hints, guys?"

Billy Ray McConkey finally broke the silence. "I didn't know you were from New York."

"I'm not, Cowboy," she replied distractedly. "Spent a summer there once. A cold-water flat down in Alphabet City . . . Avenue B and Third Street."

"And you took a grand piano with you?"

"It was his. He was studying at Juilliard. . . ." Strategy plotted, Haddix squared her shoulders and said, "Well, here goes."

She needed to make a sequence of three moves. First, insert *Ernie* into the space between the inner hull and the appliances so that its bow pointed to the rear of the submarine, its roof faced the inner hull, and its starboard flank lay lengthwise just above the floor of the submarine. Then, pivot the ROV's bow toward the ceiling until it was standing upright behind the stoves. If she got that far, all that remained would be to nose the bow down over the stove tops and glide into the galley.

The vehicle was still hovering two feet from the hull, banked to port to keep its bow parallel with the opening.

Haddix reset the vertical thrusters and pitched *Ernie* to starboard until its bow lay almost at right angles to the opening. Good, she noted; there should be enough clearance.

She nudged the ROV forward.

The camera feeds shuddered as the roof of the vehicle snubbed against the edge of the opening.

Haddix stopped eighteen inches from the nearest stove and waited for the images to stabilize. From this close range the views were unfocused, but she could see that her angle of entry was still too high; the ROV's bow had to be forced both upward and farther to starboard.

The vertical thrusters were at maximum throttle.

Haddix thought for a few moments, then extended the vehicle's left arm and clamped the pincers atop the stove. With this new leverage, she redirected *Ernie*'s bow and applied forward power.

The camera feeds danced.

"How much of me is inside?" she asked.

"Three quarters, Jonesy," Trent replied encouragingly as he consulted one of the shots from the sled. "You're looking good."

"How's my tether?"

"Tether clear," Parkhill said.

Haddix continued pirouetting the ROV into the submarine.

Suddenly, *Ernie* balked at her commands.

"What's snagging?" she barked in frustration.

"Your starboard afterthruster, Jonesy."

"Shit."

"Look, if you can't fit through here," Trent said, "we'll try down near the conning tower."

Haddix's eyes darted up to the main monitor, which displayed the feed from *Bert*'s forward camera. "Trent, request permission to blast my way in. The worst we can do is break off the protective shroud. *Ernie*'ll still fly."

"Then do it, Jonesy."

Haddix realigned the vertical thrusters, took a deep breath, and throttled up to the stops.

The feeds from the ROV's cameras began to shudder again.

On the main monitor the van crew watched the starboard after-thruster's shroud crumple—and then snap off.

Ernie's suddenly freed stern slammed through the opening and down onto the back of the stove, the impact jolting loose a cloud of rust particles.

"Great job, Jonesy . . . we're in!"

From around the van a chorus of approval.

As Haddix waited for the red snowstorm to subside, it suddenly occurred to her that she—and not Trent—had been the first to re-flexively push a vehicle beyond its capabilities. So much for her preconceived fears.

When the visibility cleared, she used the vehicle's left arm, which was still clamped to the top of the stove, and its thrusters to slowly pivot the bow counterclockwise. Trent and McConkey had been right; the space above the stoves was combed with wire shelving. The rusted metal readily gave way.

Haddix continued to bring *Ernie* around until it was standing upright, its roof still facing the inner hull.

Now, from the feeds sent by the ROV's belly-mounted cameras, they could see the far wall of the galley and part of the passageway beyond. As at the stern, these compartments were festooned with loose wires swaying in the pressure waves from the intruding vehicle. The wires also seemed to fall away at an impossible angle, though in fact they hung straight down. The optical illusion resulted from the fact that the submarine was resting far off horizontal; the boat's floorboards, to which the ROV stood perpendicular, canted severely to port and away from them.

Having gained her bearings, Haddix used the thrusters to deflect the vehicle's bow away from the inner hull.

Ernie swung down over the top of the stoves as gracefully as a Murphy bed from the wall.

Applause and sighs of relief, mixed in equal proportions, swept the van.

"Hot damn, Navy," McConkey chortled. "That was as outstanding as anything that Sigourney broad did in *Aliens*."

"Much appreciated, Cowboy," Haddix said. She checked to see that the left pincers were still mooring the ROV to the top of the stove, then pushed herself from her chair. "Why don't you all look at the pretty pictures while I try to find a pulse."

Rick Wolfe began to scan the galley with the pan-and-tilt camera.

The bottom half of the rust-streaked wall that separated the galley from the passageway was pyramided with an eclectic assortment of refuse: bottles and crushed cans, their paper labels long since eaten away; heavy skillets and pots, their black cast iron rusted into a medley of bright oranges; porcelain-coated pots, still shining white; aluminum pans, chalky from their long saline bath; sections of fallen shelving; plates and cups and glasses, some, surprisingly, intact; stainless steel utensils, untarnished as their day of manufacture.

"Doc, are we getting a reading in here?" asked Trent.

Wolfe, who had been documenting the scene with electronic stills, logged over to the gamma-ray-detector readouts. "Nope."

Haddix took another sip of Evian and finished her stretching exercises. She was returning to the ROV station when Trent intercepted her.

"Jonesy, you did good," he said softly. "Real good."

"Thanks. I kind of did, didn't I?"

He gave her a light squeeze on the arm, then headed back toward the chart table.

"How're we doing, Rick?" asked Haddix.

"Ten-four-eight . . . ten-four-nine." Wolfe looked up. "That should do it."

Haddix nodded. "Trent, where do you want to start?"

"Why don't you make a fast scan aft, into the crew quarters."

"Roger that." She climbed back into her chair and swiveled to the left to face *Bert* flyer Parkhill. "Tom, with all the twists and turns I made to get here, I figure my tether's more likely to catch on something back here than on the opening. I'm going to draw in the slack. Let me know when I get down to the last fifteen feet."

"Roger, E.J."

Haddix released the pincers that moored *Ernie* and pivoted the ROV through 180 degrees above the stoves. Then, using both mechanical arms, she patiently gathered in the buoyant tether, letting it float up in loose coils to the galley ceiling.

"Whoa . . . that's good," Parkhill finally said.

"Jonesy, how much range does that give you?" asked Trent.

"A little over forty feet."

Haddix wheeled *Ernie* around again to face the interior of the submarine. Moving forward until she was clear of the stoves, she dropped the vehicle to three feet above the floorboards to avoid the worst of the dangling wires and advanced out of the galley into the passageway.

The crew quarters lay steeply uphill to starboard.

Haddix turned into the narrow passageway, which was as off kilter as a funhouse corridor. It took her several moments to overcome the extreme disorientation and start *Ernie* climbing to aft.

Gradually, the ROV's floods began illuminating the large compartment.

"Unreal," Wolfe murmured.

Filling Monitor Two, which displayed the feed from *Ernie*'s forward camera, was what appeared to be a storm-devastated grove of white birch saplings; some of the skinny floor-to-ceiling poles were in place, but others were bent or missing.

"Aluminum stanchions," Trent said quietly. "Bunk supports . . . see how they're arranged in pairs? But where are the bunk frames? Doc, are you getting shots of this?"

Wolfe blinked, then began firing off electronic stills.

"Jonesy, I see things hanging from the stanchions," Trent said. "Can you come up higher without fouling on those wires?"

"Can do." Haddix moved deeper into the compartment and raised *Ernie* off the sloping floorboards. Spotting a cluster of intact stanchions relatively clear of the streaming wires, she sidled the vehicle over.

The hanging objects turned out to be badly tarnished brass rings. Two were affixed on opposite sides of the stanchion, slightly less than three feet off the floor, and a second pair some three feet above the first. Each stanchion seemed similarly fitted.

"What the hell was this, some kind of slave ship?" asked McConkey in an incredulous voice.

Trent thought for a moment, then said, "What's the front-to-back distance between pairs of stanchions?"

"Six, seven feet," Haddix replied.

Several of the others voiced agreement.

"I'd guess they were hammock rings," Trent said. "The quickest, most weight-efficient way to increase the number of people you can carry. Jonesy, gain as much altitude as you can so Doc can pan the area. Let's try to figure out how many they could accommodate back here."

Haddix continued climbing toward the rear of the cabin until she ran out of tether.

Wolfe slowly swiveled the pan-and-tilt camera through 360 degrees. "It's hard to see all the way to the back, but I count eleven or twelve pairs along each side."

Trent did a quick calculation at the side of his sketch.

"Eleven pairs would give them eighty hammocks," he announced. "Why? A boat this size didn't carry that large a crew. Besides, at least a third of them would've been standing watch at any given time."

"Trent, how many aboard *Dakar* when it went down?" asked Haddix.

"Sixty-nine."

"Or so the Israelis claimed."

McConkey swore softly. "If all those hammocks carried bodies, it must have been a living hell in here."

"Especially if this is *Dakar*," Trent agreed. "That boat came here all the way from the North Atlantic, nonstop. Doc, you through taking pictures? Then let's get this show on the road."

Haddix turned *Ernie* back toward the bow of the submarine and began descending back toward the galley. Nearing the entrance to the passageway, she noticed several dark shapes near the ceiling bobbing in the pressure waves.

"Look at that," she said, coming to a stop.

"Ten-seven-zero," Wolfe called out as he captured an electronic still of three rucksacks suspended from an overhead pipe by loops of lightweight chain. "Those sure don't look like standard military issue."

"Leather or rubber," Trent said. "Nothing else would have survived. And look at those other loops of chain . . . there must've been a lot of those things strung up there. Jonesy, can you give us a closer look?"

Haddix eased *Ernie* upward.

The nearest rucksack hung at an awkward angle. She probed out the vehicle's right arm, gently secured the mahogany-colored bag, and rotated it before the camera.

"There . . . a label!" said McConkey. "Is that what Hebrew writing looks like?"

"Unh-unh, it's Cyrillic," Haddix responded in bafflement. "Those are letters from the Russian alphabet."

"Ten-seven-one," Wolfe called out, pressing the red button.

Haddix said, "Trent, did the Soviets ever lose a boat out here?"

"If they did, it sure as hell wasn't a British-built T-class."

"Want me to try to open it?"

Trent hesitated, then said, "Negative. We've got too many other things to do. This boat isn't one of Ivan's, and, like Doc says, that bag's not military issue. Carry on, Jonesy."

Haddix released the rucksack, brought *Ernie* down below the heaviest snarls of wires, and descended back into the passageway.

To starboard the area opposite the galley was bulging inward, collapsed along the contours of the ravine wall. The impact had skewed one of the vertical steel partitions at a strange angle.

"Jonesy, let's take a peek behind that banged-up partition," Trent said.

She nosed *Ernie* down and turned it forty-five degrees to starboard.

The crumpled compartment held an upended table and metal chairs, all of which had gravitated to the base of the far corner.

"Looks like the officers' wardroom," Trent said. "Doc, pan the walls, will you?"

The pan-and-tilt camera picked up a quartet of rectangles grouped on the rust-stained far wall, about five feet off the floor.

Haddix advanced *Ernie* closer.

Three of the rectangles were picture frames. The glass was broken, the photographs long since consumed. Two of the frames, made of a soft wood like pine, were riddled with wormholes; the third, most probably of teak, looked as good as new.

The other rectangle was a heavily tarnished brass plaque.

The glare from the ROV's bright floods made it difficult to read the inscription. Haddix played with the arms until they deflected enough light to shadow in the lettering:

To the crew of INS Dakar
"May You Always Make Port Safely"
From the crew of HMS Totem
10 November 1967

It was McConkey who finally broke the silence. "May the souls of all those aboard INS *Dakar* rest in peace."

A chorus of soft "amens" filled the van.

"Ten-eight-two," Wolfe whispered as he captured the plaque on laser disc.

Haddix brought *Ernie* around and retreated from the wardroom.

The boat's operations area lay forward, beyond a bulkhead. Before descending down the passageway toward it she paused to check that the ROV's tether had remained unkinked, then retracted the mechanical arms.

"Jonesy, got enough line to reach the hatchway?"

"Affirmative."

When *Dakar* crunched into the ravine wall to starboard, the force had accordioned the bulkhead up ahead to just two thirds its original width. In the process the hatch had popped out like a watermelon seed and the hatchway compressed into a foot-wide slit.

Haddix coasted *Ernie* to a stop eighteen inches from the twisted metal.

Peeking into the darkened operations area through the hatchway —which listed some thirty degrees to starboard, like the hull itself —was not going to be easy because of the ROV's configuration. The forward camera was mounted in the center of the vehicle's bow, a foot above its belly, while the floods were mounted higher up and to the sides, separated like the headlights of a car. Yet the slit was so narrow that if she pointed the forward camera through it, the floods would cast their beams on the crumpled bulkhead.

Her only chance of illuminating the operations area was to tilt the ROV's bow hard to port until it paralleled the hatchway.

Haddix extended the mechanical arms and locked the pincers onto the jamb of the hatchway. Then she slowly muscled *Ernie*'s port flank downward.

"I was afraid of this," she said, studying the feed. "No matter how I position *Ernie,* I can't throw in light and get a picture at the same time."

"Play around and see what you can do," Trent replied. "Doc, any spikes on the readout?"

Wolfe consulted the data stream. "Nope. Flat as a board."

Haddix continued to jockey the ROV up and down, to and fro, in and out. Finally she said, in a heavy voice, "I'm afraid this is as good as it gets."

The display on Monitor Two was as disorienting as it was unproductive. The jamb of the hatchway, which lay just inches from the camera, appeared as an out-of-focus wedge that diagonally bisected the screen. Above it, to the right, was the operations area. Haddix had managed to angle part of the starboard flood's beam through the slit, but not enough to produce a coherent image.

"E.J."

"Yes, Rick."

"The strobe and the electronic still camera are mounted pretty close together. Can you position that camera in front of the opening? I may be able to get something that I can enhance."

Haddix forced *Ernie* upward until the pan-and-tilt camera, to which the electronic still camera was yoked, pointed through the hatchway.

"Good," Wolfe said, pressing the red button at the right of the *Bert* engineering station. "Ten-nine-one."

He keyed in the retrieve command.

Twenty seconds later an image started to form on the small monitor in front of him.

"I'll put it up on Monitor Two," he said, his fingers already working to boost the brightness. It was hopeless. The seawater was too opaque, the light too weak; no matter what tricks he tried, the picture remained as murky as an Instamatic snapshot taken at dusk without benefit of a flash.

Wolfe sank back into his chair.

And just as quickly straightened. "E.J., you know how we sometimes stack a seismographic image? If you think about it, this is the same kind of signal-to-noise problem. Why not apply the same solution? In fact, a pal of mine, a photographer, once found himself in a bind like ours . . . his lights weren't strong enough to pull off a certain shot. So he kept opening the shutter on the same frame, firing his strobe each time. He eventually got enough light on the film to burn in a usable image."

"I don't know if I can keep *Ernie* steady enough for a multiple exposure," Haddix said doubtfully.

"You don't have to. It's not like we're on assignment for *National Geographic.*" Wolfe quickly reprogrammed the electronic still camera to disable its automatic frame-advance. Then, glancing at the laser-disc counter, he said to Liz Trimble, "I believe the next shot is frame ten-nine-two."

"Check. How many exposures do you plan to make, Doc?"

"Well, as I remember it, two flashes double the amount of light, four flashes triple it. Depending on how much *Ernie* jiggles, I'm going for sixteen."

Wolfe turned to Monitor Four. The feed from the pan-and-tilt camera looked stable enough. He triggered the first strobe, waited four seconds for the capacitor to recharge, then fired again. When he finally completed the sequence, he set about retrieving and enhancing the image.

Haddix, still holding *Ernie* in position in front of the narrow hatchway, said, "Liz, can you kick the pan-and-tilt down and to the right? There's some debris down there."

Liz Trimble went to the *Bert* engineering station and reached around Wolfe to redirect the camera.

Some of the items that had collected in the lower starboard corner were from the galley, but most seemed to have sluiced down the passageway all the way from the crew quarters.

"Oh my God," Trimble gasped, "the shoes . . ."

Trent flicked his attention from Monitor Five, which displayed Wolfe's work-in-progress, to the ROV's pan-and-tilt feed on Monitor Four.

"Damn," Trent said softly. "It's like those rucksacks hanging on that pipe . . . most of those shoes aren't military issue either. And there, at about two o'clock . . ."

In the upper right-hand corner of the screen sat a small red patent leather pump, the kind a young girl might save for the special occasions in her life.

"Rick, okay if I move *Ernie*?" asked Haddix.

"What?" Wolfe looked up distractedly. "Oh, uh, sure. If we can't see it on this still, it's not seeable."

Haddix unclamped the pincers, banked hard to starboard, and lowered the ROV's right arm toward the mound of debris.

"What the hell was *Dakar* carrying?" whispered Billy Ray McConkey. "Civilians?"

As Haddix gently lifted the red pump free, the pile shifted to reveal two objects that reflected back the harsh light of the floods.

She stared at the nearest one for several seconds before comprehension belatedly set in. "Soviet civilians, Cowboy," she said in a subdued voice. "Soviet civilians of the Jewish faith. The gold necklace just left of the shoe? The pendant on it is the Star of David."

"Of course," Trent murmured, slumping into an empty chair. "That's what the sabotage's been about, that's the secret the Israelis have been trying to protect."

Most of the others in the van swung around to face him.

"We were sure this boat was part of their pipeline for fissionable materials. Instead, it was for people . . . and my guess is, they don't want it exposed because it's still in operation." Trent numbly shook his head. "Our intelligence agencies know that Israel has been smuggling Jews out of the Soviet Union since the mid-seventies. But *Dakar* went down on the twenty-sixth of January 1968. Something this elaborate, at such an early date . . . incredible, just incredible."

In the stunned silence Haddix turned back to her console. *Ernie*'s pincers still grasped the red pump. She released it, then gently uncovered the second glittering object that had caught her attention.

It was a small metal headband studded with fake emeralds and sapphires.

Suddenly, her eyes began to sting. The tiny shoe, the miniature costume-jewelry tiara—there had been children aboard *Dakar.* Children who, had they lived, would be her age now. Children who, after traveling so far and so arduously, had fallen just two days short of the Promised Land. And their parents: had they known, in those last few hours, that the submarine was doomed? Or had catastrophe descended with merciful swiftness? Haddix wiped her eyes with the back of a hand, but could not staunch the tears.

From behind her Trent said softly, "I feel like I'm desecrating a cemetery. It's time to retrieve the vehicles and head for port."

"Will we tell the Israelis about what we found?" asked Trimble in a choked voice.

"Absolutely. And knowing my boss, we'll share our videotapes, even though they show us violating international laws." He paused, then said, "Jonesy? Whenever you're ready."

Haddix had regained her composure and was about to withdraw the ROV when she spotted something else in the debris. Using the pincers, she delicately extracted a ballpoint pen and held it up to the forward camera.

The plastic barrel of the instrument was imprinted with gaily colored images of a globe, a monorail, and various fanciful pavilions befitting one of Disney's theme parks.

Haddix slowly rotated the pen.

"Jonesy?"

"Coming."

The opposite side of the barrel was inscribed:

1964 World's Fair—New York

What an odd souvenir to find aboard *Dakar,* Haddix thought. Had one of its crew visited America? She lowered the ROV's arm and laid down the pen as tenderly as a memorial wreath.

Haddix was flying *Ernie* back up the passageway when Rick Wolfe suddenly said, "Trent, there's something you'd better see."

Trent, in the midst of composing a brief message to Cliff Zeman, replied, "Can't it wait, Doc?"

"No. Monitor Five."

Forming on the screen was electronic still frame number 1092.

Wolfe's gambit had worked. Though the picture was bleached from the multiple flashes and fuzzy from the ROV's slight movements between exposures, it chillingly documented the utter devastation within the operations area. The ravine wall had flattened the starboard hull and was spiking through in several places; the periscope housing had been bent into a giant J; the toppled consoles and chairs had all slid down to the forward bulkhead.

Trent studied the scene. "I'm sorry, Doc. What am I missing?"

"The forward bulkhead hatch," Wolfe replied.

Trent's eyes swept the far wall, which appeared gray and splotched with darker rust stains, and settled on an upright black rectangle. "I'm still not follow— Wait a minute. That hatch is showing up as dark."

"Exactly," Wolfe replied. "My guess is, it's red. Kind of unusual for a submarine, isn't it?"

"Very. What color was the hatch in the rear compartment?"

"White," Wolfe said. "Now, keep your eyes on the center of the hatch, at about chest height."

The van crew leaned forward as one.

Wolfe slowly decreased the brightness while he increased the contrast. The objects strewn about the operations area became more crisply defined. Just as the starkness grew uncomfortable to look at, a white shape started to materialize in the middle of the black hatch.

It was the circumference of a circle.

Wolfe continued to boost the contrast.

"Good God," Trent said.

Within the circumference lay three white equilateral triangles arrayed around a hub like the blades of a propeller: the international warning symbol for radiation.

At last, Trent spoke. "It appears my order to cease operations was premature. Jonesy, get *Ernie* out of here. Doc, we're going into the forward torpedo room. I'd like you to work with Joe and Cowboy on finding the best sled position for supporting that entry."

With that he turned and began composing a brief message. Cliff Zeman deserved to know that his perseverance might yet be rewarded.

Another concussive salute from the Zippo Squad greeted Rick Wolfe as he emerged from the superstructure. Bladder aching from the more than a half-dozen cups of coffee downed over the past five hours, he had wisely repaired to the head before attempting to fly

Ernie into the last unprobed section of the shattered Israeli submarine *Dakar.*

Raindrops still curved down through the luminous canopy generated by the stanchion-mounted floods; the seas still crested in angry whitecaps. Wolfe picked his way across the pitching deck and entered the control van.

The air inside was sour with tension and fatigue, for the work had been nonstop since they first made contact with the furrow across Ravine C. Yet Wolfe also detected the anticipatory edge that usually accompanied the end of a mission. He peered through the red gloom at the various people now filling the van. Along the forward wall Joe Reuss sat at the navigation console next to the door, flanked by Edna Haddix, still flying the ROV, and j.g. Tom Parkhill, handling the sled. Wendell Trent stood by the sonar station conferring with Billy Ray McConkey. Liz Trimble was at the engineering station zipping through videotapes of the two earlier searches to brief navigator Leonard Heppel and flyers Sam Lippman and Ezra Schell, all three of whom had arrived in case their help was needed.

Wolfe turned to scan the large monitors on the forward wall.

Parkhill had moved *Bert* outboard of its previous position alongside the ripped ballast tank. The sled was no lower, though, for the area immediately under the breached forward torpedo compartment was guarded by a serrated file of boulders.

Haddix had maneuvered *Ernie* almost fifty feet lower and was hovering the ROV half-under the two-and-a-half-foot slab of rock that obstructed the opening.

"Ready to be relieved, E.J.?" asked Wolfe.

"And how. But let me finish this bit of digging. A few more minutes and you'll have a clear path in."

Through a cloud of disturbed sediment Wolfe could see that the slab appeared to be supported by a roundish, basketball-sized rock. Haddix was using the ROV's left hand to gingerly excavate silt to the port, or downhill, side of that rock.

"I figure if I undermine it enough, I can jump-start it with a shove from above," Haddix said. "Then gravity'll do the rest, just like with you and that hatch back there."

"Go slow," he cautioned. "If that slab settles, it'll trap the arm. If it falls, good-bye, *Ernie*."

"I hear you, Rick."

Wolfe went to the back of the van and said to Trent, "Any response from the beach?"

"They're going ape shit. Zeman's trying to arrange us a naval escort, and CIA and State are being pulled in."

"So all we have to do is produce the smoking gun."

"Exactly," Trent replied. He glanced up at the ROV's forward-camera feed on Monitor Two. "God, what I wouldn't give for a Caterpillar right now."

He watched Haddix make one more pass with the left hand, then withdraw the arm.

The scene changed as she brought *Ernie* up six feet and deflected its bow downward. Burrowing both sets of pincers into the loose debris atop the slab until they rested on solid rock, she repositioned the thrusters and applied power.

The forward-camera feed danced, but the slab refused to budge.

"Damn." Haddix retracted the arms and brought the ROV back down to the base of the slab.

She had just resumed scooping out silt when, without warning, *Ernie*'s forward-camera feed disappeared under a shower of silt, stones, and man-made debris.

"Parkhill!" she barked. "Did the slab move?"

The bobbing feed from the sled showed sediment drifting upward from the little ROV like smoke from a fire.

"I can't rightly tell yet, E.J."

Haddix looked up at the main monitor and banged the console in frustration.

"Liz, try zooming the sled's pan-and-tilt," Wolfe said.

"Zooming the pan-and-tilt," Trimble replied.

Increasing the magnification was no use; the billows were too dense.

"We'll just have to wait for it to settle, Jonesy," Trent said in a tight voice.

A welter of conflicting thoughts surged through Haddix's mind. She took a deep breath and willed herself to concentrate solely on the calamities that might have befallen *Ernie*—as well as ways to escape each.

It took three long minutes for the swirls to dissipate and for the image from the ROV's forward camera to form on Monitor Two.

The van crew numbly stared at it, their darkest fears confirmed. The slab had lurched forward and down several inches, kicking loose a good bit of the supporting silt and debris and pinning the lower half of *Ernie*'s left arm. In fact, it appeared as if that apparatus, along with the roundish, basketball-sized rock to its right, were now the keystones holding up the slab.

Finally Haddix said, "Well, the vehicle's intact, and we still have our feed. That's a start."

She tried to wiggle the arm but succeeded only in shaking the ROV. "And we still have full power."

"Jonesy. Can you use the right arm to detach the left?"

Haddix swiveled around to face Trent. "I don't have to. The designers anticipated this scenario. They built an explosive bolt into the joint so we can amputate the arm."

Relief flooded his face. "Good. Blow it."

"It's not quite that easy," she said. "The arm weighs about fifty pounds."

Trent, grasping her point, groaned. "Lose it and *Ernie* attains positive buoyancy . . . and starts to rise."

"Affirmative."

"Can't you counterbalance by adjusting the dynamic bias and playing with the thrusters?"

She shook her head. "There's no way to compensate for that much weight without adding ballast. I've figured out a way to do that, but we may not be able to take on enough. Even if we can, *Ernie* may become too unstable to control."

"Try anyway," Trent said. "I'm willing to do anything to get inside. Including lose the vehicle."

"Aye, aye, sir." Haddix spotted ROV flyer Ezra Schell at the back of the van. "Ezra . . . just the man we need. I was thinking about using the free arm to load the sample cage with rocks. No one knows the cage's clearances and capacity better than you. Mind giving it a shot?"

Schell hurried forward to take Haddix's seat.

Filling the cage welded to the vehicle's belly turned out to be more complicated than it might have seemed. The ROV's cameras were not designed to tilt down far enough to focus on the wire basket, which was also hidden from the sled's cameras by the vehicle's body. In addition to working blind, Schell's reach was limited by *Ernie*'s immobility; he could only retrieve objects within a seven-foot radius, which unfortunately ruled out several iron skillets that had spilled out of the galley. Lastly, he had no way to accurately gauge the weight of the rocks and stones that he was stuffing into the cage.

The ballast he loaded slowly drove the vehicle down until it rested on the severely sloping bed of the bear trap.

Twenty minutes later Schell turned to Haddix, who sat beside him paging through one of the ROV's manuals. "Navy, I think the cage is full. I've been trying to force a medium-sized rock in, but it won't go."

She nodded, double-checked the computer command that triggered the left mechanical arm explosive bolt, and reached past him to key it in.

"Ready?"

Schell nodded.

Behind them Liz Trimble threw the feed from *Ernie*'s forward camera onto three of the large monitors.

Haddix pressed the Enter key.

On the monitors a small geyser of silt, and then the upper part of the arm was dropping off the ROV.

As applause swept the van, Haddix anxiously studied *Ernie*'s depth gauge: Good, it was staying put on the bed of the bear trap. Wiping her mouth with the back of one hand, she said, "Ezra, can you lift off the deck?"

Schell eased the throttle forward. The thrusters raised a thick curtain of silt, but the number on the depth gauge remained unchanging.

"Negative, Navy."

"Then it's time to start off-loading. But not too much . . . if we don't maintain neutral buoyancy, we start drifting upward."

As Schell began the trial-and-error process of lightening the ROV, Haddix and Rick Wolfe studied the recalcitrant slab for ways to make it topple. It took them five minutes to agree on a plan of attack, by which time Schell was able to power *Ernie* off the bottom.

"How's it handling, Ezra?" asked Haddix.

"Like an eighteen-wheeler on glare ice. There's a noticeable list to starboard, but it flies." Schell wrestled the ROV back down to slightly below the slab. "What's the drill?"

"You volunteering?" asked Haddix.

He nodded.

"I hope you're good at Pick Up Sticks," Wolfe said dryly. He pointed to the roundish, basketball-sized rock that lay slightly uphill of the trapped arm. "E.J. and I figure that rock should act as a fulcrum. If we can pull Ernie's arm out from under, the slab ought to tilt farther downhill. If we're lucky, it'll pick up enough momentum to keep going."

Schell glanced up at Monitor One. *Bert*'s pan-and-tilt camera showed the front third of the little ROV to be hovering directly under the slab. "We better discuss escape routes," he said. "That slab pitches away from the hull, we're dead."

"That's why you'll be in full reverse-thrust mode," Haddix replied. "Think you can also come up steeply enough to angle past that big boulder directly behind your butt?"

Schell raised the ROV and studied the feed from its rear-mounted camera. "Can do, Navy."

He lowered *Ernie,* extended its remaining arm, locked the pincers around the amputated arm, and began applying power.

It was like trying to tug a bone from a pit bull; the camera feeds juddered violently as Schell advanced the throttle to its stop.

"Keep going, Ezra," Haddix urged. "Some of the silt's shaking loose!"

Five seconds, ten seconds, fifteen seconds . . .

Suddenly the slab seemed to be receding as *Ernie* shot backward, the amputated arm still locked in the pincers of its right hand, and then the monitors carrying the ROV's feeds went to black as the vehicle plowed stern first into the boulder behind it.

"Release your load and climb!"

Schell opened the right-hand pincers, dropping the amputated arm, and started to bring the vehicle up.

The monitors blinked back on.

Through the rising silt they could see the slab slowly start to tilt.

It hesitated, but the downhill end had dipped too low; heeding gravity, the slab began its long, tumultuous slide to the bottom of the Hellencian Trench.

Now a thick column of sediment boiled up as silt and debris rushed down to fill the cavity left by the slab.

"Bring the vehicles up fifty feet!" shouted Haddix.

Parkhill started to winch in the sled's cable while Schell, working without a single reference point in the growing murk, did his best to point the ROV's thrusters straight down.

The silt and debris continued to flow down past *Dakar*'s hull with ever-increasing speed.

"Jesus, don't let the sub shift," Trent said, involuntarily stepping forward several paces as if he wanted to reach into the monitors to dam the minilandslide.

Within seconds the maelstrom had mushroomed upward to envelop both vehicles and blind all cameras.

The silence in the van grew unbearable. Yet no one broke it; the crew remained frozen in the sepulchral red gloom, transfixed by the images trying to form on the monitors.

And then Haddix was slumping over the console, weak from fatigue and gratitude: *Dakar* seemed not to have moved, and the breach in its forward torpedo room seemed unobstructed.

The crew was too spent to cheer.

Trent, who was standing behind Haddix, reached down to grip her shoulders. They felt like tempered steel. He unobtrusively massaged the muscles until they began to unknot.

"Thanks," she said softly.

"I'm the one who should be giving thanks. To you, to Ezra, to Doc, to everyone in here." He straightened and said, in a louder voice, "Let's finish this mission and go home."

Parkhill began to winch *Bert* back down.

Rick Wolfe, having steadied his nerves with another half cup of coffee, replaced Ezra Schell at the *Ernie* console. The seat felt as though it had baked in a toaster oven.

He began to drop the ROV back alongside the opening. The vehicle's camera feeds jiggled as the remaining ballast shifted.

Haddix looked at the overhead shots from the sled and saw small rocks and stones streaming over the lowest edge of the wire basket. "You losing trim, Rick?"

"Some," Wolfe replied, fighting the ROV's tendency to climb to port. Arriving in front of the breach, he asked Parkhill, "How much slack tether do I have when *Bert*'s at the top of its bounce?"

Parkhill studied his monitor. "About twenty feet, Doc."

"Ouch. That means I've got less than three vehicle lengths of maneuverability." Wolfe glanced up at the clock—it was now shortly past nine P.M.—and looked over his shoulder at Haddix, who had moved back to the *Bert* engineering station. "Ready to go, E.J.? Trent?"

"Do it, Rick," Haddix replied, firing off another electronic still and calling out the frame number.

Wolfe crept *Ernie* up to the hull. The entry, tricky under the best of circumstances, seemed impossible. Size was not the problem; the gash was more than big enough to admit the vehicle. But it sloped severely to port while the ROV, unbalanced by the loss of its left arm, listed to starboard, some sixty degrees counter to the angle of the opening.

"Nothing's easy," he muttered, staring blankly at his monitor. The most straightforward solution would be to remove rocks from the starboard side of the sample cage in *Ernie*'s belly, but Schell had already lightened the load to escape the ravine floor; too much more, and the vehicle would start to ascend. "Ezra . . . how much of the cage do you figure you dumped? A quarter? A third?"

"About a third, Doc."

"Let's hope there's enough room for me to redistribute the rocks," Wolfe said grimly.

Using the remaining mechanical arm, he began sweeping the ballast to port.

The ROV slowly came to horizontal, then tipped over to port.

But not enough.

"E.J.," he said, "give me a pan of what's directly below."

Haddix switched the feed to *Ernie*'s pan-and-tilt and swept the area.

"Hold it right there!" Wolfe had spotted a large iron skillet that had cascaded down from the opening amidships. He locked the pincers of the ROV's right arm around the handle of the pan, then swung the arm leftward until the skillet extended beyond the vehicle's port flank.

The application of this fresh weight did the trick; *Ernie* was now lined up with the hole.

"Great job, Rick."

Wolfe repositioned the ROV's thrusters.

"How's my tether?" he asked.

"Tether clear," Parkhill replied.

Wolfe advanced the throttles.

"Eleven-oh-two," Haddix called out. "Eleven-oh-three."

The forward-camera feed shuddered as *Ernie*'s roof scraped the top of the opening, but the vehicle continued inching its way through.

"Eleven-oh . . . Holy fuck!"

Startled by the obscenity, all heads swiveled to Edna Haddix.

"The gamma-ray detector . . . it's off the charts," she said, reflexively capturing the readings on laser disc.

"Bingo," Wendell Trent said, breaking into a tired but triumphant grin.

HAIFA

1811 Zulu/9:11 P.M. local time

Ephraim Levenger glanced across the communications room of the Haifa Naval Station. Leon Rose, arms crossed atop his belly, appeared to be dozing in a chair off to one side. The Mossad official shook his head in wonderment. Where had Leon summoned the will to leave his beloved sweets behind when they had transferred the command post here slightly over four hours ago? Why did Leon not jump, as did the others, at every crackle of the radio? How could Leon remain impervious to tension so palpable it was almost paralyzing?

Because the man possessed unshakable confidence, Levenger realized—not only in his intricate battle plan, but also in his ability to improvise when things went amiss, as they invariably would in an operation of this scope.

Thus far all had gone without a hitch.

At precisely 1400 Zulu, on Rose's command, an Israeli Air Force E-2C AWACS* had broken out of the lazy figure-eights it was flying over the Med south of Cyprus and headed southwest. The Boeing 707, distinctively modified by way of a large, Frisbee-like disk atop its fuselage, was an electronics-packed aerial surveillance platform.

*AWACS: *Airborne Warning and Control System.*

One hundred miles from the Egyptian port city of Alexandria the plane had changed course again, turning northwest toward Crete. At the moment it was settling into a circling pattern thirty thousand feet above the southwestern coast of the Greek island.

Thirty minutes ago, on Rose's command, the Israeli task force that had sailed from Haifa at dawn on Monday began closing on *Fanning II.* At the moment the Sa'ar-class corvette and the three Dabur-class coastal patrol boats were poised just over the horizon from the American research vessel, maintaining both station and strict radio silence.

And fifteen minutes ago, on Rose's command, Levenger's Mossad team on Crete had left its hotel in a small fishing village at the western tip of the island. At the moment the Israeli Air Force pilot and the team leader were aboard the chartered helicopter, while the others were driving back to Iráklion, where the Gulfstream was being readied for its flight to Tel Aviv.

Yet if the signal from *Sabra* did not come soon, Levenger brooded, it would all go for naught. Soon the surveillance plane would attract the attention of Greek radar operators, and soon the four gunboats idling forty miles off the coast of Crete would be spotted by some passing fishing vessel.

What was Leon waiting for? Levenger began to gnaw on a fresh fingernail. Damn, he thought, this night will shorten my life by at least a year.

Ben Goren, pacing by the door, suddenly turned to check the clock. "Leon?"

Rose's eyes opened a crack.

"Leon, the seas are heavy out there. Our boats will take longer to reach the American ship. Do not leave it too late."

Rose nodded and slid his lids shut again.

Goren looked to Levenger, who helplessly shrugged back, then resumed his pacing.

"Relax, Ben," Rose said. "There is no money in the budget to replace the linoleum."

"Then I shall walk over to the commissary to get some fresh fruit," Goren replied peevishly. "Ephraim, will you join me?"

Levenger was halfway to the door when one of the radio clerks shouted, "General Rose! It is *Sabra* calling!"

Rose uncrossed his arms and stood.

"The message reads, 'ETA seventy-five minutes,' end of message," the clerk continued. "Sir, is there a reply?"

"No, son, no reply," Rose said. "Ephraim, get your chopper in the air."

Levenger headed for one of the radio consoles.

"Alert them they may be picking up a passenger as well." Rose turned to Ben Goren. "Please order our ships to commence their runs. I have placed the surveillance plane and the chopper under the command of your Captain Litvak, so make certain he has the correct frequencies and codes."

Goren nodded and hurried to another console.

"Remind him he is to evacuate Vigneron and the Israeli student, Kahane. And remember . . . if the Americans have reached *Dakar,* I want Vigneron and the videotapes placed aboard the chopper." Rose paused, then said in voice so soft it was almost a whisper, "Gentlemen, may God be with us."

SUITLAND, MARYLAND

1816 Zulu/2:16 P.M. local time

". . . two tanks, about six feet tall by three in diam—" Wendell Trent's words were garbled by a sudden hiss of static over the speaker in a secure room of the Naval Intelligence Service headquarters in suburban Maryland, across the Potomac.

Clifford Zeman waited for the burst to subside, then said, "Sorry, son. Say again."

"We found the two new tanks described in the mods, only they're in the forward torpedo room, just inside the bulkhead. About six feet tall by three, three and a half feet in diameter, and lead lined. One tank's severely damaged, but the other appears intact . . . hold on a second, Cliff."

The door to the secure room swung open.

Zeman's eyes flicked up to Ann Davis as she entered. "Any luck?"

"Shorty refuses to buck our request up to CNO," she said, her scowl darkening. "Says when and if we come up with hard proof, he'll put the whole goddamned Sixth Fleet at our disposal. In the meantime he's offering us one of the frigates up in the Sea of Crete . . . 'on his own authority.' What a smarmy bastard."

"Transit time?"

"Four, four and a half hours," Davis said. "There's got to be a way to convince him this is for real."

"Trent said the compartment is highly radioactive, so it's not heavy water, like we suspected. *Dakar* must've been transporting fissionable material. The question is, was it U-235 or—"

The speaker suddenly crackled again: "Paydirt," Trent said with thinly concealed excitement. "Oh, my God, you're not going to believe this, Cliff . . . forget Norway, it's not heavy wa—"

Zeman and Davis reflexively turned to the speaker as Trent's voice gave way to an insistent buzz like that emitted by a faulty fluorescent fixture.

Zeman punched the intercom to the communications room and barked, "What the hell's happening to my feed?"

"We're not sure, sir. We're getting the same anomaly in here. Be right back to you."

Zeman sagged in frustration. "Damn. Shorty would have his evidence by now if Vigneron hadn't diddled the microwave transmitter. What's the latest on Bart?"

"I spoke to Carol about five minutes ago. He missed his connecting flight in Chicago, so he didn't land at National until shortly before two."

"At least something's going our way."

"Not really," she said. "The senator met him at the airport."

"Shit."

"Yeah. You still want Carol to tell him where we are?"

Zeman hesitated, then nodded. "This isn't something he'll want to discuss over the phone. With early rush-hour traffic and everything, there's no way he can get out here much before three forty-five or four. By then Trent should be retrieving the vehicles and making for home."

Just then one of the communications-room technicians called on the intercom. "Mr. Zeman? The best we can figure it is, someone's jamming all frequencies."

"What?"

"Yes, sir. We've scanned the whole band, including the frequency they were using to transmit Delta cipher. We're getting the same anomaly."

Zeman balled his fists; would this convince Vice Admiral "Shorty" Brock to at least order a reconnaissance flight? "Son, can you say with certainty that the transmissions are being jammed."

After a pause the technician replied, "With absolute certainty? No, sir, not until we can work up a full analysis of the signal. It could be just a freak atmospheric disturbance. Met's reporting a heavy storm system in that area."

"Very well. Call me the moment you know," Zeman said, trying to keep the anger out of his voice. He looked up at Davis. "If Trent's being jammed, it must be from an airplane. If there's an airplane circling above that storm, it must be showing up on one of NSA's birds. Anyone over there owe us a favor?"

Davis thought a moment, then said, "Morrison."

Zeman nodded and reached for the phone.

THE EASTERN MED

1821 Zulu/9:21 P.M. local time

Having at last rooted out *Dakar*'s dark secret—something in the Israeli submarine's flooded forward torpedo room was spewing radioactivity like a mini-Chernobyl—Wendell Trent stood hunched over the control van intercom, waiting for a reply from *Fanning II*'s bridge.

"Trent?" It was Captain Nichols. "I've tried the entire UHF band. Nothing but static. VHF is clear, but there's no traffic. This storm must be keeping the local small craft in port."

"Keep trying the satellite channels, Bill. Out." Trent's foreboding deepened. There could be only one reason for jamming the transmissions of an immobile and unarmed research vessel: to mask an attack by ships that were probably already swarming toward *Fanning II*'s floodlit afterdeck like wolves to a campfire.

Realizing that he was powerless to stop them, Trent forced his attention back to Monitor Two.

Rick Wolfe had squeezed the rest of *Ernie* through the breach on the port side of the sunken boat and was now inching the little ROV around what remained of the forward torpedo room.

The compartment had been compacted to barely half its original size when *Dakar* plowed bow first into the bear trap. Much of the starboard hull had simply disintegrated; large patches of jagged rock face protruded in, some almost to the centerline. The torpedo tubes were skewed at strange angles. Of the two tanks he had been describing to Cliff Zeman, all that remained of the starboard-side unit was its top fifth, which still dangled from pipes that lead to the external ports atop the hull. The port-side tank had been jarred free from its mounting, but seemed intact. Stenciled on its side was the same symbol that appeared on the forward hatch of the operations area, the three equilateral triangles warning of radioactivity.

But what was the hot source triggering *Ernie*'s gamma-ray detector?

According to the data it was uranium. More precisely, U_{238}, an isotope more stable than the U_{235} used to fuel nuclear reactors—but also the one convertible to Pu_{239}, or weapons-grade plutonium.

The discovery of the uranium was made by Edna Haddix. While Wolfe struggled to physically search the compartment, she had conducted a video scan.

The ROV's pan-and-tilt camera had quickly located the twisted remnants of the starboard-side tank, its lead inner lining clearly visible, sitting among the bent torpedo tubes down at the nose of the compartment. Atop this debris rested some two dozen rectangular metal boxes whose black matte surfaces were stenciled with the legend U_{238}. The lead-lined lids of several had popped, spilling out the silvery-white ingots that were driving the gamma-ray detector berserk. This was the news that Trent had been trying to relay to Zeman when his transmission was jammed.

Who had supplied the uranium to Israel twenty years earlier? he wondered. They would never know for sure; according to Wolfe, scientists the world over used English letters and Arabic numbers to describe chemicals.

The image currently displayed on Monitor Two was of the intact port-side tank, which *Ernie* was again circling. The container seemed to hang in midcompartment, held up only by the pipes at the top.

"That don't compute," Billy Ray McConkey said.

"What do you mean, Cowboy?"

"No way those skinny little pipes can support that big tank, unless it was empty. Now, suppose you were *Dakar*'s captain, and you took on that load down there. Wouldn't you want to spread it around a bit, putting half the boxes in each tank?"

"Good point," Trent said. "Doc, can you slide down to the base of the tank?"

Wolfe dropped *Ernie* two feet.

The reason the port-side tank seemed able to defy gravity was that it was indeed empty; its bottom had been severed all the way around, allowing its contents to tumble out.

"Eleven-two-one," Edna Haddix called out, firing off another electronic still.

Wolfe sought a better angle from which to view the damage.

"Eleven-two-two, eleven-two-three," Haddix said. "Look back there, inside the tank's mounting pedestal. See the hole in the hull? Very few of its edges seem to be curling inward."

"Doc, can you give us a closer look?"

As Wolfe repositioned *Ernie,* Haddix pivoted the pan-and-tilt camera and zoomed.

"You're right, Jonesy, it was an explosion, not an implosion," Trent said quietly as he studied the neat eighteen-inch circle through the double hull. The edges were splayed outward. Not many saboteurs could have secreted an explosive device in such an inaccessible location, he thought, which might explain why the British commander who had supervised the mods, Victor Cowling, was now missing. "*Dakar* was sunk by a bomb placed under this tank. Real professional job too. The charge was shaped to punch downward through the hull. Once this room flooded, it didn't matter whether the watertight hatches were closed or not . . . the boat kept sinking until the other compartments imploded. The people aboard never had a chance."

Haddix began documenting the hole with electronic stills.

"Van, Bridge."

Trent moved to the intercom. "Yes, Bill."

"Radar's picking up something south-by-southeast," Captain Nichols said. "Three blips, check that, four blips, making straight for us."

"Range?"

"Four-plus miles. They're just clearing the horizon."

"Speed?"

"Better'n thirty knots."

"Damn. They sure don't sound civilian. Let me know when you make visual contact. Out." Trent turned and said, "Doc, Jonesy, grab a few insurance shots of those metal boxes at the bottom. Then let's clear out of here."

Wolfe jockeyed *Ernie* to gain the pan-and-tilt camera an unobstructed line of sight down to the submarine's mangled nose.

"That's good, Rick," Haddix said, pressing the red button. "Eleven-two-nine. Hold it here, I want to take a few more."

While the strobes recharged, Trent got back on the intercom. "Bridge, Van. Any sight of the bogies yet."

"Negative," Captain Nichols replied. "They must be running with their lights off."

"Great. Range?"

"Just under four miles. I make their ETA at about seven minutes."

At the *Bert* engineering station Haddix zoomed *Ernie*'s pan-and-tilt camera in farther. "Eleven-three-zero. Hey, what're those things down there? Trent?"

"Keep me posted, Bill. Out." Trent's eyes darted back to Monitor Two.

To the left, half-hidden under the remnants of the starboard-side tank, lay several shiny-as-new steel cylinders, each the size of a fire extinguisher.

Trent studied them for a few moments—like so much else aboard *Dakar,* definitely not standard-issue gear, he thought—then said, "Cowboy, you've served on a few boats. Ever see anything like that?"

"Negative."

"Jonesy? Parkhill? Anyone?"

After a few seconds Haddix said, "I see writing on the cylinder at ten o'clock. Rick, can you get the arm down there?"

"No, it's out of reach."

"How about moving *Ernie* back and to starboard, to give me a better angle?"

"I can't, E.J. I'm already hard up against one of the torpedo tubes."

"Any way to throw more light down there?"

"Not directly, but we can stack the image again."

"Roger that," Haddix replied, reprogramming the electronic still camera to manual frame-advance.

She had just fired off the first strobe when the intercom squawked again.

"Yes, Bill," Trent replied.

"We're being hailed on Channel Sixteen . . . those are Israeli vessels closing on us," Captain Nichols said in a strained voice. "They've ordered me to switch to Channel Six, and they want to be patched through directly to you."

"Are you taping the transmissions?"

"I can if you want. Trent, I repeat, they're asking for you by name."

"What?"

"That's right."

Trent thought for a moment. "What's their range?"

"Two-point-seven-five miles."

"Looks like the fat lady's clearing her throat," Trent muttered. He glanced at the clock on the forward wall—it was nine twenty-eight P.M.—and turned to Haddix. "Jonesy, how many more flashes to go?"

"Nine."

Trent said into the intercom, "Stall them, Bill. Tell them you're sending someone to my cabin to wake me, anything, but buy me another two or three minutes."

"I'll do my best. Out."

But just twenty seconds later Captain Nichols was back. "Trent, it's a no-go. They say if you're not on the box in ten seconds, they're opening fire!"

Trent glanced at Haddix, who pressed the red button again and held up four fingers.

"Shit. What's their range?"

"Just over two miles, and they haven't slowed yet."

"Okay, Bill, patch them—"

"Jesus H. Christ!" interrupted Captain Nichols. "I just saw a muzzle flash. . . ."

"That shot'll be aimed across our bow," Trent replied coolly. "Patch them through on the phone . . . and keep the tape running."

Haddix triggered the strobe again.

Trent picked up the receiver, his mind racing.

Suddenly, a muffled explosion off the bow of the research vessel that, though expected, nonetheless startled the van crew.

The hissing over the phone gave way to a series of clicks, and then a clipped voice was asking, "Is this Commander Wendell Trent that I am speaking to?"

"No, just plain Wendell Trent, civilian. Who the hell are you? And what the fuck are you doing shelling an American research vessel in international waters?"

The others in the van, caught off guard by Trent's bellicose response, reflexively turned—and were further surprised to see the calm expression on his face.

The man on the other end of the line also seemed to be taken aback, for he hesitated perceptibly before replying, "I am Captain Meron Litvak of the Israeli Naval Ship *Herev*. In reply to your question, Mr. Trent, we have every reason to suspect that you are violating the sovereignty of an Israeli warship, namely the submarine *Dakar*. I therefore command you to immediately cease operations."

"Listen, buddy," Trent growled in another attempt to rattle the Israeli, "we're a civilian ship and we're flying the American flag. Uncle Sam doesn't put up with this kind of crap. Now, lighten up and back off."

"Or you will call the Sixth Fleet?" Litvak replied calmly. "But as I am sure you already know, you can neither transmit nor receive on your long-range frequencies. Mr. Trent, we will allow the diplomats to earn their pay by debating the propriety of my actions. In the meantime you are to cease all operations at once and prepare to be boarded."

They sent an unflappable man, Trent thought grudgingly.

At that moment several smaller detonations from the afterdeck—the Zippo Squad, responding to the Israeli shell.

"Mr. Trent, we carry forty-millimeter guns," Litvak said. "I advise you to instruct your men on the fantail to put down their dynamite. The next round is currently targeted ten yards astern of your ship, but I can easily change those coordinates."

Trent glanced at Haddix. She was holding up one finger, so he said, "Very well. I am ceasing operations."

"Thank you. You will please begin to raise the underwater vehicles. Also, I request that you personally meet my boarding party . . . in the event not all members of your crew are aware of your decision to cooperate. The party is led by Major Amichai."

"Message acknowledged and understood," Trent replied. "Out."

Haddix fired off the final strobe and began retrieving the last set of images from the ROV.

"Trent, we done in here?" asked Wolfe.

"Hunh?" Trent, absorbed in sorting out his diminishing options, set down the receiver that was still in his hand. "Yes, Doc, that'll be all, thanks. Why don't you get *Ernie* out of there and garage it aboard *Bert*."

"What's going on?"

"Israeli warships. We're about to be boarded."

Haddix looked up sharply, then tapped Liz Trimble on the shoulder and whispered, "Relieve me for a few minutes, will you?"

Trimble nodded and, as Haddix stepped to the shelves immediately in front of the *Bert* engineering station, slid into the seat behind the console.

Trent reached for the intercom. "Bridge, Van. Bill, patch me into the rest of the ship. Everyone needs to hear this."

"Roger."

"And keep an eye on the small-arms cabinet. It's going to get crazy enough without someone running around with a gun."

Trent sensed Edna Haddix quietly gliding past behind him. Now a cool draft of damp night air from the rear of the van; he turned just in time to see the door closing. Why the hell was Jonesy going to the ship's stern at a time like this? But before he could ponder her unexpected behavior, Captain Nichols was back. "All set on this end, Trent. You're on every loudspeaker."

Trent leaned forward, sighed, and toggled the switch.

Ariel Kahane braced himself on the railing at the rear of the cabin deck, willing his heartbeat to slow. The Israeli graduate student had been dozing through perhaps the tenth screening of *The Terminator* when the shell from INS *Herev* had burst some thirty yards off *Fanning II*'s bow. As the others in the lounge scrambled out of the room, Kahane had found himself disorientedly staring at the TV screen as Arnold Schwarzenegger, back in the Los Angeles flophouse, slowly jimmied out his damaged eye.

By the time Kahane blinked himself awake and emerged from the lounge, the corridor was awash with crewmen jostling to get through the double watertight hatches to the afterdeck. Rather than join the crush, he had gone to the nearest companionway and climbed to the cabin deck, which was just below the bridge.

Kahane had hurried out onto the port deck and, ignoring the rain, scanned the heaving seas for running lights: nothing.

Another series of explosions, this time at the stern, had brought the already drenched Kahane racing to the vantage point he now occupied, overlooking the afterdeck. To his relief these last detonations were the work of the Zippo Squad.

The Israeli graduate student was debating whether to continue around to the starboard side, or go back inside to fetch a slicker, when a rapid movement down on the afterdeck caught his eye.

Some thirty yards away a figure was darting out the back of the control van.

Squinting through the driving rain, Kahane watched in bafflement as Edna Haddix, cradling something in one crooked arm like a halfback toting a football, skirted the traction unit and disappeared into one of the utility vans.

Just then several loud clicks and squeals, and a voice boomed over *Fanning II's* loudspeakers. "This is Wendell Trent speaking. I'm sure you all heard that shell across our bow. It was fired by an Israeli warship. Four of them are bearing down on us, and they've ordered us to cease operations and prepare to be boarded."

Trent paused, then continued, "The Israeli action constitutes an overt act of aggression. However, we are an unarmed civilian vessel. Therefore, I've decided to comply with their demands. We will offer no resistance—I repeat, we will offer no resistance—to the Israelis when they board. At this time I ask the following personnel to remain at their posts . . . Captain Nichols on the bridge, Chief in the engine room, Eldon Gary at the winch, and whoever's watching Vigneron in the laundry room. I want all other hands to assemble on the afterdeck at once. That is all."

Ari Kahane knew he should start down, but he remained shivering at the rail, waiting to see what Navy would do next.

She didn't keep him waiting long.

Haddix emerged from the utility van carrying an object that looked like a silvery square of vinyl. She started across the treacherous deck toward the stern, then stopped, shielded her eyes, and looked up as if to survey the floods atop the surrounding stanchions and the superstructure. After a moment of indecision she detoured over to winch operator Eldon Gary and leaned past him to briefly speak into his squawk box. Haddix was halfway to the fantail when the entire afterdeck was plunged into inky blackness.

One deck above Ariel Kahane, Captain Nichols took his hand from the master switch controlling the floodlights and waited to reacquire his night vision.

Behind him in the red gloom of the otherwise deserted bridge, the radio speaker burst to life. "*Fanning,* this is *Herev,*" the Israeli commander said urgently. "What happens to the afterdeck lights? I repeat, what happens back there? Over."

Suddenly, from starboard, several fierce long fingers of light began quartering the research vessel's darkened afterdeck.

Captain Nichols followed the searchlight beams back to their sources. He was stunned to see that the Israeli warships, still running without lights, had closed to half a mile.

"*Fanning,* this is *Herev.* Do you read me? Over."

Captain Nichols picked up the microphone. "This is *Fanning.* Over."

"I repeat, why is your afterdeck dark? Over."

Captain Nichols hesitated—Haddix had asked that the floods remain off for at least one minute—then replied, "This is Captain Bill Nichols. I'm alone on the bridge, and I hit the wrong switch. Over."

There followed a silence that, though brief, fully conveyed the Israeli commander's skepticism. "Very well. You will please turn the lights back on at once. Over."

"Sorry, if I do that, half of them'll pop. I have to wait for the bulbs to cool. Over."

"I want those lights on before my men board," the Israeli commander said frostily. "You have ninety seconds. Quite frankly, I do not care how many of them break. Over."

"Message understood," Captain Nichols said, praying that he had bought Navy enough time.

Their path hallucinatorily illuminated by random stabs of the Israeli searchlights, Edna Haddix led the three-man Zippo Squad forward from the fantail. Her bandaged right hand smarted from her recent tasks and the cold, lashing rain was starting to sap her body heat, but she was barely conscious of these discomforts. Instead, Haddix was preoccupied by what she had spotted just before asking Captain Nichols to douse the floods: a lone silhouette lurking on an upper deck of the superstructure. Who had it been? More to the point, how long had he been there—and exactly how much had he seen? She trusted Eldon Gary, manning the winch, as well as the men trailing behind her, to remain silent about her recent activities. But would the shadowy figure up on the cabin deck?

Without warning, the floods atop the stanchions and superstructure sprang back to life with an intensity that made her flinch.

The crew, she noted, was gathering by the starboard gangway.

Claiming their undivided attention were four warships—a 150-foot-
long corvette and three smaller patrol boats—ominously slicing into
the bright pool of light radiating once more from *Fanning II*'s afterdeck. The deck-mounted guns of the Israeli boats were trained on
the research vessel. In addition the deck of the corvette bristled
with a platoon of soldiers in foul weather gear, their assault rifles
leveled at the Americans.

"After you garage *Ernie* and bring the sled up past eleven thousand
nine hundred feet, turn it over to Eldon," Wendell Trent said to
Rick Wolfe and j.g. Tom Parkhill. He shoveled the last of the smok-
ing-gun videotapes into the safe beneath the chart table and spun
the lock. "You are then to leave through the rear hatch . . . and
padlock it behind you."

"I doubt that'll slow them," Wolfe said.

"So do I. But it's worth a shot. Parkhill, lock up after me."

Trent stepped from the control van. Cursing himself for leaving
his slicker back in his cabin, he started forward—and almost collided with Haddix, who was passing by on her way back from the
fantail.

Her hair was rain plastered, her clothes sodden.

"Where the hell'd you run off to, Jonesy?"

"Not now," she replied.

Trent studied Haddix's Delphic expression for a moment, then
transferred his attention to the Zippo Squad immediately behind
her. Each man was carrying several sticks of dynamite. "Jesus,
didn't you hear me say no resistance?" he barked. "One of the
Israelis sees those, his trigger finger just might start to itch. Ditch
the damned things in that barrel over there, and pull a tarp or
something over it."

Rather than force his way through the thickening crowd, Trent
crossed to the starboard railing, climbed up to straddle it, and took
his first look at the enemy.

The rain was dramatically reducing visibility, but he could see the
Israeli patrol boats veering into position some thirty yards away.

Two were heading around to port while the third swung broadside to take up station near *Fanning II*'s stern. Meanwhile the corvette —a sleek gunboat half the research vessel's length—continued to angle closer. On its deck, interspersed with the armed soldiers, were sailors busily lowering fenders over the side preparatory to coming alongside.

Now an Israeli officer on the near-side bridge wing of the corvette raised a bullhorn. "Wendell Trent," he said, his voice metallic, "please identify yourself."

Trent cupped his hands and yelled, "Over here."

The Israeli officer turned his way. "You will clear room for my men to board. And you will move forward to meet Major Amichai."

Trent acknowledged the command with a wave and hopped down from the railing.

By the time he made his way amidships, the crew of *Fanning II,* by now grown to some forty strong, had moved back to form a rough semicircle around the gangway.

The research ship and the corvette were bobbing perilously out of sync in the six-foot swells.

An Israeli sailor gauged the heave, leapt over the side onto *Fanning II,* and began to fasten a line. He was quickly followed by several others.

Trent fought to keep his emotions in check; twenty years in the U.S. Navy had done nothing to prepare him for surrendering control of his ship without a fight.

The first Israeli soldier to jump across was a wiry, green-eyed man in his early thirties. His rain-darkened beret bore the insignia of a commando unit. He immediately sought out Trent, saluted crisply, and said, "Mr. Trent, I am Amichai."

"Spare me the formalities," Trent said in a steely voice. "You and your men are in gross violation of international maritime law."

Amichai sized up the American. Behind him the last of his platoon piled onto the deck of *Fanning II* and the corvette began to pull away. Finally the Israeli said, "That is not for us to debate. All your men are present?"

Trent shook his head. "The skipper's on the bridge and the chief engineer's down in the engine room. I have a man guarding a saboteur, and three men are overseeing our underwater vehicles."

"They are all instructed to not resist? Good." Amichai turned and gave a hand signal that spurred seven of his nine men into action. One started for the fantail. A pair of commandos took up crowd-control positions, one on the afterdeck and the other halfway up the starboard-side ladder to the boat deck. Four others hurried through the nearest hatch into the superstructure.

"Now, Mr. Trent, where are the prisoners? The Frenchman, Vigneron, and the Israeli, Kahane?"

"We only have one person under confinement. Vigneron's in the laundry room . . . one deck down, port side."

Amichai fired off a command in Hebrew. One of his two remaining commandos raced into the superstructure.

Trent turned to scan the crowd. "Ari?"

Ariel Kahane raised his hand.

Amichai grunted, then said to Trent, "You are raising the vehicles?"

"Yes."

"Excellent. I want this ship under way at once."

"I can't, without losing the vehicles," Trent replied. "They're deep in a treacherous ravine . . . that's why I have three men working on the recovery."

"I see. We must wait how long?"

Trent turned to Haddix. "Jonesy?"

"Ninety minutes to bring them to the surface," she replied. "Then we have to check them out and haul them back on deck."

"This takes how long?"

"Half an hour, give or take," Haddix said. "Longer if we have to go through a full decontamination."

"I am sorry?" said Amichai. "What is this 'decontamination,' please?"

"Jonesy, I don't believe our friend got the full brief." Trent turned to the Israeli. "They didn't tell you our vehicles have been exposed to intense radiation?"

Amichai stared at the Americans, trying to figure out if this was some kind of ruse. "And if you retrieve the vehicles without this decontamination procedure?"

"Plan on having children?" asked Haddix. "Want them to have more than ten fingers?"

"Very well," Amichai said. His orders stipulated no harm to personnel as well as no damage to the underwater vehicles. "But tell me, it is not possible to move the ship before the vehicles are on the surface?"

"Once they've cleared the worst of the ravine, we can make one or two knots," Haddix conceded.

"This takes how long?"

"Five to ten minutes. But we'll have to stay over the deepest part of the Trench, and we have to come to a complete stop later, when we decontaminate and complete the recovery."

"That is acceptable," Amichai said. "You will prepare to depart on an eastward heading at a speed of two knots."

Haddix shook her head. "We might run into a wall. As long as the vehicles are at risk, we need to head southeast."

Amichai nodded.

"Jonesy, will you coordinate with Bill?"

Haddix turned and headed for the intercom at winch operator Eldon Gary's station.

Captain Nichols, alone on *Fanning II*'s bridge, ran his finger across a chart and said, "Navy, I can give you two-three-zero. That'll keep us over deep water until the vehicles are up. Over."

"Sounds good, Bill," Edna Haddix replied from the afterdeck. "What's the latest Met? Over."

"Seems like another squall system'll be arriving from the north-northwest in the next half hour." He eyed the wind gauges. "In fact, we're already getting gusts up to twenty-two, twenty-four knots. Over."

"I copy. Listen, Bill, there're some bandits coming your way. Remember, don't resist. Over."

"Don't worry, Navy, I'll treat my visitors with the utmost courtesy. Bridge out."

Captain Nichols called down to alert the engine room of their imminent departure, then crossed to the control panel. He was programming in the new course when he heard boots rapidly clumping up the passageway leading from the cabin deck. Turning to the Israeli commandos bursting onto the bridge, he said, "Shalom."

The storm had intensified by the time Roland Vigneron, rubbing his handcuff-chafed right wrist, climbed through the watertight doors onto the afterdeck. He blinked owlishly through his rain-splattered glasses, then shrank back from the hostile expressions on the faces of *Fanning II*'s gathered crew.

An Israeli commando emerged to take the French scientist's elbow and escort him toward Major Amichai.

"Just like a Frog," Billy Ray McConkey sneered as his former buddy passed by. "Either at your feet or at your throat."

Vigneron averted his face.

"Monsieur Vigneron? I am Amichai," the Israeli officer said, stepping forward. "Time is short. Where do the Americans keep the videotaped data?"

Vigneron mutely pointed to the bright blue control van.

Amichai turned to Wendell Trent and said, "You will take us there, please."

"You have no right to enter my van," Trent said. "We're a civilian vessel conducting seismic studies, and our data are proprietary."

Amichai's mouth softened into a wry grin. "As you put it so eloquently several minutes ago, Mr. Trent, 'Spare me the formalities.' I prefer not to force my way in."

Trent hesitated, then nodded. The game was up, which meant his primary mission now was to keep the growing tensions from escalating to a flash point. He was starting for the van when the sullen hush was pierced by a shrill voice.

Amichai wheeled toward the disturbance and yelled, "Arik."

Seven yards away a livid baby-faced commando stood inches from Ariel Kahane, screaming in Hebrew at the graduate student.

Kahane said something back through tight lips.

"Arik!"

The baby-faced commando, adrenalized beyond hearing, wielded his Galil assault rifle like a staff to jostle Kahane backward, then continued his harangue.

Amichai grimly fought his way through the crowd, closely followed by Trent and Haddix.

"Yo," McConkey suddenly called out. "What the fuck's your problem? Leave the kid alone."

The baby-faced commando wheeled and hissed, "Shut up, American, is not your concern."

"Come on, Cowboy, lighten up," navigator Len Heppel said, reaching out a restraining hand.

But McConkey, his fuse grown critically short, shook off Heppel and took a step forward. "Listen, punk, why don't you just run along home? Must be a couple of Arab grandmaws you ain't beat up on yet."

Before Major Amichai could reach him, the baby-faced commando sank the butt of his rifle into McConkey's stomach, dropping the American to the deck.

Amichai, his face pale with rage, said something in Hebrew and held out his hands.

The baby-faced commando froze in disbelief.

Amichai repeated his order.

Numbly, the baby-faced commando engaged the safety on his Galil and handed over the weapon. Then, with as much dignity as he could muster, he made his way back to the gangway.

Amichai knelt beside Trent, who was tending to McConkey.

The sonarman remained sprawled on the rain-soaked deck, laboring to suck in air.

"Sir, you have my profound apologies," the Israeli officer said. "My man is relieved of duty, and he shall face a court-martial when we return to port. Is there anything I can do to help you?"

McConkey snorted despite his pain. "Yeah. You can get the fuck off our ship."

Twenty feet away Haddix, having tugged Ariel Kahane free of the fracas, was now questioning him.

"They insist that I go with them," the graduate student explained. "They say Haifa has so ordered, because I am a reservist."

"That's not an order you can refuse, is it?"

"No, if they have written authorization. But such a piece of paper, this little schmuck cannot produce."

Haddix laughed lightly. "Ari, I think you've spent too much time in America. Due process isn't a universal concept."

"Navy, believe me when I tell you that there is no society more legalistic than Israel." Kahane hesitated, then said, "You and Mr. Trent, can you not persuade them that I am also an American citizen who refuses to leave this ship?"

"If that's what you want," she said. "But don't forget our talk this afternoon. If you plan to live and work in Israel, there's bound to be repercussions, even if the order happens to be technically illegal."

Kahane looked down and reluctantly nodded. "As usual, you are right, Navy. About this, about not having me in the van . . . what I do not know, I cannot tell."

She patted him on the shoulder.

"And one other thing," he said earnestly, his eyes swinging up. "Your secret is safe with me."

For a split second Haddix was at a loss. Then she said, "That was you up on the cabin deck a few minutes ago?"

Kahane nodded.

"Good. Then I have nothing to worry about. Come on, let's go see how Cowboy's doing." As Haddix led him back toward the others, she suddenly thought to ask, "By the way, what did you say to that commando to get him so angry?"

"I tell him he behaves like a Nazi."

"Oy."

When they neared the center of the crowd, Amichai was listening to his walkie-talkie.

"Ari, what're they saying?" whispered Haddix.

"The soldiers, they say they are finished removing the circuit boards and tubes from all of our radios."

But *Fanning II* hadn't been struck totally dumb, Haddix suddenly realized; for the past six hours Trent had been communicating with Zeman by way of her turbocharged CD, which was still hooked up to the PC in the van.

Amichai flicked his unit to transmit and began speaking into it in Hebrew.

"He is telling the captain of the corvette that our radios are disabled," Kahane translated, peering up into the rain with puzzlement. "He says the fly-boys can go home."

Thirty thousand feet above the southwest coast of Crete, a communications specialist aboard the Israeli Air Force E-2C AWACS that had been lazily circling over international waters for the past twenty-nine minutes punched on his intercom. "Captain, we have been instructed to terminate the present mission and resume our patrol of Sector Lima."

Ahead in the cockpit the pilot said into his headset mike, "Message acknowledged. Schwarzman, cease jamming. Levy, give me a new heading."

He began to bank the electronics-packed 707 to the north.

"Not a moment too soon," his copilot muttered.

"How is that?"

"Schwarzman tells me we have been under constant radar interrogation for the past twenty minutes. Many nations must be asking themselves, what are those Jews doing up there?"

The pilot shrugged. "Myself, I am curious to know what those Jews down there are doing."

"**A**nnie, is it my imagination, or is the room shrinking?"

Ann Davis made a show of looking around the windowless cubicle she shared with Clifford Zeman deep inside the NIS facility in suburban Maryland. "The room's shrinking. Hell, Cliff, sometimes I liked you better when you smoked."

"So did I," Zeman replied with a grunt.

In truth, it wasn't nicotine deprivation that had him on edge, or fatigue, even though he'd gotten perhaps twelve hours sleep over the past four-plus days, mostly on his office couch. Nor was it the paper chase that always seemed to end up one frustrating step late, as with the discovery of Roland Vigneron's true allegiance. Nor was it the running battles with Eugene Da Silva, the senator, assorted bureaucrats, and, all too soon, with his boss, Bart. Nor was it the mushrooming list of imponderables, chief among them how both Soviet Jews and radioactive material of unknown provenance had ended up on the same Israeli submarine in early 1968.

Instead, Zeman realized, it was his sudden helplessness that had him climbing the wall. Six thousand miles and seven time zones to the east, in the waning moments of a complex mission, his agent, Wendell Trent, had vanished from the net—and with him the last semblance of Zeman's control.

The phone rang.

Davis immediately grabbed it, listened for a moment, then said, "It's Morrison."

Zeman took the receiver: "Don, Cliff here. Anything?"

"One of our birds detected an AWACS over the coordinates you gave me," the NSA analyst replied. "An E-2C. It belongs to Israel."

"Was your bird able to paint the sea?"

"I'm afraid not. There's still one-hundred-percent cloud cover over the entire Eastern Med."

"Thanks, Don. We owe you one." Zeman was out of his chair and halfway to the door when the intercom squawked.

"Mr. Zeman?" It was one of the communications-room technicians. "The jamming's stopped."

"When?"

"Fifteen seconds ago, sir."

"Have you reestablished a link yet?"

"That's a negative, sir. We're hailing on every frequency across the band, but there's no response."

Zeman thought for a moment, then said, "Son, how long was transmission interrupted?"

"We clock it at twenty-nine minutes, sir."

"All right. Keep trying, and let me know as soon as you raise a signal—any signal." Zeman wheeled toward Davis. "Annie, get back to Morrison. See if he can find out if the AWACS has left the site, and if so, when."

"Right. Where'll you be?"

"Shorty's office. If this string of events isn't hard enough proof, that hard-nosed son of a bitch's going to learn what hurt is."

Zeman continued to the door of the secure room, opened it—and stopped short.

Standing there, his hand poised to knock, was a man with thinning hair, tortoiseshell glasses, and an expression of uncontained fury.

"Zeman," Bart growled, pushing his way into the room. "We have to talk."

"Let's do it in Brock's office."

"Who's he?"

"One of CNO's deputies," Zeman replied. "Listen, Bart, that Israeli sub in the Med? My agent found radioactive material aboard it. He was in the middle of his report when something knocked him off the air. We have confirmation he was jammed. We also have confirmation an Israeli E-2C with jamming capabilities was overhead. It just stopped . . . but now I can't raise my agent."

Bart blinked as he tried to absorb the data. Then he nodded and hurried down the hall after Zeman.

THE EASTERN MED

1851 Zulu/9:51 P.M. local time

Rick Wolfe and j.g. Tom Parkhill had just finished winching *Bert,* with little *Ernie* securely tucked in its belly, clear of the ravine when Wendell Trent entered the control van with two men in tow.

Wolfe regarded Roland Vigneron with contempt, then looked to the Israeli soldier.

"It is now safe to move the ship?" asked Major Amichai.

"Yes," Wolfe replied. "Want me to notify the bridge?"

"No, not yet."

Amichai ushered the Americans out, locked the hatch, and found the switch for the overhead fluorescent lights.

Vigneron began skimming the mission log. Working backward from the last entry, he noted that the initial sighting of *Dakar* had come shortly after four P.M.

The French scientist crossed to the shelves of videotapes.

"Merde."

"What is wrong?" asked Amichai.

"The tapes I want, they are not . . ." Vigneron spun, hurried to rear of the van, and knelt in front of the safe beneath the chart table. It was locked.

"We have plastique," Amichai said.

Vigneron shook his head. "Security was not tight at the beginning of the expedition, before Haddix and Trent took over. Several of us know the combination."

Thirty seconds later he pulled from the open safe a videocassette labeled ROV P & T / 05-31-88 / 1600–1700. As he suspected, it had not been rewound.

Vigneron carried the tape to the bank of VCRs on the van's left-hand wall and inserted it into one of the decks.

"The Americans have nice toys," Amichai observed wistfully. "But the video equipment, most of it is Japanese."

Vigneron snorted. "Patriotism goes only so far. If you are a scientist, and your project depends on telepresencing, would you settle for hardware that says Magnavox or Sylvania?"

The French scientist seated himself at the *Bert* engineering station, threw the VCR feed up on the entire row of large forward monitors, and began to fast-reverse the tape.

Across all five screens the same images of the camera's herky-jerky pan along a smooth metallic surface.

"They found the submarine," Vigneron said, glancing at the time stamp. "More than five hours ago."

"In that case you are to be evacuated with all the tapes which contain evidence," Amichai said. "How many is that?"

"Four tapes per hour, six hours . . . twenty-four."

Amichai raised his walkie-talkie and ordered that a watertight duffel be brought to the van. "Also, signal the helicopter," he said. "I want it here in five minutes. That is all."

"Helicopter?" asked Vigneron warily.

Amichai had begun to write something on a notepad. "Yes. You are to be flown to Crete. A jet waits there to fly you to Tel Aviv."

The Frenchman tried to hide his distress.

"I am to give the Americans a receipt for those things we remove," Amichai said. "Assorted radio tubes and circuits. Now, twenty-four videocassettes, is that correct?"

"Oui."

"You will gather them for me, please."

"We should also take the mission log and the videotape log," Vigneron said. "Or at least the relevant pages."

Amichai nodded and continued to write.

There was a knock on the forward hatch. Vigneron went over to admit an Israeli commando carrying an empty duffel bag, which the two men began loading with the videocassettes in the safe.

At the back of the safe the Frenchman spotted the laser disc on which Haddix had recorded the ghostly wet suit. "Of course," he exclaimed, "the Americans also record images on laser disc!"

Vigneron grabbed the data logger's clipboard. *Bon,* he thought, the disc currently in the laser recorder hadn't been changed since noon. Crossing to the *Bert* engineering station, he typed in a command to see if any electronic stills remained in the holding unit aboard the sled. No, they had all been retrieved and permanently recorded. He ejected the silvery, LP-sized disc from the recorder and reached to the shelves in front of the engineering station for an empty cardboard sleeve.

"Is there any other evidence we are forgetting?" asked Amichai as he accepted the disc and log sheets.

"They installed a radiation detector on the ROV. The data from it is stored on that computer's hard disc," Vigneron said, pointing to the central processing unit beneath the navigator's station.

"You can remove it?"

"Not before your helicopter arrives," Vigneron replied. "However, it is possible to make the data useless. Merely destroy the drive."

Amichai hesitated, then nodded.

Vigneron went to the toolbox, grabbed a hammer, and methodically smashed in the front of the central processing unit.

"I can think of nothing else," he said, panting from his exertions. "We have all the . . . *Moment.*"

Vigneron had just noticed Edna Haddix's portable CD player. Why was it jacked into the spare PC? And why did a second cable run down under the *Bert* engineering station? The French scientist returned to the rear of the van and sank to one knee. The second cable was plugged into an antenna receptacle under the console.

"Major, add this to your list, please," Vigneron said, unhooking Haddix's toy and tossing it in the duffel bag.

"We are to confiscate evidence, not loot personal effects," Amichai replied crossly.

"If that plays compact discs, I am Louis Pasteur," Vigneron said. "I believe it to be some type of miniaturized transmitter. If so, I assure you that your Mossad technicians will find it of interest."

"Very well." Amichai paused and cocked his head. A distant sound was beginning to penetrate the walls of the van. He turned to Vigneron and said, "Come."

Edna Haddix and Wendell Trent had been huddled in conversation over by the Zodiac when they picked up the distant sound of an approaching helicopter. Now the craft—a French-made Super Frelon with civilian markings—was settling into a hover 150 feet above *Fanning II*.

Across the afterdeck Major Amichai, Roland Vigneron, and a commando carrying a duffel bag were emerging from the van.

Trent started through the crowd toward them.

As Vigneron nervously peered up into the wind-lashed rain, Amichai spoke into his walkie-talkie, then issued an order to the man with the duffel bag.

That soldier and another commando hurried aft.

The pilot of the helicopter, fighting to maintain trim, jockeyed down to within one hundred feet of the afterdeck. A grounding wire snaked through the dome of light down to the deck, followed by a sling that gyrated wildly in winds now approaching Force Six. The helicopter crew was having a devilish time trying to thread the sling between the floodlight stanchions and the taut sled cable that ascended from the traction unit to the top of the A-frame.

Amichai turned and said something to Vigneron.

The French scientist emphatically shook his head.

Trent reached Amichai just in time to hear the Israeli officer say, "You prefer to swim home?"

Vigneron, looking as pale as death, reluctantly shuffled toward the middle of the afterdeck.

"What's in that duffel?" asked Trent.

"Mostly videotapes, Mr. Trent. They document the fact that you willfully violated the sovereignty of an Israeli warship."

"You have no right to take them."

"They will be returned," replied Amichai. "To prove it to you that Israel does not intend to keep your data, here is a receipt for every item we borrow."

Trent unfolded the sheet of paper. Damn it, he thought, someone —probably Vigneron—had figured out that Jonesy's CD player was a transmitter; their last link to the beach was now in that duffel bag.

Out on the afterdeck the two commandos had finally managed to strap an increasingly panicky Vigneron into the sling. One Israeli removed the Frenchman's glasses and tucked them in the scientist's breast pocket. The other was trying to get him to accept the duffel; failing that, he lashed it to the sling.

Amichai walkie-talkied the helicopter to raise the sling.

Vigneron's mouth flew open as he was suddenly yanked skyward, but his scream was mercifully drowned out by the leaden throb of the rotors. Seven feet off the deck the French scientist nearly pendulumed into the sled cable. Then he was rising to the level of the floodlights, and then he vanished into the blackness beyond.

Amichai turned and said, "Now, Mr. Trent, if you will please instruct your captain to get under way?"

"Aren't you and your men leaving the ship?"

"Not just yet, I think."

Across the way, on the bridge of the corvette *Herev,* Captain Meron Litvak lowered his binoculars. His ships were assuming escort positions two hundred meters aflank *Fanning II,* which had begun plowing southwest at two knots.

The events of the past two hours weighed heavily on Litvak.

Though the mission was being personally conducted by a cabinet-level official of his government, it wore a bad odor. Firing upon and boarding a civilian vessel in international waters; disabling all its radios; forcibly removing private property; and now, commandeering the ship—there was no word to describe these acts other than criminal. Of course, he was only obeying orders. But that was not a defense an Israeli felt comfortable making.

"Captain?"

Litvak turned and accepted a flimsy from a signalman.

The message came from the pilot of the Israeli Air Force E-2C AWACS that had been jamming the American transmissions. The surveillance plane now 140 miles to the north en route to its next mission, had just detected a pair of jets taking off from the U.S. installation at Iráklion on Crete and heading south-by-southwest; estimated time of arrival, fifteen minutes.

Jets and not helicopters, Litvak thought gratefully, just as Ben Goren had predicted. He picked up his walkie-talkie and uttered two prearranged code words.

The first instructed Major Amichai, still aboard *Fanning II,* to herd the entire crew down into the lower corridors to prevent them from signaling the approaching planes.

The second instructed the three Dabur-class coastal patrol boats to immediately close on the port side of the research vessel, against which they would tuck themselves in single file. Meanwhile, *Herev* began to veer in toward the starboard side.

The moment the Israeli warships reached their positions, Litvak issued his final command.

Suddenly, the floods illuminating *Fanning II*'s afterdeck were cut. A few seconds later every light aboard the four Israeli warships went off.

Litvak knew the stratagem would be futile against slow-flying helicopters, but it just might help them elude detection by the jets. The American pilots, upon descending over the research vessel's last reported position, would find themselves contending with low, impenetrable storm clouds and a strengthening rain that further curbed visibility. Flying virtually blind and fearful of stalling out, they would most likely be forced to rely on their down-looking radar. Accordingly, he had deployed his darkened warships to blend with *Fanning II* into a single radar image.

But even if his gamble worked, how long before the American helicopters arrived?

Litvak peered out at the driving rain—it had grown almost heavy enough to ground even the Sea Stallions, the U.S. Navy's work-horse all-weather helicopters—and began praying for it to fall still harder.

SUITLAND, MARYLAND

1923 Zulu/3:23 P.M. local time

Vice Admiral Ronald ("Shorty") Brock had the well-tanned look of an outdoorsman and the uncallused hands of one whose communions with nature took place mostly on golf courses. As one of CNO's deputies he boasted an office far more sumptuous than the windowless secure rooms at the naval intelligence facility. Fifteen minutes after scrambling a pair of A-7 fighter bombers from Crete in response to Clifford Zeman's data, Brock, two of his aides, and the DOE contingent—Zeman and Ann Davis, along with Bart, their superior—were gathered around a speaker unit, working to follow the transmission from the Eastern Med.

The A-7's were just approaching *Fanning II*'s last fix.

The lead pilot, his voice distorted by the whine of his engine and intermittent crackles of static, was saying, "Admiral, we're showing a radar target one mile due east, and, uh . . . sir, my wingman advises they are not responding to our calls. Over."

"Lieutenant, what is your altitude," Brock said.

"Nine hundred feet, sir."

"We understand the weather's pretty nasty out there."

"Affirmative, sir," the pilot replied. "We've got winds gusting to Force Six, solid squall clouds one hundred feet below us, and heavy precip at deck level. Over."

Zeman scribbled a quick note—*Can they eyeball the ship?*—and passed it to Brock.

Brock scowled and released the Talk button. "What's the exact height of your ship?" he asked Zeman. "Including its communications array?"

Ann Davis riffled through her notes until she found *Fanning II*'s specs. "One hundred twenty-five feet."

Brock pressed the Talk button and said, "Lieutenant, we understand you are carrying FLIRs."*

"Affirmative, sir."

"Can you boys drop down for a quick look-see."

"That's an affirmative, sir," the pilot replied without hesitation.

"The target rises to one-two-five feet above the deck," Brock said, "I repeat, one-two-five feet."

"I copy one-two-five feet. Piece of cake, sir. Over."

Brock released the Talk button.

"Thank you," Zeman said.

"Don't thank me, thank them," Brock growled. "For the record, what I'm asking them to do ought to rate hazardous-duty pay. Plus, don't expect much by way of an eyewitness account. They'll be flying at two hundred sixty knots just above the deck, in zero visibility. Your ship's going to look like some flashing target on a Nintendo game. We'll probably have to wait for the IR photographs."

"How long to develop and analyze them?"

Brock glanced at a small clock on his desk. "From the time the

---

*FLIR: *Forward Looking Infra-Red camera, which senses and measures heat emissions.*

A-7s return to Iráklion, less than an hour. We should have them here no later than five."

The lead pilot's voice came through the speaker again. "Admiral, we have a visual contact, a single vessel maybe the size of a coastal freighter, she's showing running lights . . . coming up dead on her stern, passing over her . . . now. Sir, there's some kind of tall gizmo at the stern. Over."

"That'll be the A-frame," Zeman said. "Sounds like *Fanning*, but its afterdeck should be all lit up."

Brock pressed the Talk button. "Lieutenant, any lights on the afterdeck."

"Negative, sir. Just the running lights, and a few cabins. We're coming around for a broadside pass. Over."

"Is the ship under way?" asked Brock.

"Hard to say, sir. If she is, it's just barely."

"Any sign of activity aboard?"

"Hold on, we're about to overfly from starboard. . . . Negative, sir, and that's kind of peculiar. My wingman and I've been buzzing her close enough to wake the dead. Didn't see a single soul come out on deck."

"And they're still not responding to your radio calls?"

"No, sir. No signal lights either."

"We copy. Lieutenant, make another photo run, then return to base."

"Admiral, request permission to make two more passes, just to be safe? Over."

"Permission granted. Out."

Zeman's frown deepened. "Fanning's carrying a crew of more than fifty, its radios are down, and not a single man comes out to wave at two low-flying jets? Something's not adding up."

Brock said to an aide, "Get me the latest Met for that area."

"Those infrared photos might clue us in on what's happening," Zeman prompted, "but a lot else could happen between now and five. Most of it bad."

"Save the sales pitch," Brock said tartly. "Weather permitting, I'm sending in a flight of Sea Stallions."

"Sir?" the aide said. "They're reporting a cold front stalled in that vicinity. Severe squalls, with winds of gale force or better, for the next three to four hours."

"Son of a bitch," Brock muttered. "Conditions like that could cost me half my choppers. Sorry, Zeman, I won't risk it until I see the IRs. But I'll put them on standby . . . they'll go at the first break in the weather. And I'll check the positions of our nearest surface vessels."

As the DOE contingent got up to leave Brock's office, Zeman looked first to Ana Davis and then to Bart. They were equally at a loss for words.

THE EASTERN MED

2018 Zulu/11:18 P.M. local time

Forty-five minutes after the two A-7s had winged off back toward Crete, *Fanning II* and its four Israeli escorts slowed to a dead stop three and a half miles due east of the *Dakar* site. The stanchion-mounted floods on the research vessel's afterdeck sprang back on: *Bert,* with little *Ernie* tucked in its belly, had been winched to a depth of fifty feet and was ready to be retrieved.

Edna Haddix and her five-man recovery team, bundled in foul weather gear, life vests, and hard hats, hurried through the unabating storm toward the fantail. The protective-suited DOE decontamination specialists trod clumsily after them.

Wendell Trent and Major Amichai took up position beside chief mechanic Eldon Gary at the middeck winch console.

The Israeli officer looked to starboard. *Herev* was idling a mere hundred meters away, but he could barely make out the corvette through the rain.

Haddix and a decontamination specialist, the one carrying a radiation detector mounted at the end of a pole, had moved to directly under the giant yellow A-frame that leaned out over the stern. They were peering down into a sea grown so angry that it was sloshing onto the deck. Rick Wolfe had positioned himself in one corner of the fantail and Sam Lippman in the other; each man wielded a twelve-foot-long metal boom tipped with a slip-knotted guide rope. Next to them the other two DOE specialists were uncoiling fire hoses from the built-in cabinets on each side of the A-frame.

The walkie-talkie on the winch console crackled to life; Haddix's voice was barely audible over the storm and the yammering diesel that powered the traction unit. "Eldon, ready when you are."

"Roger that, Navy. Coming up." Gary began winching in cable.

Suddenly, *Bert* broke the surface.

The sled inched clear of the seven-foot swells.

Haddix hand-signaled Gary to stop.

Dangling under the canted A-frame, some ten feet outboard of the fantail, *Bert* began to yaw crazily just above the boiling wave crests.

Wolfe and Lippman quickly extended their booms; their task was to use their slip-knotted guide ropes to lasso the skids at the bottom of the sled.

Amichai watched with rapt fascination. The exercise reminded him of a documentary on American rodeos that he had recently seen on Israeli TV. What the men at the fantail were attempting struck him as even more difficult than roping a fleeing calf; the cowboys, atop their horses, enjoyed a more stable platform than this pitching, rain-slickened deck, and their target was a frightened young animal, not a wildly thrashing three-ton machine.

"Most impressive," Amichai said softly to no one in particular. "Most impressive."

■ ■ ■

Captain Meron Litvak, on seeing the first of the deep-sea vehicle's skids successfully snagged, lowered his binoculars and resumed pacing the bridge of his corvette. He had been waiting more than ten minutes for a response to his request to amend his orders.

As things currently stood, Major Amichai's platoon was to remain aboard the research vessel until Haifa signaled its warships to withdraw. Evidently, the Israeli planners had not counted on any reconnaissance flights into the area. But the Americans had demonstrated the depth of their concern for the missing boat by dispatching jets into the teeth of severe squalls. Litvak reckoned the luck that had been with them when the A-7's had streaked by would never hold against Sea Stallions. He had been assured that a Mossad agent was monitoring air traffic at both NATO bases on Crete. Still, helicopters could reach his present position in roughly forty-five minutes. It would take him a full thirty minutes to bring the commandos back aboard *Herev* and sail to the horizon—and Litvak considered this far too thin a safety margin in seas like these.

"Captain? It is Ben Goren who calls."

Litvak picked up the receiver.

"Meron? This is Ben. Your request is approved."

"Thank you," Litvak said.

"You will remain in close contact with the research vessel until the order to withdraw is given?"

"Affirmative. I shall maintain a distance of two hundred meters, from which I can reboard in less than five minutes." Litvak hesitated. "Ben, the Israeli student, Kahane. What are we to do about him?"

"The Frenchman's analysis of the data from the American ship will tell us all we need to know. Kahane's knowledge is immaterial. If he wishes to remain with the Americans, let him."

"Yes, sir."

"Good luck, Meron," Goren said. "I shall pay for the dinner when you return to Haifa."

Litvak, his spirits lifting, set down the receiver and began issuing orders to bring *Herev* back alongside *Fanning II.*

■ ■ ■

On his fourth stab Rick Wolfe finally looped the slipknot over the
sled's port skid.

Behind him, j.g. Tom Parkhill quickly uncinched the guide rope
from Wolfe's boom, hustled it over to a small deck winch, and fed it
into the unit.

Twenty feet away Ezra Schell had already rigged the guide rope
from Sam Lippman's boom in a second winch.

"Okay, take up the slack," Edna Haddix shouted above the
storm and the diesel.

When the guide ropes were taut, Haddix made sure that Wolfe
and Schell had moved back from the edge, then turned to the decontamination specialist with the radiation detector. "I'll get Eldon
started. When the sled's snubbed tight against the stern, give him
the 'cut' sign."

The DOE man nodded.

Haddix retreated to the two deck winches, then raised her right
arm and made a brisk circling motion.

Chief mechanic Eldon Gary slowly began to retract the A-frame,
which was leaning out over the stern, back to an upright position, a
maneuver that brought the vehicle toward the fantail.

As *Bert* swung inward, Parkhill and Schell continued to keep
tension on the guide ropes.

The sled crashed against the stern with a resounding thud that
was audible above the storm.

The decontamination specialist hand-signaled the winch operator
to stop, then knelt.

The top of the vehicle was six inches above the deck. He consulted the radiation-sensitive badge on the chest of his protective
suit. Good, he thought; the three-mile journey from the bottom of
the sea seemed to have washed off most of the contamination. Now
he began to run his detector over the vehicle. The upper half of the
sled was clean, but when he extended the pole with the detector
lower down, where *Ernie* was garaged, he picked up hot spots.

The DOE man signaled his two colleagues to start washing.

They turned on their hoses and advanced on the sled, sluicing it with jets of seawater.

Five minutes later the specialist with the detector scanned *Bert* again. Then he ran the detector over himself. Job done, he gave Haddix the high sign.

As soon as the three DOE men were clear of the fantail, she had Eldon Gary lower the A-frame back out over the stern a few degrees. When Parkhill and Schell loosened the guide ropes, the sled swung free.

Gary winched in cable to raise the vehicle level with the deck. Then he retracted the A-frame again, stopping only after *Ernie* had crossed the fantail and was dangling two feet above the afterdeck.

Despite the tension that Parkhill and Schell were keeping on the guide ropes, the sled—which, with the ROV tucked inside, weighed some three tons—started to pendulum.

Haddix, Wolfe, and Lippman rushed forward to grab on.

Trent was about to go lend a hand when Amichai's walkie-talkie crackled. Trent glanced at the Israeli, then remembered that he understood no Hebrew and hurried toward the stern.

When the four of them had stabilized the sled as best they could, Eldon Gary payed out cable until *Bert*'s skids settled on the deck.

"Outstanding piece of work, Jonesy."

Haddix nodded. As the others began chaining the sled in place, she said, "What's going on up there?"

Trent turned.

Amichai was approaching. In the distance his commandos had started to assemble by the starboard gangway, and beyond them the Israeli corvette was veering closer and preparing to dock.

"Mr. Trent, we are leaving your ship."

"Best news I've heard in two hours," Trent replied evenly. "Now if you'll return our radio components, we can get back to our work."

"Not just yet. We shall continue to escort you eastward for approximately one more hour. You are to proceed at full speed. The vehicles are raised, so I believe you can now make ten to twelve knots?"

"Closer to ten," Trent said. "Your divers gummed up our shafts pretty good."

"Ten knots is acceptable." Amichai held forth his walkie-talkie. "You will monitor our frequency, in the event there is a change in plans."

"How do I get this back to you?"

"Keep it. A souvenir, no?"

"What about the tapes you stole?" asked Trent.

"I understand my government will return them at an appropriate time. Oh, yes, the Israeli student, Kahane—he may stay with you. And, Mr. Trent, I assure you that the man who struck your sailor shall be disciplined."

Amichai drew himself up, snapped off a crisp salute, then pivoted and started for his men.

"I wonder if all Israelis are like him," Haddix said softly.

"How's that, Jonesy?"

"A strange blend of courtesy and arrogance."

"Like Ollie North?"

Haddix laughed. Then her smile faded. "Do you think they suspect anything?"

"Amichai doesn't miss much. If he thought something was wrong, he wouldn't be leaving."

"It doesn't matter," Haddix said. "Bill says this storm'll blow past us in three hours, so that's when the cavalry should arrive. We're home free, Trent. Hell, even if Rollie tweaks to the truth, and they come back, it'd take them a full day to search this ship."

"That's what I hate about you, Jonesy. Your pessimism."

She affectionately swatted him on the arm.

Up by the gangway Amichai waited until the last of his men had hopped aboard the corvette, then turned and gave Trent the go signal.

Haddix raised her walkie-talkie and called the bridge.

Soon *Fanning II* and its four escorts were once more heading out of harm's way, running southeast at nine knots.

After two and a half days of pounding its way across the Med, then crash-diving to avoid a pair of reconnaissance planes, the Israeli submarine *Sabra* had grown almost tolerable, thought *zampolit* Nikolai Krestnikov. Not that the quarters were any less cramped or the crew any less insolent, but at last the infernal diesels were silent, the buffeting diminished to a gentle roll. Krestnikov stood in the galley making himself tea—or so the Jews called the pallid swill that even a winter-numbed Siberian peasant would scorn. Oh, how he missed *Komsomolets,* with its bottomless samovar of bracing black *chai.* The Jews had only tea bags, and no matter how many he used, no matter how long he let them steep, the result was barely better than hot water; had he only known, he would have brought his own tea leaves. With a sigh Krestnikov removed the bags, stirred in three spoonfuls of sugar, and carried his mug forward.

The operations area buzzed with the urgent air of a hospital emergency room.

Dov Halevy, feeling as haggard as he looked, stood at the chart table conferring with his navigator. On top of the series of storms that had slowed *Sabra*'s passage, the American jets crisscrossing the area had cost him another half hour. As a result he was arriving on site a few minutes before midnight, local time, nearly three hours past his original ETA.

Halevy broke off his conversation and switched to English. "There you are, Krestnikov. Come have a look."

The *zampolit*'s face tightened. Not once on this voyage had the Israeli commander addressed him by his proper military rank, a lack of courtesy that no doubt explained the crew's boorishness. Nevertheless, he stepped over to the chart table.

"We are here," Halevy said, "some forty-two-point-five kilometers southwest of Crete. As soon as we locate a stable position below the surface turbulence, we will begin to paint the target.

Perhaps you would be good enough to fetch Yuri, so that we can synchronize guidance systems?"

Krestnikov nodded and headed forward to the torpedo room.

He found torpedo specialist Yuri Tikhonov scrutinizing the bottom of the firing control box.

"Is something wrong with the unit?" demanded Krestnikov.

"No, Comrade, nothing is wrong," Tikhonov replied, casually flipping the box right side up. There was in fact a fresh curl of metal under one of the screws on the bottom of the case, suggesting that the Israelis had stolen a peek inside; and if so, they surely must have done the same with the torpedo. Three days earlier Tikhonov would have automatically volunteered his suspicion. But now, having come to appreciate the studied informality of the Israeli crew—none of whom seemed afraid to approach his commander—and having come to realize that Krestnikov was an insufferable little *govnyuk,* Tikhonov felt no qualms about keeping silent. The *zampolit* pompously prided himself on his intelligence; if he wanted specific information, let him ask specific questions.

"They begin targeting soon," Krestnikov said. "Follow me."

Tikhonov set down the firing control box and trailed his superior back to the operations area.

"Yuri," Halevy said, "is everything okay with the torpedo?"

When Krestnikov translated, Tikhonov nodded. The Soviet torpedo specialist spotted the Israeli named Menachem. Guessing that it was *Sabra*'s weapons officer who had furtively inspected the deep-diving antisubmarine system, he threw the man a wink.

Menachem blushed.

Halevy started to draw a sketch. "Our target is an underwater abutment at a depth of approximately sixteen hundred meters. Sonar is painting the exact coordinates."

When Krestnikov translated, Tikhonov nodded.

"Our position," Halevy continued. He drew another fix, then connected the two points with a line, above which he wrote a number. "Current range, thirty-one hundred meters. Is that okay, Yuri?"

Without waiting for a translation Tikhonov shook his head, picked up a pencil, and wrote *2800 m.*

"Fine, we shall move in closer." Halevy issued a command to his XO, then turned back to Tikhonov. "We are currently at periscope depth, which is sixteen meters. Will this present a problem with the firing angle?"

When Krestnikov translated, Tikhonov replied, "No, at that range, the angle of declination does not much matter."

When Krestnikov translated, Halevy said, "Good. Now, what is the speed of your weapon?"

Krestnikov hesitated—this information was most privileged—but then realized it might be vital to Halevy. When he translated, Tikhonov wrote *56 k.*

Halevy and Menachem both whistled in admiration.

"Even allowing for guidewire clearance maneuvers," Menachem murmured in Hebrew, "even allowing for the time to get up to speed, that is only about two minutes from firing until impact."

"Come," Halevy said, leading Tikhonov to the sonar console. "Let me show you the target."

Haifa had relayed from *Herev* the satellite-navigation-determined position of *Fanning II*'s work site, accurate to two feet. With *x* and *y* coordinates in hand *Sabra*'s sonar specialist was now searching for the *z* coordinate with his vertical-scanning unit.

A cross-section of the abutment was starting to emerge.

"Our experts want the detonation down here, near the base," Halevy said. "Can you do that, Yuri?"

When Krestnikov translated, Tikhonov stared at the screen for several long seconds before uttering two words that, though in English, had become universal: "No prob-*lem*."

22,000 FEET OVER THE
EASTERN MED
■▬■▬■▬■▬■▬■▬■▬■▬■▬■

2126 Zulu/12:26 A.M. local time

The Mossad agent named Rachel glanced across the cabin of the Gulfstream at the owlish passenger who had boarded at Iráklion. Since takeoff Roland Vigneron had been working virtually nonstop on the video equipment arrayed on racks in the middle of the cabin. Now he was slumping back and swiveling away from the twin monitors. Rachel made her way to him and asked, "More coffee?"

"*S'il vous plaît.*"

The French scientist took off his glasses and kneaded his eyes. His headache would not go away. Nor, he noticed, would the gamy scent he exuded. During the nightmarish ascent by skyhook from *Fanning II*'s afterdeck, Vigneron had lost control of his bladder. Fortunately, the rain had washed away the worst of it, for there had been no time to properly clean himself. The moment the helicopter landed on Crete, he had been hustled across the rain-soaked tarmac to the waiting executive jet. There was a shower aboard, but scarcely had the plane risen into the air when Leon Rose himself had come on the radio to question him closely about the images on the confiscated videocassettes. From the Israeli general's horrified reaction to the footage of *Dakar*'s forward torpedo room, Vigneron suspected that Mossad technicians would soon be busy doctoring the tapes and the logs. Rose had then read off the sequences he wanted spliced onto a single tape, a tedious process that had taken more than an hour.

"Monsieur?"

Vigneron turned to accept the mug, saw that the woman had made café au lait, and smiled gratefully. "*Merci.*"

"You are welcome. How goes the work?"

Vigneron shrugged. "Very, very amateurish . . . there is no time to do it well . . . but I am finished."

"Congratulations. I have assembled some fresh clothes for you. If you would like to bathe now . . ."

He shook his head. "First, I must review the laser disc."

"Of course. Please let me know if there is anything else I can get for you."

"When are we scheduled to arrive?"

She checked her watch and replied, "We are to land at Lod in ninety minutes."

Vigneron nodded and took a sip of the steaming coffee. Thus braced, he rejacked one of the monitors to accept the laser recorder feed and inserted the disc. A quick and straightforward task, he thought nonchalantly, one that would leave him ample time to shower and relax before they touched down in Israel.

THE EASTERN MED

2149 Zulu/12:49 A.M. local time

The sudden sound, like that of fifty toilets being flushed simultaneously, caused Yuri Tikhonov to look up. It was only seawater flooding into *Sabra*'s Number Two tube. The Soviet torpedo specialist went back to running the final tests on his firing control box. Since first seeing his target on the Israeli submarine's sonar screen some forty-five minutes earlier, Tikhonov had understood why only this particular torpedo could perform the mission at hand; no other fish in the world was capable of operating at such great depths. Still, why would anyone wish to waste his fine weapon on an underwater rock formation? No matter; the shot before him was considerably easier than some he had achieved during exercises at Lake Baikal, if for no other reason than the abutment was guaranteed to remain stationary.

Crowded into the forward torpedo room with Tikhonov were Dov Halevy, weapons officer Menachem, with stopwatch in hand, and two Israeli crewmen. Halevy had rejected Nikolai Krestnikov's demand to be present; in fact the Israeli commander, on confining the detestable *zampolit* to the operations area, also instructed his XO to throw the Russian into a supply closet if he became a nuisance.

Gradually, the liquid roar subsided to a gurgle.

"The tube is flooded, sir," one of the crewman reported.

"Open Outer Door Two," Halevy said.

The crewman activated an electric motor that whined to life.

"Outer Door Two open."

Halevy turned to Tikhonov, who had completed his prefiring sequence, and said, "Yuri, you may fire when ready."

The torpedo specialist, unable to fathom the alien words, looked up questioningly.

Halevy flashed him a thumbs-up.

This Tikhonov understood; he nodded. All systems were operational. Without further ceremony he placed his right forefinger on the large red button and pressed it.

A hiss of air as the torpedo surged out of the tube and then, over the sibilant sound of roiling water, a soft click as Menachem started his stopwatch, followed a split second later by a crewman calling out, "Torpedo away!"

Dov Halevy let out his breath. Behind him Menachem was already stepping through the hatch to the operations area. Halevy turned to follow, but couldn't resist a last glance at the Soviet torpedo specialist.

Tikhonov was hunched over his firing control box, concentrating on the ever-changing numbers that flickered across the gauges. As if sensing the Israeli's gaze on him, he sneaked a peek over his shoulder. The commander looked too worried, the young specialist decided, so he jauntily returned Halevy's earlier thumbs-up signal before going back to monitor his torpedo's progress.

"**W**hat!"

The dozen or so men in the communications room of the Haifa Naval Station cringed before the wrath of Leon Rose, even though it was directed not at them but at a French-accented voice on the speakers.

"I repeat, the laser disc is blank," Roland Vigneron said. "They must have switched it. Can you not send back your corvette?"

"Imbecile! Why did you not inform me of this earlier? My ships separated from the *Fanning* more than fifteen minutes ago!" Rose turned to Ben Goren. "Order Litvak back immediately."

"General Rose," Vigneron said, "I—"

"Forgive me, Monsieur Vigneron," interrupted Rose, quickly regaining his composure. "This problem is no fault of yours. You were busy making the new videotape, per my request. Tell me, how is it?"

"Uh, it will win no César, but on such short notice . . ."

"Good, good. Thank you, sir, and I look forward to finally meeting you upon your arrival." Rose motioned the signalman to end the transmission, then turned to Ephraim Levenger. "Raise your agents on Crete. We must know the moment that the Americans dispatch more aircraft."

"But, Leon, there is no time for a proper search."

"Then I shall sink the damned ship!" thundered Rose.

Levenger blanched—Leon Rose's threats were never idle—but he knew that now was not the time to protest.

"General, a call for you."

Rose waved his hand in annoyance.

"Sir, it is Ehud Nir. He says it is urgent."

Rose sighed, reflexively grabbed another pastry from the platter at his side, and lifted the receiver. "Yes, Ehud?"

"Leon, I must know," his press secretary pleaded. "We are running out of time."

Rose bit into the sweet. Vigneron was arriving with the videotape at two. Yet dare he risk convening the inner circle of the cabinet in light of this setback? He swallowed and said, "Call the meeting, Ehud."

"For three A.M.?"

"For three A.M."

Rose hung up and crossed to the chart table, on which Ben Goren's stopwatch lay. Nearly two minutes had elapsed since *Sabra*'s signal that the torpedo was away. He said to the radio operator, "Put *Herev* on the speakers."

"Right away, sir."

As the man patched in the feed from the Israeli corvette's underwater listening devices, an empty hiss filled the room.

Rose looked at Goren and Levenger, who were both in signals, and then the young INS communications specialists, who were moving about as if the floor were a mine field. He had come too far to be denied, Rose decided; if Major Amichai's men could not find the missing laser disc, no one would. Feeling better, Rose popped the remainder of the pastry into his mouth.

Suddenly, over the speakers, a dull *whump* that reverberated throughout the room, followed by a bass rumble that went on and on and on and on.

"Congratulations, General," the watch officer said. "The torpedo does exactly what you hoped for . . . that is the sound of avalanches."

Rose acknowledged the compliment with a nod. But the victory that he had earned would not be secure until the commandos aboard *Herev* reached the American research vessel. He reflexively reached for another pastry.

THE EASTERN MED

Edna Haddix, struggling for breath after vaulting down three ladders and sprinting across the afterdeck, slammed into the control van; Wendell Trent and Rick Wolfe, their chests also heaving, were close on her heels. The three had been up on the bridge with Captain Nichols, celebrating the withdrawal of the Israeli warships over cold beers, when *Fanning II*'s depth sounders started to dance, as if touched by Saint Elmo's Fire. The reason: a cataclysmic underwater explosion some fifteen nautical miles to the northwest.

Haddix punched a string of commands into the navigator's console.

"Come on, come on," she gasped.

A number flashed onto the computer terminal: 3545.

"The good news is, it survived that explosion."

Haddix counted to five and repeated the commands.

A new number flashed onto the terminal: 3538.

"The bad news is, it's coming up."

"How long do we have?" asked Trent.

"Fifty-five minutes."

"Shit. That doesn't leave us a lot of options, does it, Jonesy?"

She shook her head.

Trent toggled the intercom and said, "Bridge, Van. Bill, how far off are the Israelis?"

"Over the horizon."

Trent paused to collect his thoughts, then began issuing orders.

The NIS photo analyst seated in front of his computer wasn't used to working with an admiral, two aides, and three civilians looking over his shoulder, but then again, he had never seen Shorty Brock so impatient.

The analyst called up the first picture. The infrared photograph, developed at Iráklion before it was digitized and bounced by satellite to Suitland, was a stern-first view of a civilian vessel flanked by dense shadows.

"There's the A-frame," Clifford Zeman said. "That's definitely *Fanning*."

The analyst frowned.

"Admiral? Those shadows don't look right. I'd almost venture that they're bogies, running right alongside with their lights off. I'll try to enhance—"

"No, keep going . . . the pilots also captured her in profile," Brock ordered. He turned to an aide. "What's the latest Met?"

"Unchanged, sir."

"Open a line to Iráklion."

"Right away, sir."

The analyst came to the first broadside picture, taken from starboard. Within *Fanning II*'s dark gray mass lay a blacker shape.

"May I?" asked Ann Davis, pointing to a thick volume of silhouette-recognition charts.

The analyst nodded and set to work enhancing the image.

Davis glanced from one of the silhouettes in the book to the computer monitor, on which the blacker shape was gaining resolution. "I think I've ID'd it."

Brock grabbed the volume, compared the two images, and said, "Well, I'll be a son of a bitch. Zeman, you were right. That's an Israeli Sa'ar-class corvette."

"Admiral? It's Iráklion . . . they say it's most urgent."

Brock took the receiver. "Admiral Brock here. . . . Say again? . . . I see. Are the choppers ready? . . . Listen, I don't give a rat's ass what the weather is, launch those Sea Stallions."

When he turned back to the others, his carefully cultivated tan was as gray as ash. "Their listening station just picked up a detonation out in the Hellencian Trench. Big enough to make eardrums bleed."

"Good Lord," Zeman blurted, *"Fanning . . ."*

Brock shook his head. "They report that it was in the Trench, not over it. Apparently, the blast occurred at depth, because it triggered a series of underwater avalanches."

Zeman looked as if he had been shot. Finally he turned to Davis. "Annie, I don't know how they managed it, but the Israelis found a way to do what we feared most. They're burying *Dakar.*"

THE EASTERN MED

2213 Zulu/1:13 A.M. local time

As the scanning line continued to circle the screen, a cluster of blips materialized to the south of *Fanning II.* Billy Ray McConkey, hunched over the radar scope on the bridge of the research vessel, called out, "Captain, those mothers are coming back. Bearing, one-six-eight . . . range, four miles."

"Speed?" asked Captain Nichols.

"Thirty, thirty-five knots."

"We're making eleven knots, so that gives us ten minutes."

Suddenly, over the walkie-talkie left behind by Major Amichai: "Mr. Trent, this is Captain Litvak. Do you read? Over."

Captain Nichols ignored the call.

"Mr. Trent, I repeat, this is Captain Litvak. Please acknowledge. Over. . . . Acknowledge immediately, and come to all stop, or I shall open fire."

Captain Nichols hesitated; Trent had left explicit instructions not to jeopardize the ship should the Israelis return. But a reply now would surely lead to the one question he didn't want to answer. Turning to his first mate, he said, "Grab a lamp and signal that we're coming to a stop. Then explain that their walkie-talkie's on the blink, that it won't transmit."

The first mate hefted a portable searchlight and hurried outside onto the deck.

"So much for ten minutes," McConkey muttered.

Captain Nichols reached for the intercom switch. "Damn it, Cowboy, we're not supposed to put up a fight . . . but that doesn't mean we have to roll over for the bastards."

LOD, ISRAEL

2241 Zulu/1:41 A.M. local time

Even by the Spartan standards of the offices in the administrative wing of Ben-Gurion Airport, the windowless suite maintained by the Mossad-fronted charter airline was bleak. Under the merciless glare of overhead fluorescents the cinderblock walls betrayed a dinginess that no amount of fresh paint, no array of splashy travel posters, could erase; the green and blue linoleum tiles were grimy beyond the power of cleansers; the wear-stained pair of desks and the vinyl-upholstered chairs looked as if they had been purchased twenty years earlier from a secondhand store; the air was as stale as last week's bread.

As a command center the suite was clearly unsatisfactory. Leon

Rose, though, had been stripped of options: the Frenchman, Vigneron, would be touching down shortly with the all-important videotape, and the three A.M. meeting of key ministers was all but confirmed. Leaving Ben Goren to manage communications at the Haifa Naval Station, he had helicoptered down to Lod with Ephraim Levenger.

At the moment Rose was seated behind one of the desks, his eyes closed in meditation, while Levenger juggled calls on a multiline phone.

"The plane with the Frenchman is one hundred kilometers off the coast," the Mossad analyst announced. "ETA, fifteen minutes."

Rose nodded but remained silent.

Levenger switched back to the open line to Haifa and cupped the receiver. "Leon, I worry that we will not be able to properly review Vigneron's— Yes, Ben? You are certain? Yes, he is right here. Leon, the American helicopters are arriving over the blast site."

Rose's eyes sprang open as he picked up the phone on his desk and punched on line. "Ben, how far are they from the *Herev*?"

"Twenty-five kilometers."

"How much time do our men have?"

Goren hesitated. "The transmissions we are monitoring indicate the storm is still quite severe. So unless the Americans are very, very lucky, my guess is, one half hour, at a minimum."

"That should be more than enough. Keep me posted," Rose said, punching off line.

Levenger said, "But Leon, in one half hour our ships will—"

"Relax, my friend. Is not Major Amichai already back aboard the American vessel? Has he not been searching it for nearly fifteen minutes?"

Levenger wearily shook his head and murmured, almost to himself, "I think I am too old for this kind of operation."

"Nonsense. A warrior without doubt is a fool."

The cliché had an unintended effect on Levenger, who realized with a start that in all their years of serving Israel together, he had never once known Leon Rose to evince doubt. No wonder Rose could remain so unflappable in the midst of mounting chaos; to him the American research vessel was but another inconvenient nail, even if hammering it down to the bottom of the sea might put some fifty civilian lives at risk, not to mention *Herev* and the patrol boats, as well as forty years of Israeli-American friendship. Suddenly, the walls of the threadbare room seemed to close in on the Mossad analyst.

"Leon? I—I need to step outside for some air. May I turn the line over to you?"

"Certainly, my friend," Rose replied, flashing a sympathetic smile. "Would you also mind fetching us some more mineral water?"

Levenger nodded and left the room.

Rose's countenance abruptly darkened. Ephraim had been right; his nerves were indeed gone.

He punched back onto the open line to Haifa, but heard only the buzz of background activity. As he waited, he again went over his revised plan of battle. In the event the laser disc was not located, he would allow five minutes for Major Amichai to evacuate the crew of *Fanning II,* and another five for Captain Litvak to sink it from point-blank range. Goren was estimating that the American helicopters would not find the research vessel before 0210 hours, so he would permit Major Amichai to search until—

A ring, and then a second button on the phone began to flash.

Rose quickly switched lines. "Yes? That is good news indeed, Ehud. Remember, we require at least three televisions in the room, preferably ones with large screens. No, that is the wrong format. I shall bring the VCR. We will meet fifteen minutes beforehand? Good. Thank you, my friend."

Just then Levenger returned bearing fresh mineral water.

"That was Ehud," Rose said, punching back to the open line to Haifa. "We are set for three A.M."

"The ministers all agreed?"

"Of course." Rose broke into a wicked grin. "Tell me, my friend, do you know of a politician who can resist an emergency meeting, especially one which begins at this hour of the morning?"

"I would still feel better if we could review—"

Rose suddenly raised his hand for silence and pressed the receiver to his ear. "Yes, Ben? Patch him through, and stay on the line."

"Amichai?" whispered Levenger.

Rose nodded.

Another phone was but a few paces away, but Levenger remained rooted in the middle of the room, clutching a bottle of mineral water in each hand.

"Yes, Major. Tell me what you have found."

Levenger's heart sank as he watched Rose's complexion mottle with rage and the veins on his temples and neck begin to throb. Fifteen seconds passed before Rose—his expression grown as malevolent as a clenched fist—finally spoke. "Major Amichai, you are to immediately return your platoon to the *Herev*. Instruct Captain Litvak to stand by for further orders. That is all, Major. Ben, I need time to . . . No, I do not want Litvak to stand down. . . . No, I do not necessarily agree it would serve no purpose. That is for me to decide. Damn you, Ben, have you forgotten who commands this operation?"

Rose stabbed the Hold button, slammed down the receiver, and started to mentally review Amichai's devastating report.

"They failed to find the laser disc," Levenger said.

"How observant you are, Ephraim," Rose replied sarcastically.

A sense of doom descended on Levenger. "So you are sinking the research vessel."

"I have not decided. The laser disc is not all that our boys did not find. A small, inflatable chase boat is missing, as well as three members of the crew . . . our nemesis, Wendell Trent, a naval lieutenant who is a woman, and the chief scientist. Now be quiet, Ephraim. How can I think if you continue to natter?"

DAY SIX:
1 JUNE 1988

THE EASTERN MED

The rain had stopped and the winds had backed down to Force Three, but the confused seas still boiled with the unspent energy deposited by the last squall line. Low clouds carpeted the black sky from horizon to horizon, blotting out the moon and the stars.

Charging through the dark maelstrom was a solitary inflatable craft carrying three beaten and bedraggled passengers: Edna Haddix, Wendell Trent, and Rick Wolfe. Each wore a wet suit topped by an orange life vest; each was lashed by a length of polyprop to one of the safety lines atop the Zodiac's gunwales.

The two men knelt near the bow, furiously bailing the four inches of water covering the floorboards before the next breaker deposited even more over the side.

Back by the transom, hand on the stick, Haddix suddenly spotted a steep wave rushing toward them from slightly to port. She flung the stick to starboard, hoping to meet it head on. The ninety-horsepower outboard struggled to respond, but it was like trying to change an ocean liner's course with a spoon.

"Hold on!" she screamed over the snarling engine.

Without bothering to look up Trent and Wolfe grabbed for handholds.

The wave crashed obliquely over the bow and sluiced a knee-high torrent of numbingly cold water the length of the chase boat.

Haddix wiped her eyes clear and squinted forward. The men were still aboard the Zodiac, as was the small watertight duffel that contained electronic gear and her knapsack. Then she raised her left arm to peer at the luminescent dial of her chronometer: time to check the range again.

She twisted the throttle to idle and clambered toward the duffel.

Wolfe saw her and, leaving Trent to bail, headed back to join her.

"It's been five minutes?" the scientist shouted.

Haddix nodded, fumbling at the zipper with stiffened fingers. "Seemed like an hour. Here, let me help."

Now that the Zodiac was no longer hammering directly across the six-foot swells, it began to ride with an easier motion.

Wolfe took from the duffel a thick plastic disc the size of a dinner plate. The transducer—an acoustical send/listen device—had a single lead. He wrapped this wire securely around the port oarlock and lowered the unit over the side.

Haddix retrieved a portable transponder test unit. She jacked in the transducer lead and switched on the black box. Flipping to interrogation mode, she keyed in a frequency.

The transducer submerged over the side of the Zodiac beamed out an acoustical query.

A reply immediately flashed onto the portable test unit's LED display.

"Less than a quarter mile away," Haddix said. Her eyes swept the inky liquid hillocks that continued to dissolve and rematerialize. "Damn, it hit the surface more than an hour ago. We should have seen it by now. Think the beacon light malfunctioned?"

The three Americans had braved the storm-whipped seas in quest of a transponder. The seventy-pound sphere, designed to rest just above the ocean floor and transmit precise navigational fixes, was valued at $4,000, but what made it irreplaceable was its unusual cargo.

When Trent had told those in the control van of the imminent Israeli boarding, Haddix was at the *Bert* engineering station finishing the last electronic still of *Dakar*'s forward torpedo room. Fearing for the fate of the meticulous visual documentation they had amassed inside the sunken submarine—especially once the knowledgeable Roland Vigneron was freed and questioned—she had ejected the disc then in the laser recorder, inserted a fresh blank, and hurried through the control van's rear hatch.

The mud boat offered an almost endless array of hiding places. If the Israelis discovered the switch and mounted a search, however, they could always get lucky—or frustrated enough to take the ultimate step of opening *Fanning II*'s seacocks and sinking the research vessel.

But, Haddix realized, there was one sanctuary they could never violate: the bottom of the Med.

The problems were retrievability and survivability. She could solve the first by attaching the laser disc to a transponder, which would remain submerged until summoned. The second was considerably thornier. Haddix suspected the salt water might quickly corrode the disc's Plexiglas outer shell. More important, the apparently solid disc wasn't; there was a microscopically thin air pocket sandwiched between its shell and its Mylar recording surface. She knew that water pressure, which increased by one atmosphere, or 14.7 pounds per square inch, every thirty-three feet, would attack that frailty and implode the disc long before it sank the entire two and a half miles to the sea floor.

Given time, Haddix would have opened up a transponder, broken the vacuum seal on the inner plastic bubble, slipped in the disc, and repressurized the bubble.

But her leeway had been minutes, not hours.

Hoping to improvise a solution, she had rushed across the brightly lit afterdeck to one of the utility vans. It was lined with tools, spare parts, cans of lubricating oil and a bottle of mineral oil, rolls of gaffer's tape, packages of nuts and bolts; in short, everything but a container strong enough to shield the disc from the pressure, which would eventually grow to 6,250 pounds per square inch.

When Trent had come on the loudspeakers to inform the entire ship of their situation, her eyes returned to the shelf holding the various oils. What if she could displace the air inside the disc with oil, which was more viscous than water—would it be enough to brace the disc against the crushing pressure? Yet even if it did, would the oil irreparably damage the Mylar recording surface?

Haddix was out of time.

She had heated the tip of an awl and used it to delicately pierce the outer shell in half a dozen places.

Next the mineral oil, which she dumped into a large, heavy-gauge, resealable plastic bag like the kind used to store leftovers. She dropped in the disc. The thick, clear oil bubbled with air streaming out of the tiny holes she'd made; hot damn, she thought, it just might work.

Haddix sealed the bag and stuffed it inside another one, reinforcing the outer bag's seal with three strips of gaffer's tape. She carefully punched a hole through the tape above the seal, grabbed several plastic twist-ties, and dashed from the utility van.

After detouring to the winch operator's console to instruct Captain Nichols to douse the floods, Haddix had continued to the fantail. There she had twist-tied the plastic bag to a pickup ring on the nearest transponder and, with the help of the Zippo Squad, heaved the unit over the side.

Long before *Fanning II* had stopped to complete the recovery of the sled and ROV, the transponder was safely in place, moored by its 300-foot-long weighted chain to the bottom of the Hellencian Trench.

Later, when Haddix told Trent of her impromptu action, he had approved, especially after the van was stripped of their hard-earned visual documentation. As long as the plastic bags retained their integrity, he had confidently predicted, Suitland's fabled Q department would be able to salvage the data stored on Haddix's disc. In fact, after the Israelis left, she, Trent, and Wolfe had taken beers up to the bridge to fantasize about how they would summon up the transponder. Trent had voted for returning in a seventy-foot yacht. Haddix had voted for a less romantic but more secure platform—like a Sixth Fleet aircraft carrier.

And then the mud boat's instruments had started to dance, as if touched by Saint Elmo's fire, and then the mad sprint down to the van, to confirm their fear that the monstrous underwater explosion and landslide had snapped loose the transponder; free of its mooring, it had begun its one-hour ascent to the surface.

Within minutes the three of them had thrown together some gear and scrambled down into the relaunched Zodiac.

Gunning the ninety-horsepower outboard, they had roared off into the teeth of the storm. *Dakar*'s site lay only fifteen or so nautical miles to the northwest, but the conditions proved so bad that it had taken them almost an hour and a half to reach it.

Though the transponder was fitted with a blinking white beacon light, finding such a unit on a stormy night was never simple. Additionally, the task confronting Haddix, Trent, and Wolfe was complicated by three other factors:

The underwater blast had released not only the transponder Haddix had sent down, but also four of the seven that had comprised *Fanning II*'s tracking network, including one that shared the same interrogation frequency;

The unit they sought had surfaced shortly after two A.M., which meant that for the past hour it had been subjected to the vagaries of wind, waves, and current;

And lately, they had detected from time to time an ominous sound: the far-off beat of helicopter rotors.

"Over there!" cried Rick Wolfe. "Thirty degrees left of the bow!"

Haddix swung her binoculars around, adrenaline instantly banishing fatigue.

Wendell Trent stopped bailing to lend his eyes to the search.

The horizon in the direction indicated by Wolfe was blocked by a large wave rolling down on them.

The Zodiac dipped into its trough, then climbed to the top of the crest.

Nothing.

Another trough, another crest.

Still nothing.

Down plunged the chase boat, up it rose, now a glimpse of a blinking white light, and then the waves between it and the Zodiac again fell out of sync.

Haddix scrambled to the stern, cupped her flashlight, and beamed it on her compass to get a fix.

She was reaching for the throttle when Trent shouted, "Hold on, Jonesy."

Haddix could make out one of the dark silhouettes at the bow standing and twisting from side to side.

"Hear it?"

She cocked her ear.

"Yes!" replied Haddix, straining to ascertain the direction of the chopper. The wind and the low clouds were playing cruel acoustical tricks. Some time ago they had deduced that the helicopters were probably Sea Stallions, one of the few craft capable of operating in this weather. *Fanning II*'s radios had been disabled, but Captain Nichols could have steered the rescuers their way by signal-lamping in Morse code. Yet while none of them could imagine a friendlier sight on this hell-spawned night than a U.S. Navy chopper hovering overhead, they had decided against firing a flare when Trent pointed out that the Israelis and the Greeks also flew American-manufactured helicopters.

Haddix caught the sound again and illuminated her compass. "It's still north-northeast of us."

"Damn," Trent said. "They're drawing the net tighter. Jonesy, you better get a move on it."

She gunned the outboard and pointed the Zodiac in the last observed direction of the blinking white light.

As the chase boat gathered speed, the waves began depositing more water over the gunwales.

This time no one bothered to bail.

Haddix felt like she was driving in an off-road endurance race at night without benefit of headlights; the seas were steeper than any of Baja's dunes, and her sole reference point kept disappearing for waves on end.

And then the blinking white light seemed to shoot out of the depths just thirty yards dead ahead, so close they could make out the entire upper half of the transponder.

Haddix throttled back and veered slightly to port, to bring the Zodiac upwind of the unit.

Suddenly, to their left, the black sky was riven by a shaft of light brighter than the laser swords of *Star Wars*. A helicopter had crossed to their side of the horizon and was slowly approaching, its multiple searchlights methodically quartering the seas immediately below it.

Jesus, she thought, anyone glancing our way can't help but spot the beacon light. . . .

"No, Jonesy . . . full speed! Go straight for it and don't stop!" She twisted the stick.

As the Zodiac again surged toward the transponder, Trent stripped off his reflective orange life vest. Wolfe quickly followed his lead, then flopped facedown onto the floorboards and managed to gather the two vests under his body, all the while struggling to keep his nose and mouth above the sloshing seawater.

Twenty yards.

Trent freed his polyprop safety line.

Fifteen yards.

Haddix glanced over her shoulder; the helicopter was not changing course.

Ten yards.

Trent forced his aching leg muscles into a sprinter's crouch.

Five yards.

As Trent launched himself over the port gunwale in a flat dive, Haddix slammed the stick hard to starboard to swing the churning propeller blades clear. Cutting the throttle, she whipped off her own life vest, clutched it to her chest, and dived onto the flooded floorboards.

Trent broke surface ten feet from the transponder.

The helicopter continued to inch closer.

Trent found the spherical transponder too well balanced to tip upside down, its beacon light too securely mounted to be yanked free by cold, wet fingers.

Clawing for purchase, he tried to pull the frisky yellow ball beneath him, to smother the telltale light with his body.

He got his chest on top of the transponder, but then a wave

washed away what little traction his glistening wet suit had acquired on the shiny plastic casing.

Goddamned helicopter, couldn't they fly a wider search pattern?

Up again; now find equilibrium, Trent told himself, good, now all four limbs splayed out for stability.

Every time the transponder climbed a wave, his head was forced underwater.

And every time his head broke surface, he could hear the dull *whack-whacks* of the helicopter drawing ever nearer.

To camouflage the whiteness of her face Edna Haddix plastered her wet hair down over her forehead and forward along the sides of her face before raising her eyes just above the port gunwale.

The incoming helicopter seemed to be maintaining a straight-line course that would take it past some fifty yards to the east; the trouble was, that still left them within range of the searchlights.

Recognizing that the Zodiac presented a far bigger target than Trent, she crawled back to the transom, swiveled the outboard around, and twisted the throttle. Keeping the speed down so as not to leave a wake, she began heading westward.

Back atop the transponder, Trent heard the chase boat edging away and instantly understood the reason. Of more immediate concern were several prickly questions that did little to bolster his ebbing strength: How sharp were the guys manning the searchlights—could he outlast their patience? More important, there were two transponders floating in the area that answered on the same frequency—had they found the right one?

Haddix stopped the Zodiac well beyond searchlight range and brought it about.

The scene before her could have been out of an old prison-break movie: overhead beams stabbing ever closer, now circling away, now cruelly sweeping back toward Trent, now closing to under thirty yards, he had less than five seconds . . .

"Turn the light," she whispered, "turn the light," and as if in response the beam sliced away, missing Trent by less than ten yards.

Haddix waited until the chopper was seventy-five yards to the south-southeast, then sped the Zodiac back toward Trent.

Before she could come to a full stop, Rick Wolfe, armed with a wrench from the duffel bag, was in the water and swimming to the transponder.

As Trent weakly slid off the yellow ball, Wolfe smashed the beacon light into darkness.

Haddix inched the chase boat closer.

Trent needed help from both of them to climb aboard.

"You tied the bag to a pickup ring?" shouted Wolfe.

"Affirmative," she replied, trading him a flashlight for the wrench.

Wolfe took several deep breaths, then dived under the transponder.

Trent was curled in a fetal position in the water pooled on the floorboards, his teeth chattering.

Haddix pulled him up onto a seat. They had not brought blankets, so she pried his arms away from his chest and drew him tight. Her body was cold; his was colder.

Wolfe came up for air, then dived again.

"You okay?" she said softly.

She could feel Trent nod.

Wolfe broke surface again. "Got it!"

He handed up the heavy-gauge plastic bag—it seemed intact, Haddix noted—and clambered back into the Zodiac.

While the men recovered, the three of them reviewed their options. *Fanning II* lay some fifteen miles to the south, but it might still be surrounded by Israeli warships. Crete lay some twenty-five miles to the north, but the Greek security forces might now be on alert.

In the end they agreed their chances were better on Crete.

On a high floor of the Aquarium, Lieutenant General Pavel Chesnokov broke off the connection and gazed at the bottle of export-grade Stolichnaya that had remained unopened on his desk through the long evening. Having at last heard from Leon Rose, he was frankly unsure of whether to weep or to laugh or to just drink himself into oblivion, for the Israeli's update was leaving an ironic aftertaste worthy of Chekhov.

Finally, Chesnokov blinked. First things first; switching to an internal line, he called down to communications and instructed them to immediately locate Dimitri Puzanov, the Athens *residentura*. Only then did he sit back to reflect on how Rose's call seemed the fitting capstone to this, the most emotionally wrenching day of his sixty-odd years.

It had begun badly, with whispers of panic within the High Command, of Deputy Admiral Boris Patolichev being summoned for questioning about the disappearance of an experimental torpedo. Chesnokov had spent the morning vainly trying to ascertain his friend's fate. Nerves frayed from five days of conspiracy, expecting at any moment the dreaded knock on the door, he had in late afternoon gone so far as remove his service pistol from the safe and chamber a round.

Chesnokov glanced at the desktop photograph taken the previous September at a resort on the Black Sea. As melodramatic as it sounded, he owed these last few hours to his family: wife, son and daughter and their spouses, three grandchildren. By tradition the entire clan gathered every other Sunday for supper at his modest dacha northwest of the city. In the depth of his despair Chesnokov had impulsively sought their unconditional love. They had given it. Despite considerable grumbling about the short notice all had shown up at his in-town apartment for dinner. The meal had been extremely awkward—Chesnokov being unable to explain his sudden need to see them all—but afterward, he knew he could not die by his own hand.

And then it was back to the office to maintain the lonely vigil. With each passing hour Chesnokov had grown more certain that the operation had failed.

Not so, according to Leon Rose.

Apparently, the Soviet deep-diving antisubmarine torpedo had performed perfectly; *Dakar,* and its twenty-year-old secrets, were lost until the end of time. Yet Rose had passed on this splendid news in a curiously leaden voice. The reason for his concern did not take long to emerge. Unfortunately, a laser disc, on which the Americans had recorded visual evidence piped up by their remote-control probe, was missing, along with an inflatable chase boat and three members of the research vessel's crew. The Israeli warships on site were prevented from conducting a search by the American planes and helicopters that had swarmed into the area, no doubt to investigate the underwater explosion.

Then it is finished, Chesnokov had said.

Perhaps not, Rose had replied. The American aircraft had been crisscrossing a small patch of the Med for nearly ninety minutes without success, for the weather was abysmal, the visibility virtually zero. This suggested that those in the chase boat had either sunk—problem solved—or were making for land. Because of the vessel's limited range their only possible destination was Crete. It was therefore imperative that GRU Athens prod its Pasok affiliates into action; the missing laser disc was the loose end that could unravel all their hard work.

The phone on Chesnokov's desk rang.

He quickly grabbed it: "Yes?"

"Hello, Pavel Ilyich." It was not the communications room with his call to Greece, but rather a fellow GRU officer. "Have you heard about Patolichev?"

"Of course," Chesnokov replied wearily. "He was taken in yesterday morning for—"

"No, no, not that news. I mean about his release."

"What!"

"That is what they are saying, that Boris Alekseyevich survived his interrogation, and has gone into seclusion."

Chesnokov's mind reeled at the implications. It seemed inconceivable that the High Command would have summoned his friend without having in its possession the incriminating piece of paper authorizing the transfer of the torpedo. If so, there was no lie clever enough to avert swift retribution.

"What do you know of this matter, Pavel?"

"What? Oh. I regret that I know even less than you, my friend," Chesnokov replied.

If Boris Alekseyevich had indeed gone into seclusion, he could only be at his dacha, for which Chesnokov had the private number. . . .

Another button on the phone began to blink.

"There is another call," Chesnokov said to his colleague. "Where are you? Yes, I will try to learn more."

He punched to the other line.

"Yes? Very well, put him through. . . . Good morning, Comrade Puzanov. Yes, I am afraid there is. . . ."

As Chesnokov began issuing orders, his eyes lit on the set of eighteenth-century *matrushka* dolls on his bookcase. They were aligned one next to the other, rather than nestled one inside the other. A strange half-grin spread across his face. Yes, he thought, how very apt. The largest doll was Mother Russia, reduced to passive bystander after having bestowed her dowry of an advanced weapon. The middle doll was Israel, reduced to passive bystander after having delivered the advanced weapon on target. And who remained on active duty? Only the smallest doll—the ill-trained, ill-equipped, ill-disciplined operatives of Pasok.

He reached out a practiced hand, unscrewed the top of the vodka bottle, and poured himself a shot.

Puzanov was asking an operational question.

Chesnokov downed the vodka before replying.

Poor Puzanov, who would perform his new task as he had the others—with enthusiasm and distinction. The *residentura* had every reason to believe he was earning a coveted assignment to one of the capitals of Western Europe. In fact, succeed or fail, his career was doomed. Puzanov could not know that his services were in support of an operation both unsanctioned and criminal; the young man would be fortunate to escape with a posting to some African stinkhole like Ougadougou.

Yes, Chekhov would definitely have been amused, thought Chesnokov. He poured himself another shot that he knew would not be the last of this horrendous night.

JERUSALEM

0013 Zulu/3:13 a.m. local time

On noticing the hollow echo of his own aimless footsteps, Ehud Nir, press aide to Leon Rose, stopped pacing the deserted corridor of the Knesset building. Nir's agitation was understandable. Never before had he been directed to track down Israel's highest officials at this hour of the night and summon them to an emergency session; at the moment the five men were waiting in the cabinet room, growing testier with each minute. And never before had he seen his employer so manic; storming into the building fifteen minutes later than promised, Rose had shoved a Beta-format VCR into Nir's arms with orders that it be set up, then vanished behind the locked door of his office.

Now the door was opening.

Nir started to say something about the growing impatience of the ministers. But on seeing Rose's face he meekly fell in behind him.

Rose stalked toward the cabinet room, Roland Vigneron's edited videocassette firmly in hand, consumed by the thought that the most important mission of his life was turning to ashes. He had intended the matter to have been unequivocally settled. He had intended to arrive shaved, showered, and changed into fresh clothes, not like some vagrant from the sidewalks of New York. He had intended to be bursting with a sense of righteous triumph, not radiating the profound insecurities of a newly graduated attorney.

Rose stopped before the burnished doors to the cabinet room and squeezed his eyes shut.

"Leon, is there anything I—"

Rose waved the press aide away.

When at last his arguments were marshaled so that he would be able to sweep the others around the contradictions, when at last his heartbeat was stabilized, Leon Rose drew himself erect, pushed open the doors, and strode in.

The five waiting ministers turned as one.

Rose closed the doors behind him.

The minister of industry and trade studied his archrival's disheveled appearance and broke the silence. "The operation is still in progress, Leon?"

"No, it is concluded but for some minor mop-up actions." Rose squelched his anger at the barb and faced the others. "Gentlemen, my profound apologies for asking you here at such an unholy hour, and for being late. First, to answer the question foremost in your minds . . . the operation is a success. An immense success."

The prime minister broke into a sudden grin, as if he had just won another term. Several others exhaled in relief.

"However, I fear we shall be hearing in no uncertain terms from the Americans at any moment," Rose continued. "I therefore believe it vital for you to be fully briefed on the recently concluded events. Mr. Prime Minister, with your permission?"

"By all means, Leon, by all means."

Rose took his seat at the long hardwood table. Setting the videocassette before him, he reached into his pocket for a sheet of paper and smoothed out its folds.

"I should like to begin with a brief action summary.

"Gentlemen, last night, at twenty-one thirty-six hours, our time, the corvette INS *Herev* landed a platoon of Army commandos aboard the American research vessel *Fanning II.* The Americans were directly over *Dakar,* from which station they were actively violating the sunken submarine."

"How, Leon?" one of the ministers asked.

"By means of unmanned deep-sea vehicles equipped with video-cameras. I assure you, our boys put an immediate end to this shocking activity. Our boys retained control of the vessel for approximately two hours and twenty minutes, during which time they caused it to be sailed from the *Dakar* site. Upon reaching a position some fifteen nautical miles to the south, they returned aboard the corvette *Herev.*

"This morning, at oh-one-forty-nine hours, our time, a deep-diving torpedo of Russian origin was fired by the submarine *Sabra.* It detonated two minutes later and caused a massive underwater landslide. I am happy to report that the *Dakar,* the tomb of our brave sailors, and of those poor Russian Jews as well, is now safe from further desecration."

Rose paused for a sip of mineral water, hoping the minister of industry and trade wouldn't call his bluff; only the Americans, with their deep-sea robots, could tell for sure whether the submarine had truly been buried.

"I am also pleased to report to you that as per the will of the cabinet, no unnecessary force was used," Rose continued. "The operation was concluded without injury or damage to either side. Our boys did confiscate a number of items, primarily electronic recordings on which the Americans documented their activities. All such materials were accounted for in an itemized receipt. So, gentlemen, when the U.S. State Department delivers its protest, as it shall, we need apologize for no more than protecting the sovereignty of our warship, the *Dakar* . . . as is our right and our duty."

Rose looked up from his notes. "That is what happened. Unless there are questions, I should now like to show you why our actions were necessary."

The prime minister looked around the table, then gestured Rose to continue.

"Thank you, sir. Our boys confiscated a total of twenty-four videocassettes . . . the Americans were recording from four cameras at a time. Our technicians are even at this moment analyzing the originals. However, I have taken the liberty of compiling the salient scenes on a single tape. I warn you, we were forced to edit it on inferior equipment and under extreme time pressures. Its quality is not the best. Yet I believe it will convince you, as it has me, that we must resist any and all pressure the American government brings to bear on us."

The minister of industry and trade was sitting nearest the video equipment at the foot of the table.

"Would you mind, my friend?"

Rose slid the cassette down to his archrival, watched with concealed amusement as the man clumsily tried to insert the wrong end, then reached for the remote control wand.

From the first frame that popped onto the three large-screen monitors, the others in the room seemed to shrink into themselves, like witnesses to a newborn's execution. A montage of exterior shots showing *Dakar*'s sundered hull; the interior of the tail compartment, with the three shoes; the galley and the thicket of ghostly stanchions in the crew quarters. The footage unspooled in silence, for it needed no narration. Which was just as well: despite his briefing by Roland Vigneron, despite having seen frontline action in every war since Israel attained nationhood, Leon Rose was also struck mute by the scenes on the videotape.

It was the dangling rucksacks that finally undammed the tears, and once surfaced the grief only built. The tarnished brass plaque so proudly given and so briefly sailed; the mound of civilian artifacts piled against the crushed bulkhead to the operations area; the tiny red patent leather pump; the gold necklace with the Star of David pendant; a poignant close-up of a child's headband studded with costume jewelry.

"Gentlemen," Rose said in a choked voice, "there is one other sequence you must view."

He fast-forwarded to the shots inside the forward torpedo room.

The tape ended with a close-up of rectangular metal boxes whose black matte surfaces were stenciled with the legend U_{238}, next to which lay several silvery-white ingots.

Rose pointed the remote control wand and turned off the monitors and the VCR.

"Damn those Americans," one minister said softly, blowing his nose into a handkerchief. "Better that my eyes should be blind. The pain, the suffering . . . that little red shoe. No one should ever witness such scenes. No one."

Rose cleared his throat. "Very few ever shall, my friend. The videotapes shall be returned to the Americans—yes, all twenty-four—but I assure you the privacy of those who perished aboard the *Dakar* shall be preserved. Our technicians will abridge the footage to make it appear that we interrupted the Americans just as they were about to enter the crew quarters. Our documents experts over at Mossad will contour the logbooks accordingly."

"But, Leon, the footage is time stamped."

"A technical problem, easily overcome," Rose replied.

Another minister shook his head. "There are too many tapes. The Americans will know that they have been tampered with."

"Not if we return the correct number of brand-new cassettes, unused and still sealed in the original cellophane."

"They will still know."

"Even if we duplicate the lot numbers?" said Rose.

All around the long hardwood table the ministers began to shift in their seats; could Rose be right, could the Americans actually be tricked?

As if reading their thoughts, the minister of trade and industry said, "Leon's plan is sound. Of course, the Americans will be suspicious. Allow me to remind you, though, that suspicion and proof are two separate matters."

Now he turned to Rose. "Your operation is a masterpiece of improvisation, my friend, one which will be studied for generations to come. I appreciate why it was necessary to undertake . . . did I myself not vote in favor? Yet, I see no solid evidence that the *Dakar* was carrying Russian Jews, I see no solid evidence that the uranium was furnished us by the Russians."

"Agreed."

"Then tell us this," the minister of trade and industry said. "This is no longer 1968, at which time our government saw fit to falsely report the *Dakar*'s position. The Americans know many more things about us now than they did then. Why do we not simply return all the videotapes intact? What need justifies the elaborate charade you plan? What is left to conceal in the year 1988?"

Rose took another sip of mineral water.

His archrival had asked the one question that could expose him as surely as that missing laser disc. It had been anticipated and a cover story concocted. But would it work?

Rose carefully set down his glass. "Refugees? What is our nation if not one built by those who came to escape persecution? The younger ministers here know of Aliyah Bet only from the history books. The others, myself included, remember that operation with the greatest sorrow . . . ten ships turned away from our very shores, the passengers of some to perish horribly. And does not the world know of the moneys we pay the tyrant Ceausescu, four thousand dollars U.S. per head, to purchase our people transit through Romania? No, Jews returning to *Eretz Israel* is not news, although I daresay that if they are from Russia, and if they are found aboard a submarine which sinks a full twenty years ago, that will make a few front pages.

"Nuclear weapons? Since Dimona went on line, have not our enemies cringed before our newfound might?"

Rose turned to address the others. "I agree with my friend the minister. There is no reason to keep the full tapes from the Americans except for one: Jonathan Pollard."

As he had hoped, the room was stunned by his unexpected mention of the American who, along with his wife, had in 1986 pleaded guilty to passing U.S. military secrets to Israel.

"If Pollard is not caught," Rose continued, "the rest of the operation—this 'elaborate charade' I plan—is not necessary. But Pollard poisoned the well. Has not the CIA held back data on radical Arab cells who scheme against us from their sanctuaries in Western Europe? Has not the DIA grown increasingly reluctant to share its satellite reconnaissance of the dispositions of the Syrian and Iraqi forces? Today, as you well know, the motto of American intelligence has become *Cherchez le juif.*"

Two of the ministers murmured assents.

Rose leaned forward. "I invite you to think back to the authorizing documents I revealed to you at our previous meeting. Permit me now to fill in the details.

"The time is the Six-Day War, the place the Sinai. We capture a Russian SAM prototype known as the Spandrel. Naturally, the Americans expect us to ship the battery to them, for are we not a grateful client state? Fine. But then we hear that the Russians want the Spandrel back badly, badly enough to open back-channel negotiations even as they are severing diplomatic ties with us.

"What do they first offer? Uranium for Dimona, which is then under construction. Interesting, but there are other sources for uranium, including, I might add, one extremely valuable ally in Cleveland, Ohio.

"Well, then, perhaps Russian Jews? Not five nor fifteen nor fifty, not one submarine full, but a total of five thousand before 1973 . . . and we may select up to twenty per year by name.

"This offer, I tell you, receives our fullest attention. Think of it, gentlemen. Bonner, and by her side, Sakharov! Scharansky! Free, living in Israel, in the early seventies!"

Rose scanned the table. Four of the five ministers sat as if mesmerized. At that instant he knew that those men would never pierce his cruel web of half-truths.

"Now, I ask you to imagine our dilemma. The Americans are waiting for the one thing which the Russians hold of value. The solution? We send the Americans two Spandrel missiles, and inform them that the launcher was regrettably destroyed. We send the Russians the launcher and the remainder of the missiles, and inform them that the others were fired.

"Four months later, in early January of 1968, the *Dakar* leaves Portsmouth, England, and sails into the North Atlantic. There, it takes on fifty-three Russian Jews and two dozen ingots of U_{238}." Rose's voice dropped dramatically. "The last chapter of the story, you know."

After a lengthy silence the minister of trade and industry said, "Very interesting, Leon. Now you will kindly tell us how does this relate to Pollard?"

The other ministers turned to Rose's archrival in puzzlement, as if wondering whether the man's enmity was now clouding his judgment.

"Most directly, my friend," Rose replied expansively. "Yes, there is no solid proof that Russian Jews were aboard the *Dakar,* that the uranium also comes from Russia. But there are enough clues to tax coincidence. Suppose American intelligence begins to ask the correct questions. Suppose one of their agents within the Kremlin discovers some Russian documents . . . the trade, after all, was approved by Leonid Brezhnev himself. Suppose the truth dawns like the sun over Galilee. In light of the Pollard affair, I submit, it would cripple Israeli-American intelligence-sharing for a decade to come. Is that a thing you would risk, my friend?"

The minister of trade and industry sat back in his chair, trying to find a flaw in Rose's argument. "No, Leon," he finally said with a shake of his head, "I would not."

The briefing concluded, the last question answered, Leon Rose leaned back contentedly. Then he remembered to check the time.

Startled to see that it was nearly four-thirty A.M., he looked across the table.

The prime minister was busy consoling a minister who had again begun to weep softly.

"Excuse me, sir? If there are no other pressing matters?"

"Of course, Leon, of course. You must be terribly drained. Off to a well-earned sleep, eh? A little rest for the weary?"

Rose smiled wanly, stood, and retrieved the videocassette.

"Again, my personal congratulations, Leon," the prime minister said as he stood. "Our nation owes you a debt we can never repay."

"Thank you, sir."

Rose solemnly shook hands with each of the other men, then strolled from the room.

Ben Goren was not waiting in the corridor, as promised.

Rose frowned, then headed for his office.

His friend had come here, and was sitting behind the desk.

One look at Goren's face was enough to chill Rose's very marrow.

IRÁKLION, CRETE

0416 Zulu/7:16 A.M. local time

A flight-suited pilot ducked into the Greek Air Force lounge of the NATO base at Iráklion and stopped short. Two civilians were in the room, a tall man pouring himself coffee and a shorter one sprawled on a couch, newspaper in hand. The pilot muttered something that sounded like an apology, then quickly withdrew.

The man at the coffee machine broke into a self-satisfied smile. By God, these Air Force officers knew how to extend courtesies to their fellow patriots, Constantine thought, never once suspecting the real reason why he and Mavros, his partner, had managed to have the lounge to themselves for the past two hours: Not a single pilot would willingly spend time in the presence of intelligence agents from the hated Pasok.

Spooning sugar into his cup, Constantine said, "I hear that Junior Thomopoulos may fly down from Athens to assume personal command of the operation."

"Who tells you this?" asked Mavros, glancing up from his sports paper.

"Iocovazzi, over at headquarters. We all know how Junior likes to take the credit. If he travels all the way to Crete in the middle of the night, he must sense a great success."

Mavros made a rude noise. "Or total failure. Perhaps he wants to bury the mess he is making, or at least shift the blame. Our Navy and Air Force have reason to be on alert. That explosion, so close to our island, must be investigated. But think of it, Constantine . . . because Junior chooses to see spies behind every bush, our entire bureau spends a sleepless night, and half the Gendarmerie is running around putting up roadblocks. Who are these Americans, Rambo? I tell you, we waste our time."

Constantine sipped his coffee and added more sugar. His partner's pessimism was troubling.

The early-morning calls that had shattered their sleep were sufficient to stir any Greek's blood. First, a mysterious underwater blast less than forty miles off the southwestern tip of the island. Then, the entire area aswarm with American search planes and helicopters. Finally, a bulletin from Pasok central in Athens that the feverish activity was in fact a ruse to cloak the fact that three Yankee spies had smuggled themselves, and a silvery disc containing precious oil secrets, onto Crete by boat.

Ordinarily, a manhunt would have been futile; the island was big, its network of roads primitive, Greek security resources thin. But Athens had reasoned that the fugitives would attempt to rendezvous with their fellow imperialists stationed at one of two NATO bases on Crete. Pasok could do nothing to halt the American aircraft. Yet it was capable of establishing checkpoints outside both Iráklion and Soudha Bay to closely monitor all incoming traffic. It was capable of ordering the Gendarmerie to patrol the major highways, concentrating on private cars and intercity taxis carrying two men and a woman. Finally, it was capable of placing those agents not supervising the checkpoints on standby; Constantine and Mavros, for instance, were at the air base at Iráklion, ready to helicopter down-island at an instant's notice.

Still, Mavros had a point, Constantine conceded. They had been cooling their heels since five A.M., and were likely to for some time longer. If the Yankee spies possessed an iota of ingenuity, they could easily hide out until the Greek security forces tired and relaxed their vigilance.

To bolster his own morale Constantine mused, "I retain confidence in Junior. One does not attain his high position without wisdom."

Mavros grunted, not bothering to look up from his paper.

"Anyway, the Americans are worse than the Turks," Constantine continued. "You expect your enemies to steal your oil. But the Americans are two-faced. They say they are our friends, yet—"

The telephone rang.

Constantine answered it in such haste that he spilled his coffee. As he listened, his mouth fell open.

"Yes sir, right away!"

Banging down the receiver, Constantine turned and said smugly, "Stop sitting on your fat behind, Mr. Know-Everything. We are assigned the privilege of arresting the Americans!"

The two men scrambled out of the lounge and down a short corridor into the soft light of early morning.

Ninety feet away a helicopter was whining to life.

As they ran toward it, Mavros asked, "How did they find them?"

"Emergency-channel interrogation of the coastal ferries and fishing fleets. One ferry reports a rubber raft approaching the southwest coast at high speed."

"Where on the coast?"

"Ayía Roúmeli."

Constantine and Mavros clambered aboard the helicopter. Before they finished strapping themselves in, the pilot was lifting off and banking to the southwest.

Below and to their right the Gorge of Samariá, the imposing defile that ran down from Mount Kingílos, still lay in deep shadows. To their left now, the village of Ayía Roúmeli, clinging to the narrow strip of land between mountain and sea, and beyond it, a thin, charcoal-colored band at water's edge. As they descended toward the pebbly beach, they saw a black rubber raft surrounded by several uniformed gendarmes and by local gawkers.

The pilot set the helicopter down some twenty-five yards from the raft.

Constantine and Mavros hopped out.

The gendarme sporting a colonel's patch hurried toward them.

"When does this boat arrive?" shouted Constantine over the clatter of the rotors.

"Just before seven, sir, according to the villagers. We are here since minutes after."

"How many are aboard?"

"Two, sir," the colonel replied. "Two men."

Damn it, Constantine thought, there were supposed to be three spies. Where had the woman run off to? He looked to Mavros, who shrugged. Turning back to the colonel, he said, "They are safely in your custody?"

"No, sir. Our orders are to make no move until your arrival."

"Yes, of course," Constantine said, trying to hide his disappointment. "Do you know where they are?"

"Yes, sir. An *ouzeri* in the village."

The Pasok agents, their leather-soled shoes clumsy on the slippery pebbles, picked their way across the beach to the raft.

It was bare save for the ninety-horsepower outboard mounted on the transom. No doubt stripped by the villagers, Constantine thought. The peasants on this coast were known for their unscrupulous ways; it was a wonder they hadn't pilfered the engine too.

He turned to address the locals. "Those who landed in this boat are spies who come here to harm Greece. Among their personal belongings is a disc . . . it looks exactly like a phonograph record, only it is silver in color . . . a disc that contains vital information. Who knows anything of this disc?"

Constantine was met by blank stares.

"The disc can be played only on a special machine. It is of no use to you."

More blank stares.

"I am empowered to offer a reward for the recovery of the disc. A sizable reward."

"How sizable?" asked a grizzled old fisherman.

"Er, ten thousand drachmas!"

A few onlookers smirked openly.

"Fifty thousand drachmas!"

The smirks vanished, but the crowd remained silent.

Now certain that no villager possessed the disc, Constantine said to the colonel, "Come. Take us to the *ouzeri*."

It was a motley parade, consisting of two men in suits, half a dozen gendarmes, and a growing clutch of chattering villagers that marched across the beach and up into Aíya Roúmeli.

"There," the colonel said, pointing. "They are in that shop."

Constantine and Mavros nervously reached inside their jackets for their guns.

The colonel blinked—no one had informed him the fugitives were armed and dangerous—and then unholstered his own pistol. His men were quick to follow suit.

Constantine leaned toward the colonel and whispered, "Is there a back entrance?"

"In Ayía Roúmeli?" replied the colonel incredulously.

"Very well. You and your men will fan out and provide us with cover. Come, Mavros."

The Pasok agents crept forward and assumed positions on opposite sides of the door, their backs plastered against the whitewashed stucco.

Constantine slowly craned his head around the corner and waited for his eyes to adjust to the gloom.

There they were! Two men, dressed in the sinister black rubber suits worn by skin divers, stood barefoot at the bar, their backs to the door. Though his heart pounded, Constantine remembered his training and took the time to reconnoiter the rest of the room. The proprietress stood behind the bar a few feet from the spies, polishing glasses. Several of the tables were occupied by old villagers gossiping over coffee and raki.

Constantine pulled his head back.

Drawing a deep breath, he extended his gun in a two-handed grip and settled into a crouch. Then, nodding to Mavros, he pivoted through the door, shouting orders as he dived onto the floor.

The sight of an armed madman lurching into her establishment, shrieking indecipherable words at the top of his lungs, so unhinged the proprietress that she dropped the glass in her hand.

The sharp crack of glass smashing on tile caused Constantine to reflexively pull the trigger.

Nothing; he had forgotten to disengage the safety.

Trying to hide his embarrassment, he glanced around.

The old villagers stared at him passively, as if waiting for the next scene in the movie.

The proprietress was edging toward the telephone.

The two Yankee spies, curiously, had not turned. In fact, the taller one was calmly raising a glass of ouzo.

"Do not be alarmed," Constantine called to the proprietress. "I am from Pasok."

"Truly my lucky day," she muttered.

"Mavros!"

As his partner edged through the doorway, Constantine picked himself off his knees.

The spies still had their backs to the door.

Constantine disengaged his safety, took two steps toward the black-suited men, and barked, "American!"

Wendell Trent and Rick Wolfe looked at each other; then, setting down their glasses and keeping their hands in plain sight, they slowly turned from the bar.

"Po po po," Constantine said with theatrical menace—What have we here?

Trent sized up the two Greek men as the type who, as children, probably experienced dark joy in torturing cats, and decided to deflect their swaggering hostility from Wolfe.

Mavros approached the Americans and thrust out a hand. "Passport."

"Sorry, I don't have one," Wolfe confessed, shaking his head.

Trent, though, made a show of patting down his wet suit before nonchalantly shrugging.

Infuriated, Mavros backhanded Trent across the cheek.

"Mavros!" said Constantine sharply. There was time enough for rough stuff; of more pressing concern were the woman and the disc. Directing his attention to the tall, cocky American, he demanded of Trent, *"Pou ine genika?"*

"You speak any Greek, Doc?"

"I can say thank-you, but that's about it."

"Well, hell, so can I." Trent smiled sweetly at Mavros and said, *"Efaristo?"*

Mavros slapped him again.

"Mangas," Constantine sniggered—Tough guys.

"Ohi . . . re malakas!"

When the Pasok agents were finished chortling over Mavros's rude witticism, Constantine yelled for the gendarme colonel to bring handcuffs. Interrogating the Americans back at headquarters was going to be a pleasure, he thought. Even if they failed to squeeze information from this pair, he and Mavros had done more than their share; let someone else find the woman and the disc.

KHANIÁ, CRETE

0517 Zulu/8:17 A.M. local time

The Old Harbor had the synthetic charm of a postcard; the water as still as a sheet of turquoise glass, the small boats motionless in their slips. Under the strengthening sun tendrils of mist rose from the glistening cobblestones that lined the quay. Up on balconies set with pots of vividly colored geraniums, caged finches serenaded the new day with sweet chirps. Once again the ancient port town of Khaniá, on the northwest coast of Crete, had weathered a severe storm to emerge cleansed and reinvigorated.

The calm was broken by a gaggle of tanned, mostly college-aged tourists lugging backpacks and camping gear. They had just gotten off the early bus from Palaiokhóra, one of the beach resorts to the south. Informed that the connecting bus to Iráklion was running late, they were now looking for a café at which to recover from the long, kidney-bruising ride over the rugged mountain range that bisected the island.

One of the women, dressed like the others in T-shirt and cargo shorts, led the group to a flight of broad stone steps that descended to the waterfront.

"This way," Edna Haddix said, hitching up her knapsack. "There's a place down here."

Earlier in the morning, having eluded the search helicopters and run the Zodiac north-by-northeast at full throttle for more than two hours, she, Wendell Trent, and Rick Wolfe had finally made Crete by the low gray light of false dawn. Their fog-shrouded landfall couldn't have been more forbidding; at places the jagged mountains plunged uninterrupted right into the sea. Shivering with cold, they had idled eastward, prowling one cove after another until spying a cluster of pup tents nestled in a beachfront grove of pines.

Trent had brought the chase boat to within seventy yards of shore. The laser disc, still immersed in mineral oil within the double plastic bags, was now in Haddix's knapsack, along with passport, wallet, and a change of clothes. She zipped the knapsack inside the watertight duffel, gave Wolfe a kiss on the cheek and Trent a lingering hug, and slipped over the side. Then, towing the duffel with her uninjured hand, she had started to swim in.

Soon, the outboard's gentle burble had faded into silence. When she turned to peer through the fog, the Zodiac had vanished back out to sea.

Haddix had managed to stumble up onto the rocky beach unobserved. Careful not to disturb the sleeping campers, she had ducked behind a clump of scraggly bushes to quickly strip off the wet suit, briskly massage her goose-bumped skin, and climb into T-shirt and shorts. Then, after covering the wet suit and the duffel with sand, she had followed a well-worn trail into the village that sat above the beach.

The only sign of life on the main street had been a man in a white apron opening up his *kaffaneia* for breakfast. He seemed unsurprised by her appearance, for many hippies slept on the beach, and he even spoke a few words of English, for those same unkempt foreigners usually had enough money to start the morning with coffee, bread, and jam. Yes, he would gladly change her U.S. dollars for drachmas. Yes, Palaiokhóra, as the village was named, boasted a public telephone. And yes, he would help her obtain a listing from the operator.

Haddix had ordered a coffee, taken it out to the telephone kiosk, dialed the NATO base at Soudha Bay, and asked for a particular American naval officer. His welcome to her had been heartening, but not his latest news. The local security forces were mounting an intensive hunt for three American nationals—two men and a woman—carrying secret data that compromised Greek economic interests. Any other time, Navy would just send a jeep across the island to fetch her; but at the moment every vehicle into both Soudha Bay and Iráklion was being closely inspected.

As Haddix waited for them to devise an alternative plan, the strain of the past few days had begun to overtake her. Even three cups of strong Greek coffee proved no substitute for adrenaline; she felt herself growing light headed from fatigue and the fierce throb in her injured right hand.

Down the street the *kaffaneia* had filled with villagers and young campers up from the beach.

Then Haddix noticed a group of campers leaving to board a rickety, exhaust-wreathed market bus. Ascertaining that it was the only one of the day from Palaiokhóra, she had placed another quick call to Soudha Bay, then dashed after the vehicle, catching it just as it was about to pull away.

The authorities were searching for a trio of American fugitives, not a group of holidaying college students from Sweden and Germany; drawing upon the last of her nervous energy, she had struck up a conversation with the campers.

Now, having arrived in Khaniá and led her newfound friends to her rendezvous site—a café in front of the hotel at the eastern end of the Old Harbor—Haddix was covertly monitoring the cobblestoned street. Patience, she told herself; patience.

"Fräulein Jones?"

Haddix wearily turned to the blond, sun-bronzed young German settling into the adjoining chair. She had noticed him eyeing her on the bus.

"I cannot help but overhear your story," he said gravely. "It is true that you are in Palaiokhóra because in the middle of the night your traveling companion drives away?"

She nodded.

"A man?"

She nodded again.

"Unbelievable." His piercing blue eyes softened with sympathy as he casually draped one arm across the back of her seat. "We men can be such swines. But you . . . how can one leave a woman so beautiful, with so much to give?"

Resisting the sudden urge to rearrange the young man's features, she took another sip of mineral water before saying, "Easy. One of the things I gave him was herpes."

The young German paled and hastily excused himself.

Five minutes later a small white Citroën turned onto the cobble-stoned street. The driver pulled to a stop some thirty feet from the café but left the engine running.

Thus cued, Haddix stood and dropped money on the table to cover her bill.

Now a woman of about thirty got out from the passenger side. She was also casually dressed in T-shirt and shorts, but her military bearing was unmistakable. Leaving the door open, she briskly walked away.

Haddix quickly looped her knapsack over one shoulder and headed for the car.

The driver, a black man in his late twenties, was wearing a mesh tank top and bikini-style bathing trunks.

She leaned in the open door and said, "Bright Shark."

"Welcome aboard, ma'am."

As soon as Haddix climbed into the car, the driver threw the Citroën into a U-turn and headed back up the quay.

"Chief Cookson, I presume?"

He beamed. "You got that right, Lieutenant."

"Any word on Trent and Wolfe?"

Cookson's smile faded. "Negative, ma'am."

Chief Petty Officer Cookson edged the Citroën into the line of cars waiting to pass the barricades that had been set up outside the Soudha Bay base.

He shifted into neutral gear, opened the glove compartment, and took out a military passport. "Ma'am? You are temporarily gaining two stripes. Not too many women your age and hair color, so when we get to the roadblock, you'll be answering to the rank of captain."

Haddix opened the passport and studied the photo with dismay. "Chief, those Greeks better be blind."

"Some ways, they are. The show's being run by internal-security clowns, who have strong opinions about certain things."

Cookson began to outline his plan.

The short line moved slowly.

When the Citroën finally idled up to the checkpoint, Cookson handed the two military passports through the window, then popped the trunk-lock release.

A gendarme walked around to the back, looked inside the empty compartment, and slammed the lid shut.

Meanwhile, two others compared the passports against the roster of Americans on permanent or temporary assignment to the base. Finding both names on it, they passed the documents to a man in civilian clothes.

The Pasok agent studied the two photos, then stooped for a closer look at the occupants of the car.

At that moment Haddix casually placed her left hand on the inside of Cookson's bare right thigh and began to caress it.

The Pasok agent's jaw fell. Glancing up quickly to assure himself that it was a foreign whore, and not a Greek girl, so shamelessly fondling the black man, he hurled the passports onto Cookson's lap and angrily waved the Citroën through.

Comfortably cocooned in a deep and dreamless sleep, Edna Haddix turned her head to silence the annoying voice in her ear, but it would not go away.

"What, what . . ."

She forced her eyes open and winced at the strength of the sun, even through the darkened visor.

"Ma'am?" It was the pilot of the A-3. "Ma'am? Your intercom? Mind turning it on?"

Haddix cleared her throat and fumbled on the switch. "Sorry about that. How're we doing?"

"Just passing the Austrian Alps, ma'am."

She glanced out the cockpit. Scrolling past some forty thousand feet below were a series of jagged peaks, many still crested with snow.

"My apologies for waking you, Lieutenant, but you've got an incoming message on Channel Eighteen."

She dialed over.

"Haddix? Cliff Zeman. . . . They informed me you were sleeping, but I thought you'd want to know—Trent and Wolfe are safe."

"Outstanding," she said, suddenly coming fully awake. "How did—"

"Hold on a minute," Zeman interrupted, "and you can hear for yourself. Lieutenant, I look forward to seeing you at Andrews."

"Roger that, Cliff."

A few clicks and squawks, and then Wendell Trent's voice filled her helmet. "Jonesy."

"Trent," she said, fighting to contain her elation. "You okay? And Rick?"

"Better now than half an hour ago," he replied lightly.

"What happened? When I left Soudha, Cookson still hadn't heard anything."

"A long story, but I'll keep it short. A couple of security goons choppered us into Iráklion. . . . I do believe they had notions of dragging us to some dungeon and having a little fun. A few American airmen, though, didn't take kindly to the spectacle of two fellow countrymen in wet suits and handcuffs. It got tense for a few minutes, but John Wayne would've been proud."

Haddix inexplicably found herself at a loss for words. Finally, she said, "I'm—I'm glad you're safe."

"Well, Doc and I were kind of worried about you too. How's it feel to be a priority package?"

"I'm not," she said. "The disc is. But speaking for myself, I don't think I'll ever be able to fly on a commercial jet again."

He laughed.

"Trent, I can't stop worrying about the disc," she continued, reflexively patting the knapsack by the side of her seat.

"It'll be fine," he said. "Didn't you tell me they're just like compact discs? Well, a while back Matty, my son, must've thought my

CD of *The Four Seasons* was a slice of bread, because he covered it with peanut butter."

"How does it play?"

"Not bad, if you like your summers sticky."

"Oooh," she groaned. "Bad. Real bad."

"Jonesy, trust technology, trust the Q department. Everything'll be okay. Listen, they're also air-mailing Doc and me home, though we don't get a leg on an A-3. We'll be there late afternoon–early evening, Washington time."

"Then I'll see you guys at Suitland."

"Affirmative. Uh, Jonesy . . . unless Zeman wants to pump us full of amphetamines, they'll stop the debrief at some merciful hour. I don't know if you've already made arrangements for this evening, but I thought, well, if you haven't, maybe . . ."

Haddix was grateful that her darkened visor was down, for it hid the huge grin spreading across her face. She allowed him to squirm a few seconds longer, then said, "Why, Wendell Trent. Are you asking me for a date?"

There was the hiss of static, and then Trent replied, "I guess I am, aren't I?"

"Well, then, I accept. Listen, say hi to Rick for me?"

"Sure will. Out."

Haddix switched over to intercom. "Sorry to be tying up the radio with personal stuff."

"No problem, ma'am," the pilot replied dryly. "You're not the first to make a date from forty thousand feet, and you surely won't be the last. Course, you might just be the only one brave enough to ever do it so openly. You see, ma'am, most of us use some kind of code . . . lots of ears listening in, that kind of thing."

"Starting with those closest to you?"

"Who, me? A fellow naval officer and gentleman, eavesdrop?"

She laughed, then said, "When do we land at Rhein-Main?"

"Forty-five minutes, Lieutenant. Care for a wake-up call?"

"Yes, please." Long after she closed her eyes again, her smile lingered.

■ ■ ■

The same sun that Edna Haddix had seen rise over Palaiokhóra on the south coast of Crete still sat high above Andrews Air Force Base, seven time zones to the west. She emerged from the cabin of the Air Force transport carrying the knapsack in her left hand; between planes in Germany a doctor had cleaned and bandaged the other one. Though groggy, Haddix felt almost human again, having napped her way across the Atlantic.

Now, through the heat waves shimmering above the tarmac, she watched a black limousine draw near, its rear doors swinging open even before the vehicle rocked to a stop several yards from the base of the ramp. A man and a woman climbed from the limousine. Cliff Zeman, and that must be Ann Davis, Haddix thought. Slinging her knapsack over one shoulder, she started down toward them.

The technicians of the Q department at Suitland, after consulting engineers in the United States and Japan—and after receiving, in under three hours, a special machine and tools from California—had been ready to refurbish the laser disc's Mylar recording surface as soon as it arrived at the NIS facility. The procedure required two hours, giving Edna Haddix time to bathe and change into fresh clothes, which Ann Davis had thoughtfully brought along; to have her hand rebandaged in the dispensary; and to scarf down a chef's salad, two fresh fruit cocktails—and a hot fudge sundae.

Now, leaving the commissary, she glanced at a clock and turned to Davis. "I'm sorry, Ann, when did you say they were due?"

Davis suppressed her sympathetic smile and said, "Another ninety minutes. They should get here for at least part of the briefing."

"What? But Trent's the senior officer on our—"

"Shorty Brock wants to start the moment the disc's ready . . . and before more shit hits the fan."

"What do you mean?" asked Haddix.

"You single? Ever been married? Well, the only comparison that comes to mind is a sweet sixteen party. Not enough room for everyone you absolutely, positively had to invite, so some noses got bent out of shape, right?"

Haddix laughed knowingly.

"One fact you should remember about this town, E.J. People will trade a corner office for access. By this time anyone who's anyone knows that there's been some kind of event in the Med, and they all want in on the endgame. Another fact you should remember . . . the only thing more important than access is the power to deny it."

"Boys will be boys," Haddix observed tartly.

"Really. Especially Shorty. He's never been dealt this kind of hand before, and it looks like he's betting the farm on it."

"Hunh?"

"Come on, let's go find Cliff. I'll explain on the way." Davis started down the corridor. "Ever see a man purr when he says no? Shorty's made your briefing a tougher ticket than a Redskins game. Langley's screaming bloody murder because he won't let them in. Hell, the son of a bitch even tried to keep DOE out, until Cliff reminded him just who mounted this operation."

"Brock can do that?"

"Ordinarily, no. But the folks higher up the food chain happen to be out of town. CNO's out in Pearl, reviewing the Seventh Fleet, and the NSC brain trust is over in Moscow with the President."

"But what about this betting-the-farm business?" asked Haddix.

"If you've brought home a winner, Navy earns a lot of points. Enough of that glory reflects on Shorty, he gets his next stripe that much sooner. But the downside is, by keeping this tightly compartmented, there's no one to share the blame. What if the data on your disc's unsalvageable? What if we've spent a whole lot of money drilling a dry hole?"

Haddix broke stride. "Shorty's staking his future on this briefing?"

"No, only his career," Davis replied dryly.

They turned a corner and saw Clifford Zeman still in front of one of the lab's sterile rooms, pacing like an expectant father.

When he looked up, his face softened. "Haddix. Good to see you looking fit again. How's the hand?"

"Better, thank you."

Haddix peered through the plate-glass window. The scene reminded her of a scene from *E.T.*, for the sterile-room technicians wore white long-sleeve scrub-suits and booties, disposable balaclavas that covered all hair, surgical masks, and latex gloves.

Two of them were examining the mating rims of a new Plexiglas outer shell. Another was gently flowing distilled water over the old disc's Mylar recording surface, which had been removed from its original shell, to wash away the mineral oil.

"They'll start reassembly in another ten minutes," Zeman said. "Then they need to bake the new disc in that oven over there to bond the two halves."

Haddix nodded. "Anything further on the explosion?"

"The seismologists are saying it occurred one mile below the surface. Two nations have torpedoes capable of reaching such a depth . . . and I guarantee you it wasn't one of ours. But there's no way of proving the weapon was Soviet, a fact that has Shorty foaming at the mouth."

Haddix smiled.

Zeman hesitated, then added, "I must tell you that I continue to be astounded by your ingenuity. Placing the disc in the one place the Israelis could not search, figuring out a way to shield it from the sea and the depths. Remarkable."

"Thank you, sir. Let's hope the data survived."

Had a fire marshal been permitted inside the Suitland complex, he would have issued a citation for the number of people crammed into the computer room: Vice Admiral Shorty Brock and several aides seated before one large-screen monitor; a flock of NIS analysts and assorted technical experts in front of two others; and the DOE contingent gathered around the console at the back, nervously watching Edna Haddix methodically finish her systems checks.

Finally, Haddix threw a test pattern from the laser recorder onto the monitors. "Admiral, whenever you're ready."

"Proceed, Lieutenant."

"Aye, aye, sir."

An aide dimmed the overhead lights.

Without the log Haddix had to rely on her memory of where to begin. She keyboarded in a command to call up frame 1025 and pressed Enter.

The test pattern gave way to a bizarre, off-kilter image of what appeared to be coiled snakes floating above two rusty stoves.

Haddix joined the others in a collective sigh, then said, "The boat's galley, sir. Taken shortly after we gained entry amidships. Those lines are the ROV's tether."

Clifford Zeman, who was standing behind Haddix, gave her a congratulatory squeeze on the shoulder.

She reached up and covered his hand. "Admiral, what speed would you like me to take you through the stills?"

"How many images on the disc?"

"I can't say for sure without the log, sir, but from here to the end, no more than a hundred."

"Lieutenant, it's your brief, you set the pace. If anyone in the room has a question, we'll let you know. That gizmo does work in reverse, doesn't it?"

"Yes, sir, it does."

Haddix rapidly advanced through the other skewed stills of the galley and skipped directly to the crew quarters. There was considerable interest in the ghostly forest of aluminum stanchions. She reported their conclusion that the boat had been carrying civilian passengers and, by way of documentation, skipped forward to the frames of the rucksacks hanging near the ceiling.

"Could you hold that and sharpen it a bit, ma'am?" asked one of Brock's aides. He studied the label on the rucksack for several moments, then turned to his superior. "Sir, that logo identifies it as a Laika, a brand distributed primarily in the Leningrad district. Thank you, Lieutenant."

Haddix proceeded without further questions to the sequence inside the wardroom.

"Admiral, here's verification of the boat's identity," she said, freezing the frame of the heavily tarnished brass plaque presented by the crew of HMS *Totem* to the crew of INS *Dakar*.

One of the phones in the room chimed.

"Admiral, for you."

"Why don't you pause it there, Lieutenant," Brock said, accepting the receiver. "I see. Send them up. Yes, both of them . . . I don't care what his clearance is, he saw everything with his own damned eyes, didn't he?"

Brock handed the receiver back and stood. "I'm pleased to announce that two other principals of this operation have just arrived. Let's take a break until they make their way up here."

Haddix ducked her head while she marshaled her emotions, then looked up to Zeman. "Is Trent's timing always this good?"

"It's been getting better lately," he replied with a grin.

Several junior officers were carting in beverage refills when Wendell Trent and Rick Wolfe, both still in flight suits, edged into the crowded computer room.

Clifford Zeman started forward to introduce them around.

Edna Haddix observed protocol by remaining at the console at the back of the room. Even from that distance she could see the three small gauze pads taped to Trent's left cheek. Then she noticed that between handshakes, he was surreptitiously scanning the room.

Suddenly, their eyes locked.

Trent returned his attention to one of the NIS analysts. When he glanced her way again, there was a shy smile on his face.

Admiral Brock finally called the meeting back to order by reclaiming his seat.

As the others found their places, Rick Wolfe made his way to the console and gave Haddix a warm hug.

Then Zeman was leading Trent to the back.

"Hi, Jonesy."

"Hi, Trent." She took both his hands in hers and studied the gauze pads. "Damn, just when all those yellow bruises were healing."

He shrugged. "I'm famous for leading with my chin."

Zeman discreetly cleared his throat.

Haddix blushed. "Admiral, may I continue?"

"Whenever you're ready, Lieutenant."

"Aye, aye, sir."

Haddix took her seat and keyboarded a command that filled the monitors around the room with a medium-range shot of the collapsed bulkhead separating the passageway and the operations area.

"Admiral, this bulkhead was collapsed by the boat's impact with the wall of the ravine. We were able to shoot the operations area through what remains of the hatchway—that's coming up in a few frames—but may I direct your attention to the debris in the lower right-hand corner. Sir, many of the artifacts are clearly civilian. We captured them in detail on videotape but not, unfortunately, on laser disc."

Brock grunted and turned to an aide. "What's the status of those tapes."

"Sir, State's already lodged a formal demand for their return."

"Three-to-two we get them back, fifty-to-one they'll be wiped clean," Brock said sourly. "Proceed, Lieutenant."

Haddix quickly skipped to the stacked image that Rick Wolfe had made through the hatchway and began to enhance it.

The whispered conversations ceased as the utter devastation within the operations area became apparent.

"Sir, may I direct your attention to the dark rectangle at the center of the forward bulkhead," Haddix said, continuing to decrease the brightness while she increased the contrast.

The white circle with the three equilateral triangles arrayed like a propeller slowly emerged.

"Outstanding work, Lieutenant," Brock finally said. "You have my compliments."

"Thank you, sir."

Haddix skipped past the sequence documenting *Ernie*'s attempts to dislodge the slab obstructing the breach in the forward torpedo room, stopping at the point that Rick Wolfe was nosing the ROV into the hull. Back in the control van she had reflexively burned onto the disc the spike she had seen in the data stream from the ROV's gamma ray detector.

"Admiral, you'll note the time stamp on this frame . . . seventeen fifty-seven and forty-two seconds, Zulu. I believe the next frame contains a screen of data from our gamma-ray detector."

She advanced the frame.

Though those in the room had been expecting evidence of radiation, they were nevertheless stunned by the magnitude of the jump in numbers.

"Here's what caused the spike," Haddix said, quickly advancing to a still that clearly showed both the metal boxes, their black matte surfaces stenciled with the legend U_{238}, and a scattering of silvery-white ingots.

After several moments Brock said, "Zeman, you were right to pursue your convictions. Congratulations are in order not only for your accomplishments, but also for your perseverance."

Haddix skipped now to the largely intact tank on the port side of the torpedo room.

"Sir, here's what we believe sank *Dakar*."

Four frames later she stopped at the neat circular hole through the submarine's double hull.

Several of the weapons experts began quietly conferring.

"That charge almost had to have been built in," Brock mused.

"Yes, sir," Haddix said.

"I can't believe the Israelis did it. Who performed the mods, the Brits? What motive could they have had? But if it wasn't either of them, then who?" Hearing no response, he said, "Anything else on that disc, Lieutenant?"

"Yes, sir. Some unusual objects at the bottom of the compart-

ment. None of us had time to review the frames—we were being
boarded just about then—so if you'll please bear with us?"

Haddix skipped through the remaining stills until she came to the
final stacked image.

As she played with the brightness and contrast, a cluster of shiny-
as-new steel cylinders, each the size of a fire extinguisher, gained
shape.

Now she electronically cropped the image and boosted magnification on one particular cylinder.

There was writing on it.

She sharpened the focus until the characters were legible:

ВНИМАНИЕ!

ОПАСНЫЙ МАТЕРИЯ

$(CH_3)_3CHH(CH_3)OPF(O)CH_3$

"Uh, sir," ventured the aide who had earlier translated the rucksack logo, "it says, 'Attention! Hazardous Substance.' "

"Good, but what hazardous substance? Anybody?" Brock turned
and glowered at the assembled experts. "Jesus, a room full of high-
domes, and nobody passed high-school chemistry?"

A second aide hurried to a phone and placed a brief call. "Admiral, they're sending someone on the double."

Brock noticed Haddix, Trent, Wolfe, and Zeman huddled around
the console, deep in conversation. "Lieutenant, have you come up
with something?"

Haddix hesitated, then turned to Zeman.

"It's your brief, Lieutenant," he replied softly.

Her eyes flicked to Trent.

He winked back encouragement.

Haddix turned to address Brock. "Sir, we've always been puzzled
by the magnitude of the Israeli response to our operation. It would
have made sense back in '68, when *Dakar* went down . . . they

had every reason then to shield a large shipment of uranium and, as we discovered down there, a boatload of Soviet Jews.

"But today? The entire world knows of Israel's nuclear capabilities. I believe Moscow has been issuing exit visas to Soviet Jews for several years. So why would the Israelis risk an international incident to keep us from *Dakar*? Our guess is, the Soviets were shipping something else aboard that boat. Sir, we think the answer lies in those cylinders . . . or it just plain doesn't exist."

There was a knock at the door.

At Brock's nod one of his aides opened it.

A young specialist, slightly winded and lugging a thick looseleaf notebook, stepped inside. He froze, clearly unprepared to encounter the amount of brass assembled in the room.

"Come on in, son," Brock said. "We asked you here to tell us what that there symbol stands for."

"Aye, aye, sir."

The specialist edged past Brock to the nearest monitor. As he peered at the cylinder filling the screen, his eyes widened.

"Well, son?"

"With the Admiral's permission, I'd like to double-check the reference." The specialist cracked open his thick notebook, turned a few pages, then looked up and blinked. "The symbol describes the compound methylphosphonofluoridic acid one, two, two, trimethyl-propester. The compound is more commonly known as soman.

"Soman was invented by the Nazis late in World War II and tested on concentration camp inmates—"

"You mean on Jews?" asked Brock.

"Yes, sir. Today, it is one of the nerve agents stockpiled by the Soviet Union, but it is also known as 'the poor man's A-bomb' . . . we believe Libya and Iraq to be among the lesser-developed nations possessing substantial quantities."

The specialist consulted his notebook again. "When dispersed, usually by airburst, soman triggers acute vomiting and convulsions. Those suffering incidental exposure may survive, but their central nervous systems will be irreversibly damaged. Higher dosages are fatal. Death comes in less than ten minutes, usually as a result of suffocation . . . the respiratory system just shuts down.

"Admiral, soman is possibly the most lethal nerve gas on earth." The specialist looked back to the monitor. "And, sir? Three cylinders that size would hold enough to wipe out every person in downtown Chicago."

EPILOGUE

"Is this true, Leon? What the Americans say is aboard the *Dakar*?"

Leon Rose looked at his interrogator and nodded.

"Good God! Did Eshkol know about the nerve gas? Did any cabinet member know?"

"Of course not," Rose replied calmly.

The minister of industry and trade's face turned purple with rage. "How dare you! Does history teach you nothing? After what Hitler does to our people, you have the audacity to involve the state of Israel in chemical warfare weapons?"

Rose reached for his mineral water to give the other ministers a chance to compose themselves. He himself needed no such respite. For the past five days—since being informed by Pavel Chesnokov that the three Americans had escaped from Crete—he had been anticipating this very confrontation.

The suspense had finally ended that morning when a special envoy from Washington hand-delivered to the prime minister of Israel three items. The first was a laser disc onto which had been copied the electronic stills taken inside *Dakar*'s shattered hull. The second was a twenty-seven-page analysis of the key images by the U.S. Naval Intelligence Service, which also revealed why the Soviet Union had so willingly given Israel the experimental deep-diving torpedo—to destroy evidence of the explosive charge that Moscow had one of its British agents, naval officer Victor Cowling, plant in *Dakar*'s hull. Last was a strongly worded letter from the White House suggesting that, in the interest of Middle Eastern peace, Leon Rose be stripped of office.

But that would not happen, Rose thought. He had an unimpeachable defense which, for once, was predicated on only the truth, the entire truth.

"We are waiting, Leon."

Rose looked around the long hardwood table and said, softly, "Kindly try to think back to July of 1967. The conclusion of the Six-Day War. The moment of Israel's greatest triumph . . . and also of her greatest vulnerability."

He turned to the minister of industry and trade, a hero of that campaign. "Tell me, my friend, you were privy to the deliberations of the General Staff. How much longer could we have fought?"

"What bearing does this have on the present matter?" asked his archrival with suspicion.

"Our remaining stores of munitions, of fuel . . . enough for perhaps another thirty-six hours, is that not what the General Staff estimates?"

"Something like that."

"Yes, something like that." Rose sadly shook his massive head. "After which, our brave boys can be overrun by the palace guards from one of the Gulf emirates, by any soldiers who still have bullets. And tell me, my friend, when was it that our armed forces were resupplied to the level where they could again adequately defend Israel? Nearly three years, is it not? For some reason late April 1970 remains in my mind."

His archrival reluctantly nodded.

Rose now turned to the prime minister. "Sir, if memory serves, you were at that time Mossad station chief in Paris. Tell me, do you remember an operation . . . I believe its code name is 'ABC-Two'?"

The prime minister blinked, then grew very still.

Rose pressed on: "The original 'ABC' is undertaken in the early sixties, is that not correct, sir? In response to rumors that Egypt is developing atomic-biological-chemical weaponry? Does not Mossad investigate, and does not Mossad judge that the Nazi scientists which Nasser hires are not up to the task?"

The prime minister nodded.

"Yes, well, at the end of the Six-Day War, do we not hear that Nasser desires such a weapon even more? That in fact he will now pay any sum for it? Do we not hear of several large chemical corporations in Northern Europe which are said to be willing to do business with Egypt? Mr. Prime Minister, did not you yourself participate in an intensive probe of several of these corporations?"

"Yes, I did, Leon," the prime minister replied, shifting uncomfortably in his seat. "But the rumors were false. There was therefore no need—I repeat, absolutely no need—for you to soil Israel's honor with your monstrous mischief."

Rose sighed. Emphasizing every word, as if speaking to a child, he asked, "And when does Mossad issue its final report on 'ABC-Two'?"

"You expect me to remember this?" snapped the prime minister.

"I do not, sir. So permit me to tell you. The report is issued on the fourteenth of February 1969. Which means that for a full twenty months Israel—defenseless Israel—faces a calamitous new threat from that madman in Cairo. During this uncertain time during our so-called War of Attrition, an opportunity arises to obtain quantities of the chemical called soman. I took it upon myself to accept."

Rose gathered his papers.

"You, my fellow ministers, may think of me as you will. But remember that even fools become wise when they have the luxury of hindsight. Before you pass judgment, kindly try to think back to July of 1967. Had circumstances turned out otherwise, history would judge me Israel's savior."

One of the Labor ministers finally broke the silence. "Leon, I am hearing from you not an apology, only defiance."

"For behaving patriotically, I apologize to no one."

The prime minister cleared his throat but could not bring himself to look Rose in the eye. "Apologies will not save us if news of this matter ever finds its way from this room," he muttered. "Leon, I expect your resignation on my desk by the end of the day."

"You shall not have it, sir."

Stunned, the prime minister wildly looked about for support.

"Fire me if you dare," Rose continued in a steely voice. "That act alone should bring down your sorry coalition. If it does not, I shall personally complete the task. And then, perhaps, we may all go about the business of making Israel once more strong, once more righteous, once more feared by her enemies."

Five minutes later, having won amnesty for Ben Goren and Ephraim Levenger as well, and for all military personnel who participated in the mission against *Fanning II*, Leon Rose stood and calmly strolled from the cabinet room.

That same first Monday in June of 1988 a second American envoy hand-delivered to the young president of the Soviet Union an identical laser disc and summary. Accompanying them was a strongly worded letter from the White House suggesting that in the interest of Middle Eastern peace, the Kremlin persuade its Arab clients—most notably, the Palestinian Liberation Organization—to cease all terrorist operations against Israel.

By then Moscow had solved the mystery of the missing torpedo. The evidence came from Vice Admiral Boris Patolichev, who unlike his friend, GRU Lieutenant General Pavel Chesnokov, had known of the order to sabotage *Dakar*. Patilochev directed his interrogators to certain sealed archives. These revealed that in 1967, members of the High Command had convinced President Leonid Brezhnev that the Spandrel SAM launcher captured by the Israelis was worth bargaining back. The records further showed that Brezhnev had approved the release of fifty-three Soviet Jews, along with quantities of U_{238} ingots and the nerve gas soman, under one condition: The transporting vessel must never reach Israel. By way of confirmation there was also the bizarre story told by a retired British naval officer who had stormed into the Soviet embassy in East Berlin demanding asylum for past services rendered.

In earlier days Patolichev and Chesnokov would have faced a life sentence in a Siberian labor camp or, more probably, a firing squad. But the men now ruling the Kremlin were more pragmatic, less paranoid. They recognized that although the actions of these two high officers were in some ways self-serving, they had also served *Rodina* by permanently covering up a most embarrassing Soviet indiscretion. Of course the Americans had proof, but only on laser disc; and everyone knew how easily electronic images could be manipulated. Both Chesnokov and Patolichev were censured, demoted one rank, and allowed to retire early.

The subordinates who had so ably executed the operation to bury

Dakar received treatment that was kinder still. GRU's *residentura* in Athens, Dimitri Puzanov, was reassigned to Rome. The captain of *Komsomolets* was upgraded to the command of a Typhoon-class boomer and managed to take his senior officers along. (The skipper replacing him was stronger on political connections than on seamanship; the following April a fire broke out in the stern of the Mike-class boat and sank it in 5,000 feet of water north of Norway, where it remains to this day.) *Zampolit* Nikolai Krestnikov won assignment to the High Command in Moscow. And finally, torpedo specialist Yuri Tikhonov was promoted two ranks and transferred to Northern Fleet headquarters at Murmansk on the Kola Peninsula.

Two days later Eugene Da Silva drove home to Rockville, Maryland, to have dinner with his wife. Then the Department of Energy business manager returned to his office in Washington. He was prepared to spend most of the night there; the bills from Bright Shark were still arriving faster than he could log them.

On his desk lay a fresh flimsy from Langley. It had been sent to clarify an agreement, reached several months earlier by Clifford Zeman and a CIA desk officer, that committed the two agencies to share all expenses incurred on Bright Shark.

Da Silva booted up his computer and logged over to a certain interagency credit line. When he had last checked it, in midafternoon, the account showed a deficit of about $83,000.

The balance now totaled $3,000,000.

Da Silva stared at the screen for perhaps two minutes before powering down, locking up his office, and driving right back out to Rockville.

The next morning Bart, the DOE deputy director, instantly grasped the significance of the windfall: CIA was desperate for hard data. The agency had been shut out of the Suitland briefing given by Edna Haddix and was now probably being stonewalled by its friendly rivals at NIS. Bart wrestled with his conscience for all of ten seconds, then ordered a duplicate laser disc to be cut and dispatched across the river. By messenger, of course; hell, in light of Langley's generosity, it was the least he could do.

At the end of June of 1988 Clifford Zeman returned to work after a three-week vacation. Much had occurred in his absence.

The bad news was that he had become a liability to the Department of Energy. Two dozen legislators—dissimilar except for their acceptance of campaign contributions from the American-Israeli Political Affairs Committee—were threatening investigations into rumors of an unauthorized DOE operation against one of America's most trusted friends. In addition, an undersecretary at the Department of State had lodged a formal protest against Zeman for unprofessional conduct. "This man's unremitting mendacity," the complaint of J. Marshall Mear III read in part, "nearly precipitated serious misunderstandings with two of our longtime allies, Greece and Israel."

The deputy director agreed the charges against Zeman were baseless. But alas, Bart noted, the only way to refute them was with the laser disc and NIS summary—both of which would remain "Eyes Only" for decades to come. Therefore, Zeman had to be replaced in the politically sensitive post of monitoring the international traffic in nuclear technology.

Yet there was good news as well. According to the deputy director, Bright Shark and the man who ran it had fast become a legend inside the Beltway. Should Zeman choose to leave DOE, rather than accept a lateral promotion, his job offers from the intelligence community already numbered four.

Bart concluded their talk with an ironic footnote. By Eugene Da Silva's latest reckoning Zeman's operation would end up netting DOE a $716,000 profit.

In early July of 1988 Edna Haddix began a two-week furlough. She spent the first three days with Rick Wolfe's family in Mystic, Connecticut. After completing her round of interviews, and renewing acquaintances with her friends from GIO—Cowboy and Liz Trim-

ble, Ari Kahane and Len Heppel, Ezra Schell and Sam Lippman—
she flew west. Waiting by the gate at Seattle/Tacoma Airport was
Wendell Trent.

They spent the next four days discussing futures: hers, his, and
theirs.

Haddix had planned on resigning her commission and returning
to the Scripps Institute of Oceanography in La Jolla, California, to
complete her Ph.D. But now the U.S. Navy, under pressure from
Vice Admiral Shorty Brock, was trying to induce her to remain in
uniform. In addition, Rick Wolfe was trying to persuade her to
transfer from Scripps to the doctoral program in marine geology
jointly sponsored by GIO and Yale University.

Trent had planned on remaining at DOE, which had bureaus
convenient to both Scripps and GIO; he would request the appropriate transfer after Haddix made her decision. But now, with his
mentor, Clifford Zeman, being forced out of the agency by month's
end, he was having second thoughts.

Nothing was resolved by the time Erica and Matty Trent arrived
in Seattle to begin their month with Dad.

Trent originally wanted the four of them to go camping in Mount
Rainier National Park. Haddix, who numbered a divorced father
among her former beaus, talked him out of it. "After what we've
just been through, you want another Week from Hell?" She turned
out to have been right. Predictably, Matty found Jonesy "real
neat." But Erica, her every hackle raised, spent much of her time
comparing this interloper to her own mother, and loyally finding
her dad's glamorous new friend lacking. Still, Erica consented to go
to the airport to see Haddix off, and even gave her a hug. Not a big,
warm hug, but a hug nonetheless.

In July of 1988 Roland Vigneron, newly hired as a civilian consul-
tant to the Israeli Navy's main shipyard in Elat, sent for his wife and
three children. With Leon Rose's sponsorship the family was
quickly granted Israeli residency.

Later that same month Mossad agents finally tracked down

Victor Cowling, the retired British naval commander who had over-
seen the modifications on *Dakar*—which included planting the explosive charge that killed the submarine. He was staying in a heavily fortified compound in suburban Leipzig, deep inside East
Germany. Before the Israelis could mount an operation, Cowling
was flown from this transit house to his final sanctuary, an apartment outside Moscow. He lived there until his death, of cirrhosis of
the liver, in October of 1990.

In mid-August of 1988 Edna Haddix resigned her naval commission, notified Scripps that she would be continuing her doctoral
work at GIO, and leased a small house in Mystic, Connecticut.
    Shortly after Labor Day, Wendell Trent rented an apartment
within jogging distance of her place. He had resigned from DOE
following long consultations with Clifford Zeman, who had moved,
with Ann Davis, to another federal agency. Now, with a $250,000
line of credit cosigned by Zeman's new employer, Trent founded a
small company in Mystic to develop and build the next generation
of deep-sea research vehicles.
    The fourth person Trent hired was another recent alumnus of the
U.S. Navy, former Chief Petty Officer Darnell Cookson.

In November of 1988 the senator who had repaid AIPAC for its
substantial campaign contributions by covertly trying to halt Bright
Shark easily won another six-year term.

In December of 1988 the chief spokesman of the Palestinian Liberation Organization traveled to Geneva with olive branch in hand.
His followers, he announced, were now ready to recognize Israel's
statehood; to cease terrorist operations against the Zionist state;
and to call off the insurrection known as the *intifada.* If Israel would
reciprocate by granting basic liberties and protections to the two
million Palestinians who lived in the occupied territories, then the
blood feud that had riven the Holy Land for forty years would be at
an end.

The PLO spokesman did not particularly relish his role as a messenger of peace. He realized that his speech, which had been hand-crafted by the Kremlin, might land him atop the hit list of any of a dozen radical Arab cells. Yet he considered the alternative—the threatened withdrawal of all Soviet financial support—even more unpalatable.

Washington hailed the PLO initiative and urged Jerusalem to open preliminary talks. But Leon Rose and his right-wing allies pressured the coalition government into spurning the overture.

In June of 1989 Greece's eight-year experiment with socialism crumbled under the cumulative scandals besetting its aging prime minister. With the Pasok leader's personal life subject to open ridicule, and with many of his cabinet officials and top advisors under investigation for fiscal improprieties, the party lost its absolute majority in Parliament.

The results of that fateful election had been foreseen by the wealthy merchant Adonis Thomopoulos, Sr. Two months before the balloting, holding out the carrot of a full directorship in the family firm, he had persuaded his son to resign from public service. Adonis senior harbored no illusion that working for Pasok intelligence had quickened Junior's mind or honed his skills; but it had certainly taught the boy where an awful lot of bodies were buried.

In October of 1989 the two superpower heads met face-to-face on the island of Malta. It was the first summit between the Soviet leader and the American recently swept into the White House to carry on the Old Man's conservative revolution. During one of their private sessions the young Soviet president unexpectedly deviated from the set agenda. Last year, before you took office, he said to his U.S. counterpart, there was an event in the Eastern Mediterranean. As a result your predecessor and I agreed on a plan to bring lasting peace to the Middle East. Despite intense opposition from the hard-liners who wish to depose me, the Soviet president said, I have reined in the PLO and lifted the restrictions on Soviet Jews who wish to emigrate; when can we expect Washington to uphold its end of the bargain?

Eight months later the uneasy alliance that had governed Israel since 1983 finally collapsed under the strain of the *intifada,* then dragging into its thirtieth month.

Public opinion polls suggested that most of Israel's Jews favored extending to Palestinians a nominal measure of self-representation. But the nation's increasingly fractured political system allowed the conservative Likud party to form a working coalition by bribing the leaders of several small splinter groups with key cabinet appointments.

Leon Rose, denied the coveted post of defense minister, accepted the housing portfolio, which would empower him to settle the flood of immigrants from Russia on the occupied West Bank. That territory was, after all, Israel's Bible-given land.

Four hours before Rose's appointment was to be announced, the prime minister of Israel received a telephone call from Washington that he could not refuse. Nor, after being pointedly reminded of the laser disc cataloguing *Dakar*'s cargo, could he refuse the American president's wishes. The housing portfolio went to another man, one willing to publicly vow that not a single Palestinian would be displaced in favor of the arriving Soviet Jews. At least not just yet, not until world events once again changed the calculus and restored to Israel some of its lost leverage.

Over Memorial Day weekend of 1990—coincidentally, the second anniversary of Bright Shark—Clifford and Jeanne Zeman gave the hand of their daughter, Nora, to the young patent attorney whom she had been dating for more than two years.

The wedding was held in Weyers Cave, Virginia.

Among the guests were four of Zeman's valued colleagues in his new venture. Edna Haddix and Wendell Trent traveled down from Connecticut with Rick Wolfe and his wife, and Ann Davis was escorted by her new beau.

On the eve of the ceremony, following the rehearsal dinner, the veterans of Bright Shark drifted with brandies in hand to the far corner of the yard. There, around citronella torches that perfumed the sultry night, they reminisced not about the international ramifications of their success—of which they knew little and cared less— but about the others who had played key roles. In the end the most eloquent toast was proposed by Rick Wolfe, who said, simply, "To the truth."

The wedding was held in that same yard late the following afternoon. The sun was still strong, but the stately old oaks provided a leafy shade and a welcome breeze fanned the languid air.

After a minister and a rabbi led the couple through the exchange of vows and the breaking of the wineglass and the ritual kiss, the newlyweds were walking toward the guests when the bride suddenly remembered a promise she had made to her father.

Nora scanned the smiling faces, then drew back her arm.

The toss was not only errant, but also floated through the air in a soft trajectory that gave the intended recipient time to think.

Too much time, actually.

Oh, what the hell . . . Edna Haddix's grin widened as she felt Wendell Trent leaning to one side to afford her a clearer shot at catching the bridal bouquet.

In gratitude for the insight, technical expertise, encouragement, and support they patiently lent us, the authors thank:

Commander Charles W. Anderson, USN (Ret); Martin Bowen; Jackie Cantor; Christopher T. Cory; Anne Davis; Leslie A. Jay; Captain John H. Maurer, Jr., USN (Ret); Gretchen McManimin; Murdoch Matthew; Bob Miller; Alan S. Parter, Esq.; Pat Roberts; Haagen Schempf; Craig Schneider; Norman Snyder; David I. Weil, Esq.; and Lynn Yeazel, Panasonic Optical Disc Systems.

In addition, we thank our forty-two shipmates aboard *Star Hercules*, with whom we sailed the North Atlantic in May and June of 1989. During the still watches of that ultimately successful expedition to find the German battleship *Bismarck*, they generously shared not only their vast stores of marine and scientific lore but also a startling talent for conjuring up ingenious ways to perpetrate skulduggery on the high seas:

Ship's crew: Derek Latter, Master; Joe Hansen; Greg Henke; Ticky Latham; Sid Lewis; Eddie Tan; and Alan Vincent. Also, Joe Chantre; Marcelino Gomes Lima; Jorge Lucas Lopes; Jose Dos Reis Nereu; Elidio T. de Oliveira; Antao Domingos Pires; Antonio Nascimentio Silva; Canuto Santos Silva; and Armando Varela Spencer.

Scientific crew: Casey Agee; Todd Ballard; Martin Bowen; Ron Bowlin; Greg Brozio; Tom Crook; Bob Elder; Skip Gleason; Kirk Gustafson; Dr. Rachel Haymon; Jim Jones; Billy Lange; Mel Lee; Dan Martin; Jack Maurer; Cathy Offinger; Jim Saint; Haagen Schempf; Frank Smith; Dr. Elazar Uchupi; and Billy Yunck. Also, Joe Bailey; Rick Gioia; Glenn Marullo; Peter Schnall; and Chris Weber.